Praise for Joan Johnston

"Joan Johnston does short contemporary Westerns to perfection."
—*Publishers Weekly*

"Like LaVyrle Spencer, Ms. Johnston writes of intense emotions and tender passions that seem so real that the readers will feel each one of them."
—*Rave Reviews*

"Johnston warms your heart and tickles your fancy."
—*New York Daily News*

"Joan Johnston continually gives us everything we want . . . fabulous details and atmosphere, memorable characters, a story that you wish would never end, and lots of tension and sensuality."
—*Romantic Times*

"Joan Johnston [creates] unforgettable subplots and characters who make every fine thread weave into a touching tapestry."
—*Affaire de Coeur*

Texas Bride

Joan Johnston

DELL

NEW YORK

Texas Bride is a work of fiction. Names, characters, places, and incidents are the products of the author's imagination or are used fictitiously. Any resemblance to actual events, locales, or persons, living or dead, is entirely coincidental.

A Dell Mass Market Original

Copyright © 2012 by Joan Mertens Johnston, Inc.
Excerpt from *Wyoming Bride* copyright © 2012 by Joan Mertens Johnston, Inc.

All rights reserved.

Published in the United States by Dell, an imprint of The Random House Publishing Group, a division of Random House, Inc., New York.

DELL is a registered trademark of Random House, Inc., and the colophon is a trademark of Random House, Inc.

This book contains an excerpt from the forthcoming book *Wyoming Bride* by Joan Johnston. This excerpt has been set for this edition only and may not reflect the final content of the forthcoming edition.

ISBN 978-1-61793-652-4

Printed in the United States of America

Cover illustration: Alan Ayers
Title lettering: Dave Gatti

This book is dedicated to
my friend and tennis coach
Sue Gutierrez
for teaching me to love the game.

Texas Bride

Chapter One

"It's a disaster," Hannah said. "Plain and simple. We're DOOMED."

"You're the only thing standing between us and Miss Birch," Hannah's twin, Henrietta, confirmed. "Once you're gone, we're dead ducks." Hetty drew a dramatic finger across her throat, dropped her head sideways, stuck out her tongue, and crossed her eyes.

Miranda Wentworth choked back a sob. "Surely not doomed," she said with a wobbly smile, as she met the gazes of the two seventeen-year-olds sitting to the left of her on the hard dining room bench. But things were going to be bad. The headmistress at the Chicago Institute for Orphaned Children, Miss Iris Birch, had promised as much.

Miranda and her five siblings had snuck into the dining room after lights-out to sit on plank benches at a plank table set on a frigid brick floor. The whale-oil lantern in the center of the table created sinister shadows that turned their features into gargoyle faces. Miranda could see the two younger boys shivering on the bench across from her, huddled under the thin, gray wool blankets they'd taken from their beds.

"The subject of this meeting is Miranda's imminent departure from the Institute," sixteen-year-old Josephine announced from her seat beside Nicholas, the elder of the two boys.

Miranda shivered, and not just from the cold. The thought of leaving her sisters and brothers behind when she was forced to leave the orphanage on her eighteenth birthday was terrifying.

The six Wentworth children had been orphaned three years ago in the Great Chicago Fire of 1871, which had burned for three days, destroying most of the business district, including their father's bank.

It had also burned down their three-story mansion and killed their father and mother. Their wealth had gone up in flames, along with their home. Destitute and homeless, their uncle, Stephen Wentworth, had decided the best place for them was an orphanage.

Miranda had begged Uncle Stephen to let them live with him, but his home had also burned down. There was no "home" where they could all be together. So the Wentworth children had ended up at the Institute. Uncle Stephen had promised they would all be together again as soon as he could rebuild.

But that day had never come.

Repeated pleas for rescue from the cruelty of Miss Birch had gone unanswered. Letters to Uncle Stephen's last known address had come back unopened. There was no way of knowing what had happened to him.

Then, a year ago, Josie had read an article in the business section of the *Daily Herald* announcing that Mr. Stephen Wentworth was opening a new bank. It appeared Uncle Stephen was not only alive and well, but that he was rich enough to open a bank!

Miranda had immediately written to their uncle at the bank's address, asking why he hadn't come to get them as he'd promised. That letter had resulted in a visit from Uncle Stephen.

Miranda flushed every time she remembered that meeting. Uncle Stephen had told her he felt ill equipped to be a surrogate parent. They would have to stay where they were. Furthermore, she was not to contact him again. It wasn't his fault they were orphans. He wasn't the one who'd wanted a large family, his brother had. And it wasn't his fault their father hadn't kept his funds somewhere safe, so his fortune wouldn't have gone up in flames.

Miranda had been shocked at her uncle's harsh words and devastated by his unwillingness to help them escape Miss Birch. When her father was alive, Uncle Stephen's behavior had always been friendly. Obviously, appearances could be deceiving.

Ever since that day, Miranda had felt all the responsibility of being the eldest. Though the twins were only a year younger, they were flighty and silly in a way Miranda never had been. After the fire she'd been determined to rescue her siblings from the orphanage.

But three years, four months, and two days later, here they still were. Not only that, but tomorrow she would be leaving Hannah, Henrietta, Josephine, Nicholas, and Harrison behind while she escaped the tyrant who'd made their lives at the Institute so miserable.

Once she was gone, her younger siblings would be

at the mercy of the stern headmistress. No, *stern* was too kind a word. *Cruel*. That was the word for Miss Iris Birch.

"Do you have to leave, Miranda?" Nick asked plaintively.

"I must," Miranda croaked, her throat swollen with emotion. "I have no choice."

Four-year-old Harry crawled under the dining table and climbed into her lap. As his arms tightened around her neck he begged, "Please don't leave, Miranda."

Harry was small for his age, barely more than skin and bones and always sick with a cold that never seemed to go away. Miranda wiped his nose with a handkerchief she always kept with her for that purpose and pulled him close to comfort him.

"DOOMED," Hannah repeated, melodramatically placing the back of her hand across her forehead.

Miranda felt the urge to console her siblings, but the situation was likely to be every bit as bad as they feared.

"There is another option."

Every eye at the long pine dining table turned to Josie. She peered back at them through spectacles perched on the bridge of her freckled nose. Josie always had her head in a library book, and she was, without a doubt, the most educated—and practical—of them all because of it.

"What is it, Josie?" Miranda asked. "I'm willing to consider anything."

"Here." Josie unfolded a worn advertising page of the Chicago *Daily Herald* on the table in front of Miranda. She pointed a grimy finger at an advertisement circled in lead pencil.

Everyone leaned close as Miranda read:

"WIFE WANTED: Must love children, cook, sew and do laundry. Reply to Mr. Jacob Creed, General Delivery, San Antonio, Texas."

Miranda tried not to appear as crestfallen as she felt when she looked up and met Josie's owl-eyed gaze. "I'm sorry, sweetie, but I don't see how this is going to help."

"We're DOOMED," Hannah muttered.

"Forever and ever," Hetty agreed with her twin. "Or at least for the next year, until we turn eighteen."

"What about me?" Nick said. "I'm only ten. I've got *eight more years* of this hellhole to survive."

"Nicholas Jackson Wentworth!" Miranda scolded in a hushed voice. "Watch your language in front of the baby."

"I'm not a baby," Harry protested. "I'm four. And I don't want to stay here. Miss Birch is mean. Take me with you, Miranda, please!"

"I can't, Harry." Miranda's heart ached with the pain of leaving them all behind. "You're safer here. All of you," she said, meeting the stark gazes of her siblings around the table.

"Can't we at least try to make it on our own, Miranda?" Hannah asked.

"It's the middle of February," Miranda replied in a voice made harsh by the agony she was feeling inside. "I can only count on a single bed in a boarding house and a job in a kitchen. I don't have any way to take care of you. Any of you." She tenderly brushed Harry's white-blond hair away from his forehead.

On their own, they'd freeze to death or starve and be dead in a week. Or maybe two. But if they all tried to leave, disaster was a foregone conclusion. Miranda was facing an impossible choice. She couldn't stay, but she couldn't bear to go.

Josie set a tattered piece of paper on top of the newspaper ad. "Read this."

"What is it?" Hetty demanded.

"Something I wrote. Just read it, Miranda," Josie urged.

Everyone leaned close as Miranda read:

"Dear Mr. Creed,
  I'm responding to your advertisement for a wife. I'm eighteen, of sound mind—"

Miranda looked up at Josie. "Of sound mind? Really, Josie—"

"Keep reading," Josie insisted.

Miranda continued:

"and body. I have blue eyes and blond hair which curls by itself."

Miranda rolled her eyes but kept reading.

  "I can cook, clean, iron and sew."

Nick snorted. "I'll say! You can cook gruel and scrub floors and iron linens and mend torn pajamas. I don't think—"

"Shhh! Let her finish," Josie said.

Miranda kept reading.

"I love children and hope to have many of my own."

Miranda stopped as tears blurred her vision. She was headed for a life of drudgery from which there was no escape. She couldn't imagine one day having a home and a husband and children of her own to love. Her current situation was impossibly hopeless.

Josie took the paper from Miranda and continued:

"I will need first-class tickets and instructions how to meet up with you in San Antonio. I am required to leave my present circumstances by February 13, so I would appreciate a reply at your earliest convenience.

Yours sincerely,
Miss Miranda Wentworth"

"Oh, sweetie, it's a wonderful idea, a dream, really," Miranda choked out when Josie was done. "Mr. Creed must have had dozens of responses. Maybe even hundreds. He might not be interested in me. Besides, it's too late. By the time a letter like this could get all the way to San Antonio, Texas, and an answer come back, it will be far too late."

Miss Birch would have had weeks—or months—in which to lay her cane on the backs of Miranda's brothers and sisters without Miranda there to intercede. She'd been hoping beyond hope for a solution that would allow her to take her siblings away from the Institute when she left tomorrow. This was not it.

She rose to usher her siblings to their cold beds.

"Wait! Look at this!" Josie said triumphantly. She rose and unfolded a crisp piece of vellum on the table in front of Miranda.

"What is this?" Miranda asked, picking up the paper.

"Read it," Josie said.

Miranda sat back down on the bench as she read aloud:

"Dear Miss Wentworth,

I was pleased to receive your response to my advertisement. I understand your need for a quick response. Enclosed please find the first-class tickets you requested and instructions for your journey. I will meet your stagecoach when it arrives in San Antonio.

Cordially yours,
Mr. Jacob Creed"

Miranda was aghast. "What is this?" she asked as she eyed Josie.

Hannah and Hetty were goggle-eyed.

Josie replied with a grin, "You're going to Texas, Miranda. You're going to be married. You're going to have a home where we can all come and live. He must be somewhat well-to-do. He agreed to send *first-class* tickets."

"Oh. Oh." That was all Miranda could manage to say. The thousand or so things that could go wrong with such a plan ran through her head, but her chest was near to bursting—with hope. "When did you get this?"

"It came yesterday," Josie said. "I wasn't sure whether I should even show it to you, but I figured I might as well."

"Why do you suppose he said yes?" Miranda blurted.

"He was the *only one* who said yes," Josie replied.

Miranda frowned in consternation. "How many of these advertisements for a mail-order bride did you answer?"

"About fifty or so," Josie admitted.

"Where did you get the paper? And the postage?" Miranda asked, amazed at her sister's gumption.

Josie looked sheepish as she replied, "I stole them from Miss Birch's desk."

"Oh, Josie—"

"Forget about the paper and the postage!" Hetty said. "What are you going to do, Miranda?"

Miranda chewed on her lower lip as she stared at the vellum. "This was the only reply to all those letters?"

Josie nodded.

"Mr. Creed didn't ask for any other information about me? Or provide any other information about himself?" Miranda wondered aloud.

Josie looked wary as she replied, "No. Is that a problem?"

"I don't know anything about this man. He could be a murderer or a thief or—"

"He's our salvation, Miranda," Hannah interrupted. "He's going to get us out of here. Once you're married to him, we can all come live with you."

"I couldn't possibly take advantage of a stranger like that!"

"He's willing to take a wife sight unseen," Hetty said. "Maybe he wouldn't care if we came along."

"*I* would care," Miranda said. "If I went at all, I'd want to come with the honest intention of making Mr. Creed a good wife. I'm still not convinced this is a good idea."

"Why not go?" Nick asked. "It's an opportunity you won't get again, Miranda. I know you. You'd never do anything like this on your own. If Josie hadn't written all those letters, you'd be stuck scrubbing pots and pans for the rest of your life."

It was a painful truth to admit, but Miranda couldn't deny she was more mouse than lion, more likely to take a beating than to fight back. With one notable exception. She'd rescued Harry from the upstairs nursery during the Great Fire. She shuddered. She would live with that terrifying memory—and the resulting scars—for the rest of her life.

"Maybe Mr. Creed will turn out to be really rich and have an enormous house with lots of bedrooms, and you'll be able to send for us after you're married," Nick finished. "Who knows?"

The advertisement for a mail-order bride hadn't mentioned Mr. Creed's age or his looks or his financial situation. Not that Miranda was in a position to consider whether Jacob Creed was old and fat or skinny as a bed slat. This might be her only opportunity to marry.

But she was afraid to go so far from her family without knowing more. Even if she traveled all the way to Texas and married a stranger, her siblings might have to remain at the mercy of Miss Birch for a long time to come.

"Before all of you get your hopes up too high," Miranda said, "remember we don't know anything about Mr. Creed's financial situation. He could be living in a sod house. He could be as poor as a church mouse. He—"

"He had the money to send you first-class tickets on the train and on a steamship and on a packet— that's a sort of sailboat—and on a stagecoach," Josie pointed out.

"Where are the tickets?" Miranda asked.

Josie produced them from a secret pocket in her nightdress and reverently laid them on the table. "I had to keep an eagle eye on Miss Birch's mail to intercept them. Here they are."

Hannah and Hetty issued a collective sigh of awe.

Miranda was afraid to reach for the tickets. She seldom took anything for herself before offering it first to one of her siblings. Her life the past three years had been full of sacrifices. But none of her siblings were old enough to marry. She would have to do this herself.

It didn't feel like a sacrifice. She'd be going on a grand adventure to a place she knew about only from stories in the *Daily Herald*. A place full of wild broncs and longhorn cattle. A place full of cowboys . . . and Indians. It all sounded so exotic. And exciting. She'd have a husband and maybe, one day soon, children of her own, two things she'd seen as very far in the future after she'd become a destitute orphan. And with a new life outside the orphanage, there was at least a chance she could rescue her siblings.

Miranda didn't let herself dwell on the possibility that her husband might turn out to be as cruel as Miss Birch. No one could be as cruel as Miss Birch.

Speak of the devil and she appeared.

"What is this?" a piercing voice demanded.

Miranda quickly slid the vellum and tickets across the table to Josephine, who slipped them back into the pocket in her night shift. As the headmistress descended on them like a whirling dervish, Miranda whispered to her siblings, "I'll take care of Miss Birch. Go!"

Her younger brothers and sisters grabbed their blankets and scampered for the door in the dark shadows at the opposite end of the dining room, leaving Miranda behind to face their nemesis.

Miss Birch was wearing a tufted robe over her nightgown, and her long black hair, of which she was so proud, was pinned up under a nightcap. The headmistress was short and stout, with large eyes so dark brown they were almost black and cheeks that became florid when she was angry, as she was now.

"I presume that bunch who ran off was the passel of brats you brought with you to the Institute," Miss Birch said. "I've warned you before about leaving the dormitory after lights out, Miss Wentworth."

Miranda lowered her eyes in submission, knowing that was the best way to conciliate the headmistress. "Yes, Miss Birch. I was saying good-bye to my brothers and sisters, since I'm leaving tomorrow morning."

"You think the fact that you're leaving tomorrow means you can flaunt my rules tonight?"

"No, Miss Birch. I—"

A slender wooden rod whipped through the air and

hit Miranda's right shoulder without warning. *Whop*. She gasped at the pain and bit her lip to keep from crying out. She didn't want her siblings to hear her and try coming to her rescue. There was no defying Miss Birch.

Miranda kept her hands at her sides, aware that if she tried to protect herself, Miss Birch would only hit harder.

"I'll be glad"—*whop*—"to see"—*whop*—"you go!"

The pain was excruciating. Miranda felt tears of pain well in her eyes, but she didn't make a sound, not even a whimper. She refused to give Miss Birch the satisfaction.

She could hear the heavyset woman breathing hard from the effort of whipping her. Miranda raised her gaze, staring into the black eyes that stared hatefully back at her, and said with all the calm and dignity she could muster, "Are you done now? May I leave?"

She watched as Miss Birch resisted the urge to hit her again. Three cracks of the rod. That was Miss Birch's limit, no matter how bad the infraction. Miranda knew her punishment was over, which was why there had been a taunt in her calm, dignified voice.

Then Miss Birch hit her again. *WHOP!* Hard enough to make Miranda moan with pain. Hard enough to make the tears in her eyes spill onto her cheeks.

"*Now* I'm done," the headmistress said with malicious satisfaction. "Go back to the dormitory, Miss Wentworth, and stay there until it's time for you to leave."

Miranda had turned to go when Miss Birch said, "Too bad you won't be here when those brats get their punishment."

"You've already punished me!" Miranda protested. "There's no need to punish anyone else."

"They were here, weren't they? Where they didn't belong? Oh, they'll be punished, all right. Each and every one of them."

"The baby—"

"That brat is no baby! He's four years old."

"*Only* four years old!" Miranda retorted, fear for her youngest brother, whom she would no longer be able to protect, making her bold. "How can you be so mean?"

"Mean?" Miss Birch pressed her lips flat. "I enforce *discipline,* Miss Wentworth. Without *discipline,* where would we be? Those children must learn to obey the rules. They must learn there are *consequences* when they break them."

"If you must punish someone, beat me instead."

Miss Birch raised her eyebrows as she tapped the rod against her open palm. "Let me see. Three strokes times five offenses. How many is that, Miss Wentworth?"

"Fifteen," Miranda replied, her throat tight with fear.

"I'm tempted, Miss Wentworth. Oh, how I am tempted."

"Who would know?" Miranda said in a voice that was almost a whisper. "I'm leaving tomorrow."

Miss Birch laughed. "You're a fool, Miss Wentworth. I could give you fifteen strokes of the rod tonight and punish the rest of them tomorrow after you're gone."

Miranda knew very well that Miss Birch would find reasons to punish her siblings, even if there weren't any. But the tickets secured in Josie's pocket gave her courage. "Do it," she urged. "I trust you will be too tired after the effort to bother my siblings, at least for tomorrow."

"Very well, Miss Wentworth. Turn around and bare your back."

Miranda's eyes went wide. "You can't mean—"

"Bare your back," Miss Birch demanded. "Or I'll have every one of those brats back in here tonight to get three strokes of the rod."

"Yes, Miss Birch." Miranda turned and slid her shift off already aching shoulders, securing the folds of cloth against her small breasts.

She focused her terrified mind on the faceless man at the end of her upcoming journey. The man who would be her husband. The man who would be the salvation of her siblings. The man who would plant the seeds for a family of her own. The man she would somehow learn to love. The man who might someday learn to love her.

Miranda braced herself and waited for the cane to strike.

Chapter Two

"How long till we get there?"

Miranda felt her heart squeeze at the pitiful, plaintive tone in her brother's voice. "The stagecoach can only go so fast, Nick," she said, brushing at the wheat-colored cowlick shooting up like a rooster's tail at the back of his head. She was wondering, yet again, whether she'd made the right decision sneaking away from the orphanage in the middle of the night with her two younger brothers in tow.

"I'm hungry, Miranda," Harry said, peering up at her with beseeching blue eyes.

"Me, too," Nick grumbled. He pulled away from her mothering touch to stare out the open coach window at the surprisingly green rolling hills.

Miranda couldn't help marveling at the leafy trees and lush green grass in Texas, when there had been bare branches and snow on the ground sixteen days ago when they'd left Chicago.

"It feels like we've been traveling forever," Nick said. "How much farther do we have to go?"

"I don't know!" Miranda snapped. She saw the hurt look on her brother's face and said, with as much patience as she could muster, "Another hour. Maybe two. We're almost there."

Nick slumped back on the lumpy coach seat with a mulish look on his face and stared out the window.

It was too late for Miranda to regret her impulsive decision to bring her two brothers along. But after the horrific beating Miss Birch had given her, she'd been afraid to leave them behind.

She hadn't asked for permission, because Miss Birch would likely have kept her from taking the boys out of spite. She'd decided to make her escape in secret. She'd roused the girls in the middle of the night to tell them what she was doing, so they wouldn't be frightened when they awoke to find their brothers missing along with her.

The girls had wanted to come, too. It had been difficult, but she'd convinced them to stay behind. While she might pawn off two young boys on her unsuspecting husband, he could very well decide not to marry her if she showed up with five extra mouths to feed.

"You're right, Miranda," Josie had said. "Our early departure from the Institute depends upon your marrying Mr. Creed. The three of us will wait here."

That had been that.

Because she'd been in such a rush to escape undetected—and in such pain she could scarcely move without whimpering—the boys didn't even have a change of clothes. Miranda wasn't much better off. She was wearing a too-large, navy woolen dress with a starched white cotton collar that someone had donated to the orphanage. She had felt blood seeping through the fabric from the wounds on her back, but the dark stain wouldn't show against the deep blue cloth.

She'd packed a faded print cotton dress to change into once her back stopped bleeding. She would have changed into the cooler garment a couple of days ago, if only she'd had the privacy to do so. There had been none, because she hadn't traveled first class. All her tickets had been traded for cheaper fares, to provide passage for the two boys.

Besides, it didn't seem fair for her to be dressed in cotton when the boys were stuck wearing their woolen winter clothing in the sweltering Texas heat.

She used her hanky to pat at the perspiration dotting her forehead and the skin above her upper lip. Miranda worried about meeting her prospective husband looking—and smelling—like something the cat dragged in, but there was no help for it.

She'd left the rest of her meager wardrobe behind in order to stuff her carpetbag with food she'd scrounged from the Institute's kitchen. She was glad she'd packed food instead of extra clothes. The bread and cheese and dried apples had kept her and the two little boys fed during the first few days of travel.

The journey by rail to St. Louis, by steamboat down the Mississippi to New Orleans, by packet across the Gulf of Mexico to Houston, and now by stagecoach to San Antonio had been arduous. They'd been sleeping upright and eating whatever they could beg, borrow, or steal, once the food from her carpetbag was gone.

Yes, steal. It wasn't that she didn't know right from wrong. She did. But Miranda had learned a lot of hard truths over the past three years. Sometimes survival required behavior that would have appalled her parents. But Mama and Papa were long gone, and she'd had two—three, if she counted herself—empty stomachs to fill.

She and Harry had provided the distraction while Nick slipped in to steal a piece of fruit or a chunk of cheese or bread or whatever else might be found. Or Harry might throw a tantrum, drawing an attentive crowd, allowing Nick to steal a purse filled with enough money to buy them sustenance.

These last hours on the road were turning out to be the hardest—bumpy and hot and dusty. They'd had nothing to eat or drink since early morning. The boys were tired and hungry. So was she. However, her exhaustion was caused as much by fear as by fatigue.

What if Mr. Creed refuses to allow Nick and Harry to come live with us?

She and the boys could always throw themselves on the mercy of whatever church she might find in San Antonio, at least until she could find a job and a place for them to live. But that might take time. How were they going to eat and where were they going to sleep in the meantime?

This country was so . . . barren of people. And so . . . full of wild animals. Cattle with long, sharp horns. Wolves with howls eerie enough to wake the dead. Lumbering black bears with big teeth and enormous claws. Gophers that popped up out of holes and hurriedly retreated in the face of shrieking, sharp-beaked hawks. Worst of all, ugly vultures, feasting on the dead . . . and dying.

Miranda had run enough errands for Miss Birch to navigate the shadowy back alleys of Chicago with ease, but she felt totally out of her element facing this endless prairie wilderness. She had a vivid imagination, and her thoughts left her anxious and frightened.

What if Mr. Creed takes one look at me standing there with two little boys and wants back the cost of the tickets he gave me? What if he has the sheriff arrest me when I can't come up with the money to repay him? What will happen to Nick and Harry?

The thought of her two younger brothers left alone on the streets of San Antonio, or in some strange orphanage or farmed out to some family as slave labor, made her sick to her stomach.

Miranda felt like a cornered animal, ready to fight with fang and claw to defend her young. She clenched her hands into tight fists.

If Jacob Creed ever threatens my brothers' welfare, he's going to be very, very sorry.

The more Miranda thought of it, the more she realized she would have to get the Texan to marry her before he discovered the existence of her brothers. She had no idea how she was going to keep Nick and Harry out of sight until the wedding was over, but there had to be a way. Once she was married, she would be in a better position to argue to Mr. Creed that the boys came along with the wife he'd just acquired.

What if Mr. Creed wants to get married near his friends and neighbors at his ranch?

Miranda gnawed on an already tiny thumbnail as she considered her options. She would have to insist that they tie the knot before she went anywhere with her new husband. She remembered hearing Mama and Papa laughing and talking behind their bedroom door, so she knew a man and wife slept together in the same room. Actually, in the same bed. And from a girl at the orphanage who'd had a clandestine lover, she knew basically what a husband and wife did together in that bed.

The thought of being a wife intrigued her. Her mother had read her fairy tales when she was young. *Sleeping Beauty* was her favorite. Miss Birch could have been the evil witch. She wondered if Mr. Creed would turn out to be her Prince Charming, and whether they would live happily ever after.

In fairy tales, the princess was always beautiful. She wasn't nearly as beautiful as the twins, but she did have pretty blue eyes and curly blond hair. Would that be enough to balance a limp and a grotesque lower left leg?

When she'd expressed concern about her terrible burn scars, Josephine had pointed out that before they were married, Mr. Creed would only see her nice figure and pretty blond curls.

But Miranda knew the horror that was hidden beneath her floor-length skirt. She didn't limp badly, but that didn't mean a great deal of damage hadn't been done to her flesh when her skirt caught fire three years ago.

She'd been lucky to live, considering the seriousness of her burns, but she'd come away with a terror of being burned again. Her parents had been caught upstairs and she'd heard her mother's screams and her father's shouts as the blazing fire forced her back down the stairs.

Her parents hadn't gotten out of their burning home. The six Wentworth children had fled down a street on fire. Miranda had become the guardian of her siblings that night. She'd made a promise to herself, as she pulled her soot-covered siblings close, to keep them safe forever after.

Which was why she'd agreed, against her better judgment, to become a mail-order bride.

She would do anything Mr. Creed asked if he would just agree to take the boys—work her fingers to the bone, bear his children—anything.

Miranda felt a little breathless. She wished she knew more of what happened between a man and a woman behind that closed bedroom door. She'd had her first menses only a week before the fire. She'd been terrified, but her mother had explained what was happening in terms that made the bleeding sound like a blessing, instead of the curse she'd heard whispered about among her friends at school.

She was now a woman, her mother had explained, and her body was preparing itself for the seed a man planted that would cause a baby to grow. Miranda knew the basics of how that seed got transferred from male to female from her friend at the orphanage, and she remembered her mother assuring her, face blushing rosily, that her husband would tell her what was required of her when the time came.

Miranda hoped Jacob Creed would be young and handsome. But even if he turned out to be an ancient troll, she was going to marry him to save her family.

Despite her fears, Miranda still believed she'd made the right decision bringing the boys along. Knowing Miss Birch, Harry would have been left out in the cold to catch pneumonia and die before Miranda

could get back to rescue him. Nick would have suffered a fall down the stairs or some other "accident"
that ended his life. His forearm had already been "accidentally" broken once during one of Miss Birch's
private punishment sessions.

Miranda brushed the white-blond hair back from
Harry's forehead. He felt feverish. She helped him rearrange himself so he was lying with his head in her
lap. He stuck his thumb in his mouth and began to
suck it. She didn't try to remove it, even though he
was too old for such behavior, because she thought
it might keep him from remembering how hungry he
was.

Harry had been as pale as death for most of the
journey. Now he was flushed with fever and had developed a wheezy cough to go along with his Chicago
winter cold. If Harry could just survive until they
got to San Antonio—where a home with a bed and
good food would surely be waiting—she would nurse
him back to health. As Harry swiped his runny nose
across his dusty face, Miranda grabbed for her hanky.
She dabbed at the cloth with her dry tongue, then spit
on it and scrubbed at the muck on Harry's face.

"Stop, Miranda!" Harry protested. He wriggled
away from her and slipped down onto the coach
floor. He sat at her feet for a few moments before he
reached out with a dirty finger to touch the fancy silk
hem of the rotund woman passenger on the opposite
seat.

"What is that?" the woman said in a shrill voice so
reminiscent of Miss Birch that Miranda winced.

Harry froze in place. When the woman stomped
her high button shoe, he launched himself off the

floor and back onto the seat beside Miranda with a yelp of terror. He pressed himself against her like a frightened rabbit.

Despite how hot and sweaty she felt, Miranda pulled her brother close and glared at the woman on the opposite bench.

The woman looked down her nose at the three raggedy passengers with whom she shared the coach. Miranda felt angry but knew the better course was to appease the woman, if she could. This lady might become one of her neighbors in San Antonio. At least, she had the same destination.

"I'm sorry. He's very tired," Miranda said in explanation and excuse of Harry's behavior. "My name is Miranda Wentworth. These are my brothers, Nicholas and Harrison."

When the woman said nothing in reply, she continued, "We've come all the way from Chicago. We weren't expecting it to be so hot in February."

"I'm Mrs. Swenson," the woman said. "I run the Happy Trails boarding house in San Antonio. You can call me Dottie."

"Thank you, Dottie," Miranda said.

"Sorry I yelled at your brother. I've got a fear of mice. I don't really see very well, but I don't like to wear my spectacles, so I wasn't sure what it was down there. He touched my skirt just enough that I thought it was one of those awful vermin. Well, anyway, I'm sorry. You seem very young to be traveling alone."

"I'm meeting my husband in San Antonio," Miranda replied, feeling relieved that Mrs. Swenson wasn't another Miss Birch. Miranda wondered why she hadn't just admitted she was a mail-order bride and that she was meeting her *prospective* husband in San Antonio.

She turned to stare out the coach window, hoping Mrs. Swenson wouldn't ask any more questions, especially since she intended to conceal the existence of her two brothers from Mr. Creed when she arrived.

"Wentworth. Wentworth," Dottie Swenson murmured. "I don't believe I know any Wentworths in San Antonio."

Miranda felt pinned like a butterfly on a museum wall by Miss Swenson's inquisitive stare. "That's my maiden name," she admitted. "I'm meeting my husband-to-be in San Antonio."

"Oh." Mrs. Swenson smiled. "You're a mail-order bride?"

Miranda gave a jerky nod. "Yes."

"Well, I'll be a horny toad."

"A *horny* toad?" Nicholas said. "What's that?"

Mrs. Swenson grinned. "Horned toad, actually," she corrected, and then explained, "It's a lizard with spines. You'll see a lot of them around here, along with rattlesnakes and such."

Miranda's eyes went wide. "Rattlesnakes?"

"Holy cow!" Nick said.

"Nicholas Jackson Wentworth!" Miranda scolded. "Watch your language around—"

"I'm not a baby!" Harry yelled before she could finish her sentence.

Nick wasn't cowed. "I can't wait to see a horny toad and a rattlesnake." He stuck his head out the coach window, searching the terrain and exclaimed, "Look! There's another deer."

"Let me see!" Harry cried as he climbed across Miranda to the window where Nick was seated.

"It's gone now," Nick said.

"There it is," Harry said, pointing to an animal with a red hide.

"That's a cow, stupid."

"I'm not stupid!" Harry retorted. "Is that a cow or a deer, Miranda?"

Miranda scooted closer, glanced out the window and said, "It's a cow. You can tell by the long horns growing out of its head to the sides. Deer have antlers that grow up, rather than out."

"So there!" Nick said to his brother.

"There sure are a lot of cows," Harry said.

"Yes, there are," Miranda agreed.

"They're steers," Mrs. Swenson corrected.

Miranda turned to the older woman and asked, "What's the difference?"

"There are cows out there, but most of those animals are steers—male animals that have been cut so they can't reproduce."

"I see," Miranda said, although she didn't.

"Cut how?" Nick asked.

Miranda had wanted an explanation, too, but she'd been too embarrassed to ask.

"Emasculated," Mrs. Swenson said.

"What does emascu—"

Miranda slapped a hand across Nick's mouth to cut off his question and said, "I'll explain later." To change the subject she asked, "If you live in San Antonio, Mrs. Swenson, what caused you to travel to Houston?"

"I was visiting my sister," she replied.

"I miss my sisters already," Miranda said wistfully.

"Where are they?" Mrs. Swenson asked.

"I left them behind in Chicago."

"Miranda's eighteen, so she had to leave the orphanage, and Nick and I came along at the last minute," Harry volunteered. "We're a surprise."

Miranda put a hand over Harry's mouth but it was too late. The cat was out of the bag.

Mrs. Swenson's eyebrows rose all the way to her hairline. "Your prospective husband doesn't know your brothers have come along?"

Miranda shook her head.

"Oh, my. Who are you marrying, Miss Wentworth, if I may be so bold as to ask?"

She took a deep breath and said, "Mr. Jacob Creed."

"Oh, my," Mrs. Swenson repeated, putting a gloved hand to her mouth, which had opened in shock. "Jacob Creed, you say?"

"Yes. Is there something wrong with Mr. Creed?"

"I think it would be better if he explains the situation to you himself," Mrs. Swenson said.

Miranda was left to wonder and worry as Mrs. Swenson chattered on about a number of subjects that steered completely clear of Jacob Creed. Miranda was so distracted by her troubled thoughts that she was surprised when the driver shouted, "Whoa! Whoa!" and the stagecoach rumbled to a stop.

Miranda's gaze shot to the window for her first view of San Antonio. All she saw was a cloud of dust.

She turned back to Mrs. Swenson and said, "Please, I need your help. Could you take the boys with you to your boarding house? I mean, just until I have a chance to meet Mr. Creed. I promise I'll come for them as soon as I can."

"I want to stay with you, Miranda," Harry said.

Miranda ignored Harry's grip on her arm and said, "Please, Dottie?"

Mrs. Swenson took her time making up her mind. The coach door was already open by the time she said, "How would you boys like a big bowl of beef stew?"

The mention of food caused Harry's head to whip around. The mention of beef even made Miranda's mouth water.

"Real beef?" Nick said.

"Sure enough," Mrs. Swenson said. "How about it, boys?"

"Come on, Harry," Nick said as he grabbed Harry's hand and jumped down from the coach. "Let's go get some lunch."

"The boarding house is at the end of the street, just beyond the Alamo," Mrs. Swenson said as she stepped down after the boys. "They'll be fine. Come get them when you can."

"I'll be there soon," Miranda said, following after the older woman. She brushed a hand across Nick's cowlick, and wiped Harry's nose one last time, before they eagerly turned and followed Mrs. Swenson down the street.

Miranda stood, carpetbag in hand, looking around her for Mr. Jacob Creed. The street that had appeared busy a moment before was suddenly empty. Where was he? He was supposed to be here to meet her.

She felt a moment of panic. What if he never showed up? She took a deep breath and let it out. No one would have spent so much on tickets if he didn't intend to marry his mail-order bride once she arrived. She looked around and saw the coach had stopped at the front door of the Menger Hotel. That was as good a place as any to start the search for her groom.

Chapter Three

Jake Creed didn't want a wife, but he needed one. He needed someone to cook, someone to clean, someone to mend his clothes. And someone to be a mother to his two-year-old daughter.

Maybe he should have warned his mail-order bride that she was getting a ready-made family. Miss Miranda Wentworth had written that she loved kids. If she hadn't lied, things would work out fine.

Jake rubbed his belly, which was tied in several knots. Miss Wentworth was arriving on the two-o'clock stage. He would be a married man again before the day was out.

He'd tried to imagine how his future bride might look, with her blue eyes and curly blond hair, but whenever he did, he felt unfaithful to his dead wife. Priscilla's eyes had been brown. Her hair had been brown, too, and straight as an arrow. Priss had died in childbirth six months ago, and he'd buried their stillborn son along with his beloved wife.

Jake didn't have the luxury of grieving any longer. His father-in-law had cared for motherless Anna Mae over the past six months, but the old man had complained constantly. Slim Stockton hated being house-bound. The old man didn't have much choice. He'd broken his back coming off a bronc a year past and was confined to a wooden chair with wheels. Jake had felt overwhelmed taking care of both father-in-law and baby daughter.

It was the crotchety old man who'd suggested he take another wife. Jake had agreed it was the practical thing to do. However, there hadn't been much chance of getting the daughter of any of the nearby ranchers to marry him, not with the ongoing feud between him and his wealthy stepfather.

Nobody wanted to cross swords with the Englishman who'd married Jake's mother when Jake's father, Jarrett Creed, hadn't come home after the War Between the States. As far as Jake was concerned, Alexander Blackthorne had married his mother, Creighton Creed, to steal her land and then fathered children on her to steal Jake's inheritance.

Jake had taken Three Oaks, the cotton plantation willed to him by his uncle, branded as many mavericks as he could round up after the war, and eked out a living for the past ten years as a rancher. His step-father had tried to buy him out and burn him out and starve him out. But he wasn't going anywhere. The Englishman didn't scare him.

Unfortunately, no rancher with a daughter—pretty or otherwise—wanted to get on the Englishman's bad side by aligning himself with Creighton Creed Black-thorne's eldest son. So Jake had put his advertisement for a mail-order bride in newspapers in several big cities outside Texas, including Chicago.

He'd gotten numerous replies and had chosen an

eighteen-year-old with blue eyes and curly blond hair named Miranda Wentworth. On paper, his prospective bride sounded like some kind of fairy princess. He was cynical enough to believe she'd turn out to have buckteeth and crossed eyes.

No matter how she looked, he was going to marry her this afternoon. But he wasn't going to love her. Losing Priss had nearly killed him. He was never going through that kind of pain again. Having a woman in his home was necessary. But he wasn't going to let his new wife anywhere near his heartstrings.

Life here in Texas was too damned hard on females. The blue northers, the drought, the prairie fires—and the loneliness etched into the landscape by the constantly moaning wind—chewed them up and spit them out and left their husbands to bury them.

Because Priss had loved him, she'd worked herself to the bone and then been too weak to survive the birth of their second child. He felt responsible for her death. She'd hidden her exhaustion, but he should have known better. He should have made her rest more. He should have taken better care of his wife.

He was never going to make that mistake again. He would never put that second burden—a pregnancy—on another woman. He might wish for more children, but he didn't *need* them. He would hire help, rather than depend on his own sons to do the work around the ranch. He was happy to pass on whatever he had to his daughter when the time came.

The only certain way to protect his wife from pregnancy was to avoid having sexual relations with her. But he couldn't help hoping his new wife would be pretty to look at and cordial to speak with and kind to his daughter.

He was sitting inside the Menger Hotel when he heard the two-o'clock stage pull up out front. He didn't watch his future bride step down from the coach because he wanted the possibility of a fairy tale princess to last as long as possible. He forced himself to stay seated in one of the red-satin-covered Victorian chairs in the hotel's fancy lobby.

He caught himself fidgeting with a string hanging from a hole in the knee of his best denim Levi's and let it go. When his future bride still hadn't shown up in the lobby two minutes later, he realized she might not know to come inside. So he stood, intending to search her out.

At that moment, a raggedy-looking waif in a too-big dress stepped inside the lobby. She searched the elegant room with eyes as blue as a summer sky, until her gaze landed on him. She looked frightened. The blond curls of his imagination were tied up tight in a bun at the back of her head, revealing sharp cheekbones in a thin face.

Jake's heartbeat ratcheted up, and his neck and ears got hot. He felt like a cradle robber. This elfin girl—there was no evidence of a woman's figure—must be his bride. He yanked his flat-crowned black hat off his head and held it in both hands at his waist. His feet seemed to be rooted to the floor and his tongue was tied to the roof of his mouth.

He stared at her, wondering how he could have been so stupid as to choose a bride sight unseen. "Miss Wentworth?" he said at last.

She stared back. "Mr. Creed?"

He managed a jerky nod.

Then she smiled.

Jake felt his heart jump. Her full lips were bowed at the top and her teeth were white as pearls and perfectly straight. He didn't want to make the comparison to Priss, whose teeth hadn't been her best feature, but he couldn't help it. He'd loved his wife, despite her imperfections. It didn't seem fair to compare her to this intriguing stranger with a smudge of dirt on her cheek.

He took the few steps to bring them close enough to speak without being overheard by the gossipy clerk at the lobby desk. "Do you have any luggage I need to get from the coach?"

She looked down, and he saw she held a shabby carpetbag.

"I have everything I brought with me in here."

Jake frowned as he eyed the thin carpetbag. Then he took a closer look at what she was wearing. The wool dress was too warm for the weather, which was proved by the sweat stains on the dirty white collar and the small dots of perspiration above her perfectly bowed upper lip. "You didn't bring much."

"I don't own much," she said, her smile fading. "I'm an orphan, you know."

"I thought you worked at the Chicago Institute for Orphaned Children."

Her smile returned, and he felt that flutter again in his heart. He did his best to ignore it. On first glance, she wasn't much to look at. But those blue eyes of hers and that smile had taken him off guard. He hadn't expected to be so physically attracted to a perfect stranger.

He didn't like it. Especially when he was going to share the same bed with her—but keep his hands off. No touching, no kissing, no nothing. He felt an ache in his chest. It was loss he was feeling . . . the fading promise of what might have been.

He reminded himself of the price he would pay if he took the chance of loving this woman. Her eyes and that smile were enough to tempt him. But once burned, twice chary. He had no intention of getting attached to Miss Miranda Wentworth.

"I did work at the orphanage," she explained with a winsome quirk of her lips. "I simply wasn't a paid employee."

He tried to smile back, but he couldn't manage it. Smiling was something you did when you were happy. Which he wasn't.

He had some inkling how lucky he was that Miss Wentworth hadn't turned out to have buckteeth and crossed eyes. He just hoped her personality, which was far more important, turned out to be as providential as her looks. "Would you like to wash up?"

"Oh, yes, I would. Where could I do that?" she asked.

"I've taken a room at the hotel."

Her eyes rounded and her mouth dropped open in surprise. "Oh."

His ears and neck felt hot again. There was something very womanly about those wide, innocent blue eyes and that sensual mouth. He forced himself to focus on the childish smudge of dirt on her cheek. "I got the room so you'd have a place to freshen up," he said. "I didn't plan for us to spend the night. We can be back at Three Oaks—my ranch—before dark if we leave right after the ceremony."

"Oh. Yes. Well. That sounds fine." Her smile was gone again. She looked nervous. Like a new bride. Which she was.

Except he didn't intend to bed her.

He hadn't really considered what it would be like to sleep beside a woman who was his wife and not touch her. Mostly because he hadn't let himself think that far ahead. He was horrified to realize he was getting aroused at the mere thought of lying next to her. He imagined kissing that bowed upper lip and felt himself go hard as a rock.

He held his hat where it would conceal his body's unruly—and unwanted—response and made himself remember how his dead wife had looked, lying in their bed after the stillbirth of their child. That pitiful image quelled his arousal.

"The bellman can show you where to go," he said when he had himself under control. He reached into his pocket and retrieved a room key.

She held out a surprisingly work-worn hand, and he set the key in it. She'd taken a step past him, when she stopped and turned back, looking up at him with those compelling blue eyes. "What time is the wedding?"

He pulled a gold watch from the brown leather vest he was wearing over a long-sleeved, blue cotton shirt, flipped it open and said, "I have a minister scheduled to marry us an hour from now. I wasn't sure exactly when the stage would arrive. Will that give you enough time to wash up?"

"More than enough," she said. "In fact, the sooner

we're wed, the better. Do you think we could move the wedding up a half hour?"

Jake knew why he was anxious to marry. He just wanted this part over with, so he could take this woman home, where she could start being a mother to his two-year-old daughter. He wasn't as sure why *she* was so anxious to hurry the moment. Jake felt a niggling suspicion but didn't examine it too closely. He was too glad she wasn't homely, too pleased that her smile lifted his spirits, and too grateful that she seemed healthy enough to survive the life she'd agreed to share with him.

"I'll see if the minister is available earlier and get back to you." He set his hat back on his head, tugged it low, then touched a finger to the wide, flat brim as he said, "Until later, Miss Wentworth."

"Until later, Mr. Creed."

He watched her walk away and noticed her left foot dragged slightly on the carpet. He called out to her, "Miss Wentworth?"

She stopped in her tracks. When she angled her head around to face him, her blue eyes looked haunted. "What is it?"

He closed the distance between them, and she turned completely around to face him. "You're limping," he said quietly. "Are you hurt?"

Her cheeks flushed, turning her alabaster complexion bright pink. "It's an old injury, long since healed. I'm afraid the limp is permanent. It doesn't hinder me, I assure you."

"Oh." He was embarrassed for having noticed the flaw. He wondered how she'd been hurt, but he didn't want to embarrass himself—or her—by asking.

When he didn't speak again she said, "Was there anything else?"

"No. I've got a few more supplies to load on my wagon at Franklin's Mercantile before the wedding, so we can leave right afterward." He turned abruptly and left. He wished he hadn't noticed the limp. It made Miss Wentworth vulnerable, more worthy of his care and concern. He couldn't help marveling how that strange, imperfect creature was going to be his wife.

But not his lover. Never his lover.

He had to keep reminding himself why he'd made the decision he had. If he made love to her, sooner or later she was going to get pregnant. Pregnant women died in childbirth. Not always, but often enough for it to be a real threat to her survival. If he didn't want to find himself back at this hotel in a year or so meeting another bride, he had to stick to his guns. He had to keep his distance in bed.

It ought to be easy, certainly easier than making love to a woman he'd only known for a couple of hours, especially with his former father-in-law in the same house. Besides, how could you even call it "making love"? He felt no love for Miss Miranda Wentworth. He missed the pleasures of the marriage bed, but the brief satisfaction of sex with his wife was not enough to balance the certain pain of losing her in childbirth.

He'd lived with enough pain in his twenty-seven years to want to avoid it. The betrayal by his mother, when she'd married Blackthorne despite his warnings about the Englishman's true intentions, had been bad enough. Losing Priss and their newborn son had been almost more than he could bear. If the old man hadn't been so insistent, he wouldn't be here now.

He needed to be home rounding up cattle for market. He'd taken advantage of being in San Antonio for the day to buy supplies, since he'd needed a wagon to carry home his bride. The hotel room had been a luxury, especially when he didn't plan to spend the night, but it had seemed the least he could do for his bride after her long journey. Even though he could ill afford it. He'd spent more than he'd intended on those first-class tickets.

As he headed for the minister's home, he couldn't help wondering what Miss Wentworth was going to think when he didn't consummate the marriage. Of course, there was always the possibility that she was ignorant of what happened between married folk. In that case, she wouldn't know any better if all they did together in bed was sleep.

He had no idea how to find out how much she knew, other than to ask her. The prospect was daunting. He would just have to take things one step at a time. Tonight, when they were in bed together in the dark, would be soon enough to answer any questions she might have.

♢

Miranda still couldn't breathe right. One look at Jacob Creed was all it had taken. He was so handsome! Of course, his straight black hair needed a trim, and his face bore a stubble of black beard. His dark brown eyes had been inscrutable, and he'd been so somber—not even the hint of a smile. But he'd been polite and he didn't seem to mind about her limp.

She no longer feared that Mr. Creed would be unkind. He'd been more than kind, providing a room where she could refresh herself and agreeing to move up the time of the wedding. She was delighted to know he'd brought a wagon and that he was filling it with supplies. Surely there was space somewhere in the back, amidst all those bags of flour and sugar and boxes of fruit and vegetable tins she imagined he'd bought, where two little boys could hide.

Miranda felt sure that if she could just get her brothers to Jacob Creed's ranch, she could convince him to keep them long enough to let them prove their worth.

The bellman directed her up an elegant stairway to the second floor of the hotel, where she found the room number shown on the key. When she opened the door, the room had a simple elegance that reminded her painfully of her bedroom at home in Chicago, before the fire. She dropped her carpetbag and headed for the pitcher and bowl on the chest next to the window.

She stopped abruptly when she got a look at herself in the mirror hanging above the chest. "Oh, no!" She poured a little water into the bowl, wet the towel she found beside the bowl and scrubbed at the dirt on her cheek. She'd washed her face as best she could before she'd set out on the stage that morning. The sweat and dust had combined to leave her looking not at all like the princess in a fairy tale.

From the nearby window she could see Mrs. Swenson's boarding house at the end of the busy street, which reminded her she had to get word to the boys. She could also see the Alamo, just north of the hotel, where James Bowie and the other defenders had fought to the death. It seemed strange to find the famous Spanish mission on a dusty street in the middle of downtown. She hoped someday she'd get to pay her respects to the dead.

But it wasn't going to be today.

She dropped the towel and looked for paper and pen to write a note to Nick. She found both in a small writing desk. She wrote:

Dear Nick,

Mr. Creed has a wagon full of supplies at Franklin's Mercantile. We'll be leaving right after the wedding. The minute you get this note, take Harry and hide in the back of the wagon. Keep Harry quiet until we arrive at Mr. Creed's ranch.

Your sister, Miranda

Miranda sealed the note with wax and hurried back downstairs to the front desk, keeping an eye out to make sure Mr. Creed was nowhere in sight. "Could you please deliver this note to Mrs. Swenson at the Happy Trails boarding house and ask her to give it immediately to Nick."

"Is there a last name for this Nick?" the desk clerk asked.

"She'll know who I mean," Miranda said, unwilling to reveal to the clerk that Nick was her brother.

"Very well." The desk clerk held out his hand and Miranda realized he expected some compensation.

She smiled and said, "I thank you so much for your help."

The clerk brushed his open hand over hair slicked

back with pomade and smiled ruefully back at her. "Very well, miss."

Miranda hurried back upstairs. She'd used ten minutes of her half hour on the note. She needed to get herself cleaned up and changed into her one cotton dress. It was hard to believe this was her wedding day, that in a very few minutes she would be a wife.

Her stomach was full of butterflies, all trying to get out. She hoped Mr. Creed wouldn't be too angry when he realized that two little boys were part of the bargain. His advertisement had indicated that he liked children. If he hadn't lied, things would be fine.

Miranda poured more water from the pitcher into the porcelain bowl and filled her hands to rinse her face. The water felt wonderfully cool. She found soap hidden under the towel she'd dropped and realized she wanted to wash more than her face. She undid the line of buttons on the bodice of her dress and tried sliding it down her arms.

To her horror, she discovered the material was stuck tight to her skin with dried blood. It must have oozed from the welts low on her back that kept breaking open. The cuts were deep and hadn't healed as fast as she'd hoped. Fortunately, the dark dress concealed the bloodstains, but this prison of wool was the result.

She moaned. She couldn't wear this awful dress for her wedding. She just couldn't! The simple calico dress in her carpetbag wasn't the white wedding gown she'd imagined when she was a girl growing up in Chicago, but it was better than the awful wool thing she'd worn for the entire journey from Chicago.

She tugged a little and felt warm blood ooze where

the wool pulled a scab loose. It hurt. Maybe she could soak the dress free of her wounds. But she didn't have enough water left in the pitcher to do the job, and she was running out of time. Besides, she might rip open more of the scabs, and the stains would show through the light-colored calico dress.

There was no help for it. She was going to have to get married in this appalling, filthy, travel-stained dress.

Miranda felt tears welling in her eyes. She'd dreamed of being married in a white satin gown with a lace veil, with her mother and father and sisters and brothers there to help her celebrate the joyful day. None of that was going to happen.

Her heart sank as she heard a knock on the door. She quickly patted the tears from her face with the drying cloth and shoved a stray curl behind her ear. She plucked at her thin cheeks with her thumb and forefinger to add color, then turned and headed toward the door . . . and her future.

Chapter Four

"Do you, Jacob Andrew Creed, take this woman to be your lawfully wedded wife, to have and to hold, from this day forward as long as you both shall live?"

"I do," the groom said in a gruff voice.

"And do you, Miranda Elizabeth Wentworth, take this man to be your husband, to love, honor, and obey, from this day forward as long as you both shall live?"

Miranda tried to speak but nothing came out. She cleared her throat and croaked, "I do."

"Do you have a ring for the bride?" the minister asked.

"No."

Miranda felt her heart sinking even further than it had when she'd seen the disappointed look on Jacob Creed's face at the hotel, when he'd found her still wearing the navy wool dress with the stained white collar. She'd explained that her only other dress was too wrinkled to wear and there hadn't been time to iron it.

His lips had pressed flat, but he hadn't criticized or

complained. He'd simply said, "The minister is wait-ing."

Miranda was only beginning to realize that her almost-husband didn't seem very happy to be get-ting married, which made her wonder whether she'd failed to measure up to some picture he'd had in his mind of what his mail-order bride would look like.

Certainly she wasn't dressed like a bride. She didn't smell sweet or have a bow in her hair. Nor was she smiling like a bride. Instead, her eyes were brimmed with scalding tears, and she was struggling to hold back a sob that had been threatening to break free ever since the ceremony began.

The minister took her hand and Mr. Creed's, which were by their sides, held them together in his large palms and said, "I now pronounce you man and wife. You may kiss your bride."

When the minister released their hands, they fell apart.

Miranda could sense her new husband's reluctance to kiss her. She met his somber, dark-eyed gaze and waited. Nothing about this ceremony had seemed real, and it had been cut to its barest bones in the interest of saving time. She pleaded with her eyes for the kiss that would make this farce seem more real.

But she said nothing.

At last, her new husband leaned down and gently pressed his lips against the side of her mouth. The warmth of his touch lingered on her skin for a mo-ment after his lips were gone.

"Come on," he said brusquely. "Time to go."

That was the moment Miranda panicked. She was

committed in the eyes of God and the State of Texas to a stranger who didn't seem the least bit happy with the bargain he'd made. And he didn't even know yet about the two little boys she hoped were hiding in his wagon, waiting to make their appearance when they arrived at his ranch.

"Mr. Creed," she began.

"We're married now. Call me Jake," he said, his long strides eating up the distance across the wooden floor of the meeting hall that was used on Sundays—and for this wedding—as a church. "What should I call you?"

"Miranda, I guess," she said as she hurried after him. Her gait was awkward because the burn scars kept her left knee from bending easily. "Jake, could you please slow down? I can't keep up with you."

He stopped and turned and frowned as he observed how she was walking. "I forgot about your limp," he said. "Just how bad were you hurt?"

The question, so abrupt, so apparently unfeeling, reminding Miranda of all she'd lost three years ago and how different this day would have been if her parents had lived, finally released the desperate sob she'd been restraining.

Her wedding had been awful. No beautiful white wedding gown. No flowers. No music. No happy mother to cry tears of joy. No proud father to walk her down the aisle. No aisle, for that matter. No brothers and sisters to kiss her and hug her and send her on her way. Not even a ring to prove that she was a married woman.

And the groom . . . the groom was a blunt, brusque,

beautiful, beastly stranger. Miranda covered her face with her hands and broke into tears.

She heard Jake's footsteps on the wooden floor and then felt two strong arms close around her. At first she struggled, but Jake was murmuring words that sounded like comfort. So she gave up and laid her cheek against his smooth leather vest and clung to him as she cried her heart out. She felt his arms tighten around her, as though they could keep her from shattering into a million pieces.

She couldn't stop babbling, "I want to go home. I want to go home. I want to go home." But her home was gone, burned down. There was no way to go back. She could only go forward. She had to pull herself together. She couldn't afford to lose control. Nick and Harry were depending on her. Hannah and Hetty and Josie were stuck in Chicago. She had to please this man who held her life in his hands in order to save her family.

She was eighteen. She was a wife. She had to dry her tears and get on with her new life.

"Shh. Shh," he murmured.

As she quieted, Miranda made out the rest of what Jake Creed was saying.

"This was a bad idea. I'll figure out some way to send you home."

She drew back abruptly, pulling free of his embrace, and swiped at her wet eyes. "No! I can't go back. I mean, I have to stay here with you." She realized after the words were out that it sounded like being with him was a choice only slightly better than the plague. "That isn't what I meant. I meant—"

"If you don't want to be married to me, we can have this thing annulled," he said flatly.

Miranda realized that if she wasn't careful, she would end up getting sent back to Chicago whether she wanted to go or not. There was nothing left for her there. She hoped, somehow, to get the rest of her family moved here to Texas, which was only going to happen if she was married and had a home of her own.

"I'm sorry I broke down like that," she said past a throat that felt raw. She reached into the pocket of her dress for the new handkerchief she'd put there when she'd washed up at the hotel. She dabbed at her eyes and her cheeks, swiping away tears as fast as she could. Then her throat squeezed tight again. "It's just . . ."

"It wasn't much of a wedding," he finished in a curt voice. "I'm sorry. I know women set a lot of store by that sort of thing. I just . . . didn't think."

It was amazing how much better she felt hearing him say he understood her feelings. Hearing him admit he could—and probably should—have done more to make their wedding special. Miranda dabbed at her face again. "It's all right," she said.

"No, it isn't," he said angrily.

She stared at her new husband, wide-eyed. She watched a muscle in his jaw work, as though he were clenching his teeth.

Finally he said, "It's done now, for better or worse. What do you want to do?"

"I want to go home."

He closed his eyes and grimaced.

She put a gentle hand on his arm. When he opened

his eyes, she said, "I meant, I want to go to your home."

"*Our* home," he corrected.

She smiled as another tear slipped onto her cheek and said, "*Our* home."

"Shall we go, then, Miranda?"

This time, instead of hurrying off ahead of her, he offered his arm like a gentleman. She slipped hers through it and walked beside him into the hot Texas sunshine.

"You're very tall," Miranda said, looking up at him as they headed down the boardwalk.

He smiled ruefully down at her. "You're barely knee-high to a grasshopper."

She laughed at the quaint expression. "My—" She was about to say her sisters were all taller than she was, but she didn't want to reveal too much too soon. "I'm stronger than I look," she said instead.

He muttered what she thought was, "I hope so," but that sounded so ominous, she didn't ask him to repeat it.

When they got to his wagon, he was about to help her up when she said, "Oh, uh, I need to use the necessary before we leave." She needed a way to examine the back of the wagon, to be sure her brothers were on board.

"Good idea," he said. "There's an outhouse behind the mercantile."

Miranda headed down the alley between establishments to the back of the mercantile, then scampered along the back alley toward the Happy Trails boarding house. She knocked hard on the back door. When it opened, her eyes went wide at the sight of a dark-eyed, dark-skinned man with a flat nose and thin lips, whose long black hair was tied in two braids decorated with feathers.

Miranda felt certain she was seeing her first red savage. She would have been terrified, except he was wearing a linsey-woolsey shirt and trousers instead of the buckskins and breechclout she'd seen in bookplates of Indians in the library.

"Who you want?" he said in a harsh, guttural voice.

A savage who spoke English.

When he picked up a big butcher knife, gooseflesh rose on Miranda's arms. "Is Mrs. Swenson here?"

He left her standing there and returned a few moments later, butcher knife still in hand, with Mrs. Swenson.

"Oh, child, what are you doing here? I thought you were getting married."

"I am married," Miranda said. "I wanted to make sure you got my note and gave it to Nick."

"I did. The boys left right away. I'm afraid I have no idea where they are now."

"Thank you!" Miranda said. "Thank you so much, Mrs. Swenson. I'll never forget your kindness." Without waiting for the woman to say another word, she edged past the Indian with the butcher knife and ran back down the alley to the outhouse. She'd made use of the chamber pot at the hotel, so she didn't really need to use the necessary.

She snuck down an alley between buildings that led to the back of the wagon, watching to make sure Jake didn't see her as she crossed the open space on the street. She tried to spy under the canvas that covered the supplies, but it was tied down so tight she could see nothing.

"Nick?" she whispered. "Harry?"

"We're here," Nick whispered back.

Satisfied they were safe, Miranda took a deep breath and let it out. She patted her face with her hanky to remove the signs of exertion after her race to and from the boarding house, then walked to the front of the wagon, where Jake was readjusting the harness along the left-hand horse's shoulder. "I'm back," she announced.

"I was getting worried. Thought you'd run off. Or fell in."

She laughed feebly. "No. I'm here." She started to climb up onto the wagon seat by herself, but before she could, Jake was by her side. He set his big hands on either side of her waist and lifted her up so she could put her feet on the floorboards. She felt breathless when she sat down, as much from the feel of a man's hands on her waist as from the height of the wagon seat.

"You all right up there?" he asked.

"Fine." She was happy to discover the seat was padded but wished she had a hat or an umbrella to protect her from the relentless sun. But she wasn't about to ask her new husband for anything.

She'd already gotten the boys this far. Now she needed to impress Jake with how very helpful—and how little trouble—she was going to be. Before they reached their destination, she had to convince him that he hadn't made a mistake marrying a mail-order bride.

"Did you hear that?" Jake asked, glancing over his shoulder as he released the hand brake on the wagon, slapped the reins, and clucked at the horses to get them moving.

"What?" Miranda said. "I didn't hear anything."

Except Harry's sneeze . . . and a whimper . . . followed by a "Shh!"

Desperate to distract Jake from the noise being made by the two little boys, Miranda asked, "Will we be sleeping in the same bed?"

She watched his Adam's apple bob before he replied, "Married folk usually do. Is that a problem?"

Miranda blushed. "No. My parents did." Then, because she was curious, and because a great deal depended on his answer, she asked, "What is your home like?"

"It's actually an old Southern plantation house, two stories, with tall columns that hold up a second-floor gallery porch."

"That sounds enormous," Miranda said, feeling hopeful that there might be room for all of the Wentworths. "And beautiful."

"It used to be both—grand in size and magnificent to the eye," Jake said. "Part of it, one wing, was burned down after the war by carpetbaggers." His voice sounded bitter as he added, "Those bastards shot my uncle Luke and then hung every one of the freed slaves who'd stayed on at Three Oaks to work the cotton."

"How awful!" Miranda said.

Jake's face looked so fearsome it didn't invite conversation. He stared at the road that stretched endlessly before them, apparently lost in his dark thoughts.

She understood his pain because she'd endured it herself. "My house burned down in the Great Chicago Fire," she said quietly. "My parents weren't able to escape."

"Sorry to hear it," he said gruffly.

"I've been at the orphanage ever since. I was required to leave when I turned eighteen."

He raised a questioning brow. "Is that why you applied to be a mail-order bride?"

She nodded. She wondered how many rooms in Jake's plantation home had been left intact. Enough to house the rest of her family? "Have you ever thought about rebuilding the house?"

"Without slaves, there was no way I could keep planting cotton, so I've become a rancher. The demand for beef has been good, but there are problems getting my cattle to market. The closest railhead is the Missouri Pacific in Abilene. I would have had to leave my late wife—" He swore under his breath.

Miranda's jaw dropped. "You've been married before?"

He glanced at her, his eyes tortured, then turned his gaze back to the road. "I meant to tell you about Priscilla before the ceremony. I just never found the right time."

"How long ago did she die?"

"I buried Priss last August," he said through tight jaws.

That was only six months ago! Miranda tried to imagine how Jake could even think of marrying again before a decent period of mourning was past. Decent being *at least* a year. But if he'd waited, she would be washing dishes right now. She had to be grateful that, for whatever reason, he'd decided to marry again.

"I'm sorry for your loss," she said softly.

"I loved her."

Miranda gritted her teeth. Of course he had. He'd married again for the reasons he'd mentioned in his advertisement. He needed someone to cook and clean. Someone to bear his children. He'd married a housemaid. And gotten himself a brood mare. "You should have told me you're a widower." She felt angry. And sad. And discouraged.

"Would it have made a difference?"

"I hoped . . ."

"What?"

She lifted her chin and replied, "I hoped my husband might learn to love me, even though we married under such unusual circumstances." She lowered her eyes to her hands, threaded tightly in her lap. "I wonder now if your heart is free to love someone else."

He swore again.

She heard a snort from the back of the wagon that she covered with a cough of her own. "I would rather you didn't use that kind of language." She didn't want Harry, or especially Nick, who was older and more likely to try out such words, picking up bad habits.

He didn't apologize, but he didn't swear again, either.

He'd just turned to speak to her when the horse on the right shied away, then kicked out with both hind feet. Its hooves only missed her head because Jake yanked her halfway across his body at the last instant. The horses bolted and the wagon began to careen down the rutted dirt road.

"Damned rabbits!" Jake grabbed for the reins he'd dropped when he'd rescued her from the kicking horse but they were beyond his grasp. She instinctively caught them as they slid across her lap toward the edge of the seat. She shoved the worn leather toward Jake, who wrapped both hands around the reins and pulled with all his might.

"Whoa, Brutus! Whoa, Caesar!" he called in an amazingly calm voice. "Everything's all right now. Easy, boys. Slow it down now. That's it. Whoa, boys." He turned to Miranda and said, "You'd think those damned rabbits were rattlesnakes, the way they jump when one darts out in front of them."

The wagon finally rolled to a stop. In the silence that followed the excitement, Miranda distinctly heard Nick yell, "Ow! Ow! Ow!"

She stumbled down off the wagon seat and ran to the back of the wagon. Jake was a half second behind her.

"What the hell is going on here?" he demanded.

"Get this canvas off," she ordered. When he didn't move fast enough, she yelled, "Get it off! One of my brothers might be hurt."

As Jake stood stunned, Miranda yanked on the knots that held the tarpaulin taut against the top of the wagon. She freed the cover enough to pull it back, at which point two towheads popped up.

"Nick, are you all right?" Miranda asked anxiously.

"Sheesh, Miranda. What the hell happened?" Nick said.

"Nicholas Jackson Wentworth! If I ever hear you

use language like that again, I'll wash your mouth out with soap!" Miranda snapped. "Are you hurt? Or not?"

Nick held up one hand cradled by the other, and she saw one of his wrists was already swelling.

"A barrel of something fell over and landed on my arm." He moved the hand a little, but he moaned when he did. "I think maybe it's broken."

"Come here and let me see," she commanded. "You might as well get out of there, too, Harry."

Miranda purposely didn't look at Jake. She didn't want to argue with him in front of the boys. She was pretty sure he'd use language she didn't want them to hear.

Harry came scrambling toward her and launched himself into her open arms. She pulled him close and hugged him tight, then set him down. He hid behind her skirt, eyeing Jake suspiciously. Nick had trouble scooting out of the wagon with the use of only one hand. Finally, he slid down onto the ground, groaning when he landed.

"Let me see your wrist." Miranda held out her hand and Nick laid his wrist in her palm. She didn't see any obviously broken bone projecting from the skin, but when she tried to move the wrist, Nick howled.

"That hurt!"

At last, Miranda met Jake's gaze. Her chin was tipped up defensively. "Do you have anything I could use to wrap his wrist? I don't think it's broken but—"

"Let me take a look," Jake said.

Nick started to pull away when Jake reached for his wrist, but Miranda said, "Be still, Nick."

Miranda watched as Jake gently manipulated Nick's wrist.

When he was done, he said, "Move your fingers."

Nick slowly moved his fingers.

"It's not broken," Jake said. "Looks like a bad sprain, though." He pulled a red kerchief from his hip pocket and wrapped it several times around Nick's wrist to keep it from moving, then tied it in a knot. When he was done, he took a step back and said to Miranda, "I think maybe you better introduce us."

She put an arm around Nick's shoulder, although she had to reach up to do so and said, "This is my brother Nicholas, Nick for short. He's ten and a good worker."

"Not with a sprained wrist, he won't be," Jake said.

"He wouldn't have been hurt if your horses hadn't run away with the wagon," Miranda shot back.

"Who's the runt?" Jake asked.

Miranda tried to get Harry to come out from behind her, but he wouldn't. At last she gave up and said, "Harrison is four. We call him Harry."

"How did they get here?" Jake demanded. "More important, why are they here?"

"I traded in my first-class tickets to pay their passage," Miranda said. "They're here because I didn't think it was safe to leave them behind at the orphanage."

"It's a hell of a lot safer for kids in Chicago than it is here in Texas," Jake said.

"That's a matter of opinion."

"What are you planning to do with them?" Jake asked.

"I hoped they could live with us."

"There's no room."

"You just told me you have a plantation home—"

"That's half burned down."

"Half a plantation sounds pretty big to me," Miranda argued.

"It might be if there wasn't anybody but you and me living there. But my crippled father-in-law lives with me, and I've got—"

"Nick and Harry won't take up much room," she interrupted. She started to say they could sleep with her. But that wouldn't work, now that she was a wife. It was a good guess that Jake hadn't planned a wedding night that included two little boys. "Surely there's someplace in the house they could sleep. They don't need a bed, just a pallet on the floor will do."

"That's a good thing, because I don't have an extra bedroom," Jake said in exasperation.

Harry tugged on her skirt. She glanced down and automatically reached for her hanky and wiped his nose.

"The runt looks like he's sick. What's wrong with him?"

"He's got a cold."

"I can't have a sick kid living in my house," Jake said.

"It's only a cold," Miranda protested.

"Colds are contagious, right?"

"Neither Nick nor I have caught Harry's cold, if that's what you're asking. We're both fine. Harry just needs a warm place to sleep and a little food in his stomach and he'll be well in no time." At least, that was her hope.

"I'm hungry, Miranda," Harry said. "And I need the necessary."

"Didn't you eat and take care of business at the boarding house? Mrs. Swenson promised to feed you."

"There wasn't time for any of that," Nick said. "I figured we better get to the wagon lickety-split. I didn't want to risk getting left behind."

Without a look in Jake's direction to see what effect that admission had on his temper, Miranda took Harry's hand and walked off toward a patch of cactus that would provide a little privacy so he could relieve himself.

She watched Jake take off his hat, run a frustrated hand through his black hair, then slam the hat back on and yank it low on his brow. He focused his gaze on Nick and said, "When was the last time you ate, boy?"

Nick's eyes never left the ground. "I don't remember."

Jake turned to Miranda, his hands balled into fists at his waist, and said, "Why haven't you fed these kids?"

"We've eaten what we can, when we can," she said. "You can't buy food without money, and we don't have any."

"You should have left them at the orphanage where they were safe."

"That's just the point. They weren't safe there," Miranda said as she returned with her younger brother in tow. She straightened one of the braces that ran across Harry's shoulder, holding up his short pants.

Jake grimaced as Harry swiped at his runny nose

with his sleeve and said, "I can't have a sick kid in my home."

Miranda put her hands on her hips and demanded, "Why is a big, bad man like you so afraid of a little cold?"

"It's not me I'm worried about," he shot back. "It's my two-year-old daughter!"

Chapter Five

Jake watched the blood drain from his new wife's face. Finding out he'd been married before was one thing. Apparently, finding out he also had a child was something else entirely.

"What other secrets are you keeping?" she said, her voice trembling with emotion.

"I could ask the same thing."

"None!"

He might have believed her, except her brow furrowed after she spoke and her blue eyes looked shadowed. He wondered what else she'd concealed from him. Neglecting to mention her two brothers was a lie of omission at least equal to his failure to mention his daughter and the old man. His marriage was off to a roaring start, with lies and deceit on both sides.

He shook his head. Two more mouths to feed. Two more kids who would be at risk in this wilderness. A bigger chance his new wife would end up exhausted at the end of every day. A bigger chance she'd sicken and die.

It said something about the harshness of this land that, when he'd just married the woman, he already imagined her dead and buried. His Chicago-born bride didn't understand how hard life was on an isolated ranch. Endless chores, work from dawn to dusk, and even then he felt like he couldn't catch up. And there was no help to be had if disaster struck.

He hadn't wanted the responsibility of another wife, but he'd been desperate. He'd figured the rewards would balance the risks. Now he had two more small, precious lives to worry about—and protect from danger.

"Get in the wagon," he ordered Nick.

"I don't have to do what you say," the kid said sullenly.

Jake turned to his new wife and said, "I can see he's not going to be a bit of trouble."

"Get in the wagon, Nick," she said. When the older boy continued to stare through narrowed eyes at Jake without moving, she said, "Please, Nick. Do what he says."

When the boy had trouble climbing up one-handed, Jake got hold of the back of his trousers and tossed him up onto the wagon bed. The kid yelped in surprise as his butt landed on a crate of tinned peaches. The runt had a death grip on Miranda's leg and started shrieking when Jake grabbed him by his skinny ribs and tore him away.

"What are you doing?" Miranda cried, snatching at Jake's shirtsleeves. "Leave him alone!"

Jake tossed the runt onto a feed sack in the back of the wagon with the other one. "You coming or staying?" he asked as he tugged himself free of her hold and headed for the front of the wagon. He didn't offer to help his wife up.

But by the time he was ready to go, with the reins in his hands, Miranda was sitting there beside him. Spitting mad. Her teeth gritted, if the muscle working in her jaw was any measure. Her eyes narrowed and shooting blue fire.

"You're a bully and a brute!" she muttered.

"You're a liar and a cheat," he shot back.

That shut her up. For about a half second.

"I won't stand for you hurting my brothers."

"I helped them into the wagon."

"Threw them in, you mean."

He shrugged. "We needed to get moving. Daylight's wasting."

He watched her survey the skyline, where the sun was sinking fast. She looked around and seemed to realize for the first time that they were in the middle of nowhere with night falling.

"How far is it to your ranch?"

"Couple of hours ought to do it."

She put a hand to her brow to shade her eyes so she could see into the distance and asked, "Will we get there before dark?"

"Maybe. If we don't keep stopping."

"You're the one who stopped the wagon," she reminded him.

"You're the one who jumped out and untied the tarpaulin."

Jake realized he was enjoying the argument. Not the fact that they were arguing, exactly, but matching wits with someone with enough spunk to fight back. He found himself comparing Miranda to Priss, who'd given him his own way in everything. It made for a peaceful household, all right, but with Miranda, he felt the first spark of . . . excitement . . . in a very long time. And felt guilty for it.

Priss loved him, that's why she hadn't fought with him. This woman was a stranger, someone he never wanted to love, and who was unlikely ever to love him. No wonder she was so persnickety.

"What's your daughter's name?" she asked.

Jake was suspicious of the question because Miranda had changed the subject from her brothers to his daughter. He told her anyway. "Anna Mae."

"How did your father-in-law get crippled?"

Another question. But better questions than accusations, so he said, "He was breaking wild mustangs and one fell on him."

"*Breaking* them?"

"Taming them by riding them till they stop bucking."

She stayed silent long enough to imagine what he was talking about, then said, "That sounds dangerous."

"It can be."

"Do you *break* horses, too?"

"When necessary."

"What are we supposed to do if you get crippled?" she asked.

Jake turned and met her concerned gaze. He was taken aback when he looked into her eyes because he had the sensation of falling. He quickly averted his gaze, focusing instead on his horses' rumps. "This is a hard land. A man does what needs to be done. Sometimes he gets hurt. Sometimes he gets killed. Sometimes the woman in his life gets hurt. Or dies."

His throat tightened on the last word. He tried

swallowing past the pain, but it hurt too much, so he stopped talking.

It would have been a silent journey, except the irrepressible boys in back began a conversation with their sister. He listened. And learned.

His wife turned to check on the boys and said, "Don't suck your thumb, Harry."

"I'm hungry, Miranda," the runt replied.

"Will there be something to eat when we get there?" Nick asked.

"I'll make sure there's supper for everyone when we arrive," his wife promised, eyeing him sideways.

Did she think he was going to let two little kids go hungry? Fine opinion she had of him. He knew that Slim would have something prepared for supper when they got there, but he wondered what she would have done if there was nothing on the stove. Could she cook? Or sew? Or do any of the things she'd mentioned she could in her letter? Had that all been a lie, too? He would find out soon enough.

"I'd like a big juicy steak," Nick said dreamily. "I can't remember the last time I had a steak."

"What's a steak?" the runt asked.

"It's bloody red meat from a cow," Nick explained to his brother. "It's been a long time, but I can still remember that it tastes delicious."

"I don't want anything bloody," the runt said. "I want oatmeal."

Jake ignored his wife's furtive glance in his direction. She must be wondering what he thought about Nick's revelation. It was obvious they hadn't been getting steak at the orphanage. It was also clear the

Wentworths must have eaten steak at some time before they'd gone there.

The boys settled down and it was quiet, except for an occasional whimper from the older boy when his wrist got jarred and a sneeze or two from the runt.

The crickets were beginning to chirp, a herald of the evening, when he asked, "What were you thinking when you decided to bring them along?"

"I was thinking I might be able to find a better life for my two little brothers. I was thinking they could be a help to you on your ranch."

"Bears'll eat 'em. Snakes'll bite 'em. Bulls'll stomp 'em. Horses'll trample 'em. Cold'll freeze 'em. Especially the runt."

"If it's so dangerous," she said in a huff, "why are you living here?"

"I was born here. I grew up here. This is my home."

He watched her chew on a tiny thumbnail for a minute before she asked, "How did your wife die?"

"In childbirth. I buried her with our stillborn son."

"Oh. I'm sorry." She hesitated, then said, "So you needed a bride to take care of your daughter?"

He nodded. "Yeah. That's about it."

"Why didn't you just marry someone from around here?"

"That's a long story."

"It's a long ride."

He might as well tell her what she'd gotten herself into. The problem wasn't going away. "My stepfather wants Three Oaks. He thinks my mother should have inherited it instead of me. He thinks I forged the will."

In the silence that followed she asked, "Did you?"

It was a fair question. It made him mad anyway. "No. Hell, no!"

"Please watch your—"

He held up a hand to cut her off. "Fine." Priss had warned him when Anna Mae was born that he was going to have to watch his language. His daughter had already picked up a few words that he'd rather she didn't have in her two-year-old vocabulary.

"What happened to your father?" she asked.

That was another painful subject but another fair question. "He never came home from the war."

"He died?"

"He was reported killed at the Battle of Gettysburg. My stepfather is a foreigner who caught my mother at a weak moment, right after she'd heard of my father's death in battle."

"A foreigner? From where?"

"England. He was a gambler, I think, before he met her. Certainly, he took a lot of risks—and won big. There are rumors he was a lord or something in England. But if that was true, why would he have left? That bastard—"

"Jake, please!"

He lowered his voice and said, "That bastard has made my life miserable. He's determined to get my land. I'm just as determined he won't."

"He can't very well roll it up and steal it, can he?"

"He can deny me credit for feed and seed in Bitter Creek, the town closest to my ranch, so I have to travel half the day to San Antonio for supplies."

"How can he do that?" she asked. "I mean, if your credit is good."

Jake smirked. "He owns the store. He owns pretty

much everything in town. The saloon, the hotel, the mercantile. He even built the schoolhouse and the town hall. Nobody dares to cross him, because he could ruin them financially and socially and every which way."

"Which is why, I presume, you had to send for a mail-order bride from Chicago."

"Chicago, St. Louis, Kansas City, New Orleans. Anywhere away from here," he said. Funny that he'd ended up with a bride from the city farthest away. It was the damned idea of a woman with blue eyes and blond curls that had caught his fancy. The blue eyes, at least, had met—all right, exceeded—his expectations. He wasn't so sure about the blond curls, since he hadn't seen any yet. He forced his thoughts away from her attributes and back to the conversation at hand.

"My stepfather's attitude is also why life is harder for anyone living at Three Oaks," he continued. "There's no help to be had from anyone. I don't know how you're going to take care of three little ones and the old man and do all the chores, too."

"I'm very strong," she said. "And I'm a hard worker. Honestly, you won't be sorry you let the boys stay."

"I haven't made up my mind yet whether those boys are staying. And I'm already sorry."

A voice from the back piped up, "If you ask me, Miranda, he's another Miss Birch."

"You're not helping, Nick," she replied.

"Who's Miss Birch?" Jake asked.

"The headmistress at the Chicago Institute for Orphaned Children," Miranda said. "She's not a nice person."

"Humph," Jake said. He didn't appreciate the comparison. He was a *very* nice person, that is, when he wasn't lied to and deceived. Of course, he'd done his own share of deceiving—and lying by omission—so he didn't have much room to complain.

"Give Nick and Harry a chance," Miranda pleaded. "I know they can be a big help to you."

He spotted a golden curl that had escaped from the tight bun at her nape and wondered what her hair would look like if she let it down. He chastised himself for even thinking about such things. That was a can of worms he didn't want to open.

"All right," he said, coming to a decision. "Here's what we're going to do. The older boy can share my daughter's room. I don't want the runt anywhere near her until that cold is gone. He can sleep in the room with the old man until he's well."

Slim wouldn't like it, but he could lump it. Jake wasn't taking any chances with his daughter's health, and he didn't have anyplace else to put the runt except his own bed, which he intended to share with no one but his wife.

"That's the deal. Take it or leave it."

She lifted her chin and stared up at him, "Fine. I have a condition of my own."

He felt stabbed to the heart by the desolate look in her eyes. It wasn't *all* his fault that things were so messed up. "I'm listening," he said past the knot in his throat.

"I'm willing to be a mother to your daughter and take care of your father-in-law and cook and clean and do chores. In return, I expect you to treat my brothers with respect, to teach them and care for them as a father would."

"That's a tall order."

"That's the deal. Take it or leave it."

He didn't agree right away. Be a father to the kid and the runt? He barely knew how to be a father to his own daughter. Besides, his new wife was in no position to be making demands. Where could she go, what could she do, if he didn't agree?

Except, women were so scarce here, that even if she didn't have such a pretty face, she could probably find a new husband without too much trouble. And he wasn't about to go through the trouble of finding another wife.

Sending the boys back to Chicago wasn't an option. First, he didn't have the money. He'd spent most of what he had getting his bride here. The woman with the blue eyes and blond curls had demanded first-class tickets, and he'd been afraid she would back out if he sent anything less. It had seemed worth the sac-rifice to spend the extra dollars to get the right bride. After all, he was going to spend the rest of his life—or hers—living with her.

Second, he didn't have anyone he could send on the trip with the boys. He'd spent too much time and effort getting his mail-order bride here. He wasn't about to turn around and send her back to Chicago with her brothers. She might decide to stay there, and then where would he be?

Back where he started, that's where.

"All right," he said. "We have a deal." He would have shaken hands with a man to seal the bargain. He would have kissed Priss to confirm an agreement.

In this case, he guessed words were going to have to be enough.

By the time he'd reached that conclusion, he saw a small, callused hand with the nails chewed down to the nub had been extended in his direction. He switched the reins he was holding in both hands to his left one, and shook her hand with his right. "I expect you to keep your word," she said as she released his hand.

"And if I don't?" He was pretty sure he was the one in the position of power here.

She looked him in the eye and said, "I will make you very, very sorry."

She sounded like she meant it.

$\diamondsuit$

Miranda's first view of Three Oaks left her feeling breathless, but not with awe. She was suddenly filled with doubt. Maybe she'd made a mistake. Maybe she should have left Nick and Harry in Chicago. This was not the home of a maiden's dreams. This was more like something she might conjure in a nightmare.

The Southern mansion was in far worse shape than Jake had led her to believe. One wing of the house was a charred ruin, all right. But Jake had failed to mention that white paint was peeling off the rest of it, exposing black, rotted wood, and that numerous rails were missing from the once-beautiful second-floor gallery porch. She'd have to be sure those rails were replaced as soon as possible, so neither Harry nor Anna Mae accidentally fell through the gaps.

He hadn't mentioned that three enormous trees—oaks, she supposed—shadowed the house like a shroud.

He hadn't mentioned that shrubs and bushes and tall grass had grown up around the front porch, leaving only a narrow path to get inside. Or the abandoned double row of facing log cabins she'd noticed a half mile before they reached the house, which had once been home to the fifty or sixty field slaves who'd worked the cotton.

He didn't carry her over the threshold, apparently didn't even realize he was forgetting that part of the marriage ritual. She felt the loss as one more missing piece of a marriage that was a far cry from what she'd hoped or dreamed.

Once inside the house, she found chaos, the result, she supposed, of two bachelors and a baby living for six months without a woman in the house. The entryway smelled of wet horse. It was crowded with a Western saddle and horse blanket, boots, halters, bridles, rope, and other things that belonged in the stable.

Jake led them into a parlor where horsehair stuffing gaped through tears in the delicate brocade sofa and a mouse-eaten cowhide-covered chair sat behind a battered oak desk strewn with tin plates and cups and stacks of paper. A mother cat had created a nest out of a man's plaid shirt in the corner and a litter of five kittens lay nursing at her side.

"Kitty cat!" Harry cried as he made a beeline for the cat.

The instant the calico cat saw Harry, she turned into a spitting fanged creature with an arched back and a high tail.

Harry screamed and came running back to the

safety of Miranda's arms. She picked him up and said to Jake, "What's your cat's name?"

"Doesn't have one," Jake said. "Barn cat sort of moved in after Priss . . ." He stopped there and called out, "Slim? Where are you?"

Miranda heard the sound of creaking wooden floors and a man in a wheelchair with a wicker back showed up in the parlor door. A barefoot baby wearing a nightgown sat in his lap.

The baby's face lit up when she saw Jake.

Miranda's first thought was that the baby needed some warm woolen socks on her feet. Then she remembered she was in Texas. Though it was February, the night air was warm.

The little girl cried, "Daddy, Daddy, Daddy!" Her arms reached out to Jake and a moment later she was snuggled against her father's chest, her arms tight around his neck.

The old man didn't look nearly so happy. "I sent you to town to pick up a wife." He eyed Nick and Harry sourly and said, "Where'd the extra young'ns come from?"

"They're my brothers," Miranda explained, anxious to make friends with the old man, since they'd be spending all their time together in the house. "You must be Slim. I'm Miranda. This boy in my arms is Harry. The tall young man over by the fireplace is Nick."

"Let's get some light in here," Jake said, setting his daughter back in Slim's lap. She didn't want to be put down and began to whine.

"There, there, missy," the old man cooed.

Slim wasn't totally against children, Miranda thought. He obviously adored his granddaughter.

The sun was almost gone, leaving the parlor strewn with shadows. Miranda shivered. She had a dreadful feeling of foreboding and tried to shake it off.

Jake lit several kerosene lanterns situated around the parlor. Somehow, the room looked more cheerful in the lamplight.

"I smell food," Nick said, sniffing the air.

"I made stew to last for a week," Slim said. "Guess there's enough for a few extra mouths."

"Is there beef in it?" Nick asked.

"Beef and potatoes and carrots," Slim said.

"Do you think we could have some?" Nick asked, looking from Slim to Jake.

Miranda realized that for the first time, Nick wasn't looking to her as the one in charge. He was consulting the two men. She wasn't sure whether to feel insulted or gratified.

She merely felt relieved when Jake said, "Sure. There's tin plates in the cabinet, forks in the drawer. Help yourself. Just don't burn yourself on the stove."

At last Nick turned to her. "Can I, Miranda?"

"Sure. Take Harry with you."

Miranda realized there was going to be no special first dinner, where the family sat down together. Not unless she orchestrated it. "Let Harry help you set the dining room table for all of us. We'll join you in a few minutes. Don't start without us."

Nick took a lantern in one hand and Harry's hand in the other and headed for the kitchen.

"I already ate," the old man said as he watched them go. "Don't figure to eat again."

Miranda realized she would be fighting an uphill battle to get Slim to the supper table. Tomorrow would be soon enough to make it plain that, from now on, they would be eating as a family.

She turned instead to Jake and said, "Would you introduce me to your daughter?"

He picked up the little girl from Slim's lap and brought her over to Miranda. "This is Anna Mae. Honey, this is Miranda."

"Mama?" the baby said.

"No, sweetie," Miranda said, feeling a sudden ache in her throat. "I'm not your mama."

"You should go eat," Jake said to Miranda. "You must be hungry, too."

"Yes, I am. Aren't you? I thought we could all sit down together. I mean, this is our first dinner as man and wife."

"It's Anna Mae's bedtime. I usually spend some time reading to her."

"Oh, I know the boys would love to listen, if you wouldn't mind waiting and reading to her here in the parlor after supper."

He hesitated, then said, "I suppose I could do that."

"Could you—would you—join us for dinner?"

He hesitated again, and said, "I'm not sure there's room at the table for all of us."

"Oh. If the table's too small—"

"It's plenty big. It's just covered with stuff."

She brightened. "I can fix that. Give me a few minutes, then come on into the dining room. Maybe you and Slim have some things to talk about."

"Sure do," Slim said. "I wanted to see when you figure to plow me a vegetable garden."

Miranda left the two men talking about how many rows they were going to plant in corn and beans and tomatoes and watermelon and hurried down the central hall in the direction the boys had taken. Just hearing about all those fresh vegetables—and watermelon!—made her mouth water.

She was appalled when she stepped inside the high-ceilinged dining room. Jake hadn't exaggerated. Apparently the two men had been eating elsewhere, because the dining room table was completely covered with boxes and tins and papers and clothes. There was no way to sort through it and put it away a piece at a time right now, so she grabbed handfuls of stuff and dumped it in a corner of the room.

Beneath the clutter she found the most beautiful cherrywood dining table she'd ever seen. The gold-brocade-covered chairs looked new. This was a table where they could have wonderful family dinners. There were seats for twelve at the table. She mentally picked spots for Jake and herself, her five siblings, Slim and baby Anna Mae at the table. That was only nine. She began to imagine three more children she would beget with Jake, along with their aunts and uncles, all sitting down together.

"What are you doing with my stuff?" Jake demanded.

Instead of dropping the load in her arms, as she had the last four, Miranda carefully set it on top of the pile in the corner. She grabbed a bath towel she'd found and used it to wipe the remaining dust and debris off the table. "I'm moving everything temporarily, so we can eat at the table. We can go through this stuff tomorrow, and you can tell me where to put it away."

"I'm going to be busy mending fence tomorrow. The house is your business."

She stopped what she was doing and looked up at him. "So you want me to decide where to put your things on my own?"

Jake looked unhappy with his choices. Either he had to spend time with her in the house sorting through everything, or he was going to have to ask her whenever he wanted something that she'd put away for him.

"I suppose I could spend some time tomorrow afternoon helping you sort through things."

She rewarded his good sense with a smile. "Thank you, Jake. That would be wonderful." She turned and surveyed the cleared table. "It's beautiful." She didn't point out that it seemed not to fit with everything else she'd seen in the house so far, which was worn out, torn up, and dilapidated.

"The dining room set was a wedding gift from my mother. I didn't want to take it, but Priss fell in love with it."

"I can see why. It's lovely. I'm glad you kept it."

Nick showed up a moment later in the dining room, Harry trailing after him, and said, "I've been looking, but I can't find any clean plates or forks or knives in the kitchen." He shot a narrow-eyed glance at Jake and said, "Looks like we'll have to wash all those dirty dishes in the sink before we can eat."

Miranda crossed to the glass-fronted china cabinet along one wall of the dining room and began taking out beautiful china plates imprinted with tiny roses.

"Those dishes belonged to my aunt and uncle. We only use them for special occasions," Jake said.

Miranda clutched the plates to her breast and lifted her chin. "I think our first dinner together as man and wife qualifies as a special occasion, wouldn't you say?"

He didn't say anything.

Miranda was learning that her new husband didn't like to lose an argument. She accepted his tacit permission and continued taking china plates from the cabinet and setting them around the table. She pulled open the first drawer of the cabinet and found tarnished silver forks and spoons. "They aren't as pretty as they will be once they're polished again," she said, "but at least they're clean."

She pulled open a drawer farther down and found table linens. She pulled out beautiful napkins embroidered with pink roses to match the dishes and set them at each place.

"This is looking pretty fancy," Jake said in a voice that bordered on disapproval.

"It's our first dinner together, Jake. Do you really mind?"

"I guess not."

"This reminds me of our home in Chicago, Miranda," Nick said wistfully.

Miranda stopped what she was doing and surveyed the table. If not for the peeling wallpaper and the dull finish on the forest green wainscoting and the burned-down candles in the modest chandelier above the table and the tarnish on the silver, why, Nick was right. "Yes, Nick," she said softly. "It reminds me of home, too. Where's the baby's high chair?" she asked Jake.

"In the kitchen."

"Would you bring it to the table."

"It's Anna Mae's bedtime," Jake said. "She's likely eaten already."

"Could she stay up and sit at the table with us? Please, Jake? We're a family now."

He looked torn, but she kept her eyes focused on his until he relented. "I guess that would be okay." He left to go retrieve the high chair from the kitchen. Nick and Harry went with him, to carry back cups of water for everyone.

As she surveyed her work, she heard the creak of the wheeled chair on the oak floor behind her. She turned to find the old man sitting in the doorway.

"You're wastin' your time," he said.

"It's never a waste of time to set a beautiful table and eat dinner as a family."

"Jake ain't never gonna love you like he loved my Priss," the old man said. "He ain't never gonna get no babies on you, neither. He ain't gonna take the chance of killin' you, like he killed my girl. Set all the tables you like. Do all the fancy arrangin' you want. It ain't gonna make no difference. You ain't never gonna be nothin' to him."

"Slim! Shut up!"

Miranda saw Jake in the doorway to the kitchen looking white-faced, his eyes stark. Which was how she knew the old man wasn't lying. For once, somebody around here was telling the truth.

There was no way she could sit down at that table with Jake right now and force food down her constricted throat, let alone have a civil conversation. She wanted to run. She wanted to hide. But she was well and truly trapped. This was her life, like it or not.

She would just have to prove the old man wrong.

"Please get Nick and Harry," she said to Jake at last. "It's time for supper."

Chapter Six

"Please, I want to sleep with you, Miranda," Harry begged.

Miranda's heart was breaking. "You can't sleep with me, Harry." She'd snuck Harry into bed with her at the orphanage whenever a storm thundered outside or whenever her little brother felt afraid of the bogeyman. She could hardly blame Harry for being anxious under the circumstances. She was distressed herself.

"I'll be good," Harry promised. "I won't wet the bed."

"Oh, baby, it isn't that."

She turned to Jake, who simply shook his head. She hugged her little brother tight and said, "You need to sleep in your own bed tonight."

"I'll sleep with you, Harry," Nick offered.

"Not in Anna Mae's room, you won't," Jake said.

"Don't worry. We're not going to infect your precious little girl," Nick said with an ugly sneer. "We'll sleep on the floor in the parlor."

"Nick, if we want Harry to get well, he needs to sleep in a bed with warm covers."

"It's warm enough in this blasted place without covers," Nick said. "I'll make up a pallet for the two of us by the fireplace in the parlor, from stuff on the iron-rail bed in Anna Mae's room, where I was supposed to sleep. We'll be fine, I promise."

Miranda turned to Jake and asked, "Is that all right with you?"

"I'll get the mattress," Jake said to Nick. "You can get the bedding. Be careful not to wake up Anna Mae. It took me a long time to get her to sleep."

Nick glared at Jake and muttered, "I wasn't planning on singing a song up there."

Jake shot Nick a dour glance but he didn't chastise him.

Miranda couldn't understand why Nick had taken such an instant dislike to Jake. She wondered how long Jake would tolerate Nick's insolent behavior, and what he would do when he'd had enough of it. She hated feeling so helpless. She could only hope that Nick would realize that Jake was more Savior than Satan and start behaving himself.

"Are you still going to read to the children?" Miranda called after Jake as the two of them headed upstairs where most of the bedrooms were located. Slim slept in a downstairs room decorated with flowery wallpaper and ragged pink curtains, which made Miranda think it might once have been a ladies' tearoom.

"No story tonight," Jake replied. "It's late. I've got to be up at daybreak."

It was also his wedding night. Miranda felt a shiver of expectation—and a smidgeon of fear—run down her spine. Tonight, her husband would do what husbands did to wives to make babies.

Fortunately, Miranda wasn't totally ignorant. Her friend at the orphanage, who'd lost her innocence with a boy she liked before coming to the Institute, had told Miranda that sex was painful the first time, but enjoyable—really wonderful—ever after. Miranda had seen the orphanage cats mating, so she had some inkling of the process, although it looked awkward in the extreme.

She felt nervous and a little anxious about what was going to happen tonight, especially since she barely knew the man who was going to be doing those awkward things to her. But she wasn't afraid. She held on to the hope of great pleasure her friend had promised was part of a man and women making love.

Miranda supposed tomorrow night was soon enough to begin traditions like reading to the children before bed. Tomorrow she would be more organized. She would have supper on the table earlier and have the kids washed up and waiting when Jake came home from wherever he went to work. After they'd eaten, she would ready the children for bed, then sit them down in the parlor so Jake could read to them.

"Are you going to read me a bedtime story?" Harry asked as Miranda began removing his shoes and socks.

"Tomorrow I will," Miranda promised.

Harry slid the braces off his shoulders and his knee-length trousers fell to the floor, leaving him in his smalls and a blousy white shirt that hung almost to his knees.

Miranda debated whether to take off the smelly,

food-and-dirt-stained shirt, but she was afraid Harry would get a chill if the temperature cooled later in the evening. Besides, taking off the shirt wouldn't really solve the problem. The little boy's skin smelled rank.

Tomorrow, she would make sure both boys got a bath and washed their hair. Tonight, everyone was exhausted, including her. Tonight, they all simply needed to sleep in something that resembled a bed.

Jake returned in a few moments with the pallet from Anna Mae's room. Nick traipsed after him, dragging the bedding behind him, including a white sheet, a colorful patchwork quilt, and a pillow.

Miranda marveled at the delicate flowers and butterflies and bees embroidered on the white pillowcase. She envied the talent of the woman who'd done such fine work. Especially when she had no idea how to embroider. Her sewing skills only extended to mending.

She wondered what else Priscilla Creed might have been much better at than she would turn out to be.

"The boys will have to share the pillow," Jake said. "There isn't another one."

"I can sleep without one," Miranda volunteered.

"No, you can't," Jake said. "You need to take care of yourself first, the kids second. If anything happens to you, they're going to be in serious trouble. Get that through your head."

Miranda was shocked at Jake's attitude. Every thought in her head for the past three years had been about how she could take better care of her brothers and sisters. She tried to understand how Jake could say something so harsh, when she saw how loving he was with his daughter.

She didn't have to think long to realize the truth of what he was saying: Nick and Harry, and even baby Anna Mae, were going to lead better lives if she stayed healthy—and alive—to take care of them. But a pillow was just a pillow.

"I don't need a pillow," she argued.

"Harry can have the pillow," Nick said. "I can manage without one."

Miranda stared at her brother in surprise. She was the one who'd always done without. This place, these people, seemed to be having a strange effect on all of them.

As soon as Jake placed the pallet on the floor of the parlor and Nick added the bedding, Harry scooted down and made a cocoon of it. Miranda took the pillow from Nick and handed it to Harry, who set it on the pallet, plumped it up, and laid his head on it. "Is that what he's going to sleep in?" Jake asked.

"It's all he has," Miranda replied. "I decided to bring my brothers along at the last minute. We left in the middle of the night. We didn't have time to pack."

"Who were you running from?" Jake asked.

"Miss Birch," Nick and Harry said together.

"The infamous Miss Birch. I'd love to meet her sometime," Jake said.

"No, you wouldn't," Miranda said.

Nick shuffled his feet and said, "I can undress myself, Miranda."

Sometime during the past year, Nick had gotten modest about undressing in front of her. "All right," she said. He didn't like being kissed, either, but she took his head in her hands so he couldn't escape and kissed his hair, brushing at his stubborn cowlick.

She got down on both knees to wipe Harry's runny nose one last time and kiss his cheek. Jake helped her up as she said, "Good night, boys. I'll see you both in the morning."

His hold on her arm should have been welcome, but it felt more like she was a prisoner in his grasp. She tried to shake off the feeling. This was her husband. It was his right to touch her whenever—and however—he wanted.

She shuddered as she realized the power she'd placed in Jake Creed's hands.

He must have felt her sudden reluctance, because he asked, "You all right?"

"Fine. Just tired."

"Good night, Miranda," Nick said.

"Good night, Miranda," Harry echoed.

Jake started to blow out the lantern but Nick said, "I'll take care of that."

"Don't forget, boy. Fire is—"

"We know about fire," Nick said bitterly. "In case you've forgotten, our house burned down."

"Well, I don't want this one burning down," Jake said. "So be sure to blow out that lamp."

Jake didn't give Nick a chance to argue further. He'd already turned, his hand still on her arm, bringing her along with him.

Miranda could feel her brothers watching as she followed Jake from the room. She didn't turn around because she didn't want them to see the worry in her eyes. She couldn't help being a little apprehensive about what came next. She was about to join a man—a virtual stranger—in bed.

Once they were out of the room, Jake seemed to

realize he still had hold of her arm and let her go as though she were a hot potato. Her heart was in her throat as he walked ahead of her up what must once have been a very grand winding staircase. He headed down a short hall to his bedroom on the second floor. When they arrived, he stopped in the doorway and said, "I'll give you a few minutes to get out of that dress and get into bed. I'm going to check on some stock in the barn."

He wasn't just leaving the room, he was leaving the house to give her the privacy to undress and slip under the covers. She blessed him for his consideration.

Once he was gone, she turned to survey her new bedroom.

Jake had already put a lantern on the bedside table, which also held a Bible. The bed looked small for two people, but she thought maybe it was the same size as the one her parents had shared. It was covered with another distinctive patchwork quilt. She studied the tiny stitches and the beautiful star pattern. Jake's wife must have been very good with a needle.

The room itself was large, with high ceilings and tall windows draped in moth-eaten blue velvet that must have been elegant once upon a time. An enormous wardrobe stood along one wall. She turned around and found a dressing table near the window with a mirror hanging above it. It held a rose-decorated bowl and pitcher.

A breakfront nearby held a larger, plain white pitcher and bowl for washing. There was a mirror above the breakfront, too, which made Miranda wonder whether Jake might have shaved each morning there, while his wife washed her face and fixed her hair at the dressing table.

Braided rag rugs made of bright scraps of fabric lay on either side of the bed. All those cloth scraps made Miranda wonder if Priss might have left several dresses behind that she could cut down for shirts and pants for the boys and make over for herself. She was tempted to open the wardrobe and look, but she didn't want Jake to catch her snooping.

When she checked the dressing table, she discovered Jake had already filled the rose pitcher. As she poured some of the water into the bowl, she felt that it was warm. Heavenly! She was so glad to have the time, and the warm water, to finally ease herself out of her awful wool dress.

Which was when Miranda realized she would be left wearing only a chemise and pantalets. No wonder Jake had left the room. She would have been pink-cheeked with embarrassment to be seen by anyone in the raggedy garments, let alone her new husband. She would be grateful to hide under the sheets.

She'd made herself pantalets that covered her limbs down to the ankle, to conceal her scarred left leg. She never wanted anyone, and especially not her new husband, to see it. As soon as she was under the covers, she would blow out the lantern. Surely Jake could undress and find his way to bed in the dark.

Miranda unbuttoned her dress and eased it off her shoulders along with her chemise. She got both garments almost to her waist before the chemise got stuck where scabs had torn and dried blood had attached skin to fabric. The problem she faced was how to wet down the cotton, so she could pull the chemise free, without making a mess on the wooden floor.

She decided it didn't matter if she spilled a little water. She could wipe it up with the delicately embroidered hand towel that had been left on the dressing table with the pitcher. It was so beautiful, it seemed a shame to ruin it, but there was no help for it. Maybe if she rinsed out the towel right away, it wouldn't end up bloodstained.

Miranda carefully lifted the pitcher and held it over her shoulder and poured warm water down her back. She hissed as it stung her open wounds. She moved the pitcher to the other shoulder and slowly poured again. Water splattered on the floor, but when she was done, both the cotton chemise and the wool dress were sopping wet.

She set the pitcher down and carefully began peeling both sets of fabric, cotton and wool, away from her skin.

It wasn't as easy as she'd hoped, because she couldn't see what she was doing. It soon became clear that the scabs needed to soak. Except, she didn't really have time for that. Jake might be back at any moment. She had to get herself out of her dress and into bed before he returned.

"Ow!" She bit her lip to keep from crying out again. She didn't want the boys to hear and come running upstairs to help her. She could feel the scabs tearing free, feel the warm blood sliding down her back.

Her throat felt tight with despair. Even if she could blot up the blood streaming down her back before Jake returned, she didn't dare lie down in bed until the bleeding stopped. Who knew how long that would take? If she just got into bed, Jake would find blood on the sheets in the morning and start asking questions.

She didn't want his pity. She'd managed fine for the past three desperate years. She planned to pull her weight here, too, and she didn't want Jake taking one look at her back and thinking she couldn't.

She had to stop the bleeding, but she had no idea how. The worst part was that she hadn't even freed the dress from her skin yet. It seemed to be stuck tight low on her back.

A knock came on the door.

Miranda moaned like a dying animal.

The door opened suddenly, and she found herself staring into Jake's stunned eyes.

$\heartsuit$

"You sounded like you were hurt. I thought you were hurt," Jake babbled, startled by the scene before him. "I wouldn't have come in except—" He couldn't stop staring at his half-dressed wife.

She yanked her bodice up, but not before he'd seen all of one small breast and a rose-colored nipple. She held the cloth bunched tight against her and stared anxiously back at him. "What are you doing in here?"

It was a stupid question, since this was his bedroom. Their bedroom. He couldn't tear his eyes from the sight of the two slight mounds of feminine flesh exposed above the cloth, behind which she was attempting to hide.

He'd spent his time in the barn reminding himself of all the reasons he wasn't going to bed his wife. It was plain he'd returned too soon. He was about to back his way out again, when he saw the red-stained water pooled around her on the light oak floor.

"You *are* hurt! What happened?" He'd crossed half the distance between them when he realized her blue eyes had gone wide with terror. She held out one hand—the other still clutching the fabric at her chest—to keep him away.

"Don't come any closer!" she begged.

He stopped in his tracks, eyeing the puddle of bloodstained water at her feet, finding more blood on the clothes she had bunched around her, and finally staring into her wide, frightened eyes.

He held out a soothing hand and said in a voice he would have used with a skittish mare, "I'm not coming any closer, but I need to know what's going on here."

"I don't . . . I can't . . . I can't . . ."

She was gasping for air, and he wanted more than anything to reach for her and pull her close to protect her, but he was afraid that if he took another step she might scream. The last thing he wanted was to wake those two little boys and have them come running up here to find out what he was doing to their big sister.

Because he wasn't doing anything.

"Where is the blood coming from?" he asked in as calm a voice as he could manage.

She swallowed twice, hard, before she answered, "My back."

"Did you fall?" he asked, concerned.

She shook her head. A tear spilled onto her cheek.

He felt his gut clench. "I want to help you. Will you let me help you?"

She swallowed again and said, in the saddest voice he'd ever heard, "I suppose I must."

"What can I do?"

"I can't get this cloth free from the scabs on my back." She angled herself so she exposed her back to him.

Jake gasped. Her back was layered with bright pink stripes where new scabs had fallen off and red stripes where unhealed scabs had been torn away and white stripes where scars remained after past wounds had healed. He felt horror and pity and anger. "Who did this to you?"

She peeped at him over her shoulder, as though to apologize for having been so severely beaten. "Miss Iris Birch."

"Damn that bitch to hell!"

"I wish I could," she said in a quiet voice.

"Why would she do this? What did you do?"

"I met with my—" She cut herself off.

He wondered what truth she'd decided not to tell him. She continued, "I met with my brothers after lights-out, the day before I was supposed to leave the orphanage. When we were caught, I took the punishment for all of us."

He started counting the marks. There were so many of them! "Somebody should take a bullwhip to Miss Birch."

"You can see why I had to bring Nick and Harry with me. I was afraid she would beat them even worse when I wasn't there to protect them anymore."

"She beat your brothers like this?" he asked, appalled.

"Nick, yes. She only swatted Harry's palms."

"Are you telling me Nick has scars like these?"

She turned her face aside, and he saw another tear fall. "There was nothing I could do."

He felt his gut twist again. "I'm not blaming you."

Jake's mind was whirling. He felt like swearing a blue streak, but he didn't want to frighten her any more than she already seemed to be. He couldn't imagine anyone being that cruel to a young girl and two small boys. And Miss Birch was in charge of an entire orphanage of children?

He wondered if there was anything he could do about the problem from here. "I'd love to get my hands on Miss Iris Birch," he said through gritted teeth. But that would have to wait till later.

"I wanted to get my dress off before you came back," she said. "But it's stuck tight to my skin by dried blood. I need your help to get out of my clothes."

Good God! There was no question of not helping her. But the whole time he'd been checking on stock in the barn he'd been trying to figure out how he was going to sleep in the same bed as his new wife and keep his distance. The bed wasn't big enough.

He'd reminded himself again and again of the dangers of having sex with her. It made no difference to his body, which hungered for a woman.

He'd given himself a stern lecture and headed back inside. He'd been ready to sleep—and sleep only—with his wife.

He hadn't counted on having to touch her. He hadn't counted on feeling sorry for her or wanting to protect her from an evil witch who was thousands of miles away. He hadn't counted on getting a glimpse of a soft, womanly breast.

He cleared his throat, which was suddenly tight, and asked, "What do you want me to do?"

She gestured toward the pitcher and said, "I think maybe I need more water to soak the scabs free. Thank you for warming it, by the way."

"I used to do that for Priss. Or rather, she did it for me first. After she got pregnant the second time she was always so tired, I got warm water for both of us." He felt discomfited revealing parts of his life with Priss when he was about to see the naked back of the woman who'd replaced her. The words had sort of tumbled out.

He didn't know why Miranda was so much easier to talk to than Priss. Maybe it had something to do with her being a stranger. He'd grown up around Priss. She knew all his faults and foibles. This woman did not. He could start fresh with Miranda. She didn't know about—and therefore could not judge him for—all the mistakes he'd made in the past.

He supposed it was human nature to make comparisons between Priss and his new wife. But it seemed unfair to Priss to think anything about Miranda was better. Then he remembered what Priss had said toward the end of her labor, when they'd both realized she might not survive it.

"It's okay to love again, Jake."

That was all she'd said. He'd said the only thing that had mattered to him at that moment. "I love you, Priss."

Jake felt the tears of sorrow that were never far from the surface, burn his nose. At the end, Priss had acknowledged what he'd refused to admit. She was dying. He would need to marry again. Their daughter would need a mother. And he would need a wife.

He forgave himself for noticing the things about Miranda he liked. It didn't dishonor the wife he'd buried to appreciate the wife he'd married. Far from it. The better he got along with Miranda, the better mother she would be to his daughter.

He turned and collected the pitcher from Priss's dressing table, then stood behind his new wife, ready to do her bidding. Up close, he could see blond tendrils on her nape that had escaped from the tight bun—and exactly what bad shape her back was in.

"How did you travel like this? You must have been in a lot of pain."

"A little," she admitted. "One does what one must."

"Whose rule is that?"

"My mother's," she said softly. "She was . . ." Her voice broke, and he saw more tears well in her eyes.

He felt helpless to mend what seemed most broken in her—her soft heart. "What do I do?" he said brusquely.

She glanced over her shoulder and said, "You'll have to move the cloth down to see where it's stuck. Then pour more water there so the scabs can soak free."

Jake shifted the cloth as though he were stealing honey from a hive of bees and might get stung if he moved too fast. "I think it's the white cotton thing that's stuck," he said as he tugged gently at the cloth at her back.

"My chemise."

She was still holding both garments tight against her breasts, but he was tall enough, and she was so short, that he could see the swell of her breasts and the dark crevice between. He felt sweat pop out on his forehead, and his body stirred below.

What kind of beast, what kind of brute, could become aroused when she was so obviously in pain?

A man who's been without a woman for more than a year. He needed to get her out of this dress and under the covers where she was concealed from view. "I don't want to hurt you," he said, as he held the pitcher ready to pour.

"Go ahead and wet everything down. I think the scabs need to soak awhile."

He tugged lightly at the cotton, poured where he found it stuck, tugged again and poured again, until he'd soaked her back and the puddle under her feet had grown large.

"I'm done. Now what?"

She looked around the room. "I'd love to sit down while we wait for the water to do its work, but I don't see anywhere I can sit without ruining linens or the upholstery."

"Just a minute. I'll be right back." He hurried down the hall to the nursery, grateful that he didn't have to explain his appearance to Nick, since he was sleeping downstairs. He picked up the rocker next to Anna Mae's bed, where Priss had used to sit when she was nursing the baby . . . and where she had planned to sit to nurse the baby who'd died with her.

He forced his thoughts away from Priss. He knocked lightly on his bedroom door and reentered, carrying the rocker. "How's this?" He set the rocker near Miranda but out of the puddle of water.

"Thank you," she said as she sank into the wooden rocker. She let out a long sigh. "I didn't realize how tired I am."

She had to sit forward on the rocker because of her back, but at least he'd made it possible for her to sit.

"What shall we do to pass the time?" she asked, looking up at him with temptingly innocent blue eyes.

"You can tell me more about that orphanage," Jake said, crossing his arms to keep from reaching to adjust the cloth to cover more of her bosom.

"I'd rather hear about your ranch," she said. "What chores will I need to do every day?"

"I don't want you doing much of anything till your back is healed. You're lucky those wounds didn't get infected." Jake realized she was going to need something dry to wear once he got her clothes unstuck, and he headed for the wardrobe. He began rooting through it for one of his wife's nightgowns. Whatever Miranda wore tonight was probably going to get ruined, because blood was bound to seep from her wounds.

"I have a question," she said, "but I'm not sure if I should ask it."

"Go ahead and ask."

"I wondered if there might be anything in that wardrobe I could cut down for the boys or remake for myself."

He realized Miranda wanted to make use of his dead wife's clothes. He paused, because he'd passed by every one of Priss's nightgowns—which she would never use again—in favor of ruining one of his own good cotton shirts.

He put the shirt down and turned back to Miranda with one of Priss's flannel nightgowns in hand. "Priss would have given a stranger anything she had. She'd like knowing that her things were being put to good use."

"Thank you. I wish I'd known her. She sounds like a wonderful person."

She was. Jake would have said the words, except they got caught by the knot in his throat. His hands fisted around the flannel nightgown. He missed his wife. He missed loving his wife. He missed the child he'd never known. He suddenly bitterly resented the stranger in his wife's rocker. Or rather, the necessity of having her here.

"I think maybe the scabs have had enough time to soak," she said, meeting his gaze with trust in her eyes.

Jake thought of what his new wife must be feeling right now. This was her wedding night, and instead of loving his wife, he almost hated her. She didn't deserve a resentful husband. None of this was her fault.

He dropped Priss's worn flannel nightgown on her lap and took a step behind his new wife to begin the job of freeing her from her clothes as painlessly as possible. The soaking helped, but he knew he still hurt her as he eased the fabric free. Blood spurted from tiny wounds. He grabbed the towel from the dressing table and dabbed gently at her back.

He heard her hiss in a breath.

"I'm sorry. I'm being as careful as I can."

"I know."

"Do you want me to stop?" But he knew that would only postpone the problem. And how was she going to lie down and sleep, if she couldn't get the dress off?

To his relief, she shook her head. "The dress has to come off tonight. I appreciate what you're doing."

It seemed to take forever before the cloth was completely free of her flesh. "I'm done," he said at last. He realized his hands were trembling as he gazed at her mutilated back. He bunched them into fists, one of which held the towel he'd been using to sop up blood.

He took a step forward and she looked up at him.

He drew in a breath when he saw the tears streaking her face. She hadn't made a sound to let him know he was hurting her. But he obviously had.

"I'm sorry," he said. "I tried to be gentle."

"You were. Thank you."

"I think you need bandages of some sort on your back before you put on a nightgown. I have some gauze I use for the horses down in the kitchen. I'll go get it while you change."

He left her alone, hoping she would take the hint and get out of her clothes and into the nightgown while he was gone. She could just as easily hold the nightgown to her bosom and leave her back bared for the bandages he was retrieving from downstairs.

When he got back, she'd not only managed to get into the nightgown, but her ugly dress and cotton chemise were nowhere to be seen. She'd also wiped up the bloody water on the floor. She was sitting on the edge of the bed waiting for him, the gown slipped off her shoulders and held tight against her bosom. She was so tiny, her feet, which hung over the edge of the bed, didn't reach the floor. Her shoes were off, but he saw she was still wearing her white stockings.

She'd taken down her hair and apparently used his wife's brush. She did indeed have blond curls. They spilled over her bare shoulders and made a halo around her face.

His mouth went dry at the sight of her. His body responded to the knowledge that he was going to have to sit on the bed with this half-naked woman to bandage her.

"I have the gauze," he announced unnecessarily. "And some sticking plasters."

She smiled and he felt his heart jump.

If he used the gauze, he would have to wrap it entirely around her. His heart pounded at the thought of what that would entail. Better by far to use the sticking plasters.

"Ready?" he said.

She glanced over her shoulder and said, "Ready."

Chapter Seven

Miranda shivered when she felt Jake's warm breath on the back of her neck, but not from fear. She'd been frightened when he'd first shown up in the doorway, but as he tended to her wounds, she slowly relaxed. She felt almost comfortable sitting beside him on the edge of the bed.

Almost comfortable. It was impossible to forget that she was half naked, sitting next to a fully dressed man. Jake had been speaking to her quietly, treating her gently, dispelling her qualms. Despite all that, an inexplicable tension arced between them. It made her stomach feel funny.

She bit her lip to keep from crying out as he carefully blotted each wound dry. She felt him attach a sticking plaster high on her shoulder and another in the middle of her spine.

"Some of these are pretty deep," he muttered. "She must have been pretty mad to hit you so hard."

"She was."

"You must have been glad to get out of there."

"Yes. I just wish . . ." She wanted to blurt out all her troubles, blurt out the existence of her three sis-

ters, who were still suffering under the rod of Miss
Iris Birch. But she'd already sprung so many surprises
on Jake, she was afraid one more might be the straw
that made the mule sit down.

"What is it you wish?" he asked.

"That things were different."

She didn't explain what "things" she wished were
different. He must wish "things" were different, too.
That they'd courted before they married. That she
wasn't so injured that she wasn't a fit wife for a husband on their wedding night.

She was most afraid that she would never match
up to the amazing wife who'd died in childbirth, who
could create such beautiful things with a needle and
thread. Miranda's home before the fire had been filled
with servants. The only skills she had were those
she'd learned at the orphanage: how to cook simple
foods, how to mend tears and scrub clothes and cut
hair—all the things that kept orphans looking good
for the patrons whose charitable donations paid Miss
Birch's salary.

She shivered again as Jake's callused fingertips
grazed her naked flesh.

"You're cold," he said.

She was pretty sure that wasn't the problem, but
she didn't correct him.

"I'll be done in a minute and you can cover up."

She felt him attach one last sticking plaster barely
above her buttocks. She blushed with the knowledge
of what he must be seeing.

"There. All done." His voice sounded odd, kind of
hoarse. He rose abruptly from the bed and crossed to
the doorway. He turned once he got there and said,

"I've covered the worst wounds. None of the rest should bleed through the nightgown. Finish getting dressed and get into bed. I'll be back as soon as I put this gauze away in the kitchen."

They both knew he could have put the gauze away tomorrow morning, but it made a good excuse for him to leave her alone. The moment he closed the door behind him, Miranda eased the nightgown back up over her shoulders and tied the bow that closed the front. She realized how convenient the garment was for a husband, who would only have to untie that bow to ease the gown off her shoulders and leave her bare to his gaze. Did lovers ever take off all their clothes in bed? She hadn't asked her friend that question.

Miranda debated whether to turn down the lamp when she got into bed, but it seemed silly to do so when Jake had already seen a great deal of her unclothed. It wasn't until Jake knocked at the door that she realized he still had to undress.

She leaned over to turn down the lamp, but he opened the door and caught her halfway there. She pulled the covers up to her shoulders and stared at him like a deer in his gun sight.

"Can I help?" he asked.

"I was going to turn down the lamp."

She saw in his face the moment he realized why she wanted the lamp out. He crossed to the end table and turned the wick down. Without the light, the room was pitch black.

She heard him working his way around the foot of the bed to the other side. She heard the swish of cloth and something hit the floor, then the sound of a belt being unbuckled and the brush of denim.

Jake grunted as he slumped onto the bed and she realized he had to pull off his boots and socks. She heard each boot thump on the rag rug as they came off. Then she could hear—and feel—him kicking his Levi's the rest of the way off.

She wondered if he planned to strip naked. Surely not. The bedsprings squeaked as he lay down, and the covers shifted as he pulled them over himself.

Then he was still. Too still.

She felt frozen in place. The situation was ridiculous. She would have laughed if her throat hadn't been too tight for any sound to come out.

"Good night," he said at last.

Startled, she said, "Good night," back.

That was it? This was the night she'd been so anxious about? They were lying on opposite sides of a small bed, but it felt like there was an ocean between them. She stared hard in Jake's direction, but there was no moonlight, so she couldn't even make out the shape of his body in the bed.

This couldn't be all there was to being married. Her husband hadn't done what her friend at the orphanage had said he would do. He hadn't put the male part of himself inside her.

It suddenly dawned on her that Jake must be staying on his own side of the bed in consideration of the wounds on her back. She felt a flush of gratitude.

"Thank you," she whispered into the dark.

"For what?"

"I know this isn't the wedding night you must have imagined. I mean, after all your effort and the expense of getting a mail-order bride here from Chicago, you must have hoped—"

"It's all right," he interrupted. "I have a confession to make. I should have said something sooner, but the time never seemed right."

She was almost afraid to hear what he had to say. Was there some flaw in his character he hadn't revealed? She waited a long time before he spoke again.

"I don't intend for us to have marital relations."

"I know," she said. "Tonight—"

"Ever."

She sat bolt upright in the dark, hissing when the flannel nightgown rubbed against a few wounds that weren't covered. The gown was caught under her, and when she tried to move, she nearly strangled on the bow at her throat. She wriggled around and pulled the cloth out from under herself. "I don't understand." She could feel the mattress moving beside her and assumed he was sitting up, too.

"What don't you understand?"

"I don't understand why you wanted a wife, if—" She cut herself off as she realized what had been staring her in the face ever since he'd first mentioned his precious Priss. He'd loved his first wife so much that no one could replace her. What he'd needed was a babysitter and a housekeeper. That was the role he intended she should have here in his home.

Her life in that limited role stretched out endlessly before her. It was the miserable orphanage all over again, except she could always hope Jake wouldn't beat her. She would be taking care of a chair-bound old man and a baby in diapers and her two brothers and her husband. She might as well have stayed in Chicago and washed dishes. At least that way she would have earned wages.

As an unpaid wife, she would be cooking and cleaning and sewing, with maybe some gardening thrown in. Which meant canning, she supposed, although she had no idea how to do that. She would not be a loved and valued partner. She would be unpaid household help.

"Oh, my God," she whispered.

The bedsprings creaked, and she imagined him turning toward her voice. "What's wrong?"

"What if I don't like that arrangement?"

"That's the way it's going to be."

"What if I don't like that arrangement?" she repeated.

He didn't answer her right away. She wondered what he would do if she leaned over and kissed him right on the mouth, something her friend at the orphanage said would feel lovely. That was the exact word she'd used: *lovely.*

Oh, how she was tempted!

But she didn't have the nerve. She was too scared of how Jake might react. Too scared of being rejected. That would be the perfect ending to this whole miserable journey.

"On second thought, I take back my objection," she said. "The arrangement you're suggesting is fine with me."

"What?"

"I don't want to have relations with you, either." Her voice was full of anger at him—and pity for herself.

"What the hell is wrong with you, woman?"

"Not a damned thing is wrong with me!" It was the first time in her life Miranda had used a swear word. Oh, how good it felt! "You're the one with the problem," she said. "I'll thank you to keep your hands off me tonight and every night from now on, as long as we both shall live!"

It was a great speech. At least, it would have been, if she hadn't burst into tears after making it.

She felt Jake's arms close around her and fought like a wildcat, scratching and thrashing to make him let go.

She didn't make a sound. She was too ashamed that she'd fallen into such a trap, too angry that she'd let this happen. Hannah and Hetty and Josie were DOOMED. She was never going to be able to bring them here to live, when she wasn't really Jake's wife.

She struggled.

And he held on.

♡

Jake realized he'd made a bad mistake. He'd only wanted to protect his new wife's life from the dangers of childbirth, but that wasn't the way she saw it. He was afraid if he didn't hang on to her, she'd leave the bedroom—and maybe the house—and never come back. He'd been a fool and an idiot. He should have kept his mouth shut. He should have let her think he was being considerate.

"Settle down," he said. "I can feel your back bleeding again."

She suddenly slumped in his arms.

"Will you sit here if I let you go?" He was close enough to feel her head bob up and down. He leaned over and found a match and lit the lamp. He turned it up all the way. He glanced back and saw Miranda eyeing his faded red long johns. He wanted to pull his Levi's back on, but he was afraid if he didn't tend to her back right now, while she was quiet, she wouldn't let him do it at all. He ignored his self-consciousness and got out of bed.

He grabbed one of his handkerchiefs from the wardrobe and brought it back to the bed. "Turn around and undo your nightgown, so I can tend to your back."

She seemed happy to turn her back on him. He nearly gasped when she let the gown slide down her back. It was a seductive move, even though she crossed her arms around the cloth at her breasts to keep them covered and to make it clear she was only tolerating his help.

He quickly noticed that one wound was the cause of the blood he'd felt dampening her gown. He held the hanky against the wound until the bleeding stopped, then made sure all traces of blood were blotted away.

He realized that she thought he didn't desire her. That was the furthest thing from the truth. The truth was, when he was tending her wounds, he'd barely managed to avoid kissing her shoulder and her throat and that tantalizingly bowed upper lip.

He bent his head, brushed a blond curl out of the way and pressed his lips against her shoulder. He felt her quiver. He waited for her to pull away.

She didn't.

He leaned in and kissed her throat beneath her ear. "It's not that I don't desire you," he said quietly. "I want you. But . . ." He wasn't sure where to go from there.

"But?"

He sat back and said, "Women die in childbirth."

"Oh." In a moment he heard her speak another, more reflective, "Oh."

He waited for her to say something more, but instead of speaking, she turned and timidly put her hand on his cheek. Her hand urged his face down to hers and their lips met.

He felt his heart thump harder in his chest. What was she doing? What did she want from him? He wasn't going to make love to her. He wasn't going to take that kind of chance.

She broke the kiss and looked up at him shyly from beneath lowered lashes. "I'm really tired. Why don't we go to sleep?"

He found himself smiling with relief. "Why don't we?"

This time he helped her get the nightgown back around her shoulders, being careful not to touch her skin. He tied the bow at the front, keeping his eyes off the soft mounds that lay beneath it.

He waited while she lay back down before he turned down the lamp and crossed around the foot of the bed in the dark. He slid back under the covers, careful to stay on his own side. He felt a little like a fox being chased by hounds that had managed to go to ground. He was breathing hard, but he'd escaped the danger.

Then she rolled over on her side and snuggled close to him. "Is this all right?"

It was torture. It was heaven. He could feel her soft

breast against his arm. His body went rock hard. His throat went dry. He managed to croak, "It's fine."

She sighed. "You're so warm."

Warm? He was on fire! He said nothing.

"The sounds here are so different from the city," she said in the darkness.

"I suppose so," he replied. He could hardly hear himself speak over the thundering of his heart. The windows were open to allow the evening breeze to cool the room, and he listened to the familiar rustle of the oaks and the croak of the bullfrogs in the stock pond, and the lowing of cattle in the distance, as he willed his heart to slow.

"Where should I start tomorrow?" she asked.

"We can worry about that in the morning." He faked a yawn and heard her yawn in reply. Then he yawned again, for real.

"All right," she said agreeably. "Good night, Jake."

"Good night, Miranda."

He heard her breathing become slow and even and realized she was asleep. He was awake long enough to realize this sleeping arrangement wasn't going to work. Not if he wanted to keep his hands off his wife.

Chapter Eight

Alexander Blackthorne felt his wife's hand slide across his naked back in a loving caress, waking him as the pink light of dawn cracked the windowsill in their bedroom. He was immediately suspicious. Cricket rarely initiated lovemaking. Whenever she did, he knew it was because she was aware that, once sated, he would do anything she asked. Lately, they'd been on opposite sides of a very important issue. He didn't want sex to complicate the matter, so he simply asked, "What do you want, love?"

She kissed the dark curls at his nape, causing a shiver to roll down his spine. All she had to do was touch him, and he responded like a stag in rut. It had been that way since the first day he'd laid eyes on her twelve years ago, two months after the fateful battle at Gettysburg.

He'd found her sitting in a rocker on the porch at Lion's Dare, Jarrett Creed's cotton plantation southeast of San Antonio. He'd sought her out that hot September afternoon to tell her that she'd become a widow.

And that he was now the owner of Lion's Dare.

She'd been dressed in a man's fringed buckskins, her rich, auburn hair caught in a single braid that ran halfway down her back. Her almond-shaped gray eyes had narrowed distrustfully at him as he dismounted and tied the reins of his horse at the hitching post in front of the two-story wood-frame house.

She rose and took a step toward the porch rail holding a Kentucky rifle in her arms as tenderly as a baby. He'd had the feeling she knew how to use it. Not surprising, when so many grifters, rapists, and murderers were taking advantage of missing fathers and brothers and husbands—off fighting the War Between the States—to wreak havoc among the women left behind.

As he stepped up onto the porch he noticed her head came almost to his shoulders, and he was six foot four. He surveyed her high cheekbones, her small, straight nose, and her wide mouth, the lips pressed flat with hostility.

Her skin was the warm color of honey, but she looked thin to the point of gauntness. It was plain the war was taking a terrible toll not only on the soldiers who fought but on those left behind. Strangest of all was the wolf—he was sure it was a wolf and not just a dog that looked like a wolf—that stood by her side, growling low in its throat.

"How can I help you?" she asked.

He was startled by the question, which suggested she was willing to offer help to a stranger in these dangerous times. She could—and maybe should—have told him to get off her land.

Only, it wasn't her land anymore. Not since he'd won Lion's Dare in a poker game from a man who said his name was Jarrett Creed. Creed had signed a note deeding the plantation to Alexander Blackthorne. The next morning, Alex had watched that same man take a musket ball between the eyes. Jarrett Creed lay dead on the battlefield at Gettysburg with fifty thousand other brave men.

"If you're Creighton Creed, I have bad news," he said.

Her face crumpled. "Which one?"

"What?"

"My husband and three sons are fighting in this war," she said in a voice that grated with emotion. "Which one is gone?"

"Jarrett Creed died at Gettysburg."

He would never forget her ghost-white face or her ululating wail of grief. Anxious to comfort her all over again, he rolled over in bed and pulled her into his embrace, feeling his blood heat as she fitted her soft feminine curves to his hard masculine body.

To hell with differences. The woman he loved wanted him. And even with fifty-two years in his dish, he wanted her. Craved her, like a dying man craves water in the desert. Needed her, as he needed sustenance to survive.

Her hands slid around his neck and her lips found his.

His tongue sought out the sweetness within as his hands cupped her breasts. He teased the nipple of one breast with his thumb and forefinger, while his tongue mimicked the sex act.

She moaned and his body heated.

Her hands weren't idle. She sought the places on his inner thighs that she knew were sensitive, teasing him by not touching where he wanted most to be touched, until he ached with need.

He yanked at her nightgown until he could get it off over her head and feel the warmth of flesh against flesh. She was sleek as a lioness, despite turning fifty-one on her most recent birthday. Her auburn hair was laced with gray, and her face had been weathered by sun and wind and age, attesting to the hardships she'd endured.

But the woman he loved remained as spirited and strong-willed as the day he'd met her, and he found her very, very desirable.

"Come inside me," she whispered.

No words were more certain to arouse him. His body trembled where she touched. He was aware she was inciting him, wanting him to lose control, so that he would be all the more willing to please her afterward.

He didn't care.

He thrust hard and deep, and she opened herself to him, warm and wet and willing. They moved together in a dance that was even more sensual, more passionate, because they were so much in tune with one another.

She scratched and bit with nails and teeth that caused just enough pain to inflame his desire.

He sucked and bit with a ravenous mouth that claimed his mate as surely as she had claimed him.

He felt her body clench and knew from the guttural sounds she made and the frantic grasp of her hands that she was losing control. He thrust harder and faster, rushing toward the edge of the cliff with her, until he finally fell with her into an abyss of deep and immeasurable pleasure.

Breathing hard, struggling to suck enough air to survive, she wrapped her arms and legs around him and begged, "Don't leave me."

He laughed with gusto and said, "I'm going to squash you if I don't." He always marveled at the fact that she could bear his weight when he inevitably collapsed onto her after lovemaking. He was too big and she was too precious for him to stay long where she wanted him. He pushed himself onto his side and wrapped his arms around her, pulling her close and kissing her mussed hair.

"I love you," he said.

"I love you, too," she replied. "Which is why I'm asking you to back off of your ultimatum to Jake."

He'd known she wanted something even before that first kiss. The problem was, he always realized after he'd made love to his wife exactly how necessary her love and respect and happiness were to him. Which meant he inevitably gave her what she asked.

This time, he couldn't do it.

In a harsh voice that revealed just how much he was struggling to deny her, he said, "I can't do that, love."

"How can you call me your love in one breath, Alex, and tell me you're planning to ruin my son in the next?"

She had a point.

He was willing to explain. He just wasn't sure which argument would hold the most sway with her. "You don't understand."

"There's no explanation you can give that justifies what you're doing," she said. "Jake is grieving the loss of his wife and stillborn son. He's married some woman barely out of the cradle herself, who brought along her two younger brothers from Chicago. Slim can't help anymore, now that he's paralyzed. How much more weight do you think you can lay on my son's shoulders without crushing him?"

During her speech she'd pulled herself from his embrace. He knew she had friends—cowhands on the various nearby spreads and tradesmen in San Antonio—who kept her informed of Jake's comings and goings. Still, it was amazing how much she knew, when not even a day had passed since his stepson's marriage to a mail-order bride. He'd known about the wedding but not about the two stowaways.

He crossed his arms behind his head, linking his hands at his nape, and said, "I'd be as hard on any rancher who couldn't pull his weight. Why should your son be any different?"

She sat upright staring down at him, her gray eyes stormy with anger and . . . disappointment.

Cricket always expected him to be better than he was. Always expected him to show mercy, when he went for the jugular. Always expected him to be generous, when he sought more power, more land, more wealth.

She had no idea of the cutthroat family he'd left behind in England, who'd made him what he was. There, it had been survival of the fittest. He'd learned to fight tooth and claw because anything less would have left him dead. He understood the wreckage left by cruelty well enough not to condone it. That didn't mean he wasn't brutal when he needed to be.

Survival skills honed in a desperately unhappy

childhood had helped him to thrive in a savage land like Texas, where Indians or outlaws or wild animals or the ruthless weather or even the desolate land itself could kill you.

He released his hands and sat up, feeling her shiver as he brushed a stray curl behind her shoulder. He wanted her again. He half expected her to pull away, to resist his caresses until she got the answer she wanted. His wife was stubborn and persistent, almost to a fault. He knew she would give in to him if he pressed her. Her nostrils were flared to catch the scent of their prior lovemaking, and her eyes were smoky with desire.

But he didn't merely want to seduce her. He wanted her to see the reason behind his actions, to understand why he was doing what he was doing. He smiled inwardly when he realized that what he wanted was his wife's approval.

"If I'm not the one who takes Jake's land from him, someone else will," he explained. "I'd rather not have another fight on my hands with whoever that someone else is, to protect the borders of Bitter Creek. Better I should be the one who convinces Jake to give up and get out. The sooner Three Oaks becomes a part of Bitter Creek, the better."

He saw the face she made when he called his ranch by the new name he'd given it. Lion's Dare had been a part of her life with another man. She lived now at Bitter Creek, the empire he was building for her and their ten-year-old twin sons, Nash and Noah.

"Besides," he argued, "with your sister Sloan and her husband moving back to Spain, and your sister Bay and her husband running off to Boston during the war, you were the logical one to inherit Three Oaks from your half brother, not your son. How do we know that will Jake showed us wasn't a fake? Rightfully, Three Oaks should be yours, and therefore, by the law of the land, mine."

"I told Luke a long time ago I didn't want it," she said. "He must have changed his will when Jake came home so badly wounded from the war, to be sure his favorite nephew would have a place of his own, especially if Jake didn't manage to get back on his feet."

"He's back on his feet, all right," Alex muttered. "And stepping all over mine."

"Do you love me, Alex?"

"You know I do."

"Then do this for me. Step back. Give Jake room to succeed. I know he'll be fine once he—"

He couldn't let her go on asking him for mercy, not when he knew he wasn't going to do what she asked. "Jake's not going to be fine," he said in a voice made harsh by the knowledge that he was hurting his wife. "He's on a sinking ship, and he's not smart enough to get off while he still can. He's going to go down, love," he said as gently as he could. "There's nothing anybody can do to save him."

"You don't have to shove his head underwater and hold it there," she said. "You could throw him a rope. You could help to save him."

He shook his head. "How often? For how long? The rest of his life? Besides, he's too proud to take the help, even if I offered it. Which I won't. There's been a break in the fence between Bitter Creek and Three Oaks that he hasn't mended for a week. His cattle are on my land, eating grass intended for my cattle. What am I supposed to do?"

"It's just a little grass, Alex."

"It's *my* grass," he said implacably. "I want his cattle off my land. Today."

"Or what?" she said, her gray eyes flashing.

"Or they'll be my cattle at sundown."

"He just got married! He has a new wife and new responsibilities. At least give him some time to move them!"

He knew it was a mistake to give his wife a finger's worth of leeway, because she tended to turn it into an entire arm. So he said, "A day won't make any difference."

"It might. Please, Alex."

He watched her gray eyes brim with tears and felt an ache in his chest at the hurt he could see she was feeling. She knew the truth he was speaking. Out here, the strong survived. The weak—and those, like her sisters, who'd tired of the terrible death toll this land took on the living—moved on and lived out their lives somewhere more civilized.

He opened his mouth to agree to anything his wife asked and shut it again. He swallowed over the knot in his throat before he spoke.

"I can't let up, love," he said as he kissed a tear from her cheek. "Jake wouldn't want me to treat him like any less than the man he is. If he survives, if he thrives, it's because he belongs here. If he doesn't . . . then he should move on."

She looked up at him, her eyes glistening with tears, and said in a choked voice, "Do what you have to do, Alex. Just know that if you ruin my son, if you drive him away, I'll leave you."

Chapter Nine

Miranda was cold. Freezing. She pulled her stocking feet under the covers to warm them. She reached for the thin wool blanket that never kept her warm enough at the orphanage—and felt an entirely different fabric. She slowly sat up in bed, wincing when her back twinged, and looked around.

This wasn't the orphanage. She was lying in her marriage bed—alone—but it felt as cold as the icy day she'd left Chicago. In fact, she could see her breath in the air.

Miranda glanced at the window that had been left open last night to allow the breeze to cool the terrible heat from the day. It was closed and covered in a layer of frost.

"What happened?" she wondered aloud.

From beyond the closed door, she heard muffled voices that gradually became louder, along with pounding footsteps on the stairs. Then, right outside the door, "I want to see my sister *right now*!"

She recognized Nick's angry voice, and then Jake saying, "You can see her when she wakes up. Not before."

"Why isn't she awake? What have you done to her? Miranda's always the first one up in the morning!" Nick sounded almost hysterical.

"I want Miranda," Harry whined pitifully.

"I want to see my sister!" Nick demanded.

"Don't touch that door," Jake warned.

Miranda launched herself out of bed, anxious to avert violence between Jake and Nick, but her bad knee didn't bend right and her toe got caught in the sheet and she fell out of the bed onto her shoulder on the rag rug.

"Aaaaah!" She was more embarrassed than hurt. Fortunately there was no one to see her foolish fall.

"Miranda!" Nick yelled. "Are you all right?"

She freed her foot from the linens and shouted, "I'm fine, Nick."

"He won't let us come in!"

Miranda struggled to get upright and limped to the bedroom door. She opened it to find Jake with a grip on Nick's wrist to keep her brother from knocking on the door.

"Goodness gracious!" she said. "What's all this fuss?"

Harry grabbed her leg and hung on. Nick jerked his fist to get free, and fortunately, Jake let go.

"These two were determined to wake you up," Jake said in his defense. "I thought you needed your rest."

"He was lording it over us, Miranda," Nick complained. "Telling us what to do. I told him he's not the boss."

"Then who is?" Jake asked.

"Not you!" Nick said.

"Your sister—"

"Is the only one who can tell me what to do," Nick interrupted. The ten-year-old glared at Jake.

To give him credit, Jake looked more annoyed than angry.

Miranda could feel Harry shivering against her leg. The boys weren't dressed yet, and the house was cold. "We need to get some warm clothes on you two. It's cold in here."

"I've got the fireplace and the stove going downstairs," Jake said. "No sense lighting a fire up here, since you're getting up."

"Does this happen much?" she asked. "I mean, going from blistering heat one day to freezing cold the next?"

"Often enough," Jake said. "Blue northers blow in without warning. Temperature can change forty degrees in a couple of hours."

"What if you were working away from the house, and you didn't have a coat?" Miranda asked.

Jake shrugged. "You never go unprepared. That's Texas."

"Will it stay cold like this?"

Jake shrugged again. "Could be eighty degrees again tomorrow. By the way, I knew the boys must have coats, since you came from Chicago in winter. When I asked Nick where their coats are, he told me a story I couldn't believe."

Miranda made an apologetic face. "I sold our coats in New Orleans. I needed money for the boys' passage."

Jake's hands landed on his hips. "How are the bunch of you supposed to do outdoor chores without coats in this weather?"

"We weren't expecting this weather," she said pertly. "It was warm in New Orleans. It's been warm every day since." She lifted her chin and asked, "What would you like me to do about it now? I can hardly go back to New Orleans and get them."

"I have a couple of wool shirts you can cut down for the boys." He hesitated, then added, "Priss had a nice wool cape with a hood you can use."

"Thank you, Jake." She wasn't used to dealing with someone so reasonable. She shuddered to think what Miss Birch would have done if a few coats had turned up missing.

"I can see you're cold," Jake said, misinterpreting her shudder. "Go get dressed." He turned to Nick and Harry and said, "Come on. We need to give your sister some privacy."

Miranda could see Nick was reluctant to go, so she said, "I'll be down soon, Nick. Help Harry get dressed, would you, please?"

"I can take care of the runt," Jake offered.

Nick shot Jake a mulish look, grabbed Harry's hand and said, "We don't need any help from you."

Miranda watched as Nick dragged Harry down the stairs. Jake remained standing at the bedroom door shaking his head.

"That boy has a big chip on his shoulder," Jake said.

"He doesn't trust grown-ups."

Jake looked offended. "I would never lay a rough hand on either of those boys."

"Nick doesn't know that."

Miranda saw Jake's gaze drop and followed it to her bosom, where the cold had caused her nipples to form distinctive peaks beneath the flannel. She crossed her arms and saw a flush rise on his cheeks at being caught looking.

He ducked his head and said, "Slim has breakfast on the table whenever you're ready."

"In the future, I'd rather you wake me up than let me sleep. I want to do my share."

"You needed the rest."

She nodded. "Yes, I expect I did." She looked up at him, feeling grateful for his consideration, unused to small kindnesses, unsure how to respond. She felt a strange fluttering in her stomach and lowered her gaze, suddenly shy. "I'd better get moving."

He took a step back. "Yeah."

But he didn't leave.

She could feel his dark eyes focused on her.

"How does your back feel?" he asked in a quiet voice.

She looked up and met his intense gaze and felt warm all over. She tightened her arms over her breasts, trying to contain her feelings. She had to be very careful not to let herself fall in love with a man who was too heartsore to love her back. "It feels better this morning."

"That's good."

They stood looking at each other for what seemed like an eternity before he finally said, "I'll get you some warm water to wash. I figured it would get cold if I brought it before you were up."

He was gone before she could thank him.

Miranda sighed when she realized real baths for everyone were going to have to wait until the weather warmed up again. As she closed the bedroom door, she wondered how long that would be. At least she could wash her face and neck and hands. She reached into her carpetbag for the wrinkled calico dress, since the wool one was still wet.

She held the dress in her hands and smiled ruefully. She'd desperately wanted to wear it yesterday. The cold weather today made it totally unsuitable.

The knock at the door came sooner than she expected. When she opened the door, Jake was waiting with the pitcher from her dressing table in hand. She hadn't even noticed it was missing. "May I come in?"

She gestured toward the dressing table and he crossed and poured some of the steaming water into the empty bowl, then set the pitcher down next to it.

"All set?" he asked.

"Yes, except . . ." She hesitated, then said, "This calico is the only dress I have. Would you mind if I look for something warmer in the wardrobe?"

A look of agony crossed his face. It was gone so quickly she would have missed it if she hadn't been watching so intently.

"Sure." He turned and left without another word.

Despite the cold, Miranda stripped and took her time washing in the wonderfully warm water she poured into the bowl. She found a small bar of rose-scented soap on the dressing table, wet a washcloth, and created a sweet-smelling, soapy lather. It felt heavenly to wash her face and neck and hands and underarms and between her legs with the warm cloth. She left her back alone. When she was done, she felt like a new person.

She'd taken her hair out of its bun last night and it hung in ringlets around her face. Miss Birch had required all the girls' hair to be tied up tight in a bun. Miranda realized she could do anything she wanted with it. She decided to pull it up on the sides and tie it with a ribbon she'd found in the wardrobe, letting the curls hang down her back.

When she was done, she stared at herself with surprised eyes. She might almost have been pretty, if her eyes hadn't looked so haunted. The despair was liable to remain there until she could rescue her sisters. Her cheeks were too thin, but a few good meals might help that. Her hair looked almost wild. Absolutely untamed. She grinned. She liked it.

She wrapped herself in the quilt to stay warm as she crossed to the wardrobe. She felt a little like a kid at Christmas. Before the fire, her mother had dressed her in the latest fashions, but she'd possessed very little of her own at the Institute.

Miranda thought of how much her family had lost in the fire, and how different their lives might be now, if Uncle Stephen hadn't been so selfish. Looking back, she remembered moments of tension between her father and his brother. But she hadn't understood just how much her uncle resented her father until he'd refused to help his brother's children. What had gone wrong between the two brothers? She would probably never know.

Miranda forced thoughts of Uncle Stephen from her mind. It only made her sad—and mad—to remember his heartlessness and neglect.

She focused her attention instead on the entire wardrobe full of clothes she'd inherited. She had no idea whether she would like the items she found or whether they would fit, but she was grateful for the gift of them.

When she opened the wardrobe doors, she was assailed by the smell of roses. Priscilla Creed must have loved roses. They were embroidered on her linens, they decorated her water pitcher, and her soap and clothes smelled distinctly of rosewater.

Miranda reached for a rose-pink dress made of heavy linen that looked warm. The dress unfolded and unfolded and unfolded.

"Oh, dear," she murmured.

Jake's wife must have been almost as tall as her very tall husband. Miranda held the bodice against herself and saw that Priscilla Creed had been more well endowed than she was. The waist was larger, too. This dress was going to need a great deal of alteration before it would fit. She smiled ruefully as she realized how lucky she was that the other woman had been larger than her, rather than smaller.

Miranda tapped her fingers on the pair of Jake's Levi's under her hand and had a crazy idea. The trousers could be folded up at the bottom, and she could use one of Priscilla's many ribbons to hold them in at the waist. She'd never worn trousers, mostly because she'd never had a reason to do something so outlandish. But why not?

She glanced guiltily toward the door. Maybe she ought to ask before she borrowed Jake's Levi's. But she'd have to go downstairs wearing a quilt to find him, which was silly. Surely he'd understand why she'd chosen his trousers over one of his dead wife's dresses.

She folded up the legs of the Levi's, then sat on the bed

and pulled them up to her waist. They were big, but not too big to cinch in. She found a pink hair ribbon amongst Priscilla's things and ran it through the belt loops and tied it in a small bow in front.

She found a beautiful chemise embroidered with roses and put it on, then added one of Priscilla's white blouses with a frill down the front. She folded up the sleeves to her wrists and tucked the tails into the Levi's as best she could. Last, she tied a pink knitted shawl around her shoulders and felt warm for the first time since she'd gotten out of bed.

It felt strange to be dressed half in the clothes of one sex and half in the clothes of the other. However, wearing Jake's Levi's, she would be able to do chores without tripping over a too-long skirt. She took a deep breath, then opened the door and headed downstairs.

Miranda was halfway down the stairs when she heard Slim start yelling. She hobbled as fast as she could on her stiff left knee the rest of the way to the kitchen. She found Harry sitting at a long kitchen table howling his heart out. Anna Mae was screaming at the top of her lungs in a high chair. A red-faced Slim was sitting in his wheeled chair tending a pan on the stove, his back to both of them. Jake was trying to calm the baby, while Nick was hovering over Harry.

"What on earth is going on here?" Miranda said from the doorway.

Harry jumped out of his chair and came running, clinging to her waist as though he were being chased by demons. "Slim yelled at me!"

"Kid nearly burned himself on the stove," Slim muttered without turning around.

"Why is the baby crying?" Miranda asked.

"She pulled Harry's hair, and he yelled at her," Jake said. He picked up the little girl and held her in his arms, staring at Miranda as though she were a cow with two heads. "Why are you dressed like that?"

"Oh. Do you like it?" Miranda smiled self-consciously. She straightened the pink shawl on her shoulders, adjusted the pink bow at her waist, and finally ran her hands down the front of the dark blue Levi's.

"Where'd you find that outfit?" Jake asked.

"The dresses were all way too big for me, so I borrowed a pair of your trousers and paired them with one of Priscilla's blouses. The blouse is too big, too, but I was able to fold up the sleeves and this way I can work without tripping over a skirt." She realized she was babbling and shut up.

He stared at her legs as though he was noticing for the first time that women had them, too. She supposed female limbs were mostly hidden from view beneath skirts, so maybe he had a right to gape.

Slim wheeled himself around to look and said, "Damndest thing I've ever seen. What kind of woman wears pants, I ask you?"

"A woman who plans to work and needs something warm to wear," Miranda replied.

"It's fine, Slim," Jake said, never taking his eyes off Miranda. "How long is it going to take for you to cut one of those dresses to fit?"

"Depends on how much other work there is to be done around here."

"I'm starving," Nick piped up. "Are we going to eat breakfast or not?"

"Pancakes are ready when you are," Slim said, setting a few more hotcakes on a platter at the back of the stove that was already stacked high with them. "Butter and blackberry jam are on the table."

Miranda watched both boys' eyes go wide at Slim's announcement.

"Blackberry jam?" Nick asked in amazement.

"Blackberry jam?" Harry repeated.

"You both deaf?" Slim asked.

"No, sir!" Nick said. "How many pancakes—flapjacks—can I have?"

"Many as you want," Slim said.

Nick shot a glance in Miranda's direction, his blue eyes bright with excitement. Pancakes were only served on Sunday at the orphanage and each child could have a second, if he asked for it, and if he hadn't incurred an infraction during the previous week. Nick rarely got the second pancake.

"I'll take six," Nick said. "To start."

Slim grinned. "Nothing wrong with the kid's appetite," he said to Jake.

"Me, too," Harry said.

"You'll take two," Miranda said to Harry. "When those are gone, if you're still hungry, you can have more."

Jake started pouring a tin cup full of milk from a jar.

"Is that real milk?" Nick asked, his eyes glued on the cup of milk.

"Straight from the cow," Jake replied. "Milked her myself this morning."

"Can I have some?" Nick asked.

"Can I have some, too?" Harry asked.

Jake frowned and exchanged a glance with Slim before he said to Nick, "I was pouring this cup for you."

"Can Harry have some, too?" Nick asked before accepting the cup from Jake.

This time Jake exchanged a frown and a glance with Miranda, who flushed at the insinuation that she'd been depriving her brothers of the basic foods necessary for life. He handed the cup to Nick and said, "Sure."

Nick set the cup of milk in front of Harry's seat at the table and held out his hand for another.

Miranda caught another glance from Jake at this further proof that Nick didn't trust adults. She wasn't the one who'd deprived her brothers, it was the Institute, where they'd received enough food and drink to sustain life, but nothing as special as milk. Ever.

Both boys ate and drank as though they were starving, which they literally had been for the past few days.

Miranda found a seat near the baby, who'd already started on a pancake of her own, which she was eating with her hands. The child had large, dark brown eyes and long brown hair. She was pudgy with baby fat, proof that she'd been well fed.

"You don't have her using a fork?" she asked Jake.

"Don't see the point," Jake said. "She does fine like this."

Miranda pursed her lips. She could see why he needed a woman in the house. The baby wouldn't learn to use a fork and spoon without practice. She would make sure in the future the little girl got them.

Miranda smiled and said, "Good morning, Anna Mae."

The little girl looked up at her and smiled back.

Miranda's fingers got caught in tangles as she tried to brush her hand through Anna Mae's hair. She'd often put her sisters' hair in braids, and she was looking forward to doing the same with Anna Mae's.

Miranda finished her fifth pancake and looked up to see Jake staring at her.

"Where are you putting all that?" he asked.

She pointed to her mouth, which was full. She chewed and swallowed before she said, "We ran out of food on the steamboat ride down the Mississippi."

She realized how much she'd revealed about the struggles on their journey by that simple statement. She distracted Jake by asking, "What can the boys help you with today?"

"Stock has to be fed, but the boys don't have coats. You can put one of my wool shirts on each of them, and they can cart wood from the back porch to the fireplaces around the house. What are your plans?"

"Cleaning seems to be the most urgent need right now."

Slim's eyes narrowed. "You sayin' I ain't a good housekeeper?"

"Not at all," Miranda said. "We're here to help. We can make up beds and dust and do dishes and give you more time to . . ." Miranda wasn't sure what it was Slim did to fill up his days in the wheeled chair.

"Ain't much else I can do 'cept cook and clean and play with my grandbaby," Slim grumbled.

"I'd be willing to help cook, if you'll teach me some of your recipes," Miranda said.

"Got a book full of 'em," Slim said. "My Willa Mae wrote 'em down for Priss."

"Oh, that's wonderful!" Miranda had been wondering whether she'd be able to cook for the two men. Having recipes would solve the problem nicely.

"Guess you ain't gonna plow that garden today with the ground froze solid," Slim said to Jake.

"I'd better ride fence today, see if there are any breaks. Don't want to give Blackthorne an excuse to steal my cattle."

"Would your stepfather really steal from you?" Miranda asked.

"You bet that bastard would!" Slim retorted before Jake could speak.

"What's a bastard?" Harry asked.

"A no-good son of a bitch," Slim said.

"A bastard no-good son of a bitch," Harry repeated.

Slim grinned. "You got it, boy."

Miranda had her mouth open to chastise her brother, but Jake spoke first.

"That's enough of that, runt." Then he turned to Slim and said, "Watch your language around the kids. Otherwise, before you know it, Anna Mae'll be swearing like a bullwhacker stuck in mud."

Miranda rose along with Jake and watched as he put on a shearling coat, his black, flat-brimmed hat, a knitted wool scarf, and heavy leather gloves.

"When will you be back?" she asked.

"Sundown, I expect."

"You're not coming back to eat at noon?"

He pointed to a pail and said, "Packed a lunch. You

and the boys are free to make yourselves whatever you want. There's plenty of food in the pantry."

A swirl of icy wind ruffled the frills on her blouse when he opened the kitchen door and stepped out. A moment later, he was gone.

She turned and saw her brothers licking blackberry jam off their fingers. The baby's face was covered with the gooey mess. She glanced toward the pump at the sink, which wasn't so different from what they'd had in Chicago. She found a cloth and wet it at the pump, then came back to wipe jam off small faces and fingers.

"Fold up your bed linens and put them aside," she instructed Nick. "Harry, you can help him. Then come back in here. I'm going to need some help with drying the dishes and putting them away."

"You gonna tell me what to do, too?" Slim asked once the boys were gone.

Miranda had completely forgotten about the old man, who was sitting quietly at the table.

"Of course not. What do you usually do?"

"That baby takes all my time. Can't hardly turn around without changin' a diaper or wipin' a face."

"I can help with that," Miranda volunteered.

"Didn't ask for no help."

Miranda realized there was going to be no right thing to say, so she said nothing, simply went to the pump and began filling the sink to wash dishes.

Slim mumbled something under his breath, then said, "I'm goin' to my room. Don't nobody bother me." He wheeled himself out of the kitchen.

Miranda realized there was something she'd been aching to do, something she hadn't dared to do with

Jake or Slim in the room. She crossed to the high chair and lifted the little girl out of it and held her close. She nuzzled the baby's cheek with her nose. "You are about the cutest thing I've ever seen."

She sniffed. And sniffed again. "And the stinkiest," she said with a laugh. She turned to leave in search of diapers and powder when the kitchen door banged open.

She circled the baby with her arms to protect her from the rush of frigid wind and turned back to close the door.

And found a stranger standing in the open doorway.

Chapter Ten

Jake found the break in the fence at first light and followed the trail of beaten-down and eaten-down grass, hunting for the cattle he knew had made their way onto Blackthorne land. The job became difficult, and then impossible, as falling snow hid the signs of passage. He knew he should head home, but the thought of Blackthorne finding his cattle on the wrong side of the fence stuck in his craw. He wasn't about to kowtow to his stepfather to get them back.

He kicked his horse into a trot down a sloped hill, anxious to find his cattle before the weather turned any worse than it was. "Come on, Red," he urged the bay horse. "We better find those longhorns."

No sooner had he finished speaking than Red's hindquarters slid out from under him. The horse neighed when he lost his footing and lurched forward to regain his balance, but the slippery surface was unforgiving. The gelding stumbled and rolled, landing on his side—with Jake's left leg pinned beneath him.

Jake screamed as his ankle bent at an odd angle across a large stone. He waited for the crack that would tell him his leg was broken, but he didn't hear it.

His scream frightened Red, and the horse kicked out, scrambling desperately until he was back on his feet.

Jake had the presence of mind to free his legs from the stirrups, pulling the injured ankle loose with his hands as the horse found his footing and rose.

Red stood and shook off the snow and stared down at Jake.

"Little late to be worrying about me," Jake muttered. "You should have been more careful coming down that hill."

The horse whinnied.

Jake realized how lucky he was that Red hadn't bolted. It wouldn't be a pleasant ride back to the house, but at least he wasn't going to freeze to death trying to walk back with a bum leg. He stared at his ankle, wondering if it was actually broken, and he just hadn't heard the snap. He scooted closer to Red on his rump till he could loop his arm into the stirrup, then used it to pull himself upright on his good leg.

Jake set his injured foot on the ground and gently put his weight on it. He bit back an anguished cry of pain, not wanting to spook his horse again. Without taking off his boot, he couldn't tell whether it was broken or not. Once he had the boot off, he doubted he'd get it back on again. Better to wait till he got home to tend the injury.

First things first. He had to get back in the saddle. Then he had to find his cattle. He'd worry about how he was going to mend the broken fence with one good leg after he'd driven the cattle back onto his land.

He was bracing to put his foot in the stirrup when he noticed Red was standing on three legs. His right hindquarters were canted, the right rear hoof off the ground. Jake hopped carefully, and painfully, around the horse, his hand on Red's rump to let him know he was there and to keep him calm.

His heart sank when he saw the white bone sticking out. He looked to see what could have caused so much damage and found the granite outcropping near where Red had fallen. The horse must have broken his leg when he'd been kicking so furiously to get back upright after his fall.

There was no help for it. The horse would have to be put down.

He'd raised Red from a colt. Even though he knew it was dangerous to have feelings for ranch animals, he'd let himself get attached to the horse. "I'm sorry about this, Red," he said past the knot in his throat. He welcomed the pain as he hobbled back around the horse and began removing the saddle.

"This is all my fault," he said in a soothing voice. "My foolhardy pride caused this mess. I was in a big hurry and wasn't as careful as I should have been. I shouldn't let Blackthorne get under my skin. I may just have handed him the prize on a silver platter. Considering how far I am from the ranch house, and the fact that I have a bum leg and there's no one to come looking for me, I may not outlive you by much."

Jake was sobered by the thought that he might have found a mother for his daughter and then deprived her of a father, all within twenty-four hours. If he somehow survived the freezing cold and made it back to the ranch house on foot, he had no idea how he was going to run the ranch with one functioning leg. It hurt bad enough to be broken, but even a sprain was going to make it impossible to do the manual labor that had to be done every day.

Slim couldn't manage much outside the house. He doubted his wife from the big city was going to be any good at farm chores. The elder of her two brothers might be some help mucking out the barn, milking the cow, collecting eggs from the henhouse, and slopping the hogs. But how was he supposed to round up his cattle for market?

Assuming he didn't freeze to death, how long was it going to take for his injured ankle to mend? How long before Blackthorne made good on his promise to take Jake's land away from him? How long before he'd be a married man with three kids and an old man to care for with no work and no roof over their heads?

He set aside the saddle and blanket, which he could retrieve after the storm, then pulled the bridle off over Red's ears and eased the bit out of the horse's mouth. He tossed the bridle over to the pile of tack nearby, then put his arms around the horse's neck and pressed his cheek against Red's. "I'm gonna miss you, boy."

The horse stood unmoving, unaware of what was to come. Jake took a step back, pulled his Colt .45 and put it to Red's head, so it would kill the animal instantly, then pulled the trigger.

Tears froze on the corners of Jake's eyes as the horse fell in his tracks. He turned his back on the fallen animal. His job now was to survive. Somehow, he had to walk the seven or so miles back to the house. He found a crooked mesquite branch sticking out of the snow and used it for a crutch. He put his full weight on his bad ankle and cried out at the excruciating pain.

"Damn it all to hell! That hurts!"

He had to keep walking. The storm could be over in an hour, or it could last for days. There was no rescue on the horizon. He had to save himself, or die.

Chapter Eleven

"Where is he?"

Miranda shifted the baby on her hip to put her body between the child and the frightening stranger. "Who are you? How did you get in here?"

"Doors around here are never locked, young lady. Never know when a traveling man might need a meal or refuge from a storm or from a band of marauding savages." He looked past her shoulder, then repeated, "Where is he?"

Miranda frowned. Doors left unlocked? Strangers walking in unannounced? She'd never heard of such a thing. In Chicago, the last thing her father had done each night was make sure the doors and windows were all secured. Surely this stranger should at least have knocked. She realized she was totally defenseless and glanced around the kitchen for a weapon. Despite all the dirty dishes, she didn't see a single knife she could grab to protect herself.

She would have to brazen it out. "Why are you here?"

"I want to see that cowardly, back-stabbing stepson of mine."

Miranda shuddered with relief when the man identified himself as her new stepfather-in-law, even though
she was shocked at the ugly picture he'd painted of
her husband. It was easy to imagine why Jake might
despise his stepfather. She was quickly forming her
own unsavory opinion of Alexander Blackthorne.

"We haven't been introduced," Miranda said. "My
name is—"

"I know who you are and how you got here."

Miranda flushed. There was nothing wrong with
being a mail-order bride, but this tall, broad-shouldered
man, with his sharp cheekbones and silver-winged
black hair and his piercing, ice-blue eyes, made her
feel like she'd committed some crime. She lifted her
chin and said, "Then you know the man you're calling names is my husband. I'll thank you to mind your
tongue when you're in my home."

She was startled when he grinned, and even more
astounded when he said, "He's got himself a hellion
this time. Look, girl—"

"You may address me as Mrs. Creed."

The grin broadened. Then he wrinkled his nose.
"Well, *Mrs. Creed,* that baby stinks."

Miranda was immediately put on the defensive.
"I was on my way to change her diaper when you
showed up and started—"

"Tell that sorry stepson of mine I'm looking for
him," he interrupted brusquely.

The glimpse of caring human was gone and the
heartless monster was back. Her neck hairs hackled.
"I don't believe I will." Miranda didn't know what
gave her the nerve to speak so defiantly, except she'd
formed an instant dislike for this odious, larger-than-

life character, especially because she also found him both intriguing and charming. "If you want to speak to Jake, he said he'd be riding fence, whatever that is."

"He's a little late," Blackthorne said. "A bunch of his cattle are already eating grass and drinking Bitter Creek water on my side of the divide."

"Oh." That explained his appearance in Jake's kitchen. "I don't know where to tell you to find him, Mr. Blackthorne."

"Just Blackthorne," he said. "No mister."

"Is that because you're a titled gentleman? A duke, perhaps?"

Jake had mentioned his stepfather might be a lord. Miranda had been fascinated by English royalty all her life and, along with her mother, had made a study of the great families of England. Blackthorne was one of them. The line of Blackthorne dukes ran back several centuries. She couldn't resist asking whether Jake's stepfather was an honest-to-goodness nobleman.

"I believe the Duke of Blackthorne's family name is Wharton," she continued. "Are you perhaps Alexander Wharton, Duke of Blackthorne?" she asked with a whimsical smile. "Should I be addressing you as Your Grace?"

His eyes narrowed. "Keep what you think you know to yourself, Mrs. Creed. Here in Texas I'm plain Alexander Blackthorne."

"Why is that?" she asked, truly curious now, since he hadn't denied being a duke. "Why would you give up your title and come to America? Why not use the Wharton name? Why call yourself Blackthorne, if you're not going to use the title that goes with it? Of course, we don't have royalty here in America, but—"

"I'll be taking my leave now," he said abruptly. "Tell Jake to get his cattle off my land by sundown today or—" He stopped himself, growled "Bloody hell!" under his breath, then said, "If his cattle aren't gone by sunrise tomorrow, I'll consider them mine."

He left the house in a swirl of icy wind, slamming the kitchen door behind him.

Anna Mae clung to her and said, "Mean man."

"Yes, sweetie, he is," Miranda agreed. "Let's go get you changed. Then I need to talk to your grandpa."

After she'd changed the baby in a small downstairs room she found fitted out so Slim could care for the child during the daylight hours, Miranda set Anna Mae down to play on a blanket near the fire in the parlor. She picked up odds and ends that were scattered around the room and made a pile of stuff to be moved to its proper place while she waited for Nick and Harry to return with the first batch of cut logs.

"It's cold as a witch's tit out there!" Nick said as he dropped his load of logs near the fireplace.

"Nicholas Jackson Wentworth!"

"I know, I know," he said. "Watch my language. But it *is* that cold, Miranda."

Miranda cringed at the thought of going out in such weather to find Jake and give him Blackthorne's message. Maybe Slim would know better what she should do. "Would you please watch the baby? I'm going to talk to Slim."

"He won't want to talk to you," Nick muttered. "None of them want us here. Except maybe this baby here," he said, picking up Anna Mae, who clung to him like a limpet.

"Give it some time, Nick."

"It's not like we can go anywhere," he said. "It's cold as a witch's—" He stopped himself, grimaced, and said, "Anyway, it's cold."

"Thanks for the warning," she said. "I might have to leave the house for a while."

"And go where?" Nick said. "It's snowing."

"Oh, no. Really?" Miranda looked out the parlor window and, sure enough, large snowflakes were drifting down. She frowned. How likely was it she could find Jake if the trail got covered with snow? There didn't seem to be much sense in going out in this kind of weather. She was more likely to get lost than end up helping Jake.

She wondered if Blackthorne would enforce his threat in spite of the weather. How was Jake supposed to move his cattle by sunrise tomorrow if he didn't know they'd strayed? Of course, he might already have found the break in the fence and gone hunting the missing cattle on his own, which would mean she'd be heading out in this frigid weather on a useless errand.

As she left the kitchen, Miranda decided the best thing to do was tell Slim what Blackthorne had said and let him make the decision whether she should go hunting Jake.

She hesitated before knocking on Slim's door, which was on the opposite—unburned—wing of the house from the parlor. She could understand why the old man might resent her taking his daughter's place in the household. That didn't make it any easier to endure his bad temper. She took a deep breath and told herself to remain calm, no matter what the old curmudgeon said.

She knocked, and Slim called back, "What do you want?"

"I need to talk to you."

"Don't have nothin' to say to you. Go away."

"I need some advice."

A pause and then, "Do what you want. I don't care."

"The problem is, I don't know what to do. Could I please come in and talk to you?"

"Come on in," he said gruffly.

Miranda opened the door, stepped inside, and closed it behind her. Slim's dark brown eyes looked sunken in his face, and his body looked frail in the battered wooden wheelchair. She saw the unmade bed had been lowered by having the four legs cut off so the paralyzed man could slide from the chair to the bed and back.

Miranda realized Slim must do a lot of reading and, perhaps, writing when he was alone in this room. A bookcase full of heavy tomes covered one wall. A desk complete with pen and ink sat against another. Slim's bedroom also had a fireplace, and she welcomed the toasty warmth of the crackling fire.

"Thought I heard someone in the house," Slim said. "Who was it?"

"Blackthorne."

"That son of a bitch! He knows better than to come here."

"He wanted me to tell Jake his cattle had gotten through the fence onto Blackthorne land. He wants them moved by tomorrow at sunrise, or he's going to confiscate them."

"Like hell he will! That's stealin', plain and simple."

"The cattle are trespassing, I suppose," Miranda said.

"He knows you can't keep barbed wire from comin' down now and again. Weather, wind, cattle rubbin' up against mesquite posts, knockin' 'em over. He's got no right to take Jake's cattle."

"Do you think Jake will find the break in the fence and know his cattle have strayed?"

Slim chewed on the inside of his cheek. "Might. Might not."

"How likely is Blackthorne to make good on his threat?"

"Oh, he'll take 'em, all right. He's lookin' for any excuse he can find to make life hard for Jake. He wants this land."

"I considered riding out to find Jake to warn him, but it's snowing. I don't see how I could find him if I can't see the trail."

Slim tugged at the gray whiskers on his chin as he eyed the snow out his bedroom window through the tattered pink curtains. It was blowing sideways now. "I can tell you where I think Jake might be. You follow the fence, and it'll take you right to him."

"You don't think it's too dangerous?" she asked, her heart beating hard in her chest at the thought of going out all by herself in a strange place in what was fast becoming a blizzard.

"Everythin' here in Texas is dangerous," Slim said. "Sometimes you have to take risks." He sneered. "That is, if you're not too scared."

She was plenty scared. She could see Slim wanted her to fail Jake. It would be one more way he could lower her in Jake's esteem. She looked down her dainty nose at him and said, "I'm not afraid."

Slim gave her instructions where to go, told her which horse would be easiest to ride, then asked, "You know how to saddle a horse, missy?"

She could put on an English saddle. How much different could a Western saddle be? "I'll manage. I know you usually take care of the baby. Would you mind keeping an eye on Harry for me? Nick doesn't always pay him enough mind."

"The runt can play in here with Anna Mae. It's warmer than the rest of the house."

She opened her mouth to correct his use of the term *runt* to describe Harry, then closed it. No sense starting an argument now. She knew he'd picked up the term from Jake. Once she got Jake to stop using it, Slim would likely stop as well. She ended up saying, "Thank you, Slim."

"Don't want thanks. Just be sure you find Jake. Don't get lost and cause him more trouble. He's got enough on his plate as it is."

"I'll do my best," she promised.

Chapter Twelve

After leaving Three Oaks, Blackthorne joined his cowhands on the range. He'd sent them out into the storm early to move stock closer to the ranch house, in case the snow continued for several days and it became necessary to drop hay to feed them. He hadn't gone near Jake's cattle, but he knew, with their tails to the icy wind, they'd drift farther onto his land.

In light of his wife's threat, Alex had debated whether to move Jake's longhorns back across the fence but had decided against it. He'd already given his stepson an extra half day to retrieve his stock. That was as much as he was willing to bend. He would deal with his wife when—if—things came to a head.

By mid-afternoon, the lowering temperatures and blowing snow finally forced Alex to call his men in. He took the time to unsaddle and rub down his own horse, despite the fact that he had a man working in the stable. Alex had learned when he was still a tenderfoot that a good cowman took care of his own horse. He hadn't forgotten that lesson.

He'd learned a great deal more than that the first

year he'd spent in the West. Cowboys had their own code of living—not unlike Society's rules in England—that must be followed. The difference was, out here he had to earn the respect of the men he hired to work for him. In England, he had that respect by virtue of his name and aristocratic rank.

Alex felt his stomach roll as he remembered the final betrayal that had caused him to leave his patrimony behind and start life anew. He'd married Cricket because it had seemed the most expedient thing to do. Since he didn't plan to love his wife, one would do as well as another. He smiled ruefully as he acknowledged that he would have had a bloody fight on his hands if he'd tried to evict her.

Cricket hadn't believed his account of her husband's death. She'd waited for confirmation from Creed's battlefield commander. It had come a month later. Alex knew she'd agreed to marry him only because she'd wanted to be sure that her sons had a home when they returned from the war.

The hitch had come when she'd asked that the marriage be in name only.

Alex had refused. "I need sons to carry on after me. I need a wife to provide them."

Cricket had reminded him that she wasn't in the first bloom of youth. That she might not be able to give him sons. Even if she was able to conceive a child, it might be female.

It had been reckless on his part to take her to wife, because what she'd said was true. But he'd been entranced by the image of Cricket Creed standing on her front porch confronting him, rifle in hand. Imagine the kind of sons a woman like that would breed if he could get her pregnant! She was the antithesis of the women in the world he'd left behind, which was probably why he found her so desirable as a wife.

Their marriage had been fruitful. He'd been dismayed when Cricket had borne twins, which ran in the Blackthorne family. He was a twin himself, and his relationship with his brother had poisoned his life.

Of course, in England, the aristocratic title and wealth and property all went to the elder twin, with the younger receiving only what the elder chose to give him. The greed and jealousy and envy of one brother for what the other possessed had run rampant, purposely uncurbed by either parent. Alex had endured a miserable childhood.

There were no such rules of inheritance in America, where a father's fortune was split equally among his heirs. There was no need for one twin to be jealous of the other. He was encouraged to see that, from the very beginning, Cricket treated the twins equally. He realized early on that she didn't care which had been born first. The red string on the elder twin's ankle had come untied during the night so often, he wasn't sure himself whether Nash or Noah had actually been born first.

He was glad it didn't matter.

Cricket's son Jake had returned in 1864, his shooting arm badly wounded in the Shenandoah Valley campaign, and stayed. Cricket's other two sons, Flint and Ransom, didn't return to Lion's Dare until more than a year later, when the war ended. They left together soon after, driving a small herd of cattle north to the Wyoming Territory to start a new life. Alex knew his wife missed them every day, the way he knew that the loss of Jarrett Creed had left a hole in her heart.

By the time he'd learned the truth, by the time it became apparent that Jarrett Creed had not died at Gettysburg, Alex was in love with his wife. So much in love, that he couldn't imagine life without her.

Alex felt a pang of guilt for what he'd done and forced it down.

He'd made an honest mistake thinking Jarrett Creed was dead. The man who'd impersonated Creed in the poker game had died at Gettysburg, and Creed's death had been mistakenly confirmed by his commander in the field, who'd seen him fall in battle with a head wound.

Jarrett Creed had, in fact, been shot twice on the field of battle. His head had been grazed by a musket ball that had left him both blind and not knowing who he was. He'd also taken shrapnel from a cannon to his knee that had left him on crutches. Jarrett had been taken in and nursed back to health by a widow who lived near the battlefield.

His sight had never returned, but the instant he recovered his memory, he'd returned home.

Unfortunately, he was too late. Cricket had already remarried and borne Alexander Blackthorne's sons.

Alex had heard the story of Jarrett Creed's misfortune from the man's own lips. Alex had often wondered what would have happened if Cricket had been home that day instead of him. She'd gone to visit her sister Bay. She'd left the twins at home because they both had colds. Alex had been home because he was expecting the delivery of a bull he'd bought from another rancher.

If Cricket had known Jarrett was alive, Alex was almost certain she would have gone back to her husband. Even a year into their marriage, he'd loved her a great deal more than she'd loved him. But he hadn't been willing to lose her. So he'd said what was necessary to make Jarrett Creed go away and never come back.

He'd told Jarrett that Cricket loved *him* now. Creed might have his wife back but at a terrible price. Alex would keep Lion's Dare, since possession was nine-tenths of the law, and he would keep the twins his wife had borne. Creed might have Cricket back, but in the process, he would tear her in two. She could have Jarrett, but she would lose both her children and her home.

It was a testament to how much Creed loved his wife, that he hadn't insisted on speaking to her himself.

Alex hadn't trusted the man to stay gone forever. And as long as Jarrett was alive, there was always the possibility that he would run into someone who would bring word back to Bitter Creek of his existence.

So he'd offered Creed the deed to a cattle station in Queensland, Australia, which would put his rival an ocean and a continent away. It would also salve Alex's conscience, since it was clear Creed had been cheated out of his home by an imposter.

Jarrett Creed had been gone nearly ten years, but Alex had never stopped worrying that someday he might return and take back what had been stolen from him.

So Alex's heart always beat a little harder every time

he returned to the house after he'd been away. His stomach always fluttered till he crossed the threshold and saw his wife's face, her gray eyes alight with hard-won love for him.

Although he'd been willing to hire servants, Cricket had insisted she could take care of the house on her own. It gave them more privacy, she said. So they lived in the house alone.

It was eerily silent when he entered.

"Cricket? Nash? Noah?"

The house was cold. The fires in the fireplaces had been untended long enough to burn out. Alex was not the sort of man to panic, but he could think of no reason why his wife and sons should be gone so long from the house in weather like this.

"Cricket?" he called again as he sprinted up the winding staircase. His heart jumped to his throat.

Had his family been stolen away by the man he'd banished all those years ago?

The bed in their room was unmade. The boys' room had twin beds that had also been left in disarray. He checked the other rooms upstairs and found them empty.

"Cricket!" he bellowed. "Are you in the house? Answer me!"

He heard icy snow rattle against the windowpanes. He heard the whistle of the icy wind against the wood-frame house. But there was no reply to his anguished cry.

His wife and his sons had mysteriously gone missing.

Chapter Thirteen

Cricket Blackthorne wanted to meet her son's mail-order bride, but the only way to do that was to go to Three Oaks. Otherwise, their paths were unlikely to cross. Jake had stopped coming to church after the death of his first wife, and because of Alex's stranglehold on the businesses in Bitter Creek, Jake was forced to go all the way to San Antonio for supplies. She decided to bake a dried-apple pie and take it over as a welcome gift to Jake's new bride.

At least, that was the original plan.

By the time Cricket got the pie baked, she realized that the snowy weather was going to prevent Jake from moving his cattle off Blackthorne land by sundown. She could have let things come to a head between her husband and her son, but she was certain Alex would keep his promise.

And then, she would have to keep hers.

She didn't want to leave Alexander Blackthorne. She loved him despite his many flaws. Or perhaps because of them. He was not so different from her first husband, Jarrett Creed. Both were proud, stubborn, sometimes ruthless men. Both had endured difficult childhoods. It seemed Alex's had left him scarred far more deeply than Jarrett's.

Alex was less likely to show compassion. Less likely to give way in an argument. Less likely to surrender, even to the lovemaking of his wife. It was as though he was afraid that if he showed any softness at all, he would be punished for it.

Sometimes she missed Jarrett with an ache that was almost palpable. She yearned for the simple life they'd lived with their three sons and two daughters in the years before the War Between the States. The conflict had torn the country apart—and decimated her family.

Cricket still grieved the husband who'd been killed in that horrible, seemingly endless war. Her three sons had returned to find their home invaded by an autocratic Englishman. Jake had stayed, but Flint and Ransom had headed for distant Wyoming within months of their arrival.

It didn't seem fair that she should lose so much. Long before the war was even a glimmer in some Southern gentleman's eye, she'd lost her second daughter, nicknamed Muffin, to pneumonia. Cricket had never stopped mourning the lost promise of that four-year-old child.

She'd been able to bear that calamity because she'd still had her elder daughter, Jesse. Because of the war, Jesse was now gone, too. Six months before the end of the conflict between North and South, Cricket's twenty-year-old daughter had cut her hair, dressed in buckskins, and enlisted as a man to fight.

There had been no word from her daughter since. That was ten years ago. Cricket imagined Jesse somewhere too far away to write letters, married to a man she loved, surrounded by laughing children. Anything else was too painful to contemplate.

Even the cessation of hostilities hadn't brought an end to the devastation. Cricket had lost her half brother Luke to a band of murdering carpetbaggers three months after the war was over. Long ago, Luke's wife, Tomasita, and their three young children had all died of the smallpox they'd gotten from folks just moving through, to whom Luke and Tomasita had given shelter.

Don Cruz Guerrero, who'd married Cricket's eldest sister Sloan, had returned to Spain six months before the war started, unwilling to choose sides, taking Sloan and their two children with him. In thanks for his service to the king of Spain during the next several years, Don Cruz had been given an enormous grant of land near Madrid, far larger than the ranch he owned in Texas.

The Guerreros hadn't returned when the war ended. Cricket had exchanged enough letters with Sloan to know that her sister's eldest son, Cisco, had married a beautiful senorita in Spain and made her a grandmother.

Her beautiful daughter, Ana Maria, had finally, after two disgraceful broken engagements, found a third man, an English lord, to whom she was engaged—although the wedding at St. George's in England had already been postponed once.

Cricket's sister Bayleigh, one year older, still owned a ranch not far off with her half-Comanche husband, Walker Coburn, but Bay's children were grown and gone. Her daughter, Grace, had married a man headed to California, and her son, Whipp, had left to seek his fortune in the Montana Territory.

Lately, Bay and Walker had been ostracized by their neighbors because he'd argued before the Texas legislature that the Indians remaining in Texas shouldn't be hunted to extinction or moved to a reservation.

The next thing Cricket knew, they'd gone for an extended visit to friends in Boston. She'd discovered that Walker was taking advantage of his proximity to Washington to make his pleas on behalf of the Indians to members of Congress.

"Hey, Mom, is that pie for us?"

Cricket slapped at her ten-year-old son's hand as he reached for a bit of piecrust, but Nash laughed and jerked his hand away before she could catch him.

"So, is it?" Nash's twin brother, Noah, asked as he joined his brother in the kitchen.

"It's not for you. It's for Jake's new wife."

"I didn't even know he was courting," Nash said. "Who did he marry? My teacher, Miss Pettigrew, sure is pretty. That's who I'd marry."

Cricket hadn't realized what a can of worms she was opening, but there was no help for it now. She would have to explain. "Jake's new wife is a mail-order bride."

The identical twin boys, showing signs of their father's height already, with their father's straight black hair and their mother's distinctive gray eyes, made equally confused faces at each other.

"He ordered a bride? How did he do that?" Nash asked.

"Through the newspaper." As Cricket explained, she wrapped the pie in a dishtowel and tied the corners together so she'd have a way to carry it on horse-back. "The man who wants a wife advertises in the newspaper, and the woman who would like to be his bride answers the advertisement."

"I never saw any ad like that in the San Antonio paper," Noah said.

Cricket had been using the newspaper to help teach the boys to read. "He advertised in a Chicago newspaper."

"Whoa!" Noah exclaimed. "So his mail-order bride came all the way from Chicago?"

"Yes, and she brought her two younger brothers along with her," Cricket said.

"How old are her brothers?" Nash asked.

"I don't know," Cricket replied. "Would you like to go meet them?"

The minute the words were out of her mouth, Cricket realized it was a good idea. The boys could help her herd Jake's cattle back onto his land. They would also diffuse the tension, if there was any, between her and Slim and Jake's new bride. Slim hated Blackthorne and merely tolerated her, but he'd always been cordial to her sons.

"Dad won't like it," Noah pointed out.

Alex had made it clear he didn't want his sons fraternizing with Jake and Slim. "I'll take care of any objections from your father," she said.

Cricket was pretty sure Alex was going to be a lot more angry about the fact that she'd moved Jake's cattle than the fact that she'd taken her sons along to deliver an apple pie to Jake's bride. He would grumble, but it would be too late for him to counter her actions.

The snowy weather might have been an obstacle to her success, but she'd grown up at Three Oaks back in the days before statehood, when Texas was a Republic, a sovereign nation with its own president and its own army and navy. She could find her way there blindfolded.

The three of them easily located Jake's longhorns. The boys were good cattlemen, even at ten, but it took a great deal of effort to keep the cattle headed in the right direction for the three and a half long hours it took to drive them back to Jake's ranch house, with snow blowing in their faces the whole way. The wind was so cold and fierce, it was no wonder the longhorns had turned their tails to it last night and drifted so far onto Blackthorne land.

The three of them left the cattle huddled under one of the three oaks that surrounded Jake's house and took their horses into the barn. They left their mounts saddled but scrubbed the snow off their hides with clean straw and put them in stalls with a little hay to eat before they headed to the house.

"That pie's got to be near frozen by now," Nash said.

"We can heat it up on the stove," Cricket replied. "It'll taste better warm, anyway."

"You think that lady from Chicago will know she should share it with company?" Noah asked.

Cricket laughed and tugged down her son's hat. "If she doesn't, Slim does."

As they slogged through the snow the short distance to the house, Cricket wondered what kind of wife her son had picked the second time around.

The girl must have written an impressive letter, since Cricket's friend at the post office in San Antonio had told her Jake had gotten twenty-three replies. Her son had been so devastated by his wife's death that Cricket felt sure he would never have married again, if not for the need to have a mother for his daughter.

She had her fingers crossed that this wife would turn out to be not only a great mother but a great wife.

She knocked at the kitchen door and let herself and the boys in. The twins dusted the snow off their hats by swatting them against their trousers and stomped their boots on the rug inside the door to get rid of the wet snow.

"Hello? Anybody home?" Cricket called.

There was no answer.

Cricket felt a shiver roll down her spine at the eerie silence. She'd expected Jake to be gone, but where was his new wife and her two brothers? And Slim and the baby? "Hello!" she called again, louder.

A skinny boy appeared in the kitchen doorway. He looked scared until he laid eyes on the two boys. Then he looked belligerent. "Who the hell are you? What do you want?"

Cricket was taken aback by the boy's language and shot her twins a look that warned them not to say anything. The boy was nearly as tall as her twins, but he looked to be nothing more than skin and bones.

She took off her coat and hung it on the back of a kitchen chair, then checked the stove to see if it needed more wood on the fire. "I'm Jake's mother," she said. "I brought an apple pie as a welcome present for your sister. I presume you're one of the former Miss Wentworth's brothers."

"I am," the kid said.

"What's your name?" Cricket asked.

She saw the kid deciding whether he was going to tell her or not. Finally he said, "I'm Nick."

"Where's your sister?" Cricket asked.

"She rode out to find Jake."

Alarmed, Cricket asked, "Has something happened to him?"

The boy sneered at her and said, "Nothing but that Blackthorne character showing up here and threatening to steal his cattle if he didn't move them."

"My dad wouldn't steal anything!" Nash retorted as he approached the boy with clenched fists. Noah stayed by his brother's side, their shoulders brushing, presenting a deadly united front.

"Nash, Noah," Cricket warned. "Remember you're guests in this home."

"He called Dad a thief," Nash protested.

"Well, since Jake's cattle are outside under the live oaks, I guess your dad can't very well be a thief, can he?" Cricket said.

"You brought the cattle back?" Nick said. "Did you see my sister?"

"No, I'm sorry, we didn't. When did she go after Jake?"

"This morning, right after breakfast."

Cricket bit her lip. "Was it snowing?"

The kid nodded, his eyes desolate. "I told her not to go. I knew she'd get lost!"

"She's probably on her way home right now with Jake. Where's Slim?"

"He's in his room with Anna Mae and my little brother."

"Do you think they'd like a piece of pie?"

"I know I would," Nick said. "We haven't eaten since breakfast."

Cricket looked around the kitchen, noticing the unwashed dishes in the sink, the plates still on the table from breakfast. Alex must have frightened Jake's new wife into leaving the house in a hurry. She'd obviously planned to be back before lunch or she would have made arrangements to feed the kids. Cricket was surprised Slim hadn't fed them.

"Did you tell Slim you were hungry?" she asked.

"Wouldn't ask that old man for a scrap of food if I was starving to death," Nick said. "Which I am," he added under his breath.

Cricket felt her heart sink. It seemed things in Jake's household were already headed downhill, and he hadn't even been married for a day yet. She opened cupboards looking for something she could make for lunch and found a loaf of bread, a round of cheese, and a smoked ham. She searched through drawers looking for a clean knife to cut the bread.

"Noah, find a knife and cut some slices of cheese. Nash, you find another one and cut some of that ham." The three of them spread out around the kitchen, on whatever flat, empty surface they could find. Cricket looked at the boy still standing in the doorway and said, "Why don't you go get your brother and Anna Mae and Slim? After lunch we can all have a slice of apple pie."

He stared hungrily at the pie, with its lattice crust,

which she'd set on top of the stove to warm up, then turned and left the kitchen.

"What's wrong with him, Mom?" Nash asked, once he was gone.

"He's just hungry, I expect." *And lonely and scared,* she thought. "Let's get these sandwiches put together before they all get back here."

Cricket barely had the breakfast dishes cleared from the kitchen table when Slim showed up in the doorway in his wheelchair. Anna Mae was sitting in his lap. A very small boy appeared from behind the wheelchair, which he'd apparently been helping to push. His nose was running, and he swiped his sleeve across it as he said, "Nick said you have pie."

"What's your name?" she asked the little boy as she crossed and wiped his nose on a dishtowel.

"I'm Harry. Who are you?"

"You can call me Cricket."

"Like the bug?" Harry asked.

Cricket laughed. "Yes, like the bug."

"That's a funny name."

"I guess it is," Cricket agreed. "Are you hungry, Harry?"

"Starving," the boy admitted.

If Nick was thin, Harry was a wraith. When she'd wiped his nose she'd felt his forehead was hot with fever. The little boy should be in a warm bed, not running around half dressed in this cold house.

"Won't ask what you're doin' here," Slim said. "I 'spect I can figure it out for myself."

"The boys and I brought a pie over to welcome Jake's bride." She took a deep breath and added,

"Since we were coming anyway, we rounded up Jake's strays and brought them home."

Slim glanced at her sharply, then sniffed and said, "Smells good."

The pie was warming up and the smell of cinnamon wafted through the kitchen. "I don't think Jake's bride will mind if we have some of that pie before she gets back," Cricket said.

"If she gets back," Slim muttered.

"I'm surprised you'd send a tenderfoot out in a storm like this," Cricket ventured as she set ham and cheese sandwiches on plates she'd had the twins put on the table.

"Didn't have no choice," Slim said. "Had to get word to Jake about those cattle, so I sent Miranda out to find him. Didn't 'spect you to show up here."

Miranda. Cricket felt a pang of sadness. That had been her daughter Muffin's name, although they'd rarely used it. "Miranda should have found Jake by now, don't you think?"

"Probably got throwed and froze to death," Slim said.

"Miranda's a good rider," Nick said in her defense. "Or, at least, she used to be."

More likely, Cricket thought, Miranda and Jake were out on a wild-goose chase, hunting down the cattle Cricket had already returned. While everyone else started eating, Cricket found cups and pumped a glass of water for each of them to drink. Once that was done she said, "I'm going out to move those cattle into the corral. I don't want them straying again before Jake has a chance to fix the fence. When I get back, I'll cut everyone a piece of that pie."

Cricket put a hand on each of the twin's shoulders before she left the kitchen, leaned down between them, and said, "Be on your best behavior."

"I will if he will," Nash muttered, glaring at Nick.

Cricket sighed. "I'm not kidding, Nash. I mean it, Noah. When I come back in here, I expect to see you finishing up your sandwiches. Is that clear?"

"Yes, ma'am," Nash said.

"Yes, ma'am," Noah said.

She'd already turned to leave when she caught Nick smirking at the twins. She turned back and said, "That goes for you, too, Nick."

"You can't tell me what to do," Nick shot back.

She turned to Slim and said, "Aren't you going to say anything?"

"Ain't my kid." Slim was smirking, too.

"I'll be good," Harry promised. "I want pie."

"Great idea, Harry," she said to the towheaded little boy. "The rest of you, behave yourselves, too, or no pie!"

Nick scowled, but this time, he didn't talk back.

She caught Nash and Noah starting to sneer and pointed a finger at them. They'd learned over the years the power of that pointed finger. Both boys immediately filled their mouths with their sandwiches.

"I'll be back as quick as I can," she said.

Cricket was afraid to leave, afraid of the row that might start the instant she wasn't there to prevent it, but the sooner she left the sooner she'd get back. She sent one more admonishing look toward the boys at the table as she put on her coat, hat, and gloves. Then she headed back out into the cold.

Chapter Fourteen

The mustang beneath her was nothing like the gentle hacks Miranda had ridden in the park in Chicago. The Roman-nosed gray was rebellious, yanking at the bit and even crow-hopping. She was grateful for the wide stirrups, the high cantle in back, and the horn in front that kept her firmly in the Western saddle during the gelding's antics.

Miranda had discovered that instead of buckling a strap around the horse's girth, like an English saddle, the Western saddle had a strap that had to be tightened around cinch rings. She'd known enough to knee the grulla's belly to get him to release the air he held in his lungs as she tightened the strap, so the cinch wouldn't be loose as soon as the animal exhaled.

The unruly animal had fought when she tried putting the curb bit in his mouth and jerked his head up to keep her from getting the bridle over his ears. She'd resorted to bribery, offering the mustang a dried-up carrot to keep his head down long enough to get the bridle in place.

As she rode out onto the snowy landscape, Nick's woeful warning rang in her ears.

You're going to die out there, Miranda. You're going to get lost and freeze to death. Harry and I are going to be all alone here in Texas. Please don't go!

For a moment, she'd considered staying in the house. But she knew she couldn't do it. Her family's security was tied up with Jake's success. If he lost the ranch, she and her brothers would lose the roof over their heads, and whatever chance she'd had to save her sisters would be gone along with it.

She had no choice. She had to go out into the storm.

Miranda was glad she'd added extra layers of Jake's clothing under Priscilla's pink cape and that she'd thought to tie the cape at the waist with a wool scarf she'd found among the dead woman's belongings. She'd wrapped a second knitted scarf around her throat. Nevertheless, her teeth were chattering.

"Come on, you ornery cuss," she said as she kicked the gray's flanks. "Let's go find Jake."

The horse's ears flicked forward and back when she said "Jake," which made her wonder if Priscilla and Jake had ridden together, so the horse recognized his name. She wondered if Priscilla had harbored dreams as she did. Surely she had. Miranda tried not to think of the other woman's fate. That wasn't going to be her. Her life was going to turn out differently.

Especially if Jake never touched her. Imagine a man deciding never to make love to his wife because he didn't want to get her pregnant! Miranda hoped Jake wouldn't keep that promise. Otherwise, she was never going to have a family of her own. Surely he would reconsider.

But why would he?

He already had a child of his own. She'd brought

along two young boys who would grow into helpful ranch hands. Why would he want to take the risk of losing his caretaker for the children, his housekeeper and cook, his laundress and helpmate?

She thought back to his gentleness the previous night and the kiss that had followed their conversation. She had felt . . . *strange* . . . afterward. She tried to find a better word to describe her feelings.

Uplifted. Whole. Cherished.

She'd felt all of those things and wanted to feel them again. She wanted Jake's warm lips pressed against her own. She wanted his arms wrapped around her, not just in comfort, but in passion.

Passion. What an odd word for her to be using! She would never have called herself a passionate person. If anything, she was dispassionate. Over the past three years, she'd learned to curb her emotions, to stifle her feelings, to control *everything,* because anything else gave Miss Birch the opportunity to cause her pain.

Miranda suddenly realized, riding through a blizzard all by herself, that the person she'd been for the past three years was nothing like the person she'd been before she'd arrived at the orphanage. That girl-before-the-fire, eldest daughter of doting parents, had been proud and confident and daring and even, though she didn't like to remember it, mischievous.

Where had that girl-before-the-fire gone? Was she still inside somewhere? Did Miranda want that girl back? Or was it better—safer—to remain the more careful, cautious, and cowed person she'd become?

Miranda realized even before she'd finished asking

herself that final question that she couldn't remain the girl she'd been at the orphanage. This untamed land demanded more than the diminished creature she'd been in the presence of Miss Birch.

Besides, she wasn't that abject person. She never had been, not really. She might have surrendered her body to Miss Birch, but she'd never surrendered her soul. She'd had the courage, for many years, to take punishments meant for her siblings. She'd been a mother to them and kept them from feeling like the orphans they all were. And she'd had the boldness, in the end, to steal away with Nick and Harry.

Behavior that had been necessary for survival at the Chicago Institute for Orphaned Children would not serve her well in this wild place. Careful, yes. Cautious, yes. But cowed? Never.

She smiled to herself. You couldn't exactly call what she was doing right now either careful or cautious. Riding out into a blizzard? To deliver a message that probably couldn't be acted upon anyway in this snowstorm? It seemed reckless. And yet, Slim seemed to think Jake would not only want Blackthorne's message but that he would act on it, despite the weather.

The old man had instructed her to ride the length of the fence that began at the edge of the barn, looking for a break where Jake might have gone through. She wished she had a better way of telling how long she'd been riding, or even how far. The sun was up there somewhere above the storm, but the sky was an oppressively dark gray and the landscape was endlessly white, without any particular landmarks to guide her.

Snow on the rolling hills was a half foot deep now, blowing into much deeper drifts in the gulleys and along the four-foot-high barbed wire fence that was attached to mesquite posts. In some places, barely a foot of the posts remained visible.

She was so focused on the fence to keep it beside her that she was startled when she looked up and saw a figure—a man on foot—in the distance.

Miranda was alarmed. Who would be out here on foot in this weather? Probably some drifter who'd want her horse and try to take it from her forcibly. She considered riding away from the fence to escape the stranger, but she knew she'd never find her way back to the ranch. Besides, even from here she could see the man was moving slowly, limping badly. He might need help. She could make the decision whether to run away when, and if, it became necessary.

As she got closer, she thought she recognized the flat-crowned hat and shearling coat. She was almost sure it was Jake. He was using a stick for a cane and moving even more slowly than when she'd first seen him. His lower face was wrapped up in a scarf, but she would know those serious brown eyes anywhere.

"Jake!"

She kneed her horse into a jog, then dismounted and struggled through the snow on foot to reach him. "Are you all right? What happened?"

"Horse rolled on me. Hurt my ankle," he said tersely.

His taut voice and bleak eyes revealed the direness of the situation. "Is it broken?" She looked down at his boot, but it was covered in snow.

"Don't know."

"Where's your horse?"

He stared back at her without speaking, and she

felt a wave of nausea at the thought of what he must have done.

"He's dead?"

He gave a jerky nod and said, "What are you doing out here?"

She opened her mouth to tell him about Blackthorne's warning and shut it again. There was no sense telling Jake about Blackthorne's ultimatum, since there was no way he could go hunting for lost cattle now. Maybe Blackthorne would give them more time when he found out Jake had been injured.

"Slim was worried," she said instead.

"That old man needs his head examined, sending you out here like this. Come on. Weather's not getting any better."

That was all he said. Not, "Thank you for coming." Or, "Thank you for caring." Or, "It's a good thing you came along." Miranda felt miffed. Then she took another look at his face, where the scarf had slipped, and realized the agony he must be suffering. He hadn't said how long he'd been walking on his sprained—or broken—ankle.

He mounted first, biting back an oath, then pulled her up sideways into his lap, putting his arms around her to hold her in place. He kneed the gray horse and followed the fence back toward the house, moving around drifts when necessary.

She waited for him to say something, anything, but he remained silent. Finally, she couldn't stand the silence any longer.

"What happened?"

"I found a break in the fence between my land and Bitter Creek and went looking for any cattle that might have gone through it, knowing that if that English bastard found them before I did, he'd slap a brand on them and dare me to call him a thief. I was in a hurry and moving too fast and my horse slipped and broke a leg."

So Jake had already discovered his cattle were missing and had figured out the possible consequences of their straying onto Blackthorne land. She could have stayed at home.

What if she had? She shuddered to think what might have happened to Jake. Would he have made it back in this weather with a sprained, or maybe broken, ankle? He was barely moving by the time she'd found him, and she'd been riding several hours before she reached him.

"Bad luck seems to follow me around," he muttered. "I'm damned sorry I got you into this."

She heard the despair in his voice. It sounded like he was giving up. She couldn't allow that to happen.

"Couldn't you hire someone to help until you're better?"

"No."

She had to suppose there was no money to pay such a person, since Jake didn't elaborate. "I can help," she offered. "So can Nick, if you think Slim would be willing to watch Anna Mae and Harry."

"A woman and a boy can't—"

"Why not?" she interrupted. "I'm strong and, despite his size, so is Nick. What we don't know, you can teach us."

"From a rocker in the parlor?" he snarled.

"From the back of a horse. You can obviously ride, even if you can't walk. You come along and tell us what to do, and we'll do it, starting with getting those cattle back on your—our—land."

She felt his arms tighten around her in what almost felt like a hug. She was suddenly aware of the warmth of his muscular thighs under hers. Aware of his hot breath against her cheek. Aware of his strong arms holding her close.

She felt protected. She felt cherished.

Of course, those feelings were an illusion. She wanted them to be real. She warned herself to be careful, to be cautious, not to let herself become vulnerable. She didn't want to lose her heart to a man who couldn't—or wouldn't—love her back. Better to remain friends. Better to be safe than sorry.

"Weren't you afraid to come out here alone?" Jake asked.

She was surprised into admitting the truth. "Terrified."

He chuckled in her ear. "So why did you come?"

She shifted herself so she could look up at him more easily. "I didn't want to find myself a widow before I've become a wife."

"Slim couldn't have known I was in trouble. Why did you really come?"

She hesitated, then said, "Blackthorne showed up at the house."

He swore viciously, then said, "He knows better than to set foot on my land."

"He came to tell you that some of your cattle have strayed onto Bitter Creek. To give you an ultimatum, actually. He wants them moved off before tomorrow morning or—"

"Goddamn that man!"

Miranda heard the desperation and frustration and anguish of a man pushed past his limits. "We'll get them moved, Jake."

"Not before tomorrow morning," he bit out. "That bastard means what he says. I can kiss those yearlings good-bye."

"Maybe just a few got through the fence," Miranda said in an attempt to make him feel better.

"Even a few is too many. I'm living within a hairs-breadth of disaster day-to-day. I have so many things I want to do, improvements I'd like to make, none of which I can accomplish without getting every single one of my cattle to market."

"Maybe we can get him to change his mind," Miranda said.

"Blackthorne is ruthless. Heartless. The most un-scrupulous blackguard you'll ever meet in your life."

Miranda didn't disagree with him. She hadn't liked the man when she'd met him. She liked him even less, now that she saw how miserable he made Jake's life. "Then we'll just have to thwart him at every turn."

Jake looked down at her and smiled wryly. "Good luck."

"We won't need luck. We're going to do it with de-termination and hard work."

She felt Jake's arms tighten around her again. This time it really felt like a hug.

They were nearing the house when Miranda heard the distinct lowing of cattle, carried by the icy wind. Through the whipping snow she saw a small bunch of longhorns being herded by a lone figure on horseback. As she watched, the person on horseback opened the gate to a large corral next to Jake's barn, swinging a lariat to prod the cattle into it.

"Oh, Jake, look!" Miranda said, feeling a surge of relief. "Someone found your missing cattle and brought them home."

"Son of a bitch," he muttered.

"Who is that?" Miranda asked. "Do you recognize him? Is it one of your neighbors?"

"What the hell does she think she's doing?"

Miranda turned and stared up into Jake's angry eyes. "She?" She turned back to look at the slight figure on horseback. "That's a woman?"

"That's no woman," Jake said. "That's my mother."

Chapter Fifteen

"Are you crazy?" Jake shouted at his mother.

"You want to yell at me, or you want to help?" she called back.

Jake started to shove Miranda off the horse, so he could better help his mother, but the city girl clung to him and said, "Don't put me down! Those cows will stomp me."

A ranch woman would have known to climb the outside rails of the corral, where she would have been perfectly safe from the milling longhorns. Rather than explaining, he said, "Hang on."

It didn't take more than two minutes to get the last of the cattle into the corral, but his mother never let up talking the whole time.

"I'm Jake's mother," she said to his wife. "Welcome to Texas. You must be Miranda."

He grimaced when his wife politely answered, "Yes, ma'am."

"Oh, please, call me Cricket."

Jake felt a rush of resentment. His mother had never asked Priss to call her Cricket. To Priss she'd always been Mrs. Creed, and then Mrs. Blackthorne.

Of course, Priss had been a kid when she'd first met his mother and the formal address had kind of stuck.

"What happened, Jake?" his mother asked.

"Had to put Red down."

"You all right?" she asked.

"I'm fine."

His wife shot him a shocked look, but to her credit, she didn't contradict him. Of course, the instant he got off the horse, his mother was going to see the truth. He'd just have to make sure she didn't hang around that long.

He closed the corral gate on horseback, a tricky maneuver that wasn't made any easier by the woman sitting in his lap. "Thanks, Mom," he said when he was done. "I'm sorry to send you home without a cup of coffee, but the house is—"

"Oh, dear," she interrupted with a laugh. "I forgot to tell you. I brought Nash and Noah with me. They're inside right now having lunch with Slim and the baby and Miranda's brothers."

Jake groaned inwardly. There was no hiding his infirmity now. He rode to the kitchen door with his mother, then eased Miranda off the horse and onto her feet. He saw her cheeks flush when she stumbled, but she quickly caught her balance and walked up the back porch steps with his mother.

Maybe he could hang out in the barn until his mother left.

"I'm going to put the horses away," he said.

"Can you do that with your injured ankle?" Miranda asked.

Jake closed his eyes and groaned aloud.

"You're hurt?" his mother said, stopping in her

tracks. She turned back to him and asked, "How bad is it?"

Through teeth gritted with pain and frustration he said, "I don't know."

"I'll send the twins out to take the horses to the barn. You come inside so I can tend to your leg."

Jake could have refused, but that would have been biting off his nose to spite his face. There was no way to dismount without putting weight on his bad leg, which he could feel had swollen tight inside his boot. He gasped as he put his full weight on the injured leg in the stirrup so he could slide his other leg over the horse's rump.

Miranda came running back to him, pressing herself against his side and lending her shoulder for support. A shot of agony streaked up his leg each time he hopped up a stair. Getting up the three steps to the back porch felt like a huge accomplishment.

He was hurt bad. Worse than he'd hoped.

His mother held open the back door as he limped his way inside.

" 'Bout time you got back, Miz Blackthorne," Slim said as his mother closed the kitchen door behind the three of them.

"Can we have our pie now?" Harry asked.

"He's been calling me names!" Noah accused, pointing at Nick.

"He started it!" Nick retorted, pointing at Nash.

"Boys, boys, that'll be enough of that," his mother said in a calm voice. "How about some pie?"

To Jake's everlasting embarrassment, at the mention of the word pie, his stomach growled. It had been a long time since he'd tasted anything that required skill in the kitchen. He gazed longingly at his mother's apple pie, knowing it would probably all be gone before he could get back for a piece.

His mother smiled and said, "Don't worry, Jake. I'll save some for you. You'll have to wait to eat it, though, till I can see to your ankle. Why don't you go find someplace comfortable to sit in the parlor, while I serve up this pie."

As Jake hobbled to the parlor, he realized he wasn't going to be sleeping upstairs in his marriage bed anytime soon. Not unless he wanted to endure the agony of hopping up stairs. It made more sense to stay on the ground floor, where he could use a crutch.

The sofa was too short to serve as a bed, so he was going to be stuck making a pallet on the floor. Which meant he either had to kick Miranda's brothers upstairs, or share the floor near the fireplace with them.

At least he wouldn't have to worry about keeping his hands off his wife. She provided far more temptation than he'd imagined. When he'd woken up this morning, his arm had been wrapped around her waist. Her blond curls lay across the pillow and one of them was tickling his nose. He'd blown it away with a whisper of air and watched her pert nose wrinkle in her sleep.

He'd noticed she had very long, very dark lashes, despite her blond hair. Her cheeks had gotten sunburned during the wagon ride to his ranch the previous afternoon. He'd have to show her where Priss kept her bonnets, so she could protect herself from the hot Texas sun. That is, as soon as it showed its face again.

"Help me over to one of those wing chairs in front

of the fireplace," he said to Miranda, who was still supporting him. She was a lot stronger than she looked, which was a damned good thing, considering he was going to be an invalid for the next however-long.

"I need to take my coat off," he said, starting to unbutton it.

"Let me," she said, looking up at him. "You just hold on to the chair to keep the weight off your foot."

He looked down at her as she struggled to release the bone buttons on the shearling coat. He reached to help, but she brushed his hand aside and kept working. "I can do it."

When the coat was open, she drew it down off his shoulders and threw it onto the sofa. As she eased him into the chair, he felt her jerk when his arm brushed against her breast.

"Sorry," he mumbled.

"I know you didn't mean—" She cut herself off.

He glanced up and saw she was blushing, like the untouched bride she was. He felt so damned bad for her, and for himself. "I'm sorry I got you into this," he said quietly.

"I'm not," she replied. "If your accident had happened and I hadn't been here, you might not have made it back to the house. Then what would have happened to Slim and the baby? I can help you, Jake. *We* can help you."

"Yeah, but you shouldn't have to," he said. "No telling how long I'll be a cripple."

"You'll mend fast, I'm sure," she said, laying a soothing hand on his shoulder. He could feel how cold her hands still were through his shirt. She'd had no business risking her life riding out in a snowstorm. She wasn't going to last long out here if she kept taking chances like that.

He resisted the urge to tell her to go away and leave him alone. She didn't deserve his bad temper. She didn't deserve the mess he'd gotten her into. Things had been bad even before he'd gotten hurt. He didn't know how they were going to manage now.

He heard a gurgle in his throat and swallowed hard over the painful knot that threatened to strangle him.

He felt his young wife remove his hat, which he hadn't even realized he was still wearing, and watched through eyes blurred with unshed tears as she set it carefully on the table between the two chairs. Then he felt her hand gently scratching his scalp to rearrange his hair to her liking.

He turned his face away and closed his eyes, so she wouldn't see the tears of frustration welling in them.

He felt Miranda's hand withdraw an instant before his mother said, "Oh, darling, I know the pain must be terrible."

The pain was bad. The despair was killing him.

"I'll need your help, Miranda," he heard his mother say, "cutting off his boot."

He opened his eyes and said, "The hell you will! These are my best boots."

"I'm sorry, Jake," his mother said. "Your foot's swollen too much to get the boot off any other way."

"Please, Jake. It's just a pair of boots," Miranda said in a beseeching tone she must have used a hundred times with her little brothers. "You can get another pair. I can't stand to see you in such pain."

The problem was, he didn't have money to buy

brand-new boots. "Aw, hell. Go ahead." He could always ask the cobbler in San Antonio to sew this one back up.

He had to bite his lip to keep from swearing as his mother sliced her way through the supple leather. He didn't realize he was holding Miranda's hand until he heard her gasp when he squeezed it too hard.

He tried to pull his hand free, but she held on. He looked up and met her gaze and saw tears of sympathy in her eyes.

He squeezed his eyes closed. He didn't want her sympathy. He didn't want her to see him like this. He wanted Priss back. He wanted his mother gone. He wanted his life before Blackthorne had come into it back again.

But there was no going back. He could only move forward. He could only take one day at a time and live it the best he could.

"Almost there," his mother said. "That's as much as I can do. The boot has to be eased off. Brace yourself, Jake."

He screamed in agony when his mother pulled the boot off.

He heard her say, "Thank God, it's not broken."

Then he fell down a long black tunnel.

Chapter Sixteen

"Oh, no!" Miranda cried. "What happened?"

"He fainted," Jake's mother said. "We need to hurry and bandage his foot while he's out."

"How do you know it's not broken?" Miranda asked.

"He wouldn't be able to rotate his foot or move his toes so freely."

"That ankle's pretty badly swollen," Miranda said uncertainly. "Are you sure?"

"I've treated sprains and I've set broken bones. This looks like a bad sprain."

Miranda felt her body relax. "He was so afraid it was broken. I'm glad it's not."

"Me, too. It was brave of you to go out in this storm to find him," she said. "I doubt my son has thanked you, so I will."

Miranda smiled. "No, he hasn't, but there's no need. I thank you for bringing Jake's cattle home. He'd figured out for himself that the cattle must have strayed and what would happen if his stepfather found them before he did."

"My husband is . . . a complicated man."

So is mine, Miranda thought. She watched closely as Cricket wrapped Jake's ankle snugly in the gauze Miranda had sent Nick to fetch from the kitchen counter, where she'd seen it that morning.

"What happened to him? Is he dead?" Nick asked as he watched Jake's mother work.

"He's resting," Cricket replied.

Miranda had been so focused on what Cricket was doing, she hadn't realized that the three boys had come into the parlor. "Where are Slim and the little ones?" she asked.

"Slim took Anna Mae and Harry to his room for a nap," Nick replied.

Jake's eyes fluttered open, and he straightened in the chair. He winced when he tried to lift his injured foot.

"Hold on there, cowboy," Cricket said. "Let me finish."

Jake shot Miranda a worried glance, and she smiled back at him. "You're doing fine," she told him. "Your ankle's only sprained, not broken."

"Good," was all he said.

"Did you get those horses put away in the barn?" Cricket asked one of the twins.

"Yes, ma'am," he answered.

"How do you tell them apart?" Miranda asked Cricket as she looked from one twin to the other. "They look exactly the same to me."

Nash grinned.

Noah grinned, too.

"Nash has a wider smile," Cricket said with a laugh.

"What if they aren't smiling?" Miranda asked.

"Noah has a scar through his right eyebrow."

Miranda looked, and sure enough, there it was. A thin white line, right through the arch of the brow.

"Before I learned who was who, I kept a red string tied around Nash's ankle," Cricket admitted.

"Once we were old enough, me and Noah switched it so often, Mom still didn't know who was who," Nash said.

"Until we got old enough to tell her ourselves," Noah said.

"There were twin girls at the orphanage where we grew up," Nick said. "They looked so much alike, they could trade places anytime they liked. Miss Birch found out what they were doing, so she cut one's hair real short and left the other one's long, so they couldn't fool her anymore."

"I don't think I like this Miss Birch," Cricket said.

"I hate her," Nick said vehemently. "Which is why I cut off the other girl's hair for her, so Miss Birch couldn't tell them apart anymore."

"Nicholas Jackson Wentworth!" Miranda was appalled to learn her brother had been up to that kind of mischief. "That was you?"

He stuck his chest out and pointed a thumb at himself and said, "You bet it was me!"

Miss Birch had been sure it was Miranda. Miranda wished she'd thought of doing it, but she hadn't. Miss Birch had threatened to beat every girl in the dormitory if Miranda didn't confess. So she had.

"Miss Birch was always punishing somebody for something," Nick said. "Miranda most of all."

"That's enough, Nick," Miranda said. "Don't be telling tales."

"It's not a tale," Nick protested. "It's the truth."

"I can vouch for that," Jake said. "Mom, while you're here, would you take a look at Miranda's back? I did what I could last night, but she's got a lot of fresh wounds that—"

"Miranda!" Nick interrupted, his face dismayed. "You said Miss Birch didn't beat you. You lied to us!"

"It's nothing, Nick," Miranda said, shooting a dirty look at Jake and then a warning look at Nick, not to reveal the existence of the rest of the Wentworths.

"I'll be glad to take a look," Cricket offered.

"I'm fine," Miranda said, embarrassed to have Jake's mother see what a chicken-heart she'd been, surrendering her back to Miss Birch's wrath.

"Let her take a look," Jake urged. "I'm not going to be able to come upstairs for a while, and there isn't much privacy down here for me to be treating your back."

Miranda realized he had a point. Jake's treatment of her cuts last night had felt good, and her back hadn't hurt nearly so much today. "All right," she said, then asked him, "Do you need anything else before we go upstairs?"

"If I need anything," Jake said, "one of the boys can get it for me."

"I'm not your servant," Nick shot back.

Miranda glared at her brother, wondering why he was being so quarrelsome. Before she could chastise him, Jake spoke.

"Around here, everyone does his fair share. Unless you'd like to find somewhere else to lay your head at night."

She watched Nick open his mouth to make a retort

and close it again. Nick narrowed his eyes at Jake and said, "Fine."

Miranda wasn't sure whether Nick was saying, *Fine, I'll move out when the snow stops,* or *Fine, whatever you say.* Jake's mother stepped in to resolve the matter. "Why don't you three boys go clean up the kitchen?"

"Dishes are girl's work," Nash said.

Miranda and Nick exchanged a glance. Nick had done his fair share of washing dishes at the orphanage. They all had.

Jake's mother put her hands on her hips and said, "I'm not going to ask you boys a second time."

Both twins made the same face, but they turned and marched toward the kitchen.

Nick stood where he was.

"You can help, too," Miranda said to her brother. "Unless you want my hand on your backside."

Nick stared at her in amazement. She'd never laid a hand on any of her siblings, and he must be wondering what had gotten into her. The truth was, she was at the end of her emotional rope. She needed Nick to cooperate. She needed him to go along and get along. She needed him to be a help and not a hindrance. And she was desperate enough to threaten violence.

"Please, Nick," she said.

"Oh, all right," he said. "I'll go help dry."

"Thank you, Nick," she called after him.

"That boy needs a hand to his backside," Jake said, staring after Nick.

"That boy needs love and affection!" Miranda snapped at him.

Jake's head swiveled to stare at her.

He was only saying what she'd said herself. But the thought of *anyone* touching her or her siblings in violence, after they'd finally escaped Miss Birch, was loathsome. Before he could say anything more, she growled in frustration, then turned and ran up the stairs. She could hear Jake and his mother talking behind her, but she couldn't tell what they said.

When she reached her bedroom, she realized Nick must have brought loads of wood up here and set a fire in the fireplace to warm up the bedroom. Seeing his thoughtfulness, she felt even worse about threatening to spank him. A sob of loneliness built in her chest. *If our parents had lived . . .*

How many times over the past three years had she thought those five words. How futile they were! There simply was no going back to the life she'd lived before the fire. Everything had changed. She had to move forward. She had to make the best of her life with Jake.

She was disappointed in her behavior. She shouldn't have threatened Nick. She should have appealed to his better nature. He was a good, a generous boy. He must be as frightened as she was to find herself so much at the mercy of a virtual stranger's good nature and kindness.

Was Jake good? Was he kind?

So far he had been. Nick needed a man's guidance. He couldn't be allowed to do exactly as he pleased. He needed boundaries and limits and instruction. And love. He needed a father's love.

Could Jake give that to her brothers? Would he keep his promise to become a father to them?

Miranda felt a tear drip onto her nose. When she

heard footsteps on the stairs, she quickly swiped at her face. She didn't want Jake's mother to see her feeling sorry for herself. She didn't want her thinking any less of Jake's bride.

When the knock came on the door, Miranda crossed to open it and let Jake's mother in.

Once they were closed in the room together, Cricket asked, "Are you all right?"

"Yes."

Cricket lifted a brow.

"I'm fine, really."

When Cricket put a hand on her shoulder in comfort, Miranda jerked away.

"Oh, I didn't realize the wounds were so bad," the older woman said. "Come, let's get that blouse off so I can see the damage."

She spoke almost as Miranda imagined her own mother might. It felt good to hear a sympathetic woman's voice. Oh, how she would love to confide in the older woman!

She wanted to share her hopes that Jake and his stepfather would make amends, so Blackthorne no longer threatened Jake's possession of Three Oaks. She wanted to admit how tired she was of carrying the entire burden of her family on her shoulders. She wanted to admit how wonderful it would be to have someone to share that burden with.

She didn't say any of those things.

Miranda reminded herself that this woman was married to Jake's ruthless stepfather. This woman's husband was Jake's mortal enemy. If a choice ever came, Miranda had no idea whether Cricket Blackthorne would choose her husband or her son. Better not to let down her guard. Better to accept the help that was offered, but keep her distance.

♡

Cricket was so used to wearing men's clothing herself—the result of her and her two older sisters having been raised by their father as though they were sons, rather than daughters—that she was just noticing that Miranda was wearing trousers, rather than a skirt, with the feminine blouse.

It made a great deal of practical sense for women not to wear skirts in the West, but it was still frowned upon. For a girl from Chicago to have donned trousers seemed more than a little strange.

"I see Jake lent you a pair of his Levi's," she said as she waited for Miranda to unbutton her blouse. Underneath the blouse, Cricket could see Miranda was wearing, not a chemise, but one of Jake's long john shirts.

"I'm afraid I didn't have anything warm enough of my own to wear," Miranda said.

That was odd, too, especially when the girl had come from Chicago in winter. Miranda Wentworth was far prettier than Jake had any right to hope, Cricket thought, since he'd selected his bride sight unseen. But it seemed she was poor as a church mouse, with not even a warm change of clothes to her name.

Miranda also seemed overwhelmed by the situation she'd gotten herself into. Cricket tried to imagine how horrible things must have been at the orphanage where the girl had lived with her brothers, for her to have contrived to bring them secretly with her to Texas.

Even before Miranda pulled the long john shirt over her head, Cricket's stomach clenched at the sight of the blood streaking the back of it. The girl gasped as she tore the shirt away from a place where it was stuck to her skin by dried blood, then held the shirt against her breasts to preserve her modesty.

Cricket had to bite back an oath when she saw the girl's back. She wondered how her son had felt when he'd seen the results of the awful cruelty this young woman had endured. Some of the scars were flat and white and therefore old. Some of the scars had healed in raised welts, the result, perhaps, of beatings on top of beatings. The newest wounds were numerous. Some of them were well on their way to healing. Others, the ones not covered by sticking plasters, were still raw.

"You poor dear," Cricket said as she wet a cloth to wash away the blood from a seeping wound that wasn't covered by a sticking plaster. "There must be a special hell for persons like your Miss Birch."

"I hope so," the girl said fervently.

Amazing that the young woman's spirit had not been broken. Maybe she had more gumption than Cricket had first thought. It would have taken a very strong-willed person to endure this much pain and not shatter.

"You must have caused a great deal of trouble at the orphanage," she ventured.

"Miss Birch didn't need a reason to be cruel," Miranda replied.

"You must be glad to be gone from there."

"I am. I just wish—" She bit back the rest of her sentence.

"What?" Cricket prodded.

"Nothing," the girl said.

There was more to the story that hadn't been told, Cricket realized, but the girl didn't trust her enough to tell it. "Your secrets are safe with me," she said as she applied more sticking plasters, which she found on the bedside table, to the worst of the uncovered wounds.

The girl glanced over her shoulder, then turned her face away. She didn't reply. She didn't offer any further explanation.

Cricket had opened her mouth to ask another question when she heard a ruckus downstairs.

Two male voices were raised in anger. Younger male voices joined in.

"Get out of my house!" a male voice roared.

"That's Jake!" Miranda cried, as she leapt from the bed and fumbled to get the long john shirt over her head. "We have to get down there, fast!"

Then Cricket heard, "Where the hell is my wife?"

She knew that, no matter how fast they moved, they were too late.

Chapter Seventeen

Jake was sitting slumped in the wing chair with his foot propped up on a pillow, where his mother had left him when she went upstairs, when he heard a loud commotion in the kitchen.

He grimaced as he eased his ankle off the stool where it was perched, then braced his hands on the arms of the chair to get himself upright. He hissed back an oath when he accidentally bumped his sprained ankle. He was barely on his feet when Blackthorne appeared in the doorway to the parlor.

"Get out of my house," Jake snarled in a low, deadly voice.

"Where is my wife?" Blackthorne demanded in an equally quiet, yet equally threatening voice.

"Are you afraid she's left you?"

Blackthorne paled. "Did you tell her?"

"And if I did?" Jake said defiantly.

His stepfather's hands became fists. His mouth thinned and his eyes narrowed and turned as cold and hard as blue glass. "I told you what I'd do if you ever said a word of what you know. I don't make idle threats."

"What you did was despicable," Jake snarled. "You would have gotten away with it, too, if I hadn't learned the truth from my father before he went away. You kept my mother from her rightful husband. You blackmailed my father into leaving her behind. You stole my patrimony."

"He returned too late. Your mother had already borne my sons."

"An honorable man would have admitted the mistake," Jake said, his voice trembling with fury. "An honorable man would have found a way—"

"There was no going back."

"You could have let him say good-bye to her," Jake said fiercely. *And to me.* "If I hadn't met him accidentally, I would never have known he was still alive. Or the contemptible things you did to get rid of your rival."

Jake lifted his chin and confronted his stepfather. "But I did meet him. So I know how you stole Lion's Dare. I know how you deceived my father into believing my mother would never leave you or her sons. I know what a son of a bitch you really are."

Jake saw his words strike home. He knew how much his mother had loved his father, but even he wasn't sure what her decision would have been, given a choice between the two men. Blackthorne hadn't taken the chance that she would leave him. He'd arranged everything to make sure Jarrett Creed went away without ever speaking to her.

But he must have feared she would leave. Even now, he must fear it. Otherwise, he wouldn't be so determined to keep what he'd done from his wife. Jake had been angry enough at his stepfather over the years to want to tell his mother what he knew. But once his father was gone, seemingly beyond reach, spilling his guts would only have hurt his mother.

Would she have left Blackthorne to return to Jake's father a year into her marriage with another man? He would never know. Certainly, she wouldn't have left the twins behind, and Blackthorne would never have let her have them. But his mother should have been given the choice. She should have been told the truth. She should have been told that her husband was still alive.

Blackthorne had manipulated Jake's father to make him go away. He'd made the choice for his wife. For that, Jake would never forgive him.

"Did you tell her?" Blackthorne asked again, his voice tense, his shoulders hunched as though against a blow.

Jake wanted to say yes. He wanted to make his stepfather suffer as he'd suffered for long years. But he feared the repercussions for his mother if he lied. So he told the truth.

"Your filthy secret is safe."

"Smart boy."

"Nasty man," Jake shot back.

"Just so long as you keep your mouth shut, I don't care what names you call me," Blackthorne said.

"Get out of my house!" Jake roared.

"Where the hell is my wife?" Blackthorne bellowed back.

Jake swallowed back the virulent epithets that threatened to spew out of his mouth. He hated Blackthorne for the lie he'd perpetrated on Jake's mother, for the blackmail that had sent his father halfway across the world, but most of all, he hated Blackthorne because he'd allowed himself to be convinced—never threatened, but convinced, nonetheless—that the best thing to do was keep silent.

The guilt of his complicity in the lie had made him a bitter and angry man. He'd grieved the loss of his father not just once, but twice. He hated his stepfather. He pitied his mother. And he would miss—and forever wonder about—his father, who was living on a continent so far away it was unlikely Jake would see him again in this lifetime.

"Where is she?" Blackthorne demanded through tight jaws.

Jake hesitated, then said, "She's upstairs. With my wife."

Jake watched Blackthorne head through the parlor and take the first two stairs in a single step. "Stop right there!" Jake called out. "Where do you think you're going?"

Blackthorne stopped and turned, an irritated look on his face. "I'm going to find my wife."

"I told you she's tending to mine."

Jake could tell his stepfather was rattled when it seemed to dawn on him exactly where he was and what he'd been about to do. He looked upstairs with longing, then came back down to the main floor. He gripped the newel post and called up, "Cricket, get down here!"

Jake had known his stepfather had a well-developed sense of possession toward his cattle, his land, and his children—and, of course, his wife. However, this was the first time he'd seen Blackthorne looking anxious about any of them.

"I'll be down in a minute," Cricket called back from behind a closed door.

"What happened to you?" Blackthorne asked, staring at Jake's wrapped-up ankle as Jake stepped out from behind the chair.

"None of your damned business."

"That boy in the kitchen needs his mouth washed out with soap."

"I'm sure whatever he said, you provoked it," Jake said, defending Nick, even though he agreed with his stepfather.

Slim appeared in the hall from his bedroom with two crying children. "What the Sam Hill is goin' on out here? What's all the shoutin' about?"

Jake realized he needed to stay near the chair to hold himself upright. "Bring Anna Mae over here," he said to the old man. He waited for Slim to roll his wheelchair close enough for him to pick up his wailing daughter.

When Anna Mae reached back and cried, "Harry, Harry, Harry," Jake scooped up the little boy as well, wincing as he leaned back against the chair and balanced on his good leg and his bad ankle.

Nick showed up in the hall, the twins dogging his heels, and demanded, "Are these darned Blackthornes leaving, or what?"

"We'll go when we're good and ready," Nash said.

"And not before," Noah added.

At that moment, Jake's mother and his wife came running down the stairs. Miranda reached Jake first and took Harry from his grasp and set him down, murmuring soothing words and swiping the tears from the howling four-year-old's distraught face.

Jake's gaze was riveted on his mother as she crossed to his stepfather, put her hand on his heart, looked up into his face, and said in a perfectly calm voice, "I'm fine, Alex. As you can see, we're all fine. I'm so sorry you were worried."

Jake had never thought of his stepfather as anything but invincible. The slight sag in Blackthorne's shoulders when Cricket reassured him she was all right suggested that his stepfather had an Achilles' heel. Unfortunately for Jake, he would never be able to attack that weakness, because that weakness was his own mother.

When Jake finally looked at his wife, he realized she was half dressed, wearing one of his long john shirts and a pair of his Levi's. "Are you all right?" he asked in a low voice.

"I'm fine. Are *you* all right?" she said as she took Anna Mae from him.

Jake watched as Miranda smoothed Anna Mae's fine hair back from her tear-streaked face.

"How are you, sweetie?" she cooed to the little girl. She produced a hanky from Lord knew where and dabbed at Anna Mae's cheeks. "Let's wipe away those tears, so we can see your pretty little face."

His daughter wasn't used to such compliments. Priss had been far too practical, or too tired, to bother. He could see that Anna Mae liked being called pretty, or at least that she liked the attention Miranda was lavishing on her.

He was amazed how quickly Miranda managed to calm both children, splitting her attention between them. By the time he looked up at Blackthorne again, his stepfather and his mother were engaged in what looked like a tense conversation.

Abruptly his mother turned away and said, "Come on, boys. We'd better get started home."

"Isn't Dad going with us?" Nash asked, turning to Blackthorne.

"Your father can do as he pleases," she said curtly.

"I'm coming," Blackthorne said.

Ignoring Blackthorne, his mother crossed to where Jake was standing with Miranda and said, "Welcome to the neighborhood, Miranda. I hope you enjoy the pie. With any luck, the boys have finished the dishes. I'll come visit again soon."

At the last statement, Jake saw his stepfather scowl. His mother seemed unaware of—or unfazed by—his disapproval.

"Thank you, Mom," Jake said. "For everything."

She kissed his cheek and said, "You're my son. I love you. Take care of yourself, Jake. A lot of people are depending on you."

She didn't have to tell him that. He was aware every day, every hour, every moment, of how vital it was that he turn this one-time cotton plantation into a successful cattle ranch.

A moment later, he heard the kitchen door slam.

"It's stopped snowing," Nick said, pointing out the parlor window.

"Good thing, too," Slim said. "We ain't got no hay to feed them cows. Now we got to hope it melts quick."

"I'm glad I had a chance to meet your mother," Miranda said. "Would you like a piece of pie?"

Jake felt sick to his stomach. He thought if he ate

anything, he'd probably throw it right back up. "No pie for me."

"Can I have your piece?" Nick asked hopefully.

He owed the kid one for not liking the Blackthornes. "Sure. Help yourself."

To his surprise, Nick took Anna Mae from Miranda's arms and leaned her against his waist, then grabbed Harry's hand and said, "Come on. We'll split it three ways."

Once the kids were gone, Slim said, "'Less you need me, I'm gonna finish my nap."

Jake shook his head and the old man headed back toward his bedroom, leaving Jake alone with his wife.

He looked at her and said, "Are you all right?"

She grinned and said, "Are you? Your stepfather is a rather forceful personality, isn't he?"

He grunted. "You don't know the half of it. How's your back?"

She flushed and said, "Much better. Your mother tended the few cuts that haven't healed. What should we do with the rest of the day?"

He grimaced. "I'm stuck here in this chair until the swelling goes down in my ankle. There are some crutches in the attic, if you want to hunt them down."

"I'll go up there later. What can I do for you now?" she said as she crossed and put her arm around his waist. "Can I make up a pallet for you by the fire? Or would you rather sit in the chair?"

"The chair." Jake wasn't used to being pampered. He'd been the one doing whatever pampering there was to be done. But he let his pretty young wife lead him around the wing chair and make sure he was comfortable, easing his injured ankle back onto the pillowed perch where it had previously rested.

She crossed and pushed back the raggedy drapes from the parlor window and looked out. "The snow is so beautiful. Everything is so white and bright and clean."

Beautiful? He remembered Priss remarking once upon a time how beautiful the snow was. That was before they were married, before the snow had become one more trial and tribulation in their difficult lives, before it had caused so many disasters of the sort he'd managed to survive today.

"How long before it melts?" she asked.

"Hard to tell this time of year. Could be there a week. Could be gone tomorrow."

She turned back to him with a surprised look. "Tomorrow? Is that really possible?"

"Nothing about this place is predictable, least of all the weather."

At that moment, the runt appeared in the parlor doorway and yelled, "Miranda, come quick! Anna Mae is choking!"

Jake felt his stomach lurch and his heart pound as he launched himself out of the chair. By the time he was upright, Miranda was already gone from the room, along with Harry. "I'm coming, Anna Mae!" he shouted.

As though the sound of his voice was any help!

He hopped his way from one piece of furniture to the next and hobbled along using the wall for support until he reached the kitchen.

He found Miranda sitting in a chair with Anna Mae in her lap, the child smiling up at her, while Nick and Harry hovered nearby. Miranda was holding out a button that must have come off one of his shirts and saying to his daughter, "Buttons don't taste very good, do they, sweetie?"

"She choked on a button?" He stared down at the two of them, feeling light-headed at how close he'd come to a second disaster in a single day.

Miranda smiled up at him and nodded.

"How did you get her to cough it up?"

"Turned her upside down and gave her a slap on the back. Came right out and fell on the floor. Harry retrieved it for me." She brushed a loving hand over her younger brother's head.

Jake realized he needed to hold his daughter, to reassure himself that she was all right. His knees buckled under him and he sat in a kitchen chair. Miranda kissed Anna Mae on her forehead before setting her in his lap. He marveled how his new wife had recognized his need to hold his child.

"She's fine," Miranda said.

He looked into his daughter's brown eyes and she smiled up at him, apparently having already forgotten the life-threatening event. "No more eating buttons, honey," he said. "All right?"

"Okay, Daddy," she said.

"Come on, Anna Mae," Harry said. "Let's go play."

His daughter squirmed to get down and he set her on the floor, where she reached for Harry's hand.

Jake was recovered enough from his terror to realize he owed this woman, who'd been a stranger a mere twenty-four hours ago, his daughter's life.

Before the little boy left the kitchen with his daughter Jake said, "Thank you for coming to let me know Anna Mae was in trouble, Harry."

Miranda beamed at him, and Jake realized it was the first time he hadn't called the little boy "runt."

Harry shrugged and said, "Nick told me to go get help, when he couldn't get her to spit it out."

Jake turned his attention to the older, more prickly boy. "Thank you, Nick."

Nick shrugged and stared at his toe, which was drawing a circle around a knot on the wood floor. "Woulda done it for anybody."

"Thank you anyway," Jake said. "I owe you one."

Nick looked up at him. "Do you mean it?"

Jake felt his mouth turning down cynically. What kind of reward was the boy going to want? He didn't have much he could give him. "Sure," Jake said. "What do you want?"

"Would you teach me how to ride? Miranda learned before the fire, but I was too young. I want to learn to ride horseback. That way I can help you herd cattle."

Jake felt an ache in his chest. He wasn't used to these Wentworths, with their generous hearts. "I'll give you a lesson as soon as the snow melts."

"Did you hear that, Miranda? I'm gonna learn to ride!" He whooped and leaped around in circles.

"He's going to change his mind if you knock something off the counter and break it," Miranda chided. "Go keep an eye on Harry and Anna Mae. I don't like to leave them alone for too long."

He was gone without another word.

Miranda busied herself cleaning up the pie plates the boys had used, as though she'd lived there all her life.

"This has been a strange first day of marriage," he said.

She turned and leaned back against the counter, wiping her hands on a dish towel. "Full of adventure, you mean?"

"And close calls."

She smiled. "Isn't all of life like that? I'd call any day so full of averted disasters a good one."

He found himself chuckling. When had he last done that? His new wife had led a terrible life in that orphanage, yet it hadn't bent or bowed her. He was very lucky in his choice of bride. He felt a different kind of ache in his chest. An ache of longing.

He wanted to thank her with kisses for the life of his daughter. He wanted to hold her in his arms and cherish her. But he knew where that would lead. The more he liked her, the more important it was to keep his distance. Because the biggest disaster of all would be if he got her pregnant.

Thank goodness they would be sleeping on different floors of the house for the next couple of weeks.

Then she said, "I think it would be best if I join you downstairs tonight and let the boys sleep in our bed."

Chapter Eighteen

"How did you sleep?"

Miranda blushed as she entered the kitchen to greet her husband on the second day of their marriage. "Very well, actually."

Jake was sitting at the kitchen table with a steaming cup of coffee in front of him. She'd spent the night alone upstairs at his insistence, while he'd slept in front of the fire in the parlor. Her brothers had spent the night in Anna Mae's room.

"I'm ashamed to admit I fell asleep as soon as my head hit the pillow," she said. "I can't believe I slept so late!"

He smiled. "In case you haven't noticed, we're the only two souls awake in this house."

She smiled back. "It is awfully quiet." She helped herself to a cup of coffee and looked out the window where the sun was just coming up, amazed to see the snow had almost melted away. "What happened to the snow?"

Jake shrugged. "It warmed up overnight. With any luck, the rest of it will melt today, for which I have to be grateful. I would have had a hell of a time in the snow with this bum ankle." He took another sip of coffee and said, "I see you're wearing trousers again today."

"Only because I haven't had a chance to alter one of Priscilla's dresses," she explained.

"I don't mind." His eyes surveyed her body from top to toe so carefully that she flushed with embarrassment.

"You look cute in my jeans," he said at last.

She wrinkled her nose. "Cute?" she said as she sat down at the table across from him.

He pushed himself up on his arms, leaned across the table and kissed her nose. "Definitely cute. What are your plans today?"

She leaned toward him, so excited that she set her elbows right on the table and said, "I'm itching to sort through all the stuff scattered around the house and put everything away in its proper place. I also have to go up in the attic to see if I can find you some crutches.

"If it warms up this afternoon, I'd like to clean the upstairs windows and do some weeding in the front yard. Then I want to see if you can help me repair the rails on the balcony upstairs, so the kids can play out there when the weather is nice and I'm upstairs working."

She stopped talking, as she became aware of the grin on Jake's face. "What's so funny?"

"I've never seen anyone so excited about cleaning house and washing windows and pulling weeds and making repairs on a bunch of rotten railings."

"Don't make fun of me, Jake. I'm serious."

"I know you are, Miranda. I just hope I can keep up with you."

"All you have to do today is be there to tell me where things go in the house," she said. "I'll put everything away. I know the boys will want to help, too. If the weather's nice, you could sit outside and keep an eye on the little ones while I work. I'd like them to get some sunshine and fresh air."

"Have you always been a managing female?"

Miranda sobered. "Not always. Not at all. Not until after the fire."

Harry came padding into the kitchen, barefoot and wearing one of Jake's wool shirts that was serving as a nightshirt, and announced, "I'm hungry."

"Me, too," Anna Mae said, tagging along behind him hauling a doll made of corn husks.

"Where's Nick?" Miranda asked, leaning over to see past Harry.

"I don't know," Harry said. "He wasn't in bed when I woke up."

Miranda shot a look at Jake, then leaped from her chair and ran down the hall calling frantically, "Nick? Where are you?"

She was halfway up the stairs when she heard Jake yell, "Miranda, he just came inside. He was out in the barn."

Miranda turned and ran back to the kitchen. Nick's nose was red from the cold and his cowlick was standing straight up. He was already dressed for the day. "What were you doing sneaking out of the house without telling me where you were going?" she demanded, leftover fear making her voice harsh.

"You were asleep," Nick mumbled. He glanced at

Jake and said, "Everyone was asleep." He set an almost full bucket of milk beside the kitchen sink and said, "I thought I'd help out by milking the cow."

Miranda's shoulders slumped as though she were a balloon, and someone had just let out all the air. She felt horrible. "Oh, Nick. And here I am yelling at you."

She crossed to give him a hug, which he ducked. "I didn't know you knew how to milk a cow," she said.

"I watched Jake yesterday and sort of figured it out for myself."

"Thanks, Nick," Jake said.

"I didn't do it for you," Nick retorted. "I did it so Harry and Anna Mae would have milk for breakfast."

"The important thing is that you did it," Jake said. "The cow would have been in a lot of pain if you hadn't milked her early like you did."

Nick unbent enough to say, "She would?"

"Her udders get full and they need to be emptied at the same time every day. Now that you know how, milking can be your job."

"I don't take orders from you," Nick said stubbornly.

"It's up to you whether you milk the cow," Jake said. "But I won't be doing it anymore."

Miranda could see that Jake had put Nick in a tight spot. If he defied Jake, he was going to cause pain for the cow.

"Fine, you win," Nick said. "But I'm doing it for the cow. I'm not doing it for you."

"Suit yourself," Jake said.

Slim rolled himself into the kitchen doorway and said, "What's all the ruckus?"

"Nick milked the cow," Harry announced. "And I'm hungry."

"Get on up to the table, then," Slim said. "I'll have some eggs cookin' in no time."

"Do we have any eggs left?" Miranda asked.

Nick reached for a basket on the floor near the stove and held it out to Slim. "I gathered the eggs before I milked the cow."

This time Miranda didn't let Nick duck her hug. She grabbed him and held him tight and whispered in his ear, "You are the very best brother a girl ever had!"

By the time she released him, Nick's ears had turned red. He glanced at Jake and said, "Don't say it!"

"I didn't say a word." Jake held up his hands, palms out.

Nick turned to Harry and said, "How would you like to gather eggs in the morning while I milk the cow?"

"Sure," Harry said. "Can Anna Mae help?"

Miranda beamed, like a mother whose child has just performed a task perfectly for the very first time. It was only the second day they'd been living under Jake's roof, and her brothers were already proving how helpful they were going to be.

Miranda felt happy. She wondered how long the feeling would last.

♡

Nick was the one who located the crutches in the attic, but while Miranda was up there, she found several cans of white paint. She carried each one carefully down the short attic ladder and set them on the second-floor landing.

"We might have enough to repaint the front of the house," she told Jake. "And there's surely enough to paint the new railings on the upstairs balcony."

Jake wasn't nearly so enthused. "Who's going to do all this painting, Miranda? Once I can stand on two feet, I've got to get back out on the range. And after he's learned to ride, I'm going to want Nick out there with me."

"I can do the painting, Jake. Slim and Harry can help."

"You already have plenty of work to do, just managing the house. There's soap and candles to make and clothes to wash. I don't want you to wear yourself out."

"I won't, Jake," she promised him. "You'll see. We'll get it all done."

Slim wheeled himself onto the front porch to watch the work Miranda and the boys were doing in the yard, but he couldn't get off the porch to help them.

"I usually carry Slim down and then bring down the chair," Jake said. "But I can't do it with my ankle like this."

"Why don't you make a ramp down the stairs, so he can just wheel himself down?" Miranda suggested.

"What?" Jake said.

"You know, a ramp."

Jake turned to look at Slim and said, "Why didn't we think of that?"

"Been too sunk in the sullens, I 'spect," Slim said. "'Sides, didn't need a ramp till you got yourself stove up. I gotta admit, I like the idea of being able to get myself outside during the day, when you're not around."

The old man angled his chair toward Jake and said, "What do you think? Can you do it?"

"I don't see why not." Jake turned to Nick and said, "I need your help, son."

"I'm not your—"

Nick hadn't finished his angry retort before Jake said, "I know, boy." Then he set the crutches under his arms and headed toward the barn.

Nick shot Miranda a beseeching, pain-filled glance.

Her heart went out to her brother. Here was a man offering to call Nick "son." Allowing it meant admitting, once and for all, that their own father was gone forever. Miranda understood his agony.

She met his gaze and said softly, "It's all right, Nick. Go help."

Soon they were back, Nick carrying the wood Jake would need to build the ramp. The two of them spent the rest of the afternoon working on it.

That is, until Miranda decided it was time to wash windows.

"What do you want to do that for?" Jake asked. "They're just going to get dirty again."

"I can't see out," she said. "I found some rosebushes under all that brush, Jake. I plan to water them and take care of them and I want to be able to see them out the front window when they bloom."

"All right. That makes sense. But why do you have to wash the upstairs windows?"

"So I can look out and see you coming home at night."

He made a face, but he went with Nick to get the ladder from the barn.

She rinsed the downstairs windows with buckets of water, then put Harry and Anna Mae to work drying them off with newspaper.

When Jake and Nick finally had the ladder against the wall of the house, Miranda started climbing. When she was halfway up, she made the mistake of looking down. She felt dizzy when she realized how high she was. Miranda had never suspected she was afraid of heights, but it seemed she was. Try as she might, she couldn't take a step either up or down. She was frozen as solid as if she'd been a block of ice.

"Jake?" she called down to him.

"What?" he said, standing below her, braced on his crutches.

"I want to come down."

"I don't blame you. It's been a hell of a day. Come on down, then."

"I can't," she wailed.

"What do you mean?"

"I mean I can't. I'm too scared to move."

Jake put a hand across his brow to shade his eyes and looked up at her. "Just reach down with your foot and feel the rung below you, then step down one rung at a time."

Miranda looked down and felt the world swirling around her. She felt herself falling and grabbed at the ladder, barely catching it before she fell off. "I'm falling!" she screamed.

The next thing she knew, Jake was standing on the ladder behind her, his body shielding her, his arms around her.

"What are you doing climbing a ladder when you're afraid of heights?" he demanded.

She could feel him trembling and wondered which of the two of them was more afraid at the moment. "I didn't know I was scared of heights."

"Didn't you ever climb a tree as a kid?"

"No."

"Who the hell doesn't climb trees?"

"Girls who grow up in the city, that's who!"

"I don't want to see you up this ladder again, Miranda. Do you hear me?"

"You're angry," she said, pointing out the obvious.

"Damned right, I'm angry. You could have broken your pretty little neck."

"Oh, your poor ankle!" she said, realizing he would have needed to put his weight on both legs to get up the ladder. "Does it hurt?"

"Like hell," he snapped. "Come on, Miranda, let's get you down from here."

Jake took one slow step at a time down the ladder, with Miranda protected by his arms the whole way down. When they reached the ground, Miranda took one look at Jake's pasty white face and swooned.

"Oh, Jake, your poor ankle!"

Jake caught her and eased her down on the porch. "Put your head between your knees, Miranda. Do it now."

Miranda suspected she would hear Jake using that voice of authority often over the coming years. He limped back to retrieve his crutches, while she put her head down to hide her mortified face.

"Put that ladder back in the barn," she heard him tell Nick.

"What if I don't feel like it?" Nick said.

"Suit yourself."

"You mean it?" Nick asked suspiciously

"Don't suppose we'll ever need a ladder again," Jake said. "Might as well leave this one out here in the weather to rot."

Miranda peered at Nick from where her head lay in her lap and saw the look of consternation on his face, then watched as he crossed to where the ladder stood against the side of the house. A moment later she saw him hauling it toward the barn.

Jake joined her, and she felt his hand on her nape, keeping her head down when she would have lifted it up. "Stay there for another minute," he said. "All the blood rushed out of your head. That's why you felt faint."

"I have more work to do," she mumbled against her knees.

"You've done enough for today."

She tried to lift her head again, and this time he let her sit up. "I feel fine now, Jake."

"Good. But you're done for the day. I mean it, Miranda."

"I didn't get all the windows washed."

"We have the rest of our lives for you to wash windows."

"Oh." Jake's comment took a moment to sink in. Miranda had worked hard all day, but she'd hardly made a dent in what she wanted to accomplish. It didn't matter. She had plenty of time to get everything done. There was nowhere she had to go tomorrow or the next day or the day after that.

She was finally home.

Chapter Nineteen

After that first night, Miranda hadn't allowed Jake to banish her upstairs to sleep, but it hadn't made any difference. When they'd moved back upstairs ten days later, their marriage remained unconsummated. And at the end of her first month as a married woman, she was still a virgin.

Miranda had tried everything she could imagine to entice Jake to make love to her, once they'd moved back into the privacy of their own bedroom. Brushing against him by day. Standing in the light of the lamp so he would see her figure through her gown at night. Looking at him from beneath lowered lashes before she joined him in bed. Waking up curled against him in the morning. Three long weeks she'd tempted him.

Nothing had worked.

Tonight was the night. Miranda was determined to seduce her husband. Maybe if her friend at the orphanage had painted a different picture of love-making, she could have let things go on as they had. But on the first night of her marriage, when her husband had kissed her shoulder, she'd had the briefest taste of what might be in store. She'd tingled all over, and her body had felt tight and full and . . . unfulfilled. She wanted that lovely feeling again.

Miranda was determined to become a real wife, not just a housemaid and laundress and babysitter. And wives had relations with their husbands. She was not going to let Jake shirk his duty. Tonight she would confront him and . . . Miranda wasn't quite sure what she was going to do. But she knew how she wanted the night to end.

However, she had an entire anxious day to get through first. Fortunately, they'd established a routine in the mornings, so she got up and got busy as though it was another ordinary day.

Everyone gathered in the kitchen for breakfast after a series of chores that included getting Harry and Anna Mae dressed, milking the cow, feeding the pigs, chickens, and saddle stock, and gathering eggs.

Her brothers usually arrived at the kitchen table already salivating. And no wonder! As many fresh eggs and as much creamy milk as they could eat and drink, and bacon or ham every morning, along with biscuits Slim made and butter she'd churned herself. Sometimes breakfast was flapjacks with jam, which was Nick's favorite.

Miranda could almost see Harry filling out. His nose had stopped running a week ago. She knew Nick must be a half inch taller. And Anna Mae looked adorable when she smiled, her fine black hair combed into braids tied with colorful ribbons.

Slim had thawed considerably toward Miranda since Jake had finished the ramp that allowed him to get his wheelchair in and out of the house by himself. The first time Slim had wheeled himself down the ramp and into the cool shade of one of the oaks, he'd asked her, "Where'd you get the idea for a ramp?"

"I had an aunt in a wheelchair," she'd told him as she spread a quilt out under the same tree for the little ones to play on. "That is, before she died. Aunt Claire was married to my uncle Stephen."

"You have an uncle?" Jake said as he joined her on the quilt. "Why didn't you go live with him, instead of going to an orphanage?"

Miranda had no desire to air her family's dirty linen in front of her new husband. So she merely said, "Aunt Claire had passed on. Uncle Stephen thought we'd get better care at the orphanage than if we lived with him."

"You were beaten at the orphanage. Didn't he ever check on you?" Jake asked. "Didn't he look to see how you were being treated?"

Miranda was ashamed to admit the truth. But confronted by Jake's question, she said in a low voice, "He didn't care."

"He didn't care that you were being beaten?" Jake asked incredulously.

"No," she whispered.

"He ought to be hung," Jake said flatly.

"Family takes care of family," Slim said. "That's all there is to it. Hope I don't never meet that uncle of yours. Don't think I'd have much nice to say to him."

"Well, there's not much chance you'll ever cross paths, unless you go to Chicago. He owns a bank there," Miranda said, pulling Anna Mae into her lap so she could retie a ribbon that had come off one of her braids.

"Are you telling me he's *rich* and he left you in that hellhole?" Jake said through tight jaws.

Miranda swallowed hard. She didn't understand herself why Uncle Stephen had abandoned them. She only knew he had.

"That man's got a soul blacker'n a stack of stove lids," Slim muttered.

"Uncle Stephen was always good to us when Papa was alive," Miranda said lamely.

"All the more reason he should have done a better job taking care of you after your father was gone." Jake settled his arms around Harry as the little boy made himself comfortable in Jake's lap.

That afternoon, Slim had unbent far enough to allow her to cut his hair. When she'd finished with Slim, she'd offered to cut Jake's hair, too. He'd refused.

Not only had he refused, but Jake had gotten up and hobbled away on his crutches to do some work in the barn. Miranda had spent the rest of the afternoon wondering what it would have been like to have the freedom to run her hands through Jake's hair.

It finally dawned on her that the fact she would necessarily have been running her hands through Jake's hair must have occurred to him as well. Very likely, that was what had caused him to make himself scarce!

Seeing Jake at the breakfast table this morning, Miranda noticed he still needed that haircut. And she was still looking forward to the pleasure of running her fingers through his silky black hair.

"I'd be glad to cut your hair for you today," she said.

"No thanks," he replied. "You nearly scalped Slim."

"I did not!" Miranda protested. But suggesting

that she wasn't good at cutting hair—which was the truth—certainly made a better excuse than admitting he just didn't want her fingers in his hair.

Jake had been very careful to keep his distance from her, both in bed and out. She wanted to call him on it. She wanted him to admit the problem, so they could deal with it. He must know things couldn't go on like this.

He glanced at her, then averted his gaze. She stared at him, willing him to look at her.

The silent tension growing between them was broken when Harry strode into the kitchen, a woven basket on his arm, and proudly announced, "I found nine eggs!"

"Here's the milk," Nick said, joining him and setting a pail beside the sink.

A moment later Slim appeared in the kitchen with Anna Mae in his lap. "This little one folded her blanket like you taught her."

Miranda felt her heart sink. The chance to speak frankly with Jake had passed. But life had to go on.

"Wonderful!" she said, crossing to Slim and bending down to kiss Anna Mae's tiny bowed lips. "You are such a good girl!"

"Pick me up, Mama."

"Oh. Oh." Miranda looked toward Jake uncertainly. Anna Mae hadn't called her "Mama" again after that first day—until now. She didn't know whether to correct the child or not. "Is it all right if she calls me that, Jake?"

His voice was harsh with what she thought must be pain as he said, "You're the only mother she'll ever know."

"But she's not your kid," Nick said.

He sounded upset. Almost jealous. Miranda picked up Anna Mae and set the little girl on her hip, then crossed to her brother. "She's still a baby, Nick. I want her to know what it's like to have a mother, something we've all missed since our parents died. Is that all right with you?"

She could see Nick was torn. The truth was, she was the only mother he'd known from the age of seven. He must be a little jealous—and a little worried— that he was going to have to share her with Jake's daughter. She leaned down and whispered in his ear, "I won't love you any less, Nick. I promise."

He shrugged unhappily and said, "Do what you want. I can't stop you."

"I've finally caught up with repairs after spending those two weeks on crutches," Jake said to Nick. "Are you ready for that riding lesson?"

"Yeah. I guess."

"That's 'Yes, sir,'" Jake corrected.

Nick ducked his head and mumbled, "Yes, sir."

Jake had been insistent that Nick cut the profanity from his language, and that he address both Jake and Miranda respectfully. Jake had cut off her protest that she didn't need her brother to "ma'am" her, pointing out that she was an adult and Nick was a child, and therefore, her brother owed her his regard.

She'd been surprised when Nick gave in to Jake's demand without much of a fight. There were still moments like this, when her brother tried to slide by with his old habits, but Jake corrected him every time. Soon, she knew, it would become automatic, as it had been at home in Chicago, before the fire.

"You were gonna plow me a garden today," Slim reminded Jake.

"There'll be plenty of time after Nick's lesson," he replied.

"Nick and Harry and Anna Mae and I will be glad to help with the garden, Slim," Miranda offered.

"The boys can help," Jake said. "Didn't you tell me you planned to do laundry today?"

Miranda grimaced. Once a week she washed laundry and hung it on a rope strung up between a tree and a column on the back porch to dry, but it was her least favorite chore. The only good thing about laundry day was that she heated up enough extra water in the cauldron for everyone to get a bath. Smelling sweet might very well help her plans for the evening.

After breakfast, Miranda sent Nick outside for his riding lesson and started heating water on the stove. The old Southern mansion was starting to look less like a warehouse for ranch supplies and more like a home.

The burned section of the house had been boarded up long ago, and she'd talked Jake into using some of the paint she'd found in the attic to cover the wooden wall that separated that wing from the rest of the house. She'd also found a painting in the attic of a Thoroughbred racehorse and had hung it on the bare wall. She could hardly wait till the day they could start rebuilding the rest of the house.

The lack of space in the house reminded her that she hadn't yet communicated with her sisters to tell them they were going to have to wait a while yet before they could come and live with her. She hadn't written the letter because she hadn't figured out yet how she was going to get it posted, unless she appealed to Jake's mother. Maybe in the next week or so, she could find her way to Bitter Creek.

Miranda had been surprised to discover a wagon trail that Jake said led from Three Oaks to Bitter Creek. All she'd have to do was wait until Jake was gone on the range and get Slim to watch the kids while she snuck over to see Cricket.

Would Jake's mother help? If she did, would she insist on knowing what was in the letter, and to whom it was being sent? It would be difficult to conceal the recipients of the letter, since their names would be on the outside of it.

So what if Cricket did find out about Miranda's sisters? Miranda didn't have to tell her about her plans to bring them to Texas. Would she guess on her own? Would she condemn Miranda for using Jake to save her family?

Miranda forced herself to sit down at Jake's desk and write the letter. That was the least she could do. Once it was written she could decide how and when and through whom to post it. She picked up a pencil and began.

Dear Hannah, Hetty and Josie,

That was as far as Miranda got before she realized she had no idea where to start. Should she tell them the truth—that she'd arrived to discover she'd been brought to Texas to take care of a two-year-old and a crotchety old man in a wheelchair? That half the house had burned down, and the other half was falling down around their ears? And, most dreadful, that her husband had no intention of ever doing his duty to her?

She blushed at the thought of imparting that last piece of very private information. Of course she couldn't tell her innocent sisters that! When it had fallen on her to explain the facts of life, she'd told them what she knew, blushed, and then said they would learn the rest from their husbands.

Miranda grimaced. She'd been married for a whole month and still had not become a wife in the biblical sense. Making love remained a wonderful mystery to her, but one she very much wished to have unraveled.

She focused her attention back on the letter.

It's hot here in Texas.

She erased hot, which sounded uncomfortable, and inserted in much smaller letters "wonderfully warm."

It's wonderfully warm here in Texas.

Which didn't account for the blizzard the second day they'd arrived. The snow had melted so quickly, it hardly seemed worth mentioning. Except she'd saddled a horse by herself and ridden out into the blinding snow to rescue her new husband, who'd sprained his ankle and had to shoot his own horse!

She couldn't tell her sisters any of that. They'd think she'd landed in bedlam.

I have a beautiful stepdaughter named Anna Mae. Her mother, Priscilla, died in childbirth, which is why Jake advertised for a mail-order bride.

Harry's nose has stopped running! His cheeks are rosy and round from all the eggs and bacon and biscuits he's eating. Nick eats tall stacks of flapjacks and has already grown half an inch.

Should she tell them how well they were eating? When she knew her sisters were probably still getting the same gruel every day that she had come to loathe? She decided they would be happy for her and Nick and Harry. Now she came to the difficult part of the letter.

I'm sorry to say, Jake's house isn't big enough for all of us. At least, not right now. It's an old Southern mansion, but an entire wing was burned down during the war and Jake doesn't have the money—yet—to rebuild it.

I promise you, Nick and Harry and I will do everything we can to help Jake prosper so that you can join us as soon as possible—hopefully before too much more time passes.

We love and miss you all.

Your sister,
Miranda Wentworth

Miranda reread the letter and realized she'd signed her maiden name. After *Wentworth* she added the word *Creed*. Her marriage suddenly felt very real. Miranda Wentworth Creed was someone's wife. Someone's stepmother. Someone's daughter-in-law.

The note was woefully short of details about all

those changes, not to mention information about when her sisters could hope to be rescued from the fiendish Miss Birch. But she didn't want to lie to them. Her marriage was nothing like what a maiden wished for in her dreams.

And there was no hope of rescue anytime soon.

Miranda's heart ached for her sisters. She wished there was more she could do for them. There simply weren't any other options.

She folded up the letter and sealed it with wax she found in the desk.

In another year, Hannah and Hetty would be forced to leave the Institute. Where would they end up? And once they were gone, Josie would be left there all alone. What would happen to her? Miranda crossed her fingers on both hands and closed her eyes and wished for a miracle to reunite them all.

"Are you all right?"

She jerked and turned in the desk chair and stared at Jake. "I'm fine. I was just . . . writing a list," she lied.

He smiled. "A list of what?"

She smiled back. "Things I still have to do today." She stood and walked away from the desk, so he wouldn't cross to see exactly what she'd written. "Is the riding lesson over? How did Nick do?"

"That's why I'm here. I thought you'd want to come see for yourself."

"Oh, yes, I would!" She hurried toward him, scooting past him in the doorway. When he stepped aside at the door so they wouldn't touch, she turned her head so Jake wouldn't see her frown. The time had come to end the distance between herself and her husband.

Miranda felt a quiver of expectation at the thought of what she might have to do to convince a man who avoided even touching his wife that he should make love to her.

Tonight. Tonight she would finally know what it meant to be a wife.

Chapter Twenty

Night had fallen, and it was time to go to bed . . . with his wife.

The same wife who'd brushed her breast against his arm at the corral, while they watched Nick trot in a circle, his fanny bouncing in the saddle.

The same wife who'd leaned across his shoulder to serve Slim more green beans at supper, her shirtwaist falling open to reveal an enticing amount of cleavage.

The same wife who'd sat on the parlor rug at his feet after supper, leaning back against his legs as he read a story to the kids.

And the same wife who'd hugged his daughter and kissed her good night as though Anna Mae was her own flesh and blood.

Sometimes Jake wondered if having sex with Miranda would be so bad. Then he would remember his wife's screams. And the blood. And the child who'd made no sound as it came into the world born, and yet unborn.

He didn't want to take any chances with Miranda's life, because he knew just how lucky he'd been in his choice of bride.

She could have been foul tempered. She could have been lazy. She could have been bucktoothed or sharp voiced. She could have been thoughtless or spoiled.

Miranda was none of those things. Day after day, she'd revealed herself to be an almost perfect wife. Almost, because she was also a managing female who saw a problem and solved it without necessarily deferring to his judgment. Almost, because she wanted his affection, and he wasn't able to give it without also wanting to make love to her.

There were supposedly ways of preventing conception, but Jake didn't have any French sheaths, and all it would take was one accident, one time when he didn't withdraw from her body before he'd planted his seed, to cause the disaster he feared.

Was it a mere four weeks ago that he'd married a raggedy waif in a too-big dress, her hair tied in a tight bun at her nape? He'd been attracted to that stranger. He was even more attracted to the woman she'd turned out to be.

He was torn in two, wanting her and wanting to keep her safe. He hadn't expected it to be so hard to resist her. He hadn't expected to burn for her. He hadn't expected the physical ache he felt when his body sought the release he denied it.

He wanted to throw caution to the wind and make love to his wife. There it was. The bald truth. He wondered how long his willpower would last. How long could he resist his wife's delectable body? *God help me!* He was a beast to even consider making love to her, when he knew the danger to her life if he got her pregnant.

He was in the throes of yet another argument with

his conscience as he headed for his bedroom. The instant he crossed the threshold, he stopped dead and stared.

Sometime during the day, his wife had moved the copper tub from the back porch to their bedroom. Sometime after supper, she must have heated water for a bath. While he'd been saying good night to Slim, she'd undressed herself and gotten into the tub.

Jake couldn't take his eyes off the glorious shape of her small breasts in the soft light from the lamp, the nipples puckered from the cold. Which was when he realized the tub must have been filled with water earlier in the day, since it had cooled. She'd planned this moment . . . and was waiting for him to arrive and play his part.

He'd been ambushed as surely as if she'd been hiding behind a rock with a carbine to shoot him down.

He was too enthralled to care.

Miranda lowered her eyes but didn't cover her breasts. Her legs were drawn up slightly to fit into the copper bath but were hidden in the soapy water. He might only have imagined the dark, enticing V he saw between them.

"Could you hand me a towel?" she asked in a low, sultry voice. The sound slid along his spine and caused him to shiver.

Who was this seductive siren? Where had his innocent wife gone?

His heart was pounding, and his body was aroused as he reached for the towel she'd left on the bed. He'd already opened the folded cloth, planning to turn his back when she rose to receive it from him.

She didn't wait. She stood before he reached her, so

he was treated to the sight of her sleek body, water streaming from every delectable curve. Her legs from the knees down were hidden by the copper tub.

Jake stood stunned, like a boy seeing a woman for the first time, staring without moving. He didn't know how long he was frozen in awe, but it was long enough for her cheeks, and then her throat, and finally her upper chest to flush.

She didn't lower her eyes. She stared at him boldly. With need. With desire.

He was a dead duck.

He enveloped her in the towel, to cover an irresistible body he still hoped to resist.

But Miranda was having no parts of his retreat. She stepped closer to him as she left the tub, so when he wrapped the towel around her, he also wrapped his arms around her. She looked up at him, then lowered her eyes in what could have been shyness. It was a surrender he found as seductive as if she'd run her small hands over his bare flesh.

He held onto the towel with one hand, knowing that if he let go, he was going to find himself losing control. He used his other hand to raise her chin. For a while, she still didn't lift her gaze to his. When she did, he looked into her eyes—fell headlong into those deep blue pools—then lowered his mouth slowly until their lips met.

He hadn't realized how much his feelings for her had grown over the four weeks of their marriage until their mouths touched. He felt a swell of tenderness for his wife. Her lips were closed, reminding him that she was untouched. He thought of the joy to be found as they learned to please one another.

He ran his tongue along the seam of her lips, waiting for her to let him in. He felt her body tense beneath the towel and heard her hitch a breath as she opened her mouth to him.

She tasted sweet, of the peach cobbler she'd made for supper with their last can of peaches, surprising him and the children. He felt a rush of gratitude at her willingness to please him, which fed his desire. His tongue probed her mouth seeking honey. He heard her moan and felt his body throb with need.

He'd picked her up in his arms before he realized he was doing it. The most logical place to put her down again was the bed. He sat down beside her on the mattress and leaned over to kiss her again. Her hands circled his neck and roved over his hair, gripping it tightly as her tongue slid into his mouth. He felt a surge of sexual craving for his wife and reached down to shove the towel aside and cup her naked breast.

"Oh."

Her surprised voice stopped him. He raised his head and looked into her eyes. He wasn't ready for the raw desire he saw there. He wasn't ready to find a need that matched his own.

He lost his head.

She lost the towel.

Jake tore the cloth from her body and threw it aside, then ran his left hand along her body from breast to hip to thigh. He reached down to grab her calf, to wrap it around himself as he came over her, and felt wretchedly pitted and scarred flesh beneath his hand.

He looked down and felt horror.

Before he could control his features, she cried, "Don't look!" and scrambled away from him. She curled herself into a protective ball on the bed, as Jake sat dumbfounded, trying to fathom what could have caused such destruction.

No wonder she limped! It was amazing she could walk at all, with so much flesh missing from her lower leg.

"It's horrible, I know," she said breathlessly as she hid her leg—and belatedly, her entire body—beneath the sheet.

"What happened?" he asked in a shocked voice.

"My skirt caught fire when I went into our burning house to try and find my parents." Her lower lip trembled, and her eyes suddenly welled with tears. "I managed to rescue Harry."

He heard what she hadn't said, that she hadn't been able to rescue her parents. He shuddered at the thought of what it must have been like to know your parents were being burned alive.

Miranda reached out to him, laying a hand on his forearm, but he jerked himself away.

Too late, he realized she wanted to continue their lovemaking. He was still caught up in the horror of what had happened to her and the thought of how close she'd come to dying. He was thinking how easy it was for a life to be lost. He was reminding himself why he had no business making love to his wife.

He rose abruptly and said, equally abruptly, "Put some clothes on. I'm going to . . . I've got to go."

He wasn't able to think of a good excuse for leaving her. He just knew that if he didn't get out of the room, he would end up comforting her in his arms. That would lead to lovemaking, and he'd never be able to pull out in time, not when he wanted to be so deep inside her he ached.

Sure as God made little green apples, he'd get her pregnant. He couldn't take that chance.

He made the mistake of glancing back before he left the room and saw the look of despair on her face. He almost turned around. Almost. He was running by the time he made it to the barn, his stomach churning because of how close he'd come to doing what he'd sworn to himself he would never do.

He would never endanger another woman's life. It wasn't worth it. Not for all the pleasure in the world. Not even for the sake of having another child to love.

Jake leaned against the wall of the barn and put his head against his arm and fought back tears. This was too hard. Resisting was too hard. He wanted his wife. God, how he wanted her!

What was he going to do?

Chapter Twenty-one

Two weeks had gone by since Miranda's attempted seduction. Jake had spent every night of those two weeks sleeping in the barn on a pile of scratchy hay, covered by a smelly horse blanket. He'd welcomed the discomfort like a martyr wearing a hair shirt. He'd deeply hurt his wife's feelings. He deserved to suffer.

Meanwhile, she'd wrought miracles with the house and yard, smiling brightly the whole time, as though his continued absence in their bed mattered not a whit. Most of the time, she avoided looking at him directly. When she did, her eyes looked wounded.

He felt awful.

Jake had racked his brain to think of something he could do, short of making love to his wife, to salvage the situation. When the day dawned hot as Hades, he thought how nice it would be to take a dip in the creek, which gave him a brilliant idea.

Miranda was working at the sink when Jake pulled out his chair at the breakfast table. "Going to be a scorcher today," he said.

"Already hotter'n a burned boot," Slim said, swiping the sweat off his forehead with his sleeve.

Jake spoke to Miranda's back, since she was refusing to look at him. "There's a bend in Bitter Creek where the water pools deep enough that you can swim. The cottonwoods along the bend should have enough leaves to provide shade. How would you feel about taking the day off and going on a picnic?"

He held his breath waiting for her answer. He could tell she was going to turn him down by the way her whole body tensed. He figured she was still feeling self-conscious about her failed seduction and didn't want to spend any more time with him than necessary.

Fortunately, he'd asked at the breakfast table with everyone present. The horde of children and the crotchety old man never gave her a chance to say yea, nay, or boo.

"We ain't got no time for picnickin'," Slim said.

"Can we go, Miranda? Can we?" Nick said. "I want to go swimming."

"What's a picnic?" Harry said. "What's swimming?"

"Can I go, Daddy?" Anna Mae said. "What's swimming?"

Miranda turned slowly, and he watched closely as a shadow crossed her blue eyes. If Nick knew how to swim, it likely meant that the Wentworths-before-the-fire had spent time in Chicago along the shores of Lake Michigan. The fact that Harry had no idea what swimming was suggested they hadn't been near Lake Michigan in the years since Mrs. Catherine O'Leary's cow had kicked over a lantern in her barn and started the Great Chicago Fire.

Miranda didn't look at him when she replied, in a

voice so intimately soft it raised the hairs along the back of his neck, "A picnic sounds lovely."

"Whoopeee!" Nick threw up his hands in excitement and a bit of flapjack went flying off his fork.

"Nicholas Jackson—" Miranda began.

Nick giggled and said, "We're going on a picnic, Miranda!" He jumped up to retrieve the flapjack but the cat had already stolen it and was scampering away. "Too late," he said with a cackle of laughter. "Kitty got it!"

Jake saw the arrested look on Miranda's face as she stared at Nick's happy grin. She glanced quickly in Jake's direction and he saw a look that made his throat ache. It was the first time he'd heard the kid laugh. He wondered how long it had been since Miranda had heard Nick laugh.

After that, she'd simply gone to work putting together a picnic lunch.

"Are you sure you won't come, Slim?" he'd asked his father-in-law when the wagon was all loaded with food and kids and blankets and towels and they were ready to leave.

"Aw, hell. If you're all goin', I ain't stayin' here alone."

Jake lifted the old man in his arms, noticing how much lighter he'd gotten in the year since his accident. He thought of how much more active Slim had been since the Wentworths arrived, and realized they might have saved the old man's life—giving him something to fight against every day.

He set Slim in the back of the wagon with the three kids and scooted the old man's dead legs in, then went to retrieve the wheelchair, so he'd have something to sit in when they arrived at the pond. Jake wondered if he'd be able to get the old man to go into the water. Slim used to like to take a dip at the end of a hard day's work to "cool off and clean up," as he used to say.

During the half-hour trip to the bend in the creek, the kids and Slim carried on a rowdy conversation in the back. Miranda didn't say a word.

"I'm glad to see you're wearing one of Priss's bonnets," he said to break the awful silence between them. Although, really, he was irritated because she'd been using the bonnet brim the whole way to hide her face from him.

She reached up and touched her nose and said, "I started getting freckles. I thought a bonnet might help."

He peered around the edge of the bonnet to check and, sure enough, a spattering of freckles now covered her nose and cheeks. "They make you look . . . younger somehow."

She wrinkled her nose. "And I looked old before?"

He chuckled. "Of course not. I guess I meant they make you look as young as . . . you are."

She frowned.

He'd meant it as a compliment. He wondered what she was thinking. In a voice quiet enough that it wouldn't be heard by the four in the back of the wagon, he said, "I think you look beautiful."

She was startled into looking directly at him.

When he glanced back at her, he felt his heart jump. It had a way of doing that every time he looked into her eyes. He turned and focused his gaze on Brutus's and Caesar's rumps.

He waited for Miranda to say something more, but she didn't. He wanted her to be happy, the way her brothers now seemed to be. He wanted her to want to be with him.

Which was stupid, of course. She wanted to be his wife—in every sense of the word. He was the one putting the distance between them in bed at night. He'd hoped he could make up for that by being more cordial to her in the daylight.

So he said, "When I chose you as my bride, I had an image in my head from the description in your letter of what you would look like with blue eyes and curly blond hair. I've always admired blue eyes, maybe because I didn't have them myself. And blond hair, because hardly anybody I know has blond hair." He was quiet a few moments, then added, "And curls. I imagined running my hands through your blond curls."

Jake realized he was getting into deep water, and they weren't even at the creek yet. What was he doing, talking about running his hands through her hair? Just talking about it was causing a reaction in his Levi's that surprised him. Grief had killed desire for a very long time. Over the past six weeks, his body seemed to be coming back to life with a vengeance.

Still, it was disconcerting to want the woman sitting beside him in a sexual way when all he'd been trying to do was make a friend of her, so they could live together in better harmony.

He saw her eyeing him askance and felt himself flushing all the way to the roots of his hair. "What I meant to say is that I hoped you'd be pretty, and you are."

"Not beautiful anymore? Just pretty?" she said with a rueful smile.

Jake laughed. "You know what I mean."

"I think I do," she said. "I wondered what you would look like, too. I was afraid you'd be old or skinny or maybe bald."

He wasn't any of those, but he wondered if there were qualities she'd hoped for that he didn't possess. He wanted to ask what she'd thought when she'd seen him, but he was afraid of the answer he'd get.

Then she said, "I was surprised you were so tall."

When she didn't say anything more, he said, "Did you want me to be short?"

She chewed her lower lip thoughtfully. "Being with a tall man—with you—makes me feel small and dainty and . . . protected."

That sounded like a good thing.

A small smile curved her bowed upper lip, and she began to speak again. "When I first saw you at the hotel, you looked exactly like I imagined a cowboy might look, with those leather boots and Levi's and that flat-crowned black hat and the vest and shirt. I like the way you look even better when you put on your chaps."

He wore the leather chaps over his Levi's when he was working cattle to protect his jeans from tearing on mesquite thorns and other rough brush. The chaps were cut out in the front so he could make use of the buttoned fly in his jeans. Priss had pointed out that the cutout in front emphasized a man's private parts. Jake wondered if that was what Miranda meant when she said she especially liked the way he looked in chaps.

Just thinking about her thinking about his private parts made them swell a little more. Jake shifted to try to get more comfortable, but his Levi's were fitting less and less well.

"I thought your eyes were . . . fascinating," she said.

And that was all she said. He glanced over and saw her cheeks were pink along the edges of her bonnet. She didn't explain herself and he couldn't make himself ask for an explanation, even though he wanted one. She thought his plain old dark brown eyes were *fascinating*?

It was a damned good thing they were headed for the creek. He felt hot all over.

"Is that it? Are we there?" Nick asked, leaning forward between Jake and Miranda and pointing to a spot along the creek where cottonwoods created a haven of shade.

"That's it," Jake said.

"Be sure to leave your clothes somewhere they won't get soaked," Miranda warned her brother.

"Don't worry, I will!"

Jake had barely pulled the wagon to a stop and set the brake before Nick shoved open the tailgate and lowered Harry onto the ground. Then Nick jumped down, lifted Anna Mae out of the wagon, and set her on the ground. He ignored Slim and ran with the two younger kids toward the water.

"Nicholas Jackson Wentworth!" Miranda called after him. "Don't you dare let those babies go in that water before I get there."

"I'm not a baby!" Harry yelled back at her.

Jake lifted Miranda off the wagon, feeling how thin she still was. She needed to eat more. He was careful to hold her away from his body, but just the feel of her hands on his bare forearms, where he'd rolled up his sleeves, was enough to send a shiver rolling down his spine.

"You okay?" he asked, once he had her feet on the ground.

She grabbed her bonnet and straightened it, though it looked okay to him, and said, a little breathlessly, "Fine." Then she turned and hurried toward the water. "Nick, do you hear me? I said wait!"

"Where do you want your chair?" Jake asked Slim as he lifted the wheelchair from the wagon.

"Right near that rock, where it's good and shady," the old man replied, pointing to a flat stone near the pond.

"I'll be right back to get you," Jake said heading off to put the chair in place.

By the time Jake had set down Slim's chair, the boys had already stripped to their smalls, and Miranda had taken everything off Anna Mae except her diaper. Jake quickly returned to retrieve Slim, and as he placed the old man down in his chair, he saw Miranda had the three children sitting in a row at the edge of the water.

"Nick, I want to watch you swim, to make sure you remember how. Go ahead now," she said.

Nick stuck a toe in the creek and yelled, "It's coooollldd!" Then he grinned and splashed his way in, shouting and laughing, until he was in water up to his neck. He paddled around and said, "See? I can swim!"

"I want to go in, Miranda," Harry said.

"We need to wait for Jake," she replied.

"I'm here," Jake said. "Are you going in like that?" he asked Miranda.

"No. I'm going to strip down behind those bushes over there. I've just been waiting for you to get here."

Jake unbuttoned his shirt and reached for the snap on his jeans. "I'm not planning on wearing much, so you can stand and watch or head for the bushes."

He saw Miranda's cheeks turn pink before she thrust Anna Mae into his arms and ran for the bushes. Jake set Anna Mae down so he could finish undressing, but she ran straight for the edge of the water. He picked her up and dropped her in Slim's lap and said, "Hang on to her until Miranda gets back. Then you can let her go."

"I want to swim!" Anna Mae cried.

"Miranda!" Jake called. "Are you about ready?"

Jake stopped in his tracks when Miranda came out of the bushes. She was wearing a pair of bloomers that went all the way to her ankles and a chemise that revealed two shadows that had to be her nipples. His imagination filled in the rest of her breasts, and the damned cotton wasn't even wet yet.

"Would you take Anna Mae?" he said abruptly. "I'll take care of Harry."

He turned his back on her to finish undressing. The sooner he immersed a certain part of himself in cold water, the better!

"Are you going to teach me how to swim?" Harry asked Jake.

Jake planned to swim in his long john trousers for the sake of the kids—and his own sanity. "Do you want me to teach you?" he said to Harry as he sat down and pulled off his boots and socks.

Harry nodded. "Uh-huh."

"Then I will."

As soon as Jake was down to his long johns, he picked Harry up and headed into the water. He was glad to see that Miranda had taken Anna Mae into deeper water, so she was covered up to her neck. He felt her eyes on him—on his bare chest—and felt the blood rush in his veins. He could almost hear the hiss of steam as the icy water hit his heated body.

Jake focused on the little boy in his arms and tried to forget about his unruly body. "All right, Harry," he said as he put his hands under the little boy's skinny belly to hold him up. "First step is for you to learn how to hold your breath and put your face in the water."

Jake taught the little boy the way he'd been taught, one step at a time. How to hold his breath. How to blow bubbles in the water. How to hold his breath and put his face in the water. How to paddle like a dog. How to lift his face and take a breath.

"Harry, you're doing so well!" Miranda praised.

"Remember when Dad taught me?" Nick said wistfully as he eyed Harry.

"Yes, I do," Miranda replied, brushing the wet bangs out of Nick's eyes.

Jake looked up and saw the sad look that passed between the Wentworths. "Hey, how about some lunch?" he said.

Everyone trooped out of the water. As soon as Miranda and the kids were settled on the blanket with the picnic basket of food, Jake crossed to Slim and said, "How about a dip in the creek?"

Slim made a face. "Got no legs, Jake."

"You've still got arms. The rest of you will float."

"What about them kids? Don't want them watchin' me."

"They're busy eating lunch. They aren't going to bother us."

Jake picked Slim up and carried him to the edge of the pond and set him down. He waited while Slim pulled off both shirt and long john shirt, then helped him get out of his boots, socks, and trousers. He picked up his father-in-law, who was dressed now as Jake was in long john bottoms, and headed into the water.

He felt Slim's arm tighten around his neck and said, "I won't let you go."

Slim didn't say anything about the temperature of the water until it reached his waist, reminding Jake that he had no feeling below the waist. As soon as the frigid water hit Slim's belly, he hissed and said, "Damned creek's colder than a dead snake."

Jake laughed. "You ready to swim, old man?"

For a moment, Slim looked scared, then his jaw clamped and he said, "Ready as I'll ever be."

Jake eased his father-in-law away from his body and waited until Slim's arms were waving in the water before he let go. Slim started to sink, then leaned his head back and let his body float out in front of him, using the gentle wave of his arms to keep himself from sinking.

Jake thought he saw tears brim in the old man's eyes and turned away quickly so he wouldn't embarrass him. "I should have thought to do this sooner," Jake said as he paddled to keep himself upright beside

Slim, ready to catch the old man if he got too tired to keep himself above water.

"I wasn't well enough before winter set in," Slim reminded him. "And we was busy as hell for a while after that. That girl of yours has a lot of gumption," Slim said. "And a nice shape," he added with a grin.

"You weren't supposed to notice that," Jake said with a rueful laugh.

"I'm old. I ain't dead! Just wish she hadn't grabbed that towel so damn fast."

Jake was glad she had. He laughed along with his father-in-law, but it was no laughing matter. The last thing he wanted was one more image of his wife's body appearing in his dreams at night. He already had one perfect breast with its rosy pink nipple indelibly impressed in his memory.

"You about ready to get out of here?" Jake asked.

"I'm hungry enough to eat a folded tarp."

"I don't think that's on the menu today," Jake said.

"Girl can't cook worth beans," Slim said.

"She'll learn."

"We don't starve first," Slim grumbled.

"We're having sandwiches for lunch. Can't do much to ruin those."

"Looks like she's been keepin' her distance from you, son," Slim observed as he dried off and began dressing himself.

"You noticed that?" Jake sat down and dried his feet.

"Hard not to," Slim said. "Girl's been walkin' 'round with her lips stuck out like a buggy seat the past couple of weeks."

"We'll work it out," Jake said, pulling on his shirt.

"You sure 'bout that?"

"Sure as I can be." Jake wished he felt more confident that he and Miranda would end up in an amicable marriage. Amicable, but not sexual. It helped that Miranda had nowhere to go. She didn't have much choice except to agree to the terms he'd set for their marriage. Although she'd been doing a pretty good job of giving him the cold shoulder.

Slim eyed him sideways. "You really like that gal, don't you?"

Jake was surprised by the question. Surprised that Slim had asked it. And surprised by his answer. "Yeah," he said. "I do."

How had she become so important to him in such a short time? When had he started caring for her? How had Miranda Wentworth snuck her way into what he'd been so very sure was a hardened heart?

Chapter Twenty-two

The morning after the picnic, when Jake arrived in the kitchen after another miserable night spent in the barn, he was greeted with the sight of two lively boys having a contest to see who could eat the most flapjacks. Across the table, a vivacious woman was playing a game with his daughter, mother and child laughing as Miranda wiped jam off Anna Mae's cherubic face.

He felt a tiny sprig of hope. Maybe Miranda was finally getting over being hurt by his rejection. He turned away to pour himself a cup of coffee from the stove but continued watching her from the corner of his eye. And saw her shoulders slump and her mouth turn down.

She was hurting all right. Just too proud to let him see it. She still believed her ruined leg had repulsed him. But why wouldn't she? Had he said a single thing to the contrary? And he was hiding in the barn every night, avoiding even getting into bed with her.

Because you know you'd never be able to keep your hands off her if you were sleeping in the same bed together.

Yeah. But she didn't know that.

He needed to sit her down and talk to her and explain why abstinence was the only choice they had. He had to impress upon her the danger to her of them having sex. And somehow he had to make amends for running away to the barn every night, and do it without letting her know just how vulnerable he was to her seductive wiles.

He thought all that, but he said nothing at the breakfast table.

Neither did she.

He ate far more flapjacks than he wanted, thinking that any minute he'd get the courage to tell her they needed to talk. But in the end, he simply said, "I have chores to do in the barn."

"I thought you might have finished all those already," she said.

Since you spend your nights out there.

Jake heard the words, even though she didn't say them. This was the time for him to speak. This was the time to get everything out in the open.

But his stomach was churning. And his heart hurt.

"No. There's more to do," he said as he grabbed his hat and stuck it on his head.

"The boys are helping me in the house today," Miranda said.

"Fine." He practically ran from the house. And felt like a breathless idiot when he reached the barn. Scared out of his house by a little wisp of a woman . . . with wounded blue eyes.

Damn it. He simply wasn't sure how to repair Miranda's self-esteem without making love to her. And that was not an option!

Jake spent the morning mucking out stalls. It was mindless physical work that gave him far too much time to think. He must have spent an hour arguing the pros and cons of having sex with his wife. The only con was the danger to her health. There were too many pros to count.

He was so caught up in his thoughts that he was hardly aware of what else was going on around him. The whispers caught his attention, because that sound suggested secretiveness. He glanced over his shoulder to see which of the kids had come into the barn, and what they might be up to.

A second later, he dropped the pitchfork he was using to muck stalls and ran for the ladder that led up twenty-five feet to the loft, his heart in his throat the whole way. Even so, he was barely in time to catch Anna Mae, who fell from near the top of the ladder, yelping in pain when Harry, who was one rung above her, stepped on her hand.

He threw Anna Mae onto a pile of hay without thinking and grabbed for Harry, who cried out in terror as he fell from the ladder only an instant after Anna Mae.

Harry grappled for him and clung to his neck. Once Jake had Harry firmly in hand, he picked up Anna Mae from the pile of hay and clutched both children tightly to him. Turning from one woe-filled face to the other, he asked, "Are you all right?"

"I fell," Anna Mae said, sobbing pitifully.

"What were you two doing on that ladder?" Jake demanded of Harry. "Where's Nick? He's supposed to be keeping an eye on you two!"

"I'm up here," Nick said, peering down from the

loft. He was holding a six-week-old calico kitten in each hand. "I don't know how these kittens got up here, but they couldn't get down."

Jake was in no mood to hear excuses. "Get down here, boy."

He watched as Nick slipped each kitten carefully down inside his shirt, which was tucked into his trousers, then buttoned it all the way to the top, before coming down the ladder. By the time Nick was down, Jake had set the two crying children on the dirt floor of the stable.

The instant Nick was on firm ground, he unbuttoned his shirt and handed each of the smaller children a kitten. "Here," he said.

Their sobs subsided as though he'd stuck a sucker in each of their mouths.

"Go inside and find your mother," Jake said to the little ones. It wasn't until they were gone that he realized he'd told Harry to find his mother, rather than his sister. Hell, she'd been his mother since he was a baby, hadn't she?

Then he turned to the ten-year-old standing with his chin tilted up in defiance. "What do you have to say for yourself, boy?"

"I told them to stay off the ladder."

"And I told you to stay out of the loft," Jake said angrily.

"The kittens—"

"The kittens would have found their own way down. You endangered those two babies with your foolishness."

"I told them to stay off the ladder!" Nick argued.

Jake grabbed Nick's arm and leaned in close to

Nick's face, to make sure the boy was listening. "You're their older brother, Nick. You're supposed to make smarter choices."

Nick tried to jerk free, but Jake held on. He couldn't remember the last time he'd been so angry. He shook the boy and said, "Your sister would be devastated if anything happened to you kids."

"Yeah, but you don't give a damn about me or Harry," the boy replied with a sneer. "All you care about is your precious Anna Mae!"

Jake was so stunned by the accusation that he let go of Nick's arm. The boy turned and ran before Jake could grab him again. He tried to think whether he'd been favoring his daughter over Miranda's two brothers. Of course he expected more from Nick. He was older. Here in the West, a boy had a man's responsibilities long before he might have had them in a more civilized place.

Nick hadn't been gone more than a few moments when Miranda showed up in the barn.

"What's going on out here? Harry babbled something about cats and falling off ladders and Nick being in trouble with you that made no sense at all." She looked around. "Where's Nick?"

"He ran off," Jake said.

Miranda pursed her lips in a way he realized he would probably see often in the years to come. "What did you do?"

"Nothing." When she lifted a disbelieving brow, he admitted, "I chastised him. He had no business being in the loft."

"He was in the *loft*?" she nearly shrieked. She stared up the long ladder. "He could have *killed* himself!"

"Exactly what I said. I caught both Anna Mae and Harry just as they fell off the ladder."

"Oh, thank God." She put a hand to her heart in relief. "Why did Nick run away?"

"He accused me of not caring about him."

Miranda met his gaze and asked, "Do you care?"

"How can you ask that? Of course I care!" Jake spluttered. "Haven't I taught him to ride? Haven't I been teaching him how to work a ranch?"

"Have you ever hugged him? Have you ever said a kind word to him?"

"Boys don't need hugs and kind words. They need—"

"I beg to differ," she interrupted. "Everyone needs hugs and kind words. They're signs of caring. They're signs of love."

Jake felt like she'd punched him in the gut. She was telling him that she needed affection to feel loved. He should have had that talk with his wife this morning at breakfast. "If you're referring to what happened between you and me, I've—"

"You don't ever have to make love to me, Jake. Not if my body repulses you."

"Repulses me?" *Was the woman mad?* "What the hell are you talking about?"

She met his gaze bravely and said, "You took one look at my scarred leg and ran."

"I wasn't running from your scarred leg," Jake said. "I was running from you."

She frowned. "Isn't that the same thing?"

"I wanted to make love to you, Miranda. Plain and simple. It's too damned dangerous."

"Dangerous? Oh." She frowned. "You mean I might get pregnant."

He nodded. "You could die in childbirth."

"Or I could live and have a dozen healthy children."

He was surprised into laughing. "A dozen?"

"Shouldn't the choice be mine?" she asked plaintively. "If I'm willing to take the risk, why can't you?"

"I'm the one who'll be left to suffer if anything goes wrong," he said flatly.

"Do you hear the 'if' in that statement?" she asked. "What *if* everything goes right?"

Jake couldn't believe he was having this discussion—this argument—with his wife. Was he going to let her convince him to do something he knew was wrong just because he wanted the pleasure to be had from her body? But life was a series of risks and choices. Maybe she would be all right. Maybe she wouldn't die in childbirth.

And maybe he was telling himself what he wanted to hear.

"I'm young and healthy, Jake. My mother bore six healthy children, and I'm sure I—" She stopped abruptly. "I mean—" She stopped again, obviously flustered. "I don't know what I mean. The point is, I want to have children, Jake. I want to have your children. Can't we try? Please?"

He was so busy thinking up reasons to keep her at bay, it took him a moment to realize what she'd said. "Your mother had *six* children? What happened to the other three?"

"They didn't die at birth," she said tentatively.

"But they're dead, all the same," he concluded.

She looked unhappy, but she didn't contradict him.

"I don't want any more children," he said.

"What if I do? Are you going to deny me that joy?"

Sure, there were rewards to having children, but in his mind, the dangers far outweighed whatever joy either of them might have. "Look at it this way. I'm going to deny you the chance to die having a child."

She threw up her hands. "You're a fool, Jake Creed! I'm sorry as I can be that I married you!"

She turned and ran without giving him a chance to reply.

But what could a man say when his wife called him a fool . . . and he knew she was right?

Chapter Twenty-three

Jake had expected Nick to slink off and sulk for a while, then show up for supper, bowed but certainly unbeaten. The boy had too much spunk for that. However, at sundown, Nick was nowhere to be seen.

"You have to go look for him, Jake," Miranda said, her eyes wide and frightened. "It'll be dark soon. He must be scared. I would go with you, but I need to be here, in case he shows up on his own."

Jake stood in the kitchen sniffing at what looked like a delicious supper of pork chops with onions and mashed potatoes. He was hungry. He wanted to sit down and eat. That obviously wasn't going to happen. At least, not until Nick turned up.

He figured the kid was hiding somewhere in one of the slaves' quarters. As soon as Jake saddled up and rode out, Nick would show up and have a hot supper, while Jake was out hunting for him in the moonlight. But he could see Miranda was truly worried.

"All right," he said. "I'll go look for the kid. But you better have a talk with your brother. I've got to be up at daybreak to work. I can't be spending my evenings running around looking for some brat who got his feelings hurt."

The look Miranda gave him would have done Medusa proud. If Miranda's own head had been full of snakes, he'd have turned to stone.

"Do *not* call Nick a brat," she said through bared teeth. "He made a mistake. You shouldn't have thrown that cat and her kittens out of the house. If they'd been left in the bed I made for them in the parlor, he'd never have been out in the barn hunting for kittens in the first place."

"So this is all my fault?" he said incredulously.

"If the shoe fits, wear it!"

"Cats don't belong in the house. They belong in the barn chasing mice."

"We have mice in the house, too," she retorted.

"Since when?"

"Saw one myself," Slim interjected as he rolled himself through the kitchen doorway. "Sent your wife jumpin' onto a kitchen chair, then went out through a hole in the floor."

"So there!" Miranda said, crossing her arms and glaring at him.

Jake shot a Medusa look at Slim. It didn't work. "Since when do you take her side?"

"Since I saw a mouse in the kitchen," the old man said with a grin. "Better get movin'. Gettin' darker every minute."

Jake turned his back on the two of them and stomped out of the house. And realized just how close the sun was to falling below the horizon. In a while, stars would provide some light, but the moon wouldn't rise for hours.

As soon as it got dark, snakes would be out hunting for a meal, along with owls and wolves. If the kid bothered a Texas Longhorn, he could expect to get himself gored or trampled into dust. This was no place to be out running around unarmed and on foot.

Jake muttered every bad word he could think of as he saddled up a buckskin named, of course, Buck. "Come on, horse," he said as he mounted. "Let's go find the kid."

Jake looked left along the fence that framed Three Oaks, then right, toward the road that led back toward San Antonio, branching off to Lion's Dare—now Bitter Creek—along the way.

"If I was a kid running away, Buck, I'd head back to the city. Let's go check it out."

Jake didn't hurry. He looked for footprints in the last of the light before the sun disappeared entirely. He found them along the dusty road heading back to San Antonio. The boy had been gone several hours without food or water or matches or a weapon of any kind, or even a coat to keep away the April evening chill. Nick must be feeling pretty lonesome—and damned scared—by now.

Jake realized the kid might have been smart enough not to walk too far from home. On the other hand, he might have been mad enough to move fast and keep going. Jake hoped the kid was smart. This really was no place for a kid of ten, who was ignorant of the dangers that abounded, to be running around alone.

A couple of hours later, Jake still hadn't caught up to Nick. He worried that the kid might have left the road. If he had, it might be a very long night. If he had, Jake might never find him. Alive anyway. Someday he might stumble across Nick's bones, picked clean. Otherwise, he might never know what had happened to the boy.

He'd been shouting Nick's name for the past hour, hoping against hope that the boy would hear him. He was getting hoarse. And feeling guilty. Maybe he shouldn't have been so hard on him.

Every time Jake had that thought, he remembered how his own father had raised him. Mistakes were punished immediately and harshly. There was no room for blunders in the West. Even kids had to be responsible—all day, every day. He wouldn't be doing Nick any favors if he didn't hold him to the same high standards to which Jake's father had held him.

He just hoped the kid lived long enough to learn his lesson.

"Nick!" he shouted. "Nick! Where are you? Your sister's worried. Nick! Answer me. Nick!"

There was no answer.

He searched another hour but had no luck. The moon was up and he could see almost like it was day. There was no sign of Nick, not even any footprints. The kid had probably made those tracks on the road and then doubled back and come in from one of the shacks while Jake was out here on a wild-goose chase. He should probably turn around and head back.

Except, what if the kid was still out here? Alone. Scared to death. In mortal danger.

His throat hurt, but he kept calling, kept hoping the boy would answer. Then he heard a faint cry from his left. "Nick? Is that you?"

The cry came again. It was a moan, really.

Jake moved slowly, carefully, watching for predators—

animal and human—lurking in the darkness. The moon came out from behind a cloud, and he saw a patch of white under a mesquite tree near the road. The boy's shirt, he thought.

He kept his horse moving, but all the while his eyes roamed left and right. He listened intently for any sound that didn't belong. Something—or someone—had injured the boy. He didn't want to end up a victim, too.

He didn't approach Nick directly. He rode around and came from behind him, watching for an ambush. When he was sure there was no threat, he called out softly, "Nick?"

The boy was sitting on the ground, his back against the mesquite. "I'm hurt," he said in a faint voice.

Jake dismounted and hurriedly crossed the few feet to Nick. "What happened?"

"I was resting here in the shade and something bit me." He held up his left hand, which was swollen.

"Was it a snake? Did you hear rattling beforehand?" Jake asked anxiously.

Nick shook his head. "A spider of some kind. Only it didn't look like a spider exactly. It had a stinger on its tail."

"Scorpion," Jake said.

"I was just going to rest here and then walk back," Nick said. "I must have fallen asleep."

Or he'd had an uncommon reaction to the scorpion's venom and was too weak to stand, Jake thought. "When the scorpion stung you, how did it feel?"

The kid shrugged. "I don't know. How should it feel?"

"Like you'd been stung by a bee or a wasp."

"I've never been stung by a bee or a wasp."

The result of living in a city full of buildings instead of trees and grass and flowers, Jake thought. He took the kid's hand in his and examined the bite in the moonlight. A scorpion's sting might be painful, but the venom wasn't strong enough to cause more than temporary pain—unless someone was allergic to the venom.

It looked like Nick was having a stronger reaction to the bite than normal. He was breathing heavily, and he was certainly lethargic. Better get him back to the house and get some baking soda on that bite.

Jake leaned down and picked the boy up in his arms, surprised at how light Nick still was, even after all the pancakes he'd eaten.

"I can walk," Nick protested. But his arms went around Jake's neck and his head lolled onto Jake's shoulder.

"Don't worry," Jake said soothingly. "I've got you, son."

Jake bit his lip, expecting Nick to protest his use of the word "son."

It was a sign of what bad shape the boy was in that he just circled his hands tighter around Jake's neck.

When he got back to his horse, Jake pulled Nick's hands free and placed him in the saddle. Then he settled himself on the horse's rump behind the saddle, with his arms around Nick's chest to hold him upright. He could hear—and feel—just how hard the boy was breathing.

Jake gave his mount a kick and said, "Let's go home, Buck."

Nick tried sitting upright, but it was obviously a struggle.

"It's all right to lean on me, son," Jake said quietly.

Nick tensed, and Jake realized he'd unconsciously used that word again.

After an endless moment, the boy's small back leaned trustingly against Jake's broad chest.

Jake let out a quiet sigh of relief and asked, "Where were you headed?"

"Away from you."

Jake's heart sank. It was fatigue, not acceptance, that had caused the boy to relax in his arms. The kid still didn't want anything to do with him.

Then Nick said, "The more I walked, the more I realized you were right, Jake. And I was wrong."

Jake tightened his arm around the slender boy. "It takes a big man to admit that."

"Yeah, well, I also figured I'd rather eat pancakes than whatever I can find on the trail for breakfast," the boy said flippantly.

Jake found himself laughing at the kid's cheek. "I'll see if I can get your sister to make you some for supper."

"I wish I was already grown up," he said wistfully.

"Why is that?"

"If I were grown, I could go wherever I want and do whatever I want and people couldn't boss me around."

"There are always people to tell you what they think you should do," Jake said cynically. "Where would you go, by the way, if you could go anywhere?"

"Back to Chicago to get my sisters out of that hellhole Miss Birch calls an orphanage. I'd do almost anything to rescue them from the clutches of that fat old biddy."

Jake thought the boy was confused, that the scorpion bite had affected his reasoning, which was a bad thing, if it was true. The pain and symptoms of a scorpion sting were usually gone pretty quick. Jake was worried that Nick's reaction seemed far worse than normal.

"Your sister's already escaped from Miss Birch," he told the boy gently.

"Not Miranda," the boy said petulantly. "I mean my sisters Hannah and Hetty and Josie."

Jake felt faint. "You left three sisters behind?"

"Yeah. Miranda was hoping you'd have a house big enough for all of us, but you don't. That's why she wants you to rebuild what's been burnt, so there'll be room for all six of us."

"All *six* of you," Jake murmured, remembering how Miranda had slipped up in the barn and mentioned the number of children that her mother had birthed. It appeared all six were alive and well, although three had been left behind in Chicago.

He felt like the fool she'd called him more than once. He'd been congratulating himself on having the perfect wife. She was far from perfect. Miranda Wentworth Creed was a liar and a conniver and a cheat.

Jake supposed that was the problem with putting any woman on a pedestal. It was damned hard to keep her up there for very long before she fell off.

"What's Miranda planning to do about your sisters, now that there's no room at Three Oaks for the rest of the family?" Jake asked.

"Oh, Miranda wrote a letter, telling them they'll have to wait. I don't think she's figured out how to mail it though, without you finding out."

"I see," Jake said. Did the boy realize what he was revealing?

The kid just kept talking. "Hannah and Hetty will stay until they turn eighteen—that's one more year. Poor Josie's only sixteen. Miss Birch hates her, because Josie's so smart. She reads a lot. That place'll be hell on earth, once Josie's there all by herself."

Jake felt sorry for the lot of them, but he was also aggrieved at his wife for keeping their existence a secret from him and for conspiring to bring them to Texas without his knowledge.

He would have been glad to help, if only she'd asked. Didn't she know how much he cared for her? Obviously not, if she was keeping secrets—like the existence of three more sisters—from him.

Jake realized he might lose Miranda even if he never had sex with her. She might decide to move out and set up housekeeping with the rest of her family. All of his self-denial would have been in vain.

He didn't need much of an excuse to do what he'd been wanting to do from the first night he'd spent in bed with his wife. He'd been at the end of his tether for far too long. After he got Nick fed and doctored and tucked in for the night, he was going to make love to his wife.

And he was going to enjoy every minute of it. He wasn't going to think once about the risk to her, or how devastated he would be if something happened to her.

Then he'd ask her exactly how she planned to rescue her sisters, since he hadn't turned out to be as rich a fool as she'd hoped, and just see what his wife had to say.

Chapter Twenty-four

Miranda noticed Jake was acting strangely when he returned to the house with Nick in tow, but she was so grateful he'd found Nick, and that Nick seemed to be recovering so well from his adventure, that she didn't ask what was troubling him.

Now that the house was quiet, her husband had come into their bedroom and started undressing. That was odd in the extreme. Since her failed seduction, he'd been sleeping—and therefore undressing—in the barn. There had been no chance of either one seeing the other in dishabille.

She stared at him warily from the bed, where she sat under the covers in her nightgown, wondering what had caused this change. "Are you all right?"

"Aside from being hungry, I'm fine."

"I kept your dinner warm. I could get it for you now, if you like," she said, starting to shove the covers aside.

"Stay where you are." He met her inquiring gaze and said, "I'm hungry for something else right now."

"Really? What is that?"

"You."

Miranda gaped. "Oh." What did he mean? Was he, at long last, going to make love to her? "Have you changed your mind?"

He nodded.

It was the curtness of the nod that made her feel anxious. Maybe he was as nervous about what was to come as she was. Although, she didn't think anyone could be as nervous as she was.

"What changed your mind?" she asked.

"Let's not spend time talking that we could spend doing things that are far more enjoyable," he said as he crossed to the bed.

Jake's chest and feet were bare. His belt was gone, as well, but he hadn't taken off his Levi's. The jeans hung low, revealing sharp hipbones. She couldn't take her eyes off the dark line of hair that began at his navel and disappeared beneath the metal buttons that held his fly closed.

The part of his body beneath his fly seemed to grow before her astonished eyes, pressing against the fabric, creating a very visible, very male outline.

Jake's face suddenly blocked her view, looming over her as he sat on the side of the bed. "I want you, Miranda," he said in a husky voice. "I've wanted you from the moment I laid eyes on you."

They were heady words. "I . . ." She swallowed over the sudden knot in her throat and managed to croak, "I want you, too, Jake."

"Good."

There was something in his voice, something not quite . . . right. She closed her eyes as he lowered his head and waited for his kiss.

Miranda was expecting tenderness. She was expecting the same gentle exploration that had begun their aborted attempt at lovemaking. She wasn't prepared for the sudden thrust of Jake's tongue or the resulting sensation that exploded in her belly and worked its way up to her breasts and throat, setting her body on fire. She met his tongue thrust with one of her own as her hands clutched at whatever part of him she could reach.

He made a low, guttural sound before he reached for the tie of her nightgown and yanked it free. He reached inside with both hands to hold her naked breasts, but the gown was still in his way. He roughly shoved it off her shoulders and jerked it down to her waist.

Miranda should have felt abashed. But it was excitement, not shame, that she felt as Jake perused her naked body. She wondered fleetingly why he'd changed his mind, why he no longer seemed concerned about getting her pregnant.

What he did next pushed every rational thought away.

She came willingly as he pulled her into his embrace, her naked breasts crushed against his naked chest. As he pressed fervent kisses to her throat, she bent her head to kiss his throat in return.

He tasted salty. And he smelled of hard-working man, an acrid scent that was not at all unpleasant.

He sucked on her flesh, and she heard a grating sound of pleasure come from deep in her throat. She'd been resisting the urge to bite him, but her teeth nipped in response to the pleasure and pain of what he was doing with his mouth.

He pulled away to look into her face, and she stared up into his glittering, heavy-lidded eyes. She barely had time to wonder what the look in his eyes meant before he lowered his mouth to her breast and took her nipple in his mouth.

"Ahhhh," she moaned.

She didn't know what to do with herself. She was caught up in the exquisite pleasure Jake was creating as he touched her in places she couldn't have imagined allowing a man to touch.

But she needed to touch as well.

Jake groaned as her hand slid along his hip all the way to his inner thigh.

"My God, girl. What are you doing?"

"You don't like it?" Miranda started to pull her hand away, but he caught it and held it where it was.

"I like it too much."

She didn't understand what he meant. "Should I stop?"

He gave a harsh laugh. "No. Don't stop."

She let her fingertips slide higher, toward that part of him that was particularly male. She watched as his eyes squeezed closed.

A moment later he'd laid her flat and was pushing her knees apart. She caught a glimpse of him and thought there was no way he would ever fit! She panicked.

One of his hands was caught in her hair while the other had moved down between her legs.

"Shh," he said. "Easy, love. Easy now."

His voice was soothing, coaxing, and she relaxed enough to gaze up into his eyes, which still held that strange, glittery look. His hands were warm on her, and she felt embarrassed to realize she was wet down there.

When she glanced away, he said, "That's the way it's supposed to be, girl. It's how your body readies itself for mine."

"Oh," she said meekly, turning to meet his dark-eyed gaze.

His features were taut, his jaw tight. He didn't look much like he was enjoying himself. She reached up to put a hand on his cheek. He pressed his face against her hand and closed his eyes as though he needed her touch as much as she needed his.

For a moment anyway. Then his eyes flashed open and he focused his dark eyes on her and his lips flattened.

She felt confused by his contrary behavior. And aroused by what he was doing with his hand. And frightened of what was to come.

Her eyes widened as he began to touch a part of her he hadn't touched before. "Oh," she said in surprise. "Oh, that feels good."

She reached for his shoulders to hold on, as her body began to move under his hand. She arched her hips upward and felt male flesh.

"Uh," he said in surprise.

Miranda didn't know exactly what it was she wanted as she cried, "Please, Jake! Please!"

But Jake did. He spread her legs farther apart with his knees and reached beneath her with his hands to angle her so he could more easily push himself inside.

Miranda felt stretched impossibly wide. Her body tensed against the intrusion and she gripped Jake's shoulders hard, digging her fingernails into his flesh as pleasure turned to pain. "Jake, it hurts!"

He paused, but not for long. "Yes, I know. Just this once. There's no help for it." Then he plunged deep inside her, till he was seated to the hilt.

Miranda felt like she'd been torn in two. Her whole body was trembling as she stared up at Jake, fearing more pain.

"That's the worst of it," he said in a quiet voice.

"Are you done?"

She heard him chuckle as he huffed out a breath. "No. There's more."

"Will it hurt?"

"I hope not." He hesitated, then added, "Do you want me to stop?"

Miranda didn't know why Jake had changed his mind and decided to have sex with her, but she didn't want him to change his mind now. Not if there was more. She wanted to know what that more was.

"Don't stop." She braced herself for more pain, but as he began to move inside her, she heard the wetness again that had so embarrassed her and realized it made it possible for him to love her without hurting her. She relaxed enough to lift her hips, to create a sort of rhythm with his movements, and began to feel the goodness of what he was doing.

He laid his head beside hers as he worked in her, and she felt her insides begin to clench and tighten and lifted her body to meet his in a rhythm as old as the ages. She felt an inexplicable tension and her breathing became erratic. She clutched Jake's shoulders, striving to hold onto something solid when the ground was shifting beneath her. Until, at long last, deep inside her, she felt Jake release his seed.

He pulled her close as he separated them, his chest a bellows that matched her own. Miranda leaned her cheek against his chest and smiled to herself at the knowledge that she had finally, at long last, become a wife.

He rolled onto his back, releasing his hold on her, and threw an arm over his eyes, hiding his face from her.

Miranda felt bereft. She wanted to be held. She wanted the closeness she'd felt when he was inside her to continue beyond their lovemaking.

Abruptly, he leaned across her and turned off the lamp, which was when she realized it had been on the entire time. She marveled that she hadn't been more shy. She wondered what had caused him to finally make love to her.

"Why did you change your mind?" she asked in the darkness.

"I figured I might as well get what I want out of this marriage," he said. "Before I end up with a lot more of your relatives on my doorstep."

Miranda felt cold inside. How had he found out? "What are you talking about?"

"Your three sisters in Chicago."

Miranda began searching frantically for her nightgown in the dark. She wanted to be dressed for this conversation. She finally located it on the floor and put it on, then found a match and lit the lamp. She took one look at Jake, lying naked on the bed, and said, "Cover yourself!"

He smiled sardonically. "It's a little late to play the

innocent maiden, Miranda. You're no longer a virgin. And you sure as hell aren't innocent!"

She felt her heart hammering in her chest. "I don't know what you're talking about."

He grabbed his Levi's and pulled them on, then stood up, towering over her. "I know about your three sisters in Chicago. Nick let the cat out of the bag. I'm just wondering what your plans are, now that it turns out I'm not a rich enough dupe to provide a home for them."

"Oh, Jake, it isn't like that."

"Oh, no? Then what is it like, Miranda? Are you telling me you didn't plan to bring your sisters here to live?"

She thought about lying, but instead said, "If you'd had the space, and if you were willing, yes, I would have loved to have my whole family together again. You can't know what it's like, Jake, to be at the mercy of forces beyond your control."

"Can't I?" Jake demanded. "You think I haven't been fighting a power greater than I am for the past ten years? You don't know Alexander Blackthorne!"

"Then perhaps you can understand how desperate I was. How desperate I am," she corrected. "Now that you know, perhaps you'd be willing to post a letter from me to my sisters the next time you're in San Antonio."

"I can't afford to go to town right now."

"When will you be going?"

"I have no idea."

She put her hands on her hips. "Then you won't mind if I take the letter to your mother and ask her to post it for me."

"You stay away from Bitter Creek!"

She arched a disdainful brow. "Is that an *order* from my loving husband?"

"It's for your own good."

"It's not my own good I'm worried about. I'm the one married to a kind and good man," she said with a sneer that showed just how much she meant the exact opposite. "It's my poor sisters I'm concerned about."

"Do what you want," he snarled, thrusting an agitated hand through his hair. "You always do! I'll find somewhere else to sleep tonight." He grabbed his shirt and belt and boots and left the room without a backward glance.

He was headed back to the barn. Again. Making love hadn't changed anything.

Miranda felt like bawling. Instead she turned out the lamp and got into bed. She wanted to be up early to make the trip to Bitter Creek. She hoped Jake tried to stop her, she really did. She would make a scene the likes of which he'd never seen.

Miranda felt a hot tear trickle down her cheek and angrily brushed it away. She hoped, she fervently hoped, she was pregnant. She was going to have that baby and the two of them were going to live happily ever after. That would show him!

Chapter Twenty-five

Miranda slept badly and woke early. Jake had not had a change of heart during the night. He had not come back to bed. She wondered just how uncomfortable it was to sleep on a bed of scratchy hay, then told herself she didn't care. She was determined to do what she'd threatened. She was going to saddle up a horse and ride over to Bitter Creek today and ask Jake's mother to post her letter for her in San Antonio.

Then she heard the spatter of raindrops against the window. The sun had shone so persistently every day since the snowstorm that Miranda was surprised by the change in weather. She got out of bed and crossed to the window and peered out. Not only was it raining, it had apparently been doing so all during her restless, sleepless night. Rainwater had pooled around the corral and lay in wide puddles across the backyard.

"Darn." She wasn't going to be riding anywhere today, not unless she wanted to get soaked through. The roads would be deep in mud, so slippery that her horse might take a fall. She was going to have to wait until the rain stopped and the road dried out to make her grand gesture.

She saw a light in the barn and wondered how long Jake had been awake. She hoped he'd slept as badly as she had!

She sighed. Marriage was a lot harder than she'd thought it would be. Talking with a husband was much more difficult than talking to a sibling. There was so much room for misunderstanding. She hadn't meant to hurt Jake's feelings. She hadn't realized she *could* hurt Jake's feelings. She was sorry she had.

She'd liked what he'd done to her in bed. It had made her feel close to him, closer than she'd ever felt to another human being. It had hurt at first, but as both Jake and her friend at the orphanage had promised, the pain was over quickly.

What had come afterward had been nice. Very nice. Until Jake admitted his reasons for making love to her. That *loving* was no part of what he'd done. That he'd been *taking* rather than *giving*.

She hoped they'd made a baby last night. Then it wouldn't matter if Jake never touched her again for the rest of her life. She'd still have a little one to love.

She sighed again. Marriage was for life. She would be smart to make peace with her husband. Unfortunately, she'd never been able to go along to get along. She had the stripes on her back to prove it. Maybe there was some middle ground. She would have to see if she could find it.

Miranda was about to move away from the window when she saw a strange-looking wagon with a white canvas top appear over a slight rise in the road. She knew what it was, of course. She'd seen pictures of Conestoga wagons in the Chicago newspaper, in stories about wagon trains heading west. But how had a single Conestoga wagon ended up here at Jake's ranch?

As she watched, the wagon slipped precariously from side to side on the muddy road as the six mules pulling it struggled for footing. The large back wheels seemed to be stuck for a moment and the man on the bench seat used a bullwhip to urge the mules to pull harder. The wagon slid again and the left rear wheel fell into a gully alongside the road. The mules kept pulling, and the wooden wheel snapped in two with a crack so loud Miranda heard it even through the closed window.

She watched in horror as the wagon began to topple sideways. The man on the bench yanked hard on the reins, trying to keep the frightened mules from bolting. He finally managed to calm them, then jumped down, slipping and sliding and falling on one knee, before grasping the back of the wagon. He reached his arms up and came away with a stout woman wearing a heavy skirt.

He set her carefully on the ground, then stood back at arm's length to look at her, brushing at her face and leaving a streak of mud from his hand. When the woman turned sideways, Miranda saw she was very, very pregnant.

The man looked toward the house and Miranda realized she could be seen through the window in her nightgown. She stepped back out of view and stared down at the couple. She was turning away to dress when she caught sight of movement from the corner of her eye. She leaned back in time to see Jake ride out from the stable on horseback to greet the couple.

He spoke with them briefly, then took the woman up before him on his horse, while the man followed behind on foot. Miranda realized they were headed for the house and hurried to dress herself. She was glad she'd taken the time to alter some of Priscilla's clothes and pulled on a dark blue skirt and white blouse over her chemise and pantalets. She pulled on long socks and hooked a pair of half boots onto her feet and then ran down the stairs.

She was halfway down when she realized her hair was still in its night braid. She started to turn around and go back up, but she wanted to be there when Jake arrived in order to greet their company. She realized that Jake had lit a fire in the kitchen stove before he'd left the house—or had come into the house from the barn before dawn to do so. He'd put a kettle on to heat water for washing, and it smelled like he'd also brewed a pot of coffee.

She wondered how a man could be so thoughtful—and so judgmental and stubborn and foolish—all at the same time.

Miranda opened the back door when she heard the three of them dropping their muddy shoes on the back porch. "Welcome," she said. "Come in and get dry."

She saw the woman was very young and had wide-spaced brown eyes and a beaked nose. Her husband, who had astonishingly blue eyes and a nose as straight as a ruler, couldn't have been more than a year or two older than she was. What on earth were they doing out here in the middle of Texas all by themselves?

"This is my wife, Miranda," Jake said, making the introductions as the couple entered the kitchen in stocking feet. "Miranda, this is Mr. and Mrs. Mueller. They're on their way to Fredericksburg, west of Austin, to live with Mr. Mueller's brother, Augustus."

"I am Heinrich," the young man said with a heavy German accent, taking off his dripping hat and holding it in front of him, nodding in greeting to Miranda. "This is my wife, Gretta."

"So nice to meet you," the young German woman said with a smile, her hands wrapped around her belly. Her English was even more heavily accented than her husband's.

"It's nice to meet you, too," Miranda said. "Come in and sit down where it's warm. Are you hungry? I was just about to make breakfast for—"

"She's in labor," Jake interrupted in a harsh voice.

Miranda stared at the young woman. She looked perfectly normal. "Really?" she asked, not quite believing what Jake had said. Miranda's mother had gone to bed at the first hint of labor and stayed hidden in her bedroom with the midwife—moaning and groaning and crying out in pain—until each of her children were born.

Gretta lowered her eyes shyly. "I am afraid it is true. The baby was not due for three more weeks, but I have been having pains for four hours already. I am sorry to be so much trouble."

Miranda looked at Jake and said, "Is there a doctor close by you can call to come help with the delivery?"

Jake shook his head.

She looked at him mutely. *Then who's going to de-*

liver this baby? "Maybe your mother can help," she suggested.

"I can't get across Bitter Creek," he said curtly. "With this much rain, the water will be running too high and fast."

"It is our first child," Heinrich said. "We planned to be at my brother's home in Fredericksburg when Gretta's time came. My brother's wife has six children. She would know what to do."

"Heinrich says neither of them has any experience with birthing a baby," Jake added.

"I don't either," Miranda admitted. She looked Jake in the eye and said, "You're the only one who does."

He shook his head. "I can't help her. I'm sorry. I can't."

His voice was shaky, Miranda noticed, and a little frantic.

"Having a baby is a natural thing," Gretta said, the calmest of them all, Miranda thought. "We will make do, yah?"

"I'll go milk the cow," Jake said.

Miranda recognized the offer for the excuse it was to escape, since it was Nick's job to milk the cow.

"I'll see if Slim can make breakfast for everyone while I take care of Gretta," she said. She met Jake's panicked gaze and asked with her eyes, *Are you going to help me with this?*

"I'll be in the barn," he said.

Apparently not, Miranda thought with dismay. "Please help yourself to a cup of coffee," she told Heinrich. "I'm going to get Gretta settled upstairs."

She started toward the kitchen doorway with Gretta, but the woman suddenly stopped in her tracks. Her eyes closed and she put her hands on either side of her enormous belly, panting through her mouth.

"She is having a contraction," Heinrich said.

Miranda stared, entranced. The young woman didn't make a sound. Her face didn't scrunch up in pain. She wasn't even lying down, she was standing in the middle of Miranda's kitchen. Within a very short time, Gretta took a deep breath and let it out. Then she opened her eyes, met Miranda's concerned gaze, and smiled. "We can go now."

"Aren't you in pain?"

Gretta shook her head as she followed Miranda to the stairs. "The pains come only for a few seconds. Between the pains, there is nothing. At the end, the pains will be longer and closer together. Now, I am fine."

Miranda was astonished. "Is it the same for all women?" She'd imagined her mother in pain every moment she was in labor. Gretta shrugged. "I do not know. This is what is true for my mama and my sister and me."

Miranda wondered if Gretta's labor would be any shorter than her own mother's had been. Miranda's mother had sworn that she'd spent sixteen hours trying to push her first child from her body. The rest of her siblings had come in less time, between eight and twelve hours, with Josie coming in only four.

She stopped by Slim's room and knocked and explained the situation to him through the crack in the door, whereupon he readily agreed to help with breakfast. Then she headed upstairs with Gretta. She wanted to make sure they weren't still on the stairs when the young woman had her next contraction.

"Miranda? I heard strange voices downstairs," Nick said. He was only half dressed and crossed his arms over his bare chest when he spied the strange woman on the landing at the top of the stairs.

"This is Mrs. Mueller, Nick. She's in labor. She and her husband are going to stay with us until she has her baby and they're able to get the wheel fixed on their wagon. Why don't you help Harry and Anna Mae get dressed. I've asked Slim to make breakfast."

"I saw Jake leave the house," Nick said.

"He's milking the cow. I'd appreciate it if you'd go gather some eggs. I think Slim has an extra rain slicker you can use. We're going to need all the eggs we can get with company here."

"Sure," Nick said, eyeing the pregnant woman as he backed his way down the hall to the room he now shared with Harry and Anna Mae.

"You have three children?" Gretta asked.

Miranda laughed. "No. I have two brothers, and Jake has a daughter."

"You have no babies together?"

"Not yet," Miranda said. Not *yet*? Not *ever* if Jake got his way. "Here we are," Miranda said as she led Gretta into her bedroom. "I'm sorry everything is such a mess." She realized both her clothes and some of Jake's from the previous night were strewn around the room. She quickly gathered them up. "Let me change the sheets before you lie down."

"I will help," Gretta said. "If you do not mind, I would rather sit in the rocker as long as I can. Maybe Heinrich can bring my crocheting to me. I am making a cap for the baby. I want to finish it before he—or she—is born."

Miranda was frankly agog at how little Gretta seemed to be affected by her labor. "How far apart are the pains right now?"

Gretta pursed her lips, apparently calculating, and said, "Fifteen minutes, I think."

"How close will they be at the end?" Miranda asked.

"They will come practically on top of one another and be very powerful." Gretta caught her lower lip between her teeth and for the first time looked like the inexperienced almost-mother she was. "I am a little worried about the end," she admitted. "My mama said it hurts worse than anything a woman can imagine. But one is rewarded in the end with a child to love, so it is all worth it."

"Can I get you something to eat?" Miranda asked.

Gretta shook her head. "My mama tells me it is not good to eat once labor begins. I will eat after."

Miranda thought how fortunate she was to have this experience. Not that she wasn't a little frightened, but she was learning a great deal about childbirth she hadn't known. Perhaps her mother would have told her all about it at some point, but Gretta's experience seemed very different from that of Miranda's mother. Now she would see for herself exactly what childbirth was all about.

What if something went wrong?

Miranda didn't mention that possibility to Gretta, who remained cheerful over the next four hours as her labor progressed, happy to crochet between contractions. The pains did in fact begin to come closer together and they were longer and stronger, too.

Miranda hadn't seen Jake since he'd brought the

couple to the house that morning. He hadn't come in for breakfast or lunch. She wanted to be sure he would be available to help if there were any problems when the baby started to come.

"Would you mind if I leave you for a little while?" Miranda asked the young German woman.

"I am—" Gretta stopped speaking, dropped her crochet needles and the tiny cap in her lap, and gripped the arms of the rocker so hard Miranda thought she might break them in half.

Miranda stood mesmerized as the contraction went on. And on. She heard a low groan issue from Gretta's throat that also went on. And on.

"That was a hard one," Gretta said after the contraction ended. "It will not be long now. I think I will get in the bed."

Miranda helped Gretta into the bed, on which the young woman had instructed her to lay newspaper. "My mama said there will be blood. We do not want to stain your sheets."

At the word *blood,* Miranda felt the inherent danger of the situation for the first time. "I need to speak with my husband," she said. "I'll be back as soon as I can. If you need help, just yell."

The German girl grinned. "I will."

Miranda found herself grinning back. The sweat on Gretta's forehead proved that labor was hard work, but the girl also made the pain of labor seem manageable. Her eyes, however, looked less certain than they had several hours ago. In fact, they looked a little frightened.

"I'll be right back!" Miranda called over her shoul-

der as she ran down the stairs. She was still running
when she reached the kitchen.

Heinrich leaped up from his seat at the kitchen
table and caught her arm before she reached the back
door. "Is my wife all right?"

Miranda managed to smile and say, "She's fine. Her
labor is progressing normally. It won't be long now."
She tried to take another step, but Heinrich wouldn't
release her arm.

"Are you sure everything is okay?" he demanded.

"I believe so, yes," Miranda said. "Please, I need to
speak with my husband."

Heinrich seemed to realize he was still holding her
arm and let her go. "I am sorry," he said. "I am worried."

She smiled sympathetically. "I would tell you if
anything was wrong. It isn't."

"Thank you," he said.

Miranda hurried out the back door before he could
ask her any more questions. Too late, she realized it
was still drizzling. She hadn't brought a shawl or anything else to cover her hair. Once it was wet, it tended
to curl even tighter. She began to run.

Miranda felt her feet sliding out from under her
and tried to stop her momentum by leaning forward,
then backward again. Her body was too unbalanced,
and she quickly realized her only choice was whether
to fall forward or backward. She landed on her rump
in the mud, breaking her fall with her hands.

She lifted her muddy hands and stared at them.

"Are you all right?"

She looked up to find Jake standing over her. He
reached down and pulled her upright.

"I'm fine. Just a little muddy."

"A little?" he said.

She shook her hands to sling off the extra mud, then wiped them on her skirt. "I was coming to talk to you."

"I figured that. Let's get out of the rain."

He opened his rain slicker and pulled her inside and headed back toward the barn.

She grabbed his belt in back and stopped walking, bringing him to an abrupt halt. "Why don't we go back to the house to talk? I need to get cleaned up."

"You can clean up in the barn."

He slid an arm around her waist, and she found herself being swept in the direction of the barn again. She didn't fight him. His body was as taut as the barbed wire that fenced Three Oaks.

The barn smelled of manure and hay and horses, a smell she'd come to like. He led her to a pump at one end of the barn and pumped water into a pail. "You can wash up here."

"Jake," she said as she stepped up to the pail and began rinsing her muddy hands. "I can't deliver that baby without your help."

"How far apart are the contractions?"

She stared at him, surprised by the question. "About five minutes, I guess."

"Then what are you doing out here?"

"What do you mean?"

"That baby's not going to wait much longer to be born."

"That's why I'm out here," Miranda said. "I don't know what to do, Jake. You do."

"I'll tell you what to do, but I'm not going in there."

Miranda turned to him, wiping her hands dry on a clean spot on the front of her skirt and said, "Jacob Creed, I'm only going to say this once. You are coming into that house and you are going to help me deliver that baby. Do you hear me?"

"It would be hard not to, since you're yelling."

Miranda's face flared with heat. "This is no time for joking. Gretta's life may depend on your experience with childbirth. You are not going to cower out here in the barn and let her die. And that is that!"

"All right."

Miranda had been expecting him to fight her. Having him agree took the wind out of her sails. "All right?"

His face had never looked so grim as he said, "I'll help deliver the damned baby."

Chapter Twenty-six

Jake had spent a miserable morning in the barn reliving every detail of his first wife's final hours. Reliving his futile efforts to help his child be born. Reliving his frustration and despair as he tried to breathe life into his lifeless son.

It did no good to remind himself that Anna Mae had been born with no trouble at all. Priss had woken up in labor, and before the sun had set, she'd presented him with a wailing baby daughter. He'd sent for help, but it hadn't arrived in time.

He was the one who'd caught the tiny little girl in his hands as she slipped from his wife's body. He was the one who'd tied off and cut the cord. He was the one who'd handed their daughter to his wife, both of them laughing and crying at the same time. Finally, he was the one who'd wrapped the afterbirth in newspaper and removed it to be buried behind the house.

He'd expected the second birth to follow the same course, with the same happy ending. But Priss had labored and labored and the child had not been born. When at last, exhausted, she'd expelled the child, the cord had been wrapped around its neck. The perfectly formed little boy was blue.

Jake had known his son was dead, but he'd tried to breathe life into the child anyway. It hadn't worked.

He couldn't bear to go through anything like that again.

All morning he'd been telling himself that this wasn't his child. If it died, he might be sad, but his heart wouldn't be torn from his chest. It did no good. Whenever he thought of going anywhere near Gretta Mueller, his hands trembled and his body shivered and he felt as though he was going to throw up.

He felt Miranda grasp his hand and twine her fingers through his. As they stepped onto the back porch, she turned to him and said, "You can do this, Jake. I'll be there to help. Heinrich is a little anxious, though."

Jake opened the back door and found himself greeted by a man who was beside himself with worry.

"I want to see my wife," Heinrich begged.

Miranda looked to Jake for guidance.

"You should wait down here," Jake said flatly. If things went wrong, it would be better if Heinrich wasn't in the room. "We'll call you if we need you for anything. Come on, Miranda."

This time Jake grabbed her hand. He needed to hold onto something, or he thought he might turn around and run as fast as his legs could carry him back to the barn.

Miranda pulled him into the bedroom behind her and announced, "I brought Jake."

"I thought you forgot about me," Gretta said.

Jake was surprised to see Gretta still sitting up in bed with a pillow behind her, rather than lying down. She'd definitely been laboring hard. Her brown hair was plastered to her brow with sweat, and her hands were twined in the sheets as though she'd been gripping them tightly.

"How far apart are the pains?" he asked.

"Close. Oh, no. Here comes another one," she said with a moan.

"Close the door," Jake ordered Miranda. No sense having Heinrich hearing his wife's agony as she brought their child into the world. Jake shut out the sounds she made, giving orders to Miranda about what he would need to deliver the child when it came.

She'd already put newspaper on the bed under Gretta, but he sent her to find a knife to cut the cord and string to tie it off and hot water to wash mother and child after the birth. "I'll stay here with Gretta," he said.

He sat on the edge of the bed and waited until the powerful contraction passed. "You can scream if you want," he said.

"It would only frighten Heinrich," she said breathlessly.

Before she got the sentence out, she groaned again and reached for his hand. He was amazed, as he had been with Priss, at how mighty this small woman's grasp became as she fought against the pain of childbirth. He watched her belly ripple as her body contracted to expel its burden, and the baby moved within her.

He knew he needed to check to see how far along she was, but he didn't want to embarrass her. "I need to look," he explained, "to see how the baby is doing."

"All right," she said.

"Let's get you comfortable first," he said as he rearranged the pillow, then scooted her down in the bed. He'd barely gotten her settled when she was gripped with another powerful contraction. She grabbed the sheets and waged war with the pain.

"Don't fight it," he said.

He watched her grit her teeth and growl and realized she was starting to push. "Wait," he said.

"I caaaannnnn't!" she yelled. Her feet were flat on the bed and her back was arched like a bow.

He shoved the sheet up. There was no time for modesty now. The baby was coming . . . or it was not. He needed to be ready in case the child's nose and mouth needed to be cleared.

"Miranda!" he shouted. "Where are you?"

She arrived at the door in the next instant, carrying all the supplies he'd asked for. "I'm here!" She stopped cold when she realized he had the sheet pushed up, exposing . . . everything. Her eyes went wide in shock and, he thought, a little in horror.

The baby's head had crowned. The sight had frightened Jake the first time he saw it. He knew it meant the birth was imminent. "Put that pitcher of hot water on the chest beside the bed, then bring everything else over here," he said brusquely.

"It's coooommmmmming!" Gretta grated out as her body contorted.

"Set those things on the bed and be ready with the towel," Jake ordered Miranda.

He saw the baby was coming headfirst and facedown, which he knew was good. Maybe it was going to be all right. Maybe there would be no difficulties. Maybe this baby would be born alive and well.

Despite Gretta's prediction, the baby didn't come. Contractions continued wracking her body at short intervals, but the baby's head didn't move.

"Is the baby stuck?" Miranda whispered to him.

He didn't want to say it, because he didn't want it to be true. It was his own personal nightmare come to life.

"Is there anything we can do?" Miranda asked.

"What's wrong?" Gretta said. "Why are you—" Her body was wrenched with another contraction so hard it cut off speech.

When the contraction passed, Jake tried to tell whether the baby's head had moved. He wondered how long the infant could stay like this without suffocating. He wondered whether the cord might be wrapped around its neck.

"I have to do something," he said.

"What can you do?" Miranda asked in a frightened voice.

"Give me the knife," he said.

"What are you going to do?"

"Give me the damned knife, Miranda." His hand was shaking when he took it from her. He'd thought about doing what he was about to do when his wife had been in so much trouble. He'd talked himself out of it, telling himself everything would be fine. He wasn't going to take that chance this time. There was something he could do to help the baby be born. He just needed the courage to do it.

"Go get a needle and some thread," he said.

"Now?" she asked skeptically.

"Now!" He didn't want Miranda to see what he was about to do. If it worked, as he hoped it would, she would need to sew up the cut he was about to make. He met Gretta's frightened gaze and said, "I'm going to make a small cut, so there'll be more room for the baby's head. I think maybe it'll help. I don't have anything to deaden the pain."

"It cannot be any worse than the pain I am enduring now," she said, panting as another contraction began. She bit down on her lip to stop a scream.

And Jake used the knife to cut a wider opening for the baby's head.

The timing must have been right, or maybe the baby had just needed a little bit more time before it came into the world. In any case, as Gretta bore down, the baby's head slid out of her body, followed by the shoulders, arms, and legs.

"It's a boy," Jake said. His shoulders were hunched as he waited to see whether the baby would take a breath. He shoved a finger in its mouth and came away with a ball of mucus. He held the boy up by his legs and heard a tiny wail.

He grinned. "He's got good lungs."

Gretta smiled tiredly.

Miranda appeared in the doorway, needle and thread in hand. "I heard a cry. Is the baby—"

"He's fine," Jake said as he wrapped the baby in the towel Miranda had left open on the bed. He laid the baby in its mother's arms, then crossed to Miranda. "I had to make a cut. You'll need to sew it back together as soon as she delivers the placenta."

Gretta's feet were still flat on the bed, her knees

holding up the sheet, revealing Jake's handiwork. He watched closely to gauge the look on Miranda's face when she saw the small cut he'd made. It was bleeding, but not very much.

"Oh, Jake, what a good idea," she said, looking at him, her eyes bright with tears. "You saved the baby."

Jake felt a painful knot form in his throat. Maybe he had. Maybe the baby would have come anyway. He was just glad both mother and baby were fine.

He waited for the afterbirth and wrapped it in the newspaper and set it aside. "I'll leave you to do your sewing. When you're done, come down and get Heinrich."

Jake left the room and headed downstairs. He met Heinrich at the bottom landing and said, "You have a son."

"Can I go upstairs now?"

"In a few minutes," Jake said, putting a hand on Heinrich's shoulder. "Miranda is making Gretta pretty for you."

"Are they both all right?" Heinrich asked. "Mother and baby both?"

"Both are fine," Jake reassured him. "I have to go outside for a minute. Miranda will call you when you can go up."

Jake hurried outside and barely made it past the porch before he leaned over and lost the contents of his stomach. Not that there was much in it to lose. He hadn't eaten all day. He went to the pump and rinsed his mouth out.

Then he headed for the stable. He hadn't finished mucking out the stalls. Maybe the work would help the trembling to stop.

He hadn't been working long when he heard Miranda call, "Jake? Are you in here?"

"Here," he called from one of the stalls.

"Why aren't you in the house? Heinrich has a bottle of champagne in his wagon. He wants to celebrate."

"I hope you got a good look at what you'll be subjected to if you get pregnant," Jake said.

"It was miraculous," she gushed.

Jake knew she was still basking in the glow of happiness she'd seen on Gretta's face when the new mother had held her son in her arms.

"She could have died and left her husband a widower with a baby to raise," Jake said.

"But she didn't," Miranda pointed out. "They have a son, Jake. A son to love and raise into a fine man."

"You just don't get it," he said in disgust.

"I get it, Jake," she said quietly. "I know there are risks. Oh, but the rewards, Jake. The rewards are worth it."

"You say that because you aren't going to be the one left behind to mourn. You aren't going to be the one—" He couldn't finish. His throat had swollen closed.

She took him in her arms and pulled his head down beside hers and crooned words of comfort in his ear as he fought back tears.

His arms tightened around her. He didn't want her ever to get pregnant. No child was worth the risk of losing her. Somehow, she'd found her way into his heart. He wasn't just *in love* with her. God help him, he *loved* her.

Chapter Twenty-seven

Miranda thought her sisters must be worried sick. She'd been in Texas for nearly two months, and she still hadn't sent them a letter telling them that she and the boys had arrived safely and that she was married. She'd never imagined how difficult something as simple as posting a letter would be.

Her plans to get Jake's mother to help her post her letters had been postponed by the arrival of Gretta and Heinrich Mueller's new son. The young couple had stayed at Three Oaks almost a month, giving Gretta time to recover enough to complete their journey to Fredericksburg and allowing Jake and Heinrich time to repair the broken wheel on the Muellers' wagon.

During that time, Miranda checked daily on Gretta to make sure her stitches were healing and that she didn't develop an infection. She'd also observed closely as Gretta breastfed her newborn, watching to see how the baby suckled and grew, both curious and fascinated. She'd changed the baby and played with him and watched him sleep, marveling at his tiny fingernails and delicate eyelashes, burping him and listening for the gurgling sounds he made while he slept.

All that experience was going to be very worthwhile. Because Miranda was pretty sure she was pregnant.

In all the excitement of having company, she hadn't noticed when she'd missed her monthly courses. She was a week late when she finally realized, with some shock, that she had not bled since the night her husband had made her his wife.

Miranda hadn't immediately assumed she was pregnant. She might simply be excited or anxious. Just . . . late. Not that she'd ever been late even once during all the years she'd been having her monthly courses. But there was always a first time for everything.

She could only pretend for so long. As the days passed with no sign of her courses, her breasts had become tender, and lately, she felt bilious in the morning.

Miranda still wasn't absolutely, positively certain she was with child. The only way to know, really, was to wait and see if her courses came after the Muellers left . . . or whether her body started to increase as the baby grew inside her.

At the orphanage, when Miranda had dreamed of marriage to a handsome prince and imagined living happily ever after, part of that dream had been seeing the look of joy on her husband's face when she told him she was going to bear his child.

She tried to imagine that delighted look on Jake's face. She couldn't. Jake wasn't going to be happy to hear she was pregnant. In fact, he might even be furious. It was disappointing, to say the least, to be married to a man who was opposed to his wife getting pregnant.

Knowing Jake's likely reaction dimmed her own joy. She felt resentful, even though she understood the reasons for his attitude. Besides, the situation she found herself in wasn't entirely her fault. It took two to make a baby, after all. Miranda figured there was no sense telling Jake anything until she was certain herself.

But first things first. She wanted that letter sent to her sisters.

The morning the Muellers left, Miranda waited for Jake to head out onto the range to check on his cattle, then made her preparations for a visit to Bitter Creek. She tucked her precious letter into a pocket of Jake's Levi's. She'd considered wearing a skirt for her first visit to Bitter Creek, but she planned to ride horseback and Jake had no sidesaddle. Trousers were far more practical.

Besides, if trousers were good enough for Jake's mother, they were good enough for her.

Miranda asked Slim to watch the kids while she went for a long walk to get some fresh air, after having been confined to the house for so long with Gretta. She'd debated whether to tell Slim the truth about where she was going, but she knew how he felt about the Blackthornes, and she didn't want to argue with him.

She did tell Nick where she was going. "I'll probably be gone till suppertime. You can tell Slim where I am after I've gone."

"Can't I come along?" Nick asked. "I can ride as well as you now."

"I need you to stay here, in case Slim needs you."

"Aw, Miranda. I never get to have any fun."

It was amazing to Miranda that Nick felt himself entitled to have "fun." Fun had been no part of their lives at the orphanage. She suddenly felt glad that she'd brought the two boys with her. She promised herself right then and there that she would try to make fun a bigger part of their lives from now on.

She brushed at Nick's cowlick as he ducked away, and said, "We'll go on another picnic soon, down by the creek. Maybe Jake will teach you to fish. How would that be?" She could see the idea of fishing appealed to him.

"That sounds great! When can we go?"

"How about Sunday afternoon?"

"I can't wait to tell Harry. Come back safe!" Nick whispered as he hugged her.

"I will."

Miranda figured that so long as she stayed on the road, she couldn't get lost. In addition, she was less likely to run into wildlife on a well-traveled road. She urged her horse to a mile-eating trot, feeling excited at the thought of the adventure ahead of her.

She learned over the next several hours that calling this road "well-traveled" might be a Texan's idea of a joke. She'd known Jake's ranch was isolated, but after growing up in a city where one was never alone, there was something eerie about riding half the morning without seeing another living soul. She felt relieved when she reached the turnoff to Bitter Creek.

The sun felt good on her back. Since she was dressed in trousers, she'd worn the flat-crowned Western hat Slim had loaned her a few days after she'd arrived at

Three Oaks, rather than one of Priscilla's bonnets, so she wouldn't get sunburned. She had to constantly brush at horseflies, and she could feel her shirt getting damp as she perspired in the heat, but otherwise, she was enjoying herself enormously.

Nevertheless, Miranda had heard enough warnings from Jake about the hazards in this wilderness that she kept a constant watch for danger. When she saw the three cowboys on horseback in the distance, she felt concerned but not alarmed. When she realized they were herding cattle, she relaxed. These must be cowhands working for Blackthorne. As such, they should be no threat to her.

Mrs. Swenson had explained to her on the stage that women were revered in the West because they were so scarce. Any man harming a woman could expect to be hunted down and hanged.

When the cowhands changed their direction so they were moving the cattle to cross her path, she decided they were doing so because they wanted to say hello. Perhaps they wanted to meet her, since she was new to the neighborhood. Once she identified herself as Blackthorne's daughter-in-law, they were sure to be courteous.

She didn't move any faster or slower to avoid them.

She didn't feel concern even when the cowboys left their cattle and rode in a group to cut her off on the road.

"Hello, missy," the cowboy in the middle said. "What are you doing out here all alone?"

"I'm Mrs. Creed," Miranda said, identifying herself so there could be no mistake who she was.

"Never saw a pretty little filly like you wearin'

trousers," the cowboy in the middle said. "Those are nice gams you got there, missy."

"Watch it, Call," the cowboy on the right said. "She's a lady."

Call snorted. "You ever seen a real lady wearin' trousers? I think maybe she's some other kind of female."

"I'm not—"

Miranda had never seen anyone move so fast. Call spurred his mount close, slid an arm around her waist, and yanked her off her horse. He pulled her tight against his chest, leaving her feet dangling off the ground.

She tried to draw breath to scream, but fear had caused all the oxygen to leave her lungs. She was left with her mouth open wide in terror but no sound coming out.

"Hey, Call!" the cowboy on the left said. "Put her down."

"Ain't done with her yet," Call said with a smirk, leaning down to try and kiss her.

Miranda was too frightened to scream, but she reached out with her nails and scratched four bloody furrows down the cowboy's cheek.

"You bitch!" He dropped the reins and slapped her hard across the face.

The blow left Miranda seeing stars.

"You're buyin' yourself a heap of trouble," one of the cowboys said. "Lady's the wife of the boss's stepson."

"The boss hates his stepson," Call said. "He ain't gonna mind if we play a little bit with Creed's wife."

"You're wrong about that."

The voice came from behind Miranda. All three cowboys whirled their horses so they could see the intruder, Call holding her tight around the waist as they turned their mounts. Miranda's eyes went wide when she realized the man who'd objected to her rough treatment was none other than Alexander Blackthorne.

"Put her down easy, Call," Blackthorne said.

The cowboy slid Miranda down along his horse onto the ground. She stumbled when her knees threatened to buckle but managed to stay on her feet. As she backed away from Call, one of the other two cowboys led her horse over to her.

"Here you go, ma'am. You need any help mounting?"

Miranda didn't want to be touched by anyone, but her legs felt so boneless she couldn't lift her foot up to the stirrup.

A moment later Blackthorne was standing by her side. He clasped his hands together and said, "Put your foot here, and I'll boost you up."

She did as he instructed and found herself back in the saddle. "Thank you," she said.

"Wait here a minute, and I'll give you an escort to the house."

"I'm fine—"

"Wait here."

It was an order. She decided to wait.

She wasn't ready for what happened next. Blackthorne turned and grabbed the cowboy named Call by the front of his shirt and tumbled him from his horse. Once the cowboy's feet were on the ground, Blackthorne hit him hard with his fist, right on his chin. Call was stocky enough that the punch didn't knock him down. And stupid enough to swing back at Blackthorne.

The older man ducked the blow and hit Call hard in the solar plexus. Call was bent over double, at which point Blackthorne hit him again in the chin from below, so his head snapped back and he fell down. Miranda thought he was out cold.

"Put him back on his horse and get him out of here," Blackthorne ordered.

The other two cowboys quickly manhandled Call facedown over his saddle.

"The three of you pick up your wages and be off Bitter Creek before noon. Any of you still around after that will be shot on sight."

"Me and Lonnie didn't do nothin'!" one of the cowboys protested, as the two left standing gathered up the reins of their horses, and that of the unconscious man, and stepped back into their saddles.

"That's right," Blackthorne said in a harsh voice as he remounted his horse. "You sat there and watched that piece of trash manhandle a woman and did nothing."

"That's not fair," the cowboy named Lonnie said. "How were we supposed to stop him?"

Blackthorne snorted. "Fair? Far as I'm concerned, you all ought to be shot. Matter of fact—"

When Blackthorne reached for the rifle in a boot on his saddle, the two cowboys spurred their horses and galloped away, dragging the third horse and its unconscious burden behind them.

Miranda's whole body was trembling, and she couldn't seem to get it to stop. Her teeth were chattering as she said, "Thank you. I don't know what would have happened if you hadn't come along."

"I do," he said curtly. "It wouldn't have been pretty. What the hell are you doing out here all by yourself?"

The cowboy who'd attacked her had pulled several strands of hair out of her braid and the wind was blowing them across her mouth. When she raised her shaking hand to push the blond curl away, she heard Blackthorne say, "Goddamn it, I should have shot those sons of bitches!"

She dropped her hand, which felt as heavy as lead, and stared down at the saddle.

He kneed his horse closer and said, "You're in shock. Here, drink this."

She took the silver flask from him with hands that shook and took a sip. The bitter liquid burned her throat and made her cough. She could feel it all the way down to her belly. She was still shaking when she handed the flask back, and now her eyes were watering.

"Come on," he said. "Follow me."

He kicked his horse into a canter, and she did the same to her own. The rocking motion of the horse was calming, she discovered, and knowing that she had a protector with her did a great deal to settle her nerves.

She couldn't believe how close she'd been to her destination. She could have spurred her horse and escaped the cowboys and been at the Bitter Creek ranch house in minutes.

But she hadn't realized the danger the cowboys presented. She'd thought she was safe. She'd expected civility. She hadn't been prepared for such unfeeling brutality.

Miranda shivered. She was so very cold. She felt so very dirty. She wanted Jake. "I want to go home," she said in a small voice.

"Cricket!" Blackthorne yelled as they rode up to the back door of a beautiful two-story mansion. "Come on out here."

Jake's mother arrived on the back porch so quickly, Miranda figured she must have been in the kitchen.

"One of the hands assaulted her," he said.

Miranda wasn't aware of much that happened after that. Except she distinctly heard Cricket say, "You better go get Jake."

Chapter Twenty-eight

Jake saw Blackthorne before his stepfather saw him. Jake was in a gully, trying to move a longhorn cow and her calf out of the brush. He considered letting his nemesis ride by without saying anything, but he felt galled by the fact that Blackthorne was riding across Three Oaks as though he already owned it.

Jake spurred his horse up out of the gully and came out in front of the other man's horse, forcing it backward. "What are you doing on my land?"

"Your wife was attacked by one of my cowhands. She needs you."

Jake felt like he'd been sucker punched. All the air left his lungs, and he was speechless for a moment. "Is she all right?"

"She's shaken up pretty bad." Blackthorne hesitated, then added, "She's got a bruise on her cheek."

Jake felt the blood leave his head in a rush and grabbed the horn to keep himself from tilting out of the saddle. He made himself ask, "Is that all?"

"I got there in time to keep anything else from happening."

"What about the man who attacked her? What happened to him?"

"I sent that mangy cur off with his tail between his legs."

Jake stared at his stepfather in disbelief. "You let him go? To maybe do the same thing to another woman someday? You didn't punish him?"

"Are you going to sit there ranting at me, or do you want to go see to your wife?"

Jake didn't understand Alexander Blackthorne. The Englishman played by a different set of rules than Jake had learned. Blackthorne seemed merciless in business. He *was* merciless in business. But he didn't have the strict sense of justice—the willingness to become judge and jury and executioner—that Jake had grown up with in the West.

There were no judges out here and very few lawmen. Once a man was identified as an outlaw—as a rustler or a horse thief or a man who interfered with women—he was killed like the vermin he was. Otherwise, he became a nuisance and a plague on the land.

"You should have shot him on the spot," Jake muttered as he spurred his horse toward Bitter Creek.

"What was your wife doing on the road to Bitter Creek by herself?" Blackthorne asked as he roweled his mount to ride at Jake's side.

Jake had no answer. "That isn't the point. She should have been safe no matter whose land she was on."

"She gave a good account of herself," Blackthorne said.

"What do you mean?"

"Scratched up that cowboy like some she-cat."

"Good for her." Jake knew from his own experience that his wife gave as good as she got. "You could have sent someone to find me. Why did you come yourself?"

Blackthorne smiled wryly. "My wife sent me. She said I wasn't to come back without you."

"You could have simply brought my wife home."

"Oh, you don't know? Your wife has a visitor at Bitter Creek. That was the reason I happened to be out on the road when she was attacked."

A visitor? That was news to Jake. Had Miranda's sisters somehow found their way to Texas? "Who is it?"

"Her uncle, Stephen Wentworth. Apparently he was looking for his niece at Three Oaks and took the wrong road and ended up at Bitter Creek. Very coincidental that your wife was on her way to my house today, don't you think?"

"That's exactly what it was," Jake said. "Coincidence. Miranda hasn't had any communication with her family since she married me."

"That still doesn't explain what she was doing on her way to Bitter Creek today."

"How should I know what got into her head?" Jake said irritably. "When I left the house, she was going to have Slim teach her how to make lye soap."

Jake also didn't believe in coincidences. He just couldn't figure out how Miranda could have communicated with her uncle. Unless she'd planned all along to meet him on a certain date. He realized he didn't know much about his wife and her family, except that she'd lied to him about how many of them there were.

It was the uncle who'd put them in the orphanage, and left them there.

So what was her uncle doing here in Texas?

"He's an officious bastard, that uncle of hers," Blackthorne said. "And rich as avarice, unless I miss my guess."

Jake wasn't sure what *officious* meant, or *avarice* either, but the contempt in Blackthorne's voice matched Miranda's description of her uncle's unsavory behavior toward his nieces and nephews. "Wonder what he's doing here."

Blackthorne eyed Jake cynically. "Parents dead, kids in an orphanage, who gets all the money?"

"Miranda's father owned a bank, but it burned down."

"Wentworth let it slip that his brother was *the* Chicago banker for anyone who is anyone in that town."

Jake had known Miranda's father had a bank, but he hadn't focused on what that meant. Probably because Miranda had never acted like someone used to being waited on, someone with a lot of pretty dresses, someone used to having her every wish granted. She was helpful and hardworking. She'd seemed satisfied with what little he could give her. And she'd come to him a desperate woman, a mail-order bride.

"Do you suppose she had some money coming to her on her marriage that she didn't know about?" Jake asked. "And that's why he's here? To give it to her?"

Blackthorne laughed scornfully and shook his head. "I doubt that chap plans to give up a penny of whatever money he's stolen from your bride. I figure he's here to make sure he gets to keep whatever he took from her when she was too young to know better."

Miranda rich? Jake couldn't imagine it. Would she stay with him if she didn't need to for financial reasons? Or would she go back to Chicago and set up housekeeping with her sisters and brothers? It was a sobering thought.

"You might be wrong," Jake said. "He treated Miranda and her siblings badly. Maybe he wants to make amends."

"I might be," Blackthorne conceded. "But I don't think I am."

Jake didn't say another word for the rest of the trip. Neither did Blackthorne. They rode their mounts hard, so that by the time they reached the impressive Southern mansion at the heart of Bitter Creek, their horses were lathered.

Jake followed Blackthorne in through the back door of the house, feeling nostalgia at the familiar smells in the kitchen, and anger at the changed, and much improved, furnishings. He stayed a step behind his stepfather all the way up the expensively carpeted stairs, to the bedroom where he understood his wife was being cared for by his mother.

"She's in there," Blackthorne said as he stood to the side of the door.

Jake was afraid to go inside, afraid of what he'd find. His mother was sitting in a wing chair beside a four-poster canopied bed with a gold-and-maroon-patterned top and bed curtains held back at each side with gold tassels. His wife was sitting upright under a fancy maroon coverlet.

"Jake!" she cried when she saw him.

She reached out her arms and Jake went straight to her and sat on the bed and pulled her into his embrace. He held her so tight she laughed and said, "I can't breathe."

He eased his hold a little, a very little, and leaned back to look at her. Blackthorne hadn't lied. She had a purple bruise on her cheekbone. He raised a hand to touch it and then didn't, when his insides twisted. "How are you?" he asked.

"I'm fine, as I keep telling your mother. She's the one who insisted I need to rest."

"My mother is a very smart woman."

"I'll leave you two alone to talk," his mother said as she rose from the wing chair, closed the book she'd been reading, and tucked it under her arm.

Jake left his wife long enough to cross to his mother and hug her. "Thank you for taking care of her."

"You're very welcome. When you've finished your talk with Miranda, your father and I will be in the parlor with Mr. Wentworth."

Jake watched as his mother closed the bedroom door behind her, then turned back to his wife. He felt a murderous rage toward the man who'd hurt her. And a corresponding wrath at his wife for putting herself in danger.

Instead of crossing to sit beside her again, as he'd intended when he'd watched his mother out the door, he put his balled fists on his hips and demanded, "Why didn't you tell me this morning you were planning to leave the house? What the hell were you doing on that road alone?"

"I'm pregnant."

Jake's knees suddenly buckled, and he collapsed

onto the bed. If she'd said she was dying of cancer he couldn't have felt more stricken to the heart. He didn't ask if she was sure. He could see from her anxious face that she was sure. "How did this happen?"

He realized the ridiculousness of his question before it was even out of his mouth. "I mean, how do you know?"

She met his gaze, her eyes begging him for a blessing he knew he couldn't give, and said, "The way any woman knows."

"Did you tell my mother?"

"I asked for her advice."

"Is that why you came here today?"

She shook her head yes. "That. And I wanted to send a letter to my sisters, and I hoped your mother could help me get it to San Antonio so it could be posted."

He frowned. "Then you didn't come here to meet your uncle?"

"No. Your mother only told me he was here after she'd taken away my clothes and put me into bed, otherwise I would have gone downstairs to find out what he's doing here."

"You weren't expecting him to come?"

"Why would I? He abandoned us, Jake." She reached out to lay a hand on his. "You haven't said how you feel about the baby."

"How do you think I feel?" Jake was surprised at the virulence in his voice. He pulled his hand free of hers and took a deep breath to calm himself, but his heart was still beating so hard he thought it might burst. "How should I feel, Miranda, when I've buried a wife and just done surgery on a woman who could easily have died in childbirth?"

"Happy," she said, tears welling in her eyes. "You should feel happy."

"How can I feel happy when I know what you have ahead of you? Weren't you watching when Gretta went through labor and the birth of her child?"

"Yes, I was watching. Were you?" she asked in a quiet voice. She blinked and a tear slid down her cheek.

"It isn't worth it." He couldn't look at her and not feel her sorrow at his reaction. His heart ached. "I can't go through that again. Not if there's a chance I can lose you."

She looked endearingly startled. "You care that much for me?"

"You little fool! I love you!"

"Oh."

Her mouth looked so kissable that he leaned forward and kissed it. Her arms circled his neck, capturing him when he would have pulled away. He held her tight and said, "I'm so scared, Miranda. I want a baby with you, I do. But I know just how dangerous it is. I wish I hadn't gotten you pregnant."

She leaned away and brushed the hair from his brow, then kissed his closed eyes and his cheeks and finally pressed her lips to his. "Say you're happy," she whispered.

"I'm not."

"Say you're happy," she urged with another breathless kiss.

"I'm not."

"Please, Jake." She kissed him once more.

He groaned. "I'm terrified."

"But happy," she said.

"I'm terrified. And happy," he said at last.

He could feel her lips lift slightly in a smile against his. His heart squeezed with terror. He would have to start now to distance himself from her, just in case. He would have to guard his heart or this time, if the worst happened, it might truly shatter him.

He pulled himself from her embrace and said, "I need to go meet your uncle and see what he wants." He intended to find out why that blackguard had come hunting his niece.

"I wish your mother hadn't taken my clothes," Miranda said. "Come back as soon as you can, and tell me what you find out."

"I will."

"I mean it, Jake. Uncle Stephen didn't want anything to do with us for three years. I can't imagine why he's come looking for me now."

"Stay in bed and rest. I'll be back as soon as I find out what he wants."

Chapter Twenty-nine

Jake had learned to take the measure of a man in seconds, because his life might depend on it. He felt his neck hairs hackle the moment he laid eyes on Stephen Wentworth.

He didn't like the northerner's blond, slicked-back hair, parted perfectly down the middle and combed away from his narrow face. He looked like a dandy in his fancy suit and tie. And how had his shoes stayed so shiny in the Texas dust?

Those were all trappings that could be changed at will. It was the insincere smile of greeting, a curve of thin lips to express a feeling that never reached the northerner's cold blue eyes, that told Jake he was looking at a charlatan and a fraud.

"You must be my dear Miranda's husband," Wentworth said as he extended his hand.

There was no way Jake could avoid taking it, unless he wanted to give away his true feelings for the bastard who'd abandoned his own brother's children to the cruelty of a petty tyrant like Miss Birch. He shook Wentworth's hand once and let it go, then angled his eyes to meet his stepfather's gaze.

Blackthorne lifted a brow slightly, silently asking if Jake agreed with his assessment of the man. Jake nodded equally slightly. For once—for the very first time, in fact—he and his stepfather were in perfect agreement.

The problem before Jake was how to get Stephen Wentworth to reveal his perfidy and wrest the Wentworth children's money from him, assuming there was any, no matter how little of it was left.

"Shall we all sit down?" Jake's mother invited.

Jake looked around him and saw the changes in the parlor since his father's departure. He was surprised to find his father's horn-and-hide chair angled near a desk, and he crossed over to sit in it. He was pleased to see that the room was still furnished with leather and wood rather than silk and brocade. That was his mother's doing, he would guess, as much as his stepfather's.

His mother and stepfather sat in wing chairs positioned side by side near the fireplace, leaving the Victorian sofa across from them for their guest.

Jake waited for Wentworth to speak, to explain the purpose of his visit. He didn't have to wait long.

"I have some papers I need my niece to sign."

There it was. The thief wanted the trappings of legality to cover his theft.

"Do you have the papers with you?" Jake asked.

"Yes, of course," Wentworth said.

"May I see them?"

"They're pretty complicated," Wentworth said. "I promise you I have my niece's best interests at heart."

"I believe you," Jake lied. "I'd just like to see what you want her to sign."

"It's merely a power of attorney," Wentworth said, without producing the papers.

It was unlucky for Wentworth that when Jake's father had left to fight in the war, he'd granted Jake his power of attorney. Jake knew the document granted whoever possessed it the authority to act in legal matters as though he were that person in fact.

"What is a 'power of attorney'?" Jake asked, to see how Wentworth would answer.

"It's a legal paper that allows me to make decisions in Miranda's best interests," her uncle said earnestly.

That certainly put a pretty face on ugly intentions, Jake thought.

"Exactly what decisions are we talking about?" Jake asked.

"There's a buyer for the land on which my brother's business sat before the fire. I need permission from any children over eighteen to sell it. Of course the proceeds will go into a trust for the benefit of all the children."

"Who controls the trust?" Jake asked.

A flash of annoyance crossed Wentworth's face, but he quickly schooled his features. "Why, I do, of course."

"What if Miranda wanted her share of the proceeds as soon as they become available?" Jake asked.

"I think it would be wiser to invest the proceeds."

"What if she wanted them instead?" Jake persisted.

"I think I should be discussing this with Miranda," Wentworth said, the friendliness gone from his voice.

"Then that's what you should do," a female voice said from the doorway.

Jake rose as he saw his wife step into the parlor.

Blackthorne and his mother also stood, along with Stephen Wentworth.

His wife smiled an apology to his mother as she said, "I couldn't wait to see my uncle. I borrowed some clothes I found stored in a chest in the bedroom. I hope that's all right."

His mother was staring with tortured eyes at the once-fashionable dress Miranda was wearing. And Jake suddenly knew why she was so upset.

The dress had belonged to his sister Jesse. It seemed his sister and his wife were nearly the same size. He couldn't help noticing how pretty his blond-haired, blue-eyed wife looked in the robin's-egg blue dress.

Miranda seemed oblivious to his mother's pain as she crossed the room. She was still a foot away from her uncle when she stopped. She threaded her fingers together in front of her and said, "I'm surprised to see you, Uncle Stephen. How on earth did you find me here in Texas?"

Jake hadn't thought to ask that question. He waited with interest to hear the answer.

"I went to the orphanage looking for you. I hadn't realized you'd be required to leave the Institute when you turned eighteen. I discovered your direction from your sisters. I could hardly believe you'd gotten married in such a rash manner."

Jake could tell Miranda was annoyed by her uncle's censure.

He watched her jaw firm as she replied in an arch voice, "It was either marriage or washing dishes and sleeping on an iron cot at the Palmer Hotel. I chose to become a mail-order bride."

Good for you! Jake thought.

"Shall we all sit down?" Wentworth said.

Jake figured Miranda's uncle knew he'd trod amiss with her and was buying time to figure out a new strategy for getting what he wanted.

They all sat back down where they'd been. His wife joined her uncle on the sofa, but on the far edge of it, close to Jake.

"Now, Uncle Stephen," Miranda said. "Tell me why you're here."

Wentworth went through the same explanation he'd made to Jake while Miranda listened attentively, a crease forming between her eyes.

"I thought Papa's fortune burned up with his bank in the fire," she said. "I didn't know he owned the land under the bank. How much is it worth?"

That was clearly an unexpected question and Wentworth hedged. "I don't exactly know."

"You must have had an offer," Miranda said. "Otherwise, you wouldn't be here to get my permission to sell."

Jake appreciated his wife's ability to smell a rat. She was more astute in business matters than he'd expected her to be. Although, when he thought about it, she'd managed to get herself and her brothers from Chicago to Texas on a single set of travel vouchers, no mean financial feat.

"To be honest, I have had an offer," Wentworth admitted.

If the man had an honest bone in his body, Jake was a pink raccoon.

"How much?" Miranda asked, her hands gripped tightly in her lap. "Enough to provide a home for all of us?"

Jake noticed she didn't specify where that home would be.

"I'm afraid not," Wentworth said, shaking his head. "Not nearly that much. Maybe, if it's invested and allowed to grow, it might be enough someday. That's why I'd like your power of attorney. I can invest the proceeds for you in my bank and give you a very good return."

Jake was watching Miranda intently, so when she lifted her eyes and met his gaze he saw how devastated she was that there was no fortune to be had, after all. "I didn't know your father was such a famous banker," he said to her.

"I never thought much about it. He owned the First State Bank in Chicago."

"Owned it?" Jake said. "All of it?"

Miranda nodded. "The bank burned down. Everything was lost. Isn't that right, Uncle Stephen?"

She turned to her uncle, who said, "Yes, Miranda dear, that's right."

Jake turned to his stepfather. "Aren't most bank vaults fireproof?"

"Should be," Blackthorne said.

Jake turned back to Wentworth. "What about your brother's bank? Was his vault fireproof?"

Wentworth slid a finger into his collar, as though it had suddenly tightened around his throat. "It was."

"Then the money my father kept at his bank didn't get burned up in the fire, like you said?" Miranda asked in a tremulous voice.

"Not all of it," Wentworth said.

Miranda rose on what appeared to be shaky legs and asked, "How much was left?"

Wentworth glanced first at Jake, whose expression left no doubt about his feelings toward a man who would cheat his brother's children out of their inheritance and abandon them for years to the viciousness of Miss Birch, and then toward Jake's stepfather, whose gaze was equally threatening.

"A few million is all," he said at last.

Jake paled.

Miranda gasped. "Dollars? A few million *dollars*?"

"Yes, dollars," Wentworth said irritably. "As I said, the money should be invested—"

Miranda burst into tears.

Jake leaped from his chair and had her in his arms a moment later. She pounded his chest, fighting to be free, and when he let her go, she whirled on her uncle like an avenging fury.

"I will sign nothing, do you hear?" she said through bared teeth. "I want my portion of Papa's money, and I want it as soon as the papers can be signed. How *dare* you put us in that awful orphanage! How *dare* you!"

Miranda's outrage at her uncle's dastardly behavior far outstripped any emotion Jake had seen from her since he'd met and married her. The fiery look in her eyes, the proud tilt of her chin, and the squared shoulders belonged to a girl who'd grown up to know her own worth.

That worth, as it turned out, was considerable.

"I never meant—," Wentworth began.

"You meant to steal your brother's inheritance from his children," Jake said implacably from his wide-legged stance at Miranda's shoulder. "We'll be taking steps to see that you no longer control their funds."

"I've managed their money wisely," he argued.

"The point is, it wasn't your money to manage," Miranda interjected. "It belonged to me and my sisters and brothers."

Jake's mother rose from her chair and said, "We don't want to keep you from beginning your journey back to Chicago."

Blackthorne rose and stood next to her, much as Jake was standing behind his own wife, a strong arm backing a strong-willed woman.

"I came here with the best intentions," Wentworth spluttered.

"You came here to cheat me out of my inheritance," Miranda said in a cold voice. "You came here to take advantage of me. Papa would have been ashamed of you, Uncle Stephen. He loved you, he supported you, and—"

"I hated him!" Wentworth said, venom in his voice. The mask he'd worn fell away and exposed the greedy swindler.

At Wentworth's admission, Miranda put up a hand as though to ward off a blow. Jake took a step forward to intercede, in case Miranda's uncle actually threatened her with physical violence.

"Why?" she asked in a tormented voice. "What did Papa ever do to you?"

"He never trusted me. He never gave me any authority. He always kept me under his thumb," Wentworth ranted. "He promoted other men ahead of me. Me! His own brother!"

It was clear why Miranda's father hadn't trusted his brother. Stephen Wentworth had turned out to be untrustworthy.

"You won't have to worry about being under my thumb," Miranda said. "I will hire someone else to manage my money, so it will no longer be a burden to you. And I will be taking whatever legal steps are necessary to protect the financial interests of Hannah and Hetty and Josie and Nick and Harry," she finished breathlessly.

There spoke a wealthy banker's daughter, Jake thought.

"Good-bye, Uncle Stephen," she said. "I won't see you to the door. I'm sure you can find your own way out."

He glanced out the window at the vast Texas prairie and said, "I'm not sure I can make it back to San Antonio before dark. What if I lose my way?"

"Then you'll spend the night alone in the dark," Miranda said. "Be sure to watch out for snakes. And bears and panthers and wolves," she added with relish.

Honestly, Jake hadn't seen a wolf in quite a while, except his mother's pets. And most of the bears and panthers were found in more heavily wooded areas farther east or west. But he applauded Miranda's efforts to upset her uncle.

Wentworth focused his gaze on Miranda and said, "I wasn't going to tell you, but you'll find out anyway. You may have trouble locating your sisters."

"What are you talking about?" Miranda said. "You told me they'd given you my direction."

He smirked. "Miss Birch got the information about where you'd gone from one of Josie's confederates. Your sisters are no longer at the orphanage. Miss

Birch contacted me the day they disappeared. That was almost a month ago."

"Disappeared?" Miranda said in a faint voice.

"Gone without a trace," Wentworth said with malicious satisfaction.

Tears filled Miranda's eyes and she covered her mouth to stifle the wail of despair Jake could hear growing behind her hands.

"You must have some idea where they've gone," Jake said.

"Some idea, yes," Wentworth said.

"Where are they?"

"Apparently, they joined a wagon train heading west."

Miranda turned and grabbed Jake's arm. "Oh, no! Oh, no!"

"I'm glad you're unhappy, Miranda," Wentworth said. "Because I certainly am."

"Get out," Jake said. "Out! Before I throw you out."

Wentworth bowed and turned to leave. He couldn't resist one last parting shot. "If the girls are gone, and if anything should happen to you and your brothers, I believe I am next in line to inherit."

Jake caught Stephen Wentworth by the scruff of his neck and the back of his trousers and pitched him out the door.

Chapter Thirty

Miranda cried most of the way back to Three Oaks. By the time she got into bed in one of Priscilla's cotton nightgowns, she was dry-eyed, but her heart was heavy. The incident with the three cowboys that she had found so soul shattering had faded to insignificance in light of the knowledge that her three sisters were missing.

She pulled a brush through her curls, wondering what she could have done to avoid what had happened. "I never should have left Chicago," she murmured.

Jake was undressing for bed—in their bedroom, no less—but she hardly noticed him, her mind was in such turmoil.

"I think Nick and Harry would have suffered from that choice," he said.

He was right about that, Miranda conceded.

"And without the perspective you had here, you might have signed those papers when your uncle brought them to you and lost your fortune."

"Instead, I'm rich," she said in wonder. "We can

rebuild the burned wing of the house. We can paint. We can buy more cattle."

"We aren't going to use your money to improve Three Oaks."

"Why not?"

"Because it's your money."

"It's *our* money," she said. "But it doesn't mean anything to me if I can't find my sisters. Where do you suppose they are?"

"If they left with a wagon train, they're certainly headed west. The question is, how did they get someone to take them along? The trip west is expensive. Any wagon master worth his salt requires each wagon to be outfitted properly with oxen or mules and enough supplies to last till the end of the journey."

"So how did they manage to join a wagon train?" Miranda wondered.

"Maybe they didn't," Jake said. "Maybe Josie told her friend that was what they were doing to put Miss Birch off their trail. Maybe they're on their way here right now."

"Oh, do you think so?" Miranda said, feeling her heart lighten for the first time since she'd heard her sisters had fled the orphanage. Then she remembered how difficult it had been for her and the boys to make that journey—how often she'd been offered the chance to sell herself to buy food—and shivered with foreboding.

"They also might have stowed away on someone's wagon," Jake said.

But they couldn't remain hidden forever. They would have to reveal themselves at some point. She knew from her experience in Texas that it wasn't so easy to hide on the wide-open prairie. It wasn't a matter of whether they'd be discovered but when. "What will happen when they're discovered?"

"It'll depend on how far the wagon train has traveled. If they're close enough to some settlement, they may just leave them there."

"Strand them in the middle of nowhere?"

Jake's lip quirked. "It wouldn't be the middle of nowhere. There would be some town close by."

"How would I know which one? How could I find them?"

"We can hire a detective, if it comes to that. But your sisters have been resourceful so far. I suspect they'll send a letter to you when they can."

Miranda had thought of another way her sisters might buy passage on the wagon train. One of them might try to do as she had done. One of them might marry a man if he agreed to bring her sisters along on the trip.

"I want to hire a detective right away," she said.

"You'd be better off waiting for word of their direction," Jake said.

"What if a letter never arrives? I have to find them, Jake. I have to! This is all my fault. I should have stayed in Chicago."

"You've talked yourself in a circle, Miranda, right back to where you started."

Miranda bit the inside of her cheek. Life was so unpredictable. Now that she possessed the money to bring her sisters to Texas, she didn't know where to send it. Of course, they would need somewhere to live when they got here, so the sooner she and Jake got started repairing Three Oaks, the better. "Jake, you have to let me use some of my money to rebuild the burned wing of the house."

"No."

She looked up to argue further and caught sight of bare male flesh. She dropped the hairbrush to her lap, staring wide-eyed as Jake dropped his long john shirt on the floor, then stepped out of the bottoms, leaving him naked.

"I can think of something better to do with our mouths than argue," he said, leaning over to kiss her softly on the mouth.

He sat down beside her on the bed, took the hairbrush from her limp hand, and, to her amazement, began brushing her hair. "I've wanted to do this ever since the first time you let these golden curls out of that awful bun you were wearing the day we got married."

Miranda glanced over her shoulder and asked, "Why didn't you?"

"I was keeping my distance. I didn't want to be tempted to make love to you."

Did that mean he was now willing to be tempted? And was he going to *make love* to her? Miranda shivered as the brush moved through her hair and his large hand followed after it. "That feels good."

He brushed her hair aside with his hand and bent to kiss her nape.

Miranda shivered with excitement. "What are you doing, Jake?"

"Making love to my wife."

"I thought you didn't want to do that."

"That was when I was worried about getting you pregnant."

"Oh, I see. I'm already pregnant," she said, pointing out the obvious.

"And I want you."

They weren't the three words she yearned to hear spoken again, but they were nice, nevertheless. And, Lord help her, she wanted him. She felt an ache that began in her belly and traveled up to her breasts all the way to her throat, as the blood hummed through her veins.

"I thought you would be stubborn and deny us this pleasure," she said as she leaned her head back so he could kiss her throat more easily.

He stopped kissing her to speak. "That was my thought at first," he admitted. He continued caressing her, his hands sliding up her ribs until he took the weight of her breasts in them, teasing the nipples into peaks. "But after what happened today," he said, "I changed my mind. If there's a chance I'm going to lose you—for any reason—I want to have this to remember."

She turned in his arms, her body fully aroused, aching and wanting, and rose onto her knees, which put her breasts level with his mouth. Jake stripped the cotton nightgown down past her shoulders and teased her nipples with his teeth.

She thrust her hands into his hair, keeping him where he was, and tried to continue their conversation. "I'm determined to make Three Oaks the beautiful home it once was," she said, panting as he brought her a kind of bliss she hadn't imagined. "And to bring the rest of my family here to live."

"We can discuss it later," he said, pulling her down onto his lap so he could reach her mouth.

Miranda suddenly wasn't interested in talking anymore.

It was a long time later before she had the breath to speak at all. She felt too languorous to argue, and she knew that bringing up the subject of money would start another argument. But she was determined to have her way.

Jake slid his arms around her and pulled her close, his nose in her hair. She felt safe and secure in his embrace, two things that had been lacking in her life for the past three years.

And she felt loved.

He'd already said the words. She had not. But she thought she loved him. She really thought she did.

"I want you again," he murmured in her ear.

She could feel him growing hard against her belly. She hadn't imagined he could want her again so soon. He reached down between her thighs with his hand, and she ducked her head at the grin on his face when he said, "I see you want me again, too."

The second loving was slower, and as Jake moved within her, Miranda's body began to quake. She felt herself losing control and didn't know what to do.

"Don't be afraid, Miranda," he rasped. "Come with me."

Her body spasmed with such force, it wrenched a raw, primitive sound from her throat.

Jake's body was arched backward as he spilled his seed with a savage cry of satisfaction.

He came to rest atop her so they were still joined, both their bodies heaving. She held him close, welcoming the solid weight of him. When they could both breathe easily again, he separated them and lay by her side, pulling her close.

"We should turn out the lamp," she murmured sleepily.

"Give me a minute and maybe we can do this again."

She raised her head to look into his face and saw his teasing smile. She swatted his chest and laughed. "I almost believed you."

"Almost?" he said, chuckling. "I was serious." But he leaned across her and turned out the lamp.

It should have been dark, but a soft blush of light remained outside the window.

Jake sat up, a frown wrinkling his brow. "What is that?"

Miranda bolted upright, staring hard at the orange-yellow glow. She felt her blood run cold. Her heart hammered in her chest and her body began to tremble.

She looked at Jake, her eyes wide with fear, and croaked, "That's fire."

Miranda had never seen Jake move so fast.

He already had his Levi's on and was pulling his boots over bare feet as he said, "It's the barn! Wake up the boys. They can help carry buckets of water. Get Slim out of bed. He can man the pump in the yard. I'll go get the stock out of there."

"Jake!" she cried. "Be careful!"

He was gone before she could say anything more. Miranda hurried to dress and ran to wake the boys. She did it quietly. With any luck, they could put out the fire in the barn without waking the baby and scaring her to death.

Nick scrambled out of bed and said, "Fire? Where?"

"Shh," Miranda warned. "We don't want to wake Anna Mae." When she had the two boys in the hall and the bedroom door closed behind them, she said, "It's the barn."

"My horse!" Nick said, his eyes wide with fear.

"Jake's getting him out." Miranda remembered every detail of the fire that had burned down their house in Chicago. The ferocious heat, the wind that fanned the scorching flames and sent burning ashes into the air, and the horrible, choking black smoke. And afterward, the soot that covered every pore, as the roaring fire—a dangerous, living thing—destroyed everything she loved.

Nick had been seven. She wondered how much of that awful night he remembered. His trembling body and his terrified face told her the answer. He remembered everything, too.

She laid a hand on Nick's shoulder and said, "It's only the barn. Jake will rescue the animals. Go wake up Slim," she said. "Take Harry with you. I'll meet you outside."

Miranda had pulled on trousers and a shirt and shoes almost as quickly as Jake, so she was a step ahead of the boys and Slim as she headed outside to help Jake. She didn't realize he wasn't alone until she'd almost reached the barn. She could see Jake outlined in the firelight.

Three men on horseback surrounded him.

Chapter Thirty-one

Miranda knew without seeing their faces who the three cowboys were. Just then, one of them turned his horse, and, in the light of the fire, she saw the bloody furrows she'd scratched in his cheek that morning.

"Let the barn burn," Call said.

"At least let me save the stock," Jake said in what Miranda thought was an amazingly calm voice.

"Let them burn, too," Call said.

"Why not let him get the stock out?" one of the other cowboys said.

"That bitch made us outlaws," Call said viciously. "Wearing clothes that showed her legs like no proper woman would. Tempting decent men. Better her man should know her for what she is. Won't any spread in Texas hire a man who's touched a woman against her will. We're outcasts no matter what we do from now on. The blame for all of this falls on her!"

Miranda felt sick. She backed away into the house to stop the others from coming outside. She ran into Slim and the two boys in the kitchen, where Nick had already pumped a pail full of water, which was sitting by the sink.

"The fire was set by the three men who attacked me this morning," she told them. "They've got Jake surrounded. They're forcing him to let the barn burn." She didn't mention the fact that the stock might burn as well. She was afraid Nick would run outside to try to save his horse.

"Nick, go get the rifles," Slim said, rolling himself toward the kitchen door.

"Sure, Slim," Nick said.

Miranda called after him, "Who are you planning to shoot?"

"Give you three guesses," Slim said.

"You can't kill them all, Slim."

"I can. And I will."

"Here's yours, Slim," Nick said, handing one of two Winchester rifles he'd retrieved to Slim and keeping the other for himself.

"How did you know where to find those guns?" she asked Nick.

Before he could answer, Harry piped up, "Slim's been teaching us how to shoot."

Miranda's brows nearly reached her hairline. "Both of you?"

"Both of them," Slim said. "Now, boy," he said to Nick, "remember what I taught you."

Miranda gripped the barrel of Nick's rifle and said to Slim, "My little brother isn't going out there with a gun in his hands. Those men are liable to shoot first and realize he's only a boy of ten when he's dead."

To her surprise, it wasn't Slim who argued the matter. It was Nick.

"I know what I'm doing, Miranda. I'm a good shot. Those cowboys might not settle for burning the barn.

They might decide to shoot Jake and come after you again. After they've burned the barn and killed Jake and attacked you, they're not going to leave any witnesses."

Miranda hadn't let herself imagine that sort of savagery. Clearly, Nick had. "I still think you're too young to be threatening grown men with a gun."

Too late, Miranda realized she'd said exactly the wrong thing.

Nick's shoulders squared and he tightened his grip on the Winchester, jerking the barrel from her grip. "This rifle will even things up."

"The boy's right," Slim said. "We're wastin' time talkin'. Open the door and let's get this over with."

Miranda wished she'd never suggested Jake build that ramp. If Slim was trapped on the porch by his wheelchair, Miranda was sure he wouldn't have sent Nick out there alone. She grabbed Harry's wrist when it looked like he planned to follow the other two males out the door. "You stay here with me."

She hadn't expected Harry to resist, so she didn't have a tight grip on his arm. To her surprise and dismay, he yanked free and ran after the other two. There was no question of Miranda staying behind. She hurried out onto the back porch to watch the showdown with the bad men.

Miranda heard Slim say, "We've got them covered, Jake. Go get the stock." She was glad to see Harry standing behind Slim, protected by—yet ready to push—his wheelchair.

"Thanks, Slim!" Jake yelled as he edged past the mounted cowboys and ran for the barn door.

Miranda's heart leaped to her throat when Jake

disappeared inside the burning building. A moment later, neighing horses began bolting from the open barn door, followed by the bawling milk cow. Miranda held her breath, waiting for Jake to reappear.

There was no sign of him.

Where was he? Had a burning timber fallen on him? Why was he still in there? Was he struggling with some animal too frightened to move? Jake was going to choke to death on the thick black smoke billowing from the barn door if he didn't come out soon.

Miranda wanted to rush into the barn and save Jake, as she'd saved Harry all those years ago. But her feet had somehow gotten rooted to the porch, and her knees threatened to buckle if she took another step.

Her nostrils filled with the scent of smoke, and she heard the crackling of the fire as though she was surrounded by it. All the terror, all the horror and pain and suffering and grief of that fateful night in Chicago, came flooding back. Miranda couldn't help Jake. She couldn't help anyone. She was literally paralyzed by the awesome power and destructive fury of the distant fire.

Her position on the porch gave her a perfect view of the dramatic standoff. She saw Call reaching for his gun and shouted, "Watch out!"

Everything happened very quickly after that.

Miranda felt her knees finally give out, and she collapsed onto the porch in a heap, watching the bloody scene playing out before her in slow motion. The fight was uneven, three grown men against a crippled old man and a boy. Was there any chance Slim and Nick could win?

Slim shot first and he shot straight. One of the cowboys fell out of the saddle without a sound, his gun dropping from his hand before he'd even raised it to fire.

Miranda heard Slim cry out and drop his rifle, apparently shot. But how badly? She cried out in terror when Harry picked up the rifle Slim had dropped. "No, Harry!"

She stumbled to her hands and knees and shoved herself upright, running for the little boy, who was trying to lift the heavy rifle in his skinny, four-year-old arms. "Don't shoot!" she cried to one and all. "Don't shoot!"

Her words fell on deaf ears. She heard two almost simultaneous shots and saw another of the cowboys sway in the saddle and fall from his horse. *Two down,* she thought.

But Call was the worst of them, and he was still in the saddle.

Nick was crouching near Slim's chair, his rifle wavering as he tried to aim it.

"Nick, you're hurt!" Miranda cried as she pulled the rifle from Harry's hands and dropped beside Nick behind the wheelchair. She could see a dark patch on Nick's shirt that looked like blood.

"Just a scratch," Nick said, wincing as he cocked the Winchester.

"A scratch so bad you can barely hold your rifle," Miranda snapped, angry because she was so frightened.

"Put down your gun, boy, and you, too, bitch, and I'll let the old man live," Call said, aiming his Colt at Slim. "Do it now!"

Miranda dropped the rifle she was holding where

Call could see it. "Put it down, Nick," Miranda pleaded, when her brother didn't follow suit. Call would kill Slim without a second thought. She could see it in the cowboy's eyes.

"Goddamn these useless legs!" Slim raged, pounding on his thigh with his fist. "You wouldn't be so high and mighty if I had my legs, you varmint," he yelled at Call from his chair.

"Shut up, old man."

Miranda could see tears of frustration in Nick's eyes when he laid his Winchester on the ground. When he stood again, Miranda lifted her chin and said, "What are you going to do now? Murder the four of us in cold blood?"

"I'm thinking about it," Call said.

"Think again," a voice said from behind him.

In the desperation of the moment, Miranda had completely forgotten about Jake. It seemed he was going to sacrifice himself to give them a chance to live. She grabbed for the rifle Nick had dropped, but she heard three shots in quick succession and knew she was too late.

"Jake!" she cried as she rose. She turned with the rifle just as Call fell from the saddle. In the bright light of the burning barn, she saw Jake was still standing, his face black with soot, a smoking gun in his hand.

She dropped the rifle and ran, flinging herself into Jake's arms. "You're safe! You're safe! I never saw you come out of the barn. I thought you'd burned to death in there."

"Lucky for me, my barn is in sad need of repair," Jake said. "I kicked a hole in the back wall and crawled out."

"Where did you get the gun?" Miranda asked in wonder. "I didn't know you had a gun."

"I had it tucked in the back of my jeans." He hesitated, then said, "I thought I might need it if any of the animals were too badly burned to save."

She turned at last to observe the three bodies on the ground. "Are they dead?"

One of the men groaned.

"Apparently not," Jake said. "Stay here." He crossed, gun in hand, to kneel by the first cowboy who'd been shot. "He's not dead," Jake announced, "but he's not long for this world, either."

Miranda joined Jake in time to hear the cowboy say with his last breath, "Sorry about the house, ma'am."

Miranda wondered what he meant. It was the barn they'd set on fire. She glanced over her shoulder at the house, and felt a sense of déjà vu. The house glowed and pulsed as though it was breathing fire.

Miranda realized the cowboys must have set the front of the house on fire at the same time they'd fired the barn, knowing everyone would leave the house from the kitchen door to try and save the barn, and that the fire would remain undiscovered until it was too late.

All of them had been so focused on the threat from the cowboys and the raging fire engulfing the barn, they'd never noticed the fire growing larger and larger at the front of the house.

That was the smoke she'd smelled so strongly on the back porch. Smoke from the fire at the front of the house, not smoke from the distant fire in the barn. In the next instant, Miranda realized they were not all safe. She turned to Jake and cried, "Anna Mae! I left her sleeping upstairs!"

Miranda didn't think, she just ran.

"Miranda, stop!" Jake shouted after her. "The fire's too big. Stop!"

Both Nick and Slim grabbed at her as she passed by, but she tore free and sprinted for the back door.

"Miranda, stop!" Nick cried. "You'll die if you go in there."

"Miranda, stop!" Harry screamed. "Stop!"

She yanked the screen door open and ran through the kitchen to the hall. She was met by a blistering conflagration, a wall of flame taller than she was. She fell backward into the kitchen, stunned by the heat. Then she saw the pail of water Nick had pumped when they'd thought all they'd have to fight was the fire. She dumped it over her head, wetting herself from hair to heels.

Then she took a deep breath and held it as she ran. She was already scampering through the licking flames by the time she heard Jake come pounding through the kitchen door after her.

Miranda knew if she stopped, the fire would engulf her, so she kept running until she was free of it. A moment later, Miranda realized the fire wasn't the greatest danger.

She couldn't breathe. Smoke was suffocating her. The whole bottom floor of the house was thick with acrid air that burned the back of her throat. She felt her way to the bottom of the stairs, holding her wet sleeve against her nose, gagging on smoke. She felt dizzy from lack of air.

Miranda was giddy with relief when she found the

bannister at the bottom of the stairs. She held onto it as she ran to the top. The smoke was even thicker on the second floor and she realized Anna Mae must be having difficulty breathing, too. She shoved open the door to the children's bedroom, frightened when she heard no sound from the crib.

"Anna Mae!" she cried. "Anna Mae!"

The child was balled up in a corner of her crib with a blanket pulled over her head. For a moment, Miranda thought the little girl was dead. She pulled the cover away slowly, and discovered a pair of wide, frightened eyes staring up at her.

"Mama! Mama!"

The little girl scrambled to her feet and threw herself into Miranda's open arms. Miranda quickly wrapped a blanket around the trembling child to keep her safe from the smoke and fire and pulled her close. "We're going downstairs now, sweetie. Close your eyes and hold on tight, and we'll be outside before you know it."

Miranda left the bedroom and hurried to the landing at the top of the stairs. That was as far as she got. Fire had snaked its way down the front hall and engulfed the stairs.

There was no way out.

Chapter Thirty-two

Jake had spent his life making painful choices in a land where every decision had life-and-death consequences. When he'd seen how the fire raged through the house, he'd known the chances of rescuing Anna Mae were small. But he had to try. He loved his daughter, and she was all he had left of Priss.

He'd yelled for Miranda to stop, because if there was any risk to be taken, he would be taking it. If there was any saving to be done, he'd do the saving. Or die trying.

But Miranda hadn't hesitated. She was gone before he could stop her, running into a burning house to save a child that wasn't even her own flesh and blood.

"That fool woman! She doesn't have the sense God gave a grasshopper," Jake muttered as he raced after her. He caught up to Nick and Harry, who were running for the kitchen door, too, and grabbed each boy by an arm.

Nick yelped and said, "My arm!"

Jake let him go. "You were shot?"

"I'm okay," Nick said, cradling the wounded arm. "We have to save Miranda."

"You boys stay out here and take care of Slim. I'll go get your sister."

"I can't believe she ran in there," Nick said, tears streaking the soot on his face. "She's scared to death of fire!"

Yet, she'd run into a burning house anyway. Jake marveled at the courage of the woman he'd married. He went down on one knee and put an arm around each boy and pulled them close enough to smell the smoke on their shirts and the stench of fear in their sweat.

He looked first at Nick, then at Harry, and said, "Do you trust me?"

Each nodded in turn.

"Then believe me when I say I'm going to get both of our girls out of that house. Alive. Now go take care of Slim."

He gave them each another quick hug, then jumped up and ran for the house. He expected to find Miranda trapped in the kitchen, because the fire seemed to have consumed the front half of the house. He was praying the hall wouldn't yet be blocked by fire. If it was, he would have to think of some other way of getting to Anna Mae's bedroom. Maybe he could use the ladder to climb up to the bedroom window, if that side of the house wasn't already on fire.

First, he had to get Miranda out of the house.

Smoke filled the kitchen and he could hardly see a foot in front of his face. "Miranda!" he called. "Where are you?"

He'd made it halfway across the kitchen when he caught sight of Miranda—her hair plastered to her scalp and her clothes soaking wet—running straight into a wall of flames.

His heart clutched with fear, and he was robbed of breath. He gasped, but there was no oxygen to be had. He dropped to the floor, looking for air that wasn't full of smoke. He found enough to fill his lungs and lurched toward the hallway.

He was met by a searing wall of flame that stretched high over his head, reaching out to lick at the paint on the kitchen walls, curling it into ashy feathers that flew into the air, making it even more difficult to breathe.

"Miranda!" he shouted again. He could barely hear himself over the sound of the roaring flames and the crash of falling timbers as the wooden beams in the front of the house fell, eaten away by the fire.

Jake saw the empty bucket by the pump and thought about wetting himself down, as Miranda obviously had, and following her into the fire.

He couldn't make himself do it. He would have given his left arm to save her. But a fire didn't take parts of bodies. It stole entire lives. He couldn't help Miranda if he got himself burned to death in the fire. He had to find another way to rescue her.

If she'd made it up the stairs, she would head for Anna Mae's bedroom. He stumbled back out of the smoky kitchen to the back porch and started around the side of the house toward his daughter's room.

The boys came running toward him.

"Where is she?" Nick cried.

"Where did you leave the ladder the last time you used it?" Jake asked.

"I put it away in the barn, like you told me," Nick said.

Both of them looked toward the barn. The barn, and the ladder inside it, had been consumed in a ball of fire. Jake brushed at the cowlick on Nick's head and said, "Good boy."

Jake realized he wasn't going to be using a ladder to climb up to Anna Mae's window. "Stay with Slim," he ordered.

"I want to help!" Nick said.

"You can help by staying with Slim," he said grimly. He didn't want Nick to hear his sister's screams, if Miranda was trapped in Anna Mae's room and the fire came hunting her.

And he didn't want anyone to see his face when he discovered whatever was waiting for him around the side of the house. Would Anna Mae's room be filled with flames?

Jake held his breath as he turned the corner. The air whooshed out of him in relief when he saw the upper window was still intact, not blown out by the heat of the fire, as the windows had been on the front of the house. He hoped she'd made it up the stairs. He hoped she'd had made it all the way to Anna Mae's room, and that his daughter was still alive when she got there.

"Miranda!" he shouted. "Come to the window! Miranda, open the window! Can you hear me? Open the window!"

There was no answer. He doubted she could hear him over the noise of the fire. He found a rock that Miranda had used to edge her rose garden, where deer had eaten away all the buds before the roses could bloom, and heaved it as hard as he could at the window twenty-five feet above him.

The window exploded as the rock sailed through it.

A moment later, Miranda's face appeared in the hole he'd made in the glass. She held a bundle in her arms.

She set the bundle aside, carefully shoved the window open wide and called down to him, "Anna Mae is fine. But we're trapped, Jake. The fire is blocking the stairs. Go get the ladder—"

"The ladder was in the barn."

"Oh, no!"

Jake surveyed the side of the house, looking for any way Miranda could climb down the side of the house. There were no footholds he could see. The fire was moving fast. The fierce heat was already peeling off what little paint was left on the side of the house.

He gauged the distance from the window to the ground and said, "Throw Anna Mae down to me."

"It's too dangerous," she said.

"Do what I tell you!" he shouted. "Throw my daughter down to me and do it *now*!"

"Don't you yell at me, Jacob Creed!" she shouted back.

"Please, Miranda. Do it." He held his arms out, so she would have a place to aim. He could see her talking to Anna Mae, watched her wrap the blanket more securely around his daughter, and then lean out the open window with the bundle in her arms.

"Here she comes. Don't drop her, Jake."

"Let her go. I'm ready."

Anna Mae screamed all the way down.

Jake was unnerved by his daughter's wail of terror but forced himself to stay focused and calm. The window seemed a terrifying height above the ground. He kept his eyes on the wriggling bundle and lunged at the last moment, catching her just before she hit the ground.

He pulled her close and hugged her tight, then pushed the blanket away so he could see her face, to assure himself she was all right. "Daddy, I fell," she whimpered.

"You sure did. But you're fine now." He wrapped Anna Mae tightly in her blanket and set her at the base of the nearby well, where she'd be safe from the fire. "Sit right there, honey, and don't move."

When he turned around, his heart nearly pounded out of his chest. He could see a glow beyond the bedroom window. Anna Mae's bedroom was on fire.

He focused his gaze on Miranda, who was still leaning out the window and yelled, "Your turn, sweetheart. Jump!"

"I can't," she said. "I want to, but I can't."

"Come on, Miranda. If you can run through fire, you can jump out a window. It's easy. Come on, jump!"

She shook her head, then stared back over her shoulder. Her eyes were wide with fright. "I can't. I love you, Jake."

He realized she was saying good-bye to him. It seemed she was more terrified of falling than she was of the fire. But the fire wasn't close enough yet to burn her. When it was, it might be too late. He had to convince her to jump *now*!

"Miranda Creed, if you don't obey me, I swear I'm going to come in there and get you."

"You can't, Jake. The fire—"

"Fire or no fire," he roared. "I love you, Miranda. And I'm not about to lose you and our baby this way. Get your pretty little butt out that window! Now!"

He heard a voice calling his name and turned to find Nick leading Call's horse toward him. Slim was following behind, half wheeling himself and half being pushed by Harry.

"Slim and Harry and I had an idea how to get Miranda down from Anna Mae's room," Nick said excitedly. "You can stand on the saddle, and Miranda can tie some sheets together and hang them out the window and crawl over the sill and drop into your arms. It's perfect!"

Perfect so long as Miranda was willing to do her part, Jake thought.

He could see the whites of the horse's eyes and the skittish animal was sidestepping to get away from the fire. "We need to blindfold that horse," Jake said.

"Take my shirt," Slim said, ripping at the buttons and pulling it down off his arms. He handed it to Harry, who handed it to Nick.

"As soon as you get that horse blindfolded, bring him over here," Jake told Nick. Then he called up to Miranda, "Tie the sheets together to make a rope you can use to climb down. I'm going to be standing under the window, waiting to catch you when you drop."

"Why didn't I think of that?" she said.

She disappeared from the window but was back a moment later. "I could only get one sheet."

He realized the other sheets must already be on fire. "Tie it off on Nick's bed," he said. *Hurry, Miranda!*

He thought the words but he didn't speak them. His throat was too constricted by fear to speak.

Miranda was running out of time.

"I'm coming, Jake," she said. "Where are you?"

"Bring that horse over here next to the house," Jake ordered Nick.

As Nick maneuvered the horse, Jake put a hand on the horn and threw himself into the saddle without using the stirrups. Then he pushed himself up to the length of his arms to get his feet under him on the broad seat. "Keep him steady, Nick."

"I'm trying," Nick said. "He's scared, Jake."

"Keep talking to him. You'll do fine." Jake was standing upright now and realized he was too far from the house to lean against it to steady himself. He balanced himself on the saddle as best he could and looked up. His hands were shaking. The window seemed a long way off.

Suddenly, there was no more time for terror. At long last, Miranda was crawling over the windowsill.

The horse beneath him suddenly bolted when a flaming ash hit his flank.

"Watch out!" Nick cried, hanging on to the reins for dear life.

Jake spread his legs and dropped into the saddle. He was safe, but when he looked up, he saw that Miranda was dangling twenty-five feet above the ground, and the frayed sheet, the only thing that kept her from falling like a stone, had caught fire.

"Bring us closer to the house," Jake said. "Move it, boy!"

"I'm trying," Nick sobbed.

Jake was already pushing himself up, trying to regain his footing on the saddle. He was halfway up-right when Miranda cried out and started to fall. He could see the tied end of the sheet had burned through.

He reached out to grab her and almost missed. He caught her around the waist and felt himself falling. He leaned backward to catch his balance, then slid down into the saddle with Miranda in his arms.

"You got her!" Nick said with a hoot of excitement.

"You got her!" Harry shouted.

"You got her!" Slim said with a grin.

"I got her," Jake said, smiling down at Miranda. "Now let's get the hell away from this burning house. You can take that blindfold off, Nick."

"When you're done, Nick, would you please hand Anna Mae to me?" Miranda said.

Nick handed Slim back his shirt, then retrieved the little girl, who was sitting by the well crying, and handed her up to Miranda.

"You're fine, sweetie," Miranda said, holding the little girl close. "We're all fine."

She was saying the words, but Jake could feel her whole body still trembling. How brave she was! How wonderful she was! How lucky he was to have chosen her for his wife.

"Come here, runt," Slim said to Harry, affection rife in his voice, as he lifted the four-year-old into his lap. "Let me give you a ride."

"I'll push," Nick said.

"What about your arm?" Jake asked.

"I think I was more scared than hurt."

Jake's arms tightened around the two females in his

life as they all moved a safe distance back from the house.

"I don't think I want to watch it burn to the ground," Miranda said quietly as she stared back at the inferno destroying the house. She looked up at him and said, "Let's leave here, Jake."

"And go where?" he asked.

"To Bitter Creek, of course."

"No." He had nothing left. The loss of both the barn and the house had ruined him. He wasn't about to go crawling to his stepfather and admit defeat.

He felt Miranda's hand on his arm. "You don't have to stay there with us," she said. "But the children need a roof over their heads and a hot meal in the morning. Please, Jake."

Jake felt so tired. She was right, of course. If he'd been alone, he would have slept under the stars. But Slim's arthritis bothered him in the morning damp. Harry was susceptible to the chilly night air. Anna Mae was fussy when she didn't get a full night's sleep and was ravenous every morning. Nick was hurt, whether he was admitting it or not.

And Miranda, his beloved wife, had just been through a hair-raising experience that would have left a lesser woman devastated. His pregnant wife deserved more than a bed on the hard ground.

Jake couldn't think only of himself. He had to think of all the loved ones who depended on him. "All right," he said at last. "Let's gather up those other two cowboys' horses and hitch them to the wagon. Thank God that wasn't in the barn. Then let's go visit my mother."

"Everything will be okay, Jake," Miranda said as

they rode the short distance to the corral where the wagon was kept.

"I've lost everything, Miranda. I have nothing."

"You have me, Jake. And our children. And a million or so dollars to build it all back up again."

"I won't take your money, Miranda," Jake said through tight jaws.

"Fine. Because I'm not giving it to you," she retorted. He eyed her askance.

"However, I'll be happy to loan it to you. You can pay it back . . . over the next fifty or so years."

Jake chuckled. "You never give up, do you?"

"Never. I love you, Jake. Did you mean what you said? Do you really love me, too?"

"Don't you believe me?"

"It's hard to believe, yes."

"Then I guess I'll have to prove it to you . . . over the next fifty or so years."

Miranda laughed.

Jake leaned down and kissed his wife.

Epilogue

Miranda was in labor. It was two weeks before the due date Jake had calculated. He'd made arrangements for his mother to be there to help her through the labor, but she'd woken up with pains that were startlingly close together, making it questionable whether his mother would arrive before the birth.

Miranda was tucked up in bed in her new bedroom in their new house, which had been built in the months right after the fire. The two-story house had impressive columns in front and a second-floor gallery porch. The live oaks that had once shrouded the house had been reduced to blackened stumps, but she'd insisted they plant three more. "Because the ranch is called Three Oaks," she'd explained.

Jake had laughed at her, but he'd planted the trees.

The house had an office for Jake and a sewing room for her, and rooms for her brothers and his daughter and the children she hoped they would have. She'd also insisted on rooms for her missing sisters.

It was a veritable mansion.

Miranda hoped she survived this pregnancy to enjoy it.

Jake had wanted to ride to Bitter Creek to get his mother the moment she'd admitted to the first contraction, but the labor had progressed so fast, he'd changed his mind at the last minute and stayed home.

He was pacing the bedroom floor, more anxious than she'd seen him at any time since he'd stood on a horse next to a house on fire, waiting for her to climb down a burning sheet and drop into his arms.

"I'm fine, Jake," she said. "Everything is—" She stopped speaking to concentrate on breathing through the contraction that threatened to tear her in two. It was one thing to see another woman in labor, to imagine how much work it was to deliver a child. It was quite another to endure those fierce pains oneself. Her time was close. The pains were becoming much worse and coming much closer together.

"It won't be long now," she said, once the contraction had passed. She eyed Jake and said, "You look a little green."

"Promise me we won't do this again."

"Oh, no," she said. "I plan to have five or six more."

"Good lord." He dropped onto the edge of the bed. "I should have thrown your first letter in the trash."

"It was my sister Josie's letter. She was the one who answered your advertisement for a bride."

Saying Josie's name reminded Miranda that they hadn't yet located her sisters. It seemed one of her sisters had married a man planning to travel with the wagon train and had arranged to bring her two sisters along. Because of some sort of fracas, their wagon had left the security of the train. No one had heard from any of them since.

Miranda had seen from the look in Jake's eyes that he believed her sisters were dead—from illness, from an Indian attack, from starvation, or from one of the myriad hazards to be found on the trail.

But she knew how resilient her sisters were. She knew they were still alive . . . somewhere. She'd hired a Pinkerton detective to hunt them down. She had high hopes he would find them.

There was always the chance the girls had continued their journey west, that they were fine, and that they would land somewhere at last and send her a letter telling her where they were. She waited every day in hopes that some word would come.

"Oooooowwwww." More than once during her labor, Miranda had wanted to howl like a dying animal, but she didn't want to scare Jake out of his wits. She'd settled for moans and groans and wails and whining.

"You can scream, Miranda. It's okay with me."

She hissed like a snake.

"I'm not kidding. I can handle it."

She whimpered like a kicked puppy. "Rub my back," she begged pitifully.

He sat on the bed and pressed his knuckles against her back.

"Harder."

He pushed harder.

"Harder." The strong pressure wasn't quite enough to counteract the pains in her belly, but it felt good. "Thank you, Jake. Oh, thank you!"

"What can I do?" he said in an agonized voice. "Tell me how I can help."

When she turned to look at Jake, she saw his brow

was covered with beads of sweat. It was snowing outside, so he'd built up the fire to keep the room warm. Obviously, it was too warm for a man who'd spent the morning pacing the floor in agitation.

She laid her fingertips on his nape and drew him close and kissed a salty eyebrow. "I'm—"

That was all she got out before her body attacked her again. The sound she made was all raw pain. "I have to push," she said, surprised at how fast the moment had come. She'd only been in labor for four hours. Or was it five?

"Are you sure you have to push?" He knew it was too soon, too.

She looked at him uncertainly, but her body was sure. "I need to push," she screamed.

She hadn't meant to scream, but this pain was worse than everything that had come before. And it never seemed to end. "Jake, help me! It hurts! It hurts!"

"Come on, Miranda, you can do this," he said, suddenly all business. He shoved the sheet up to her knees and checked, as he had through the day. "I can see the baby's head."

She barely had time to take three deep breaths before another contraction assaulted her belly. "Aarrrrgggh," she growled deep in her throat.

"Push, Miranda!" he commanded.

Miranda struggled to expel the baby, suddenly afraid that something would go wrong and she would push and push and push and the child would never be born. "I'm trying," she gasped in the moment between contractions. "I'm—" She grunted as she felt the urge to push and pushed to end the pain.

Jake waited at the foot of the bed, his face as pale as a ghost. "I love you, Miranda."

"I love you, tooooooooo." Miranda felt the baby moving down the birth canal, felt her body expelling its burden, and gripped the sheet with both hands and held on. At last she felt the child slip from her body and groaned with relief.

Her relief was short-lived. There was no sound of a crying baby. Into the silence she whispered, "Jake?"

Her knees were up and the sheet kept her from seeing what he was doing. She pushed herself upright and dropped her knees and said, "What's happening? Why isn't the baby crying?"

Jake held a tiny form in his hands. He had tears in his eyes.

Miranda felt tears spring to her eyes. "Jake?"

"He's beautiful, Miranda. Perfect."

"Yes, but why isn't he crying?"

"I don't know. He's just looking at me. Should I make him cry?"

"Is he breathing?" Miranda asked.

"Of course."

"Can I hold him?"

"Let me tie off the cord and cut it. And you have a little more work to do first."

Miranda felt the urge to push again and remembered there was the afterbirth to deliver. Jake handed her their son and then wrapped the afterbirth in newspaper and removed it from the bed. He came back to her a moment later and sat beside her.

"He's perfect," Miranda said.

"Perfect," Jake agreed. "I guess that wasn't so hard, after all."

"Oh, no," she said. "I'm not going through that again anytime soon. Labor's hard. And it hurts!"

Jake grinned. "Glad to hear we're finally in agreement."

Miranda knew the memory of the pain would fade. It was one of the things her mother had told her that she'd never forgotten. But there was no sense making Jake worry. That could wait until she was pregnant again.

"What should we name him?" she asked. She hadn't been willing to choose a name before the baby was born, because it might bring bad luck.

"How about naming him after your father?"

"Oh, Jake, that's a lovely idea. You wouldn't mind?"

"I promised Nick and Harry we would," he admitted sheepishly.

"Welcome to the family, William Jarrett Creed," Miranda said.

Jake looked startled.

"It's only fair he should be named after both our fathers," Miranda said.

"Hello, Will," Jake said as he reached out to his son. The baby gripped his finger and held on. "I forgot how small they are when they're born."

"He'll grow fast." *And we'll give him lots of brothers and sisters to play with.*

"Can we come in now?" Nick called from the doorway.

"Come on in," Jake said. "Just be careful not to jostle your sister."

Nick and Harry scrambled onto the bed and crawled to Miranda's side so they could look at the baby. Slim wheeled his chair in with Anna Mae in his lap.

Jake sat beside Miranda and slid his arm protectively around her shoulder. Harry cuddled up close and Nick sat cross-legged at the foot of the bed. Slim wheeled his chair close enough for Anna Mae to leap into Jake's arms.

"Baby Will!" she said delightedly.

"I'm sorry it's not a sister," Miranda said to the little girl. "I'll try to do better next time."

Jake shot her a stunned look, but she just laughed. She refused to think of the past or the future. She looked around her and felt . . . happy.

Life as a mail-order bride was not what she'd expected. Life was never what one expected. But she loved and was loved. What more could one ask?

Letter to Readers

Dear Faithful Readers,

I hope you enjoyed *Texas Bride,* the first book in my Mail-Order Brides series. Watch for *Wyoming Bride* (Hannah's story), *Montana Bride* (Hetty's story), and *Blackthorne's Bride* (Josie's story).

The Blackthornes were first featured in my Regency-era Captive Hearts series. The Creeds were introduced in my Sisters of the Lone Star series. You can find a list of the books in both series in the front of this book.

Be sure to check out my website, www.joanjohnston .com, for more information about the Creeds and Blackthornes, for publication dates, to contact me personally, or to sign up to receive an e-newsletter when the next book is in stores.

Happy reading,

Joan Johnston

Did Texas Bride steal your heart?

You won't want to miss
the adventures
of the other Wentworth sisters
as they seek love in the Wild West!

Read on for a sneak peek at

Wyoming Bride,

the story of Hannah Wentworth.

Chapter One

Hannah had never been so scared in her life, but running wasn't an option. If she didn't go through with her part of the marriage bargain, Mr. McMurtry might not go through with his. Her husband had left her alone in their room at the Palmer House Hotel to ready herself for bed. It had taken less than no time to strip out of her dress and put on the flannel night-gown that was all she owned. She paced the outlines of the canopied bed without ever going near it.

The room was luxurious enough to remind Hannah of the life she and her three sisters and two brothers had lost when their parents were killed in the Great Chicago Fire. That life had turned to ashes three years ago, when the six of them had ended up in the Chicago Institute for Orphaned Children at the mercy of the cruel headmistress, Miss Iris Birch.

The view of the fire escape through the fourth-floor hotel window blurred as tears of anger—*terrible* anger—and regret—*enormous* regret—filled her eyes.

Hannah felt trapped. Trapped by a moment of unself-ishness that she regretted with her entire being. Why, oh why had she listened to her tormented sister Josie's plea?

Two months ago, their eldest sister, Miranda, had left the orphanage in the middle of the night with hugs and tears, stealing away with ten-year-old Nick and four-year-old Harry to become a mail-order bride in faraway Texas. Hannah; her twin sister, Henrietta; and Josie had been left behind to await news of whether Miranda's new husband might have room for all of them in his home.

They'd waited . . . and waited . . . and waited for a letter from Miranda. During the past two months, there had been no news that she'd even arrived safely. No news that she was now a wife. No news at all as to whether there might be a place for the three who'd been left behind.

Hannah and Hetty had been prepared to wait the entire year until they turned eighteen and were forced to leave the orphanage, if it took that long, for Miranda to send word to come. Josie had not.

Hannah tried to remember exactly what tactic her youngest sister had employed to convince her to answer that advertisement in the Chicago *Daily Herald* seeking a bride willing to travel to the Wyoming Territory.

"We should wait for Miranda to contact us," Hannah remembered arguing.

"That's easy for you to say," Josie had replied. "You only have one more year of beatings from Miss Birch to endure. I won't be eighteen for two endless years! You know she's been meaner than ever since Miranda left with Nick and Harry. I can't stand two more years here. I can't stand two more days!"

Hannah had taken one look at the desperation in Josie's blue eyes, owlish behind wire-rimmed spectacles, and agreed to marry a man sight unseen.

At least she'd had the foresight to get a commitment from Mr. McMurtry that he would bring her two sisters along on the journey, which entailed three arduous months traveling by Conestoga wagon along the Oregon Trail.

They would all probably die of cholera, or drown crossing a river, or be scalped by Indians, or trampled by a herd of buffalo long before they got to Fort Laramie. Besides, she and Hetty and Josie were headed *away* from Miranda and Nick and Harry, with little chance of ever seeing them again. Agreeing to marry a total stranger headed into the wilderness was seeming more corkbrained by the moment. What on earth had possessed her to do something so very . . . unselfish?

Hannah was used to thinking of herself first. That had never been a problem when she was the spoiled and pampered daughter of rich parents. It had even served her well at the orphanage, where food and blankets were scarce. Before Miranda had left to become a mail-order bride, Hannah had been perfectly willing to let her eldest sister do all the sacrificing.

Now she was the eldest, at least of the three who'd been left behind. Now it was her turn to sacrifice. Although marrying a perfect stranger seemed a pretty big leap from giving up food or blankets.

She was lucky the groom hadn't turned out to be seventy-two and bald. In fact, he was only middle-aged. Was thirty-six middle-aged? To a girl of seventeen, it seemed ancient.

Her brand-new husband had a thick Irish brogue and an entire head of the curliest red hair she'd ever seen on a man or a woman. His nose was a once-broken beak, but it gave character to an otherwise plain face. His eyes twinkled, like two dark blue stars caught in a spiderweb of wrinkles. Oh, yes, she felt very lucky.

And very, very sad.

Her tall, gawky, rail-thin groom wasn't the man of her dreams. He wasn't even close.

Hannah was trying to decide how difficult it would be to open the window and retreat down the fire escape when she heard a firm—but quiet—knock at the door.

She scurried away from the window as though her presence there might reveal her desperate hope of avoiding the wedding night before her. There was no escape. She'd been well and truly caught in the trap Josie's agonized eyes had laid for her.

Her husband had arrived to make her his wife.

Even knowing who must be at the door, she called out, "Who is it?" Her voice sounded hoarse to her ears, but no wonder, when her throat was swollen nearly closed.

"It's Mr. McMurtry," a quiet—but firm—Irish voice replied. "May I come in?"

Hannah realized her husband expected to find her in bed. She stared at the gold brocade spread that still covered the sheets. She needed to pull it back and get in the bed. But she couldn't do it. She couldn't!

To hell with being unselfish! She *hated* what she was being forced to do. She should have let Hetty do it. After all, Hetty was only a *minute* younger! Hannah should have insisted they wait until Miranda contacted them. She should have told Josie *no*, in no uncertain terms. She should have run when she had the chance.

But she was married now, like it or not.

Hannah curled her hands into angry fists and fought the tears that burned in her eyes and nose. She hoped the coming journey was as dangerous as it was touted to be. Maybe her husband would die and leave her a widow and—

She brought herself up short and looked guiltily toward the door, behind which stood the man she was wishing dead. Being selfish was one thing. Wishing another person *dead* was something else entirely. That wasn't how she'd been raised by her parents. Hannah was ashamed of having harbored such an unkind thought.

No one had forced her to marry Mr. McMurtry. She'd volunteered to do it. She had to *grow up*. She had to put away childish hopes and dreams. This was her life, like it or not.

Hannah stared at the bed. She tried to imagine herself in Mr. McMurtry's arms. She tried to imagine kissing his thin lips. She tried to imagine coupling with him. She couldn't. She just couldn't!

She groaned like a dying animal.

"Are you all right in there?"

Once again, Josie's agonized gaze appeared in her mind's eye. Hannah choked back a sob of resignation, then yanked down the covers, scrambled onto the bed, and pulled the covers up to her chin.

"Come in," she croaked.

"Mrs. McMurtry? Are you there?"

Hannah cleared her throat and said, "You can come in, Mr. McMurtry."

The door opened slowly. Mr. McMurtry stepped inside and closed the door behind him, but he didn't move farther into the room.

Too late, Hannah realized she'd left the lamp lit, and that Mr. McMurtry would have to remove his hat, string tie, chambray shirt, jeans, belt, socks, and hobnail boots—and perhaps even his unmentionables—with her watching. Unless she took the coward's way out and ducked her head beneath the covers. Or he had the foresight to put out the lamp.

Her new husband swallowed so hard his Adam's apple bobbed, and said, "I had a cup of coffee downstairs."

"Coffee will keep you awake." Again, too late, Hannah realized there was a good reason why Mr. McMurtry might not want to go right to sleep.

Neither of them said anything for an awkward moment.

Then he said. "I'd better . . ."

Hannah watched as Mr. McMurtry blushed. His throat turned rosy, and then the blood filled his cheeks, causing a whole face full of freckles to disappear in a pink pool of blood.

He stammered, "I've dreamed about this . . . My whole life, I . . . You are so beautiful."

Hannah found herself staring back into her husband's very blue eyes with surprise. She'd known she was pretty, but this was the first time a grown man had remarked on the beauty of her blond curls and wide-spaced, sky blue eyes, full lips, and peaches-and-cream complexion. It was surprisingly gratifying to hear such words from her husband.

Despite Mr. McMurtry's speech, he came no farther into the room.

Why, he's scared too! Hannah realized.

Her fear returned and multiplied. The situation was

already mortifying in the extreme, but if *he* was inexperienced, who was going to tell *her* what to do?

"I'm really tired," she blurted. Hannah put her hands to her cheeks as they flamed with embarrassment. "I don't believe I said that."

He chuckled.

She glanced sharply in his direction. "Are you laughing at me?"

"No, Mrs. McMurtry," he said. "I was laughing at myself."

She narrowed her eyes suspiciously.

He continued, "I've just married the most beautiful woman I've ever seen, and I'm standing rooted to the floor a half a room away from her." His smile turned lopsided as he admitted, "You see, I've never undressed a woman before . . . or before a woman."

Hannah swallowed hard and whispered, "Never? Not even a . . ." She couldn't say the word *prostitute* or *soiled dove* or even *lady of the night*. Ladies didn't speak of such things.

He shook his head. "I'm Catholic. Fornication is a sin."

"Oh." Hannah couldn't breathe. It felt like all the air had been sucked from the room. He was thirty-six, and he'd never been with a woman? This was going to be a disaster.